Some Kind of Hero

'A warm-hearted, funny and affecting read'
York Evening Press

'Just when you think it's a comedy, the Kleenex moments sneak up on you' *More*

Such a Perfect Sister

'This tale will make you love your own sister more than ever!' *Company*

'[A] witty novel about tangled relationships' *Hello*

'A fun and witty beach read' *B magazine*

Kiss & Tell

'A very funny novel that soap fans will love'
Woman's Own

'Sparks fly and so do the pages in this irresistible book about love in the noughties' *Now magazine*

'Do you love soaps and sordid kiss-and-tell stories? Then this is the novel for you . . . Hilarious, and with a ring of truth that keeps you reading' *19 magazine*

Donna Hay's first novel, *Waiting in the Wings*, won her the RNA New Writers' Award, and since then she has attracted praise from critics for *Kiss & Tell* and *Such a Perfect Sister*. She writes regularly for *TV Times* and *What's On TV*, and has a weekly soaps page in *Chat* magazine. *Some Kind of Hero* is her latest novel in Orion paperback, and her latest hardback novel, *Goodbye, Ruby Tuesday*, is also available from Orion. She lives in York with her husband and daughter.

BY DONNA HAY

Waiting in the Wings
Kiss & Tell
Such a Perfect Sister
Some Kind of Hero
Goodbye, Ruby Tuesday

Some Kind of Hero

~

DONNA HAY

ORION

An Orion paperback

First published in Great Britain in 2003
by Orion
This paperback edition published in 2004
by Orion Books Ltd,
Orion House, 5 Upper St Martin's Lane,
London WC2H 9EA

Second impression 2004

Copyright © Donna Hay 2003

The right of Donna Hay to be identified as the author
of this work has been asserted by her in accordance
with the Copyright, Designs and Patents Act 1988.

All rights reserved. No part of this publication may be
reproduced, stored in a retrieval system, or transmitted,
in any form or by any means, electronic, mechanical,
photocopying, recording or otherwise, without the prior
permission of the copyright owner.

All the characters in this book are fictitious,
and any resemblance to actual persons,
living or dead, is purely coincidental.

A CIP catalogue record for this book
is available from the British Library.

ISBN 0 75285 907 2

Typeset by Deltatype Ltd, Birkenhead, Merseyside

Printed and bound in Great Britain by
Clays Ltd, St Ives plc

www.orionbooks.co.uk

To Ken, and Harriet
with love, as always.

Chapter 1

Tess woke slowly, opening her eyes to the morning sunshine which streamed through the open window. She stretched, luxuriating in the feel of silk sheets against her bare skin.

And then she saw him, standing at the foot of the bed, his dark hair ruffled by the soft breeze. It was Colin Firth. In one hand he held a bottle of champagne, in the other a carton of Häagen-Dazs.

As their eyes met, he smiled enigmatically and said, 'Miss Doyle, the video's finished.'

Tess dragged her attention away from the rain drizzling down the window pane and back to the thirty expectant faces in front of her. She reached for the remote control. Damn, she'd been so busy daydreaming she'd missed the bit where Colin – sorry, Mr Darcy – emerged from the lake, all lean thighs and dripping masculinity. Her finger hovered longingly over the rewind button, then she stopped herself.

'Right, so what does that tell us?'

'That Mr Darcy's really sexy?' Becky Whiting sighed.

'Leave it out, he's ancient!' Jason Fothergill looked affronted. He was supposed to be Becky's boyfriend, but at fourteen years old, with terminal acne and an ink-stained shirt, there was really no comparison.

'I'd rather have him than you.'

Wouldn't we all? Tess thought. At least Becky Whiting *had* a boyfriend. Drooling over Darcy was the closest thing Tess had to a love life these days. 'I was thinking more of his relationship with Elizabeth Bennett. What does it tell us about that?'

'They haven't got one,' Jason muttered, fiddling with his biro. 'She's a right snotty cow. I wouldn't go out with her.'

'Nice tits, though.' A paper missile sailed from the other side of the classroom and caught him on the side of the head. Jason snatched up his exercise book and flung it, as the rest of the class, sensing a fight, began to jeer.

Tess took off her glasses and rubbed her eyes. Two weeks into the new school year and she was already counting the days until half-term. She had a headache throbbing in her temples, thanks to covering Marjorie Wheeler's double lesson with 9C earlier on. Most of them didn't know a simile from a smack in the face and didn't want to, either. Tess had spent half the lesson explaining Thomas Hardy's view of fatalism, and the other half trying to stop them shutting each other's heads in the desks.

'That's enough.' Her voice rose above the din. They all turned back reluctantly to face her. 'Can anyone say what this tells us about Darcy's feelings for Elizabeth?'

Thirty blank faces stared back at her. They couldn't have looked less comprehending if she'd asked the question in Swahili. 'No one got any ideas?' No reason why they should have. She'd only been telling them every day for the past fortnight.

She glanced at Paris Malone, who ducked her head and pretended to search for her pencil sharpener. Poor Paris. She'd learned the hard way that it didn't pay to be too clever at Haxsall Park Comp.

Just as Tess was wondering if she should take up a more rewarding career, like septic-tank cleaning, a voice piped up from the back of the classroom. It was the new girl, Emily Tyler. 'He's in love with her, but he doesn't know how to say it.'

Tess looked at her with surprise and gratitude. Everyone else just stared.

2

'Exactly. That's exactly what he feels.' Tess smiled encouragingly.

Emily went red and retreated behind her book.

'Then why doesn't he just come out and say it?' Mark Nicholls asked. He was the class stud – dark, brooding and brainier than he let on. Unfortunately, he preferred to direct his intelligence into making life hell for his teachers. 'Why doesn't he just say, "Fancy a shag?"'

Tess faced him. 'Because it would be a very short book.'

'Good.' Everyone smirked appreciatively at his joke, especially the girls. Tess ignored him.

'So how do we know he feels like that? Can you find any examples in the text?' she pressed on. But Mark had the class' attention now and was making the most of it.

'No offence, Miss, but why are we bothering to learn this old stuff? I mean, it's not exactly relevant to us, is it?'

Here we go. Tess suppressed a sigh. The kids always tried this argument when they wanted to distract her. If they were lucky, they could sometimes spin it out until the end of the lesson.

But not today. She met his eye unflinchingly. 'I'm sure it would be nice to study something relevant to you, Mark. But sadly *Loaded* magazine has yet to make it on to the GCSE syllabus.'

Everyone sniggered. A dull red flush crept up his neck. Normally Tess would never have set out to embarrass one of her pupils, but Mark Nicholls was too cocky for his own good.

She turned back to the class. 'Maybe Mark's got a point,' she said. 'How do you think Elizabeth and Darcy's relationship would go if Jane Austen was writing it today?'

That started a lively discussion. It might not have been quite what was in her lesson plan, but at least it kept them interested and stopped them throwing chairs out of the window.

The only one who didn't join in was Emily. She sat at

the back, listening to Leanne Hooper and Jordan Nuttall gossiping on either side of her. Tess watched them consideringly. It was odd that she'd made friends with those two. They didn't seem to have anything in common. Leanne and Jordan had streaked hair, lipgloss and lovebites; Emily wore not a scrap of make-up and her dark hair was pulled back in a messy ponytail. Tess hoped she wouldn't start following their example too closely. She seemed such a nice girl.

Her father had seemed nice too, when he came to meet Tess before the start of term. The family had only recently moved to York from Leeds, and he was worried how Emily would settle in.

'We've had a few family problems recently,' he'd explained. Tess guessed that meant there'd been a divorce. If so, Emily certainly wouldn't be alone; she couldn't think of more than half a dozen kids in the class who had both parents still living at home. Some lived with their mothers, some with stepfamilies, others were being brought up by their grandparents. One lad was with foster parents after a long stint in a children's home.

It was the way things were in Haxsall. To the outside world, it seemed like a tough place to live, a 'problem area'. The local paper was always carrying stories of bored teenagers roaming the streets, vandalising shops and torching cars on the recreation ground. The bus company had refused to take passengers there after dark for a while after a gang threw stones at one of the buses. They made it sound like Beirut. There was even a joke about it in York: What do you call someone from Haxsall in a suit? The accused.

But Tess had lived there all her life and she knew there was a different side to the area. The papers only reported the bad news about a troublesome few. They didn't want to know about the close-knit community, where everyone knew and looked out for everyone else. They never printed stories about the good things that happened, the local shopkeepers who went round to the elderly checking if they needed anything, or the pubs that organised fund-raising events for local youngsters. Tess had more reason than most to appreciate the big-hearted people of Haxsall.

And it wasn't all rundown, either. Apart from the sprawling council estate in the centre, there were the tidy redbrick semis of the old town, built by Joseph Rowntree so his factory workers could escape the slum dwellings of the old inner city. Then there were the big houses on the fringes of Haxsall, the solid Victorian villas on Fox Lane and the smart new executive development on Hollywell Park overlooking the common.

She was fairly certain this must be where Emily and her family lived. No one from the council estate wore an expensive designer suit like Mr Tyler's. Not even the accused.

Ten minutes later the bell went for the end of the lesson. As they all made a dash for the door, Tess called Emily over. She came reluctantly, dragging her feet.

'I haven't had much chance to chat since you started here. I just wanted to make sure you're all right?'

'Fine, thanks.' Emily shrugged. She was as thin and leggy as a baby giraffe, and painfully conscious of it too, from the way she stooped, her arms folded defensively across her body. Tess felt like telling her how lucky she was; at barely five feet four, she envied any woman with supermodel height.

'So you're settling in all right? No problems?' Emily shook her head. 'I notice you've made friends with Jordan and Leanne?'

'They're all right.' She fiddled with a tendril of hair escaping from her ponytail. Her nails were bitten right down, Tess noticed.

'What about at home? Your dad mentioned you'd been through a bad time recently—'

'Everything's fine,' Emily cut her off. She glanced

longingly at the door. Tess decided to put her out of her misery.

'Okay then, you can go. But don't forget, if you ever need anyone to—' But the door was already slamming behind her. Through the glass panel, Tess could see Leanne and Jordan waiting outside. When Emily emerged, they prised themselves off the wall and joined her. They talked for a moment and Emily jerked her head back towards the door. Then they all laughed and headed off down the corridor together.

Tess shook her head regretfully. Maybe she should have kept a closer eye on her, made sure she didn't get too well in with those troublemakers. She'd meant to, but like the aerobics classes she'd signed up for and the big pile of ironing in her airing cupboard, she hadn't got round to it.

This was her first term as Head of English, and since her promotion she'd been rushed off her feet, writing reports, planning lessons, dealing with staffing crises and making ends meet on her pathetically limited budget. Actually teaching the kids had become the easy bit, and the only part of her day Tess looked forward to.

She pressed the eject button on the video. Bringing in her precious tape of *Pride and Prejudice* had been a last desperate attempt to bring the text alive for her bored Year 10 class. But she had to admit, for all his attitude, Mark Nicholls had a point. How did she expect a bunch of stroppy fourteen-year-old boys to take an interest in Regency romance? It might be easier if they had the chance to read something modern too. But judging from the state of the stock cupboard, no one had bought any new books since Dickens produced his last masterpiece.

But all that would change once she got the extra money she'd asked for in her budget. Tess had already made a list of all the new novels she would buy. There would be some play texts too, and poetry. And she'd get rid of all the old grammar books, the ones that went on about syntactic structures and prepositional phrases and said nothing about how to write a really great story. She couldn't wait.

Then we'll see who's not relevant. She gathered up the homework books that had been dumped on her desk and put them in her oversized satchel bag, then made her way to the staffroom to grab a quick coffee before she went home.

Back in the 1960s, Haxsall Park had been a shining beacon in the new comprehensive system, a sprawling modern building of glass and concrete. But like the textbooks, it was beginning to look old and tatty around the edges. The beige paintwork in the corridors was peeling, and rain filled the potholes in the playground as Tess splashed through them towards the Portakabin that housed the staffroom.

It was always busy at the end of the day, as teachers gathered their coats and belongings before heading home. Some huddled around the windows, contemplating the dash through the rain to the car park. Others had retreated around the kettle. A few keen ones were catching up on their homework, hacking through essays with their red biros.

Helen Wesley held up a mug. 'Coffee?'

'Please.' Tess swept a pile of QCA reports off one of the armchairs and flopped into it.

'Bad day?'

'Not bad. Just exhausting.'

'Aren't they all?' muttered Jeff Kramer, Head of Science. He was busy circling jobs in *The Times Ed*. 'Never mind. Another ten weeks and it'll be Christmas.'

'It sounds like a lifetime.' Tess rested her head back against the cushions and stared at the cracks in the ceiling. 'Remind me again why I wanted to be a Head of Department?'

'The power? The glamour?' Helen handed her her coffee. She was Head of PE and Tess' closest friend at the school. In her late twenties, blonde, bouncy and like Melinda Messenger in a tracksuit, she was the reason no Haxsall Park boy ever missed games.

'Do I look glamorous to you? On second thoughts, don't answer that.' Tess shook the rain off her short dark hair. It was badly in need of a wash, but she had a feeling it wouldn't get done tonight, with the mountain of marking she had to do.

'Ah, so it's got to you already, has it?' Jeff lit up a cigarette and grinned at her through the curling smoke. He was a big, untidy-looking man in a shapeless sweater. 'Blimey, I thought you were supposed to be the enthusiastic one? What happened to the woman who was full of ideas? The one who was going to show us cynical old sods how it's meant to be done?'

'You try being enthusiastic when you've got that old cow Frobisher breathing down your neck.'

Helen smiled sympathetically. 'Still giving you a hard time, is she?'

'Like you wouldn't believe.' Cynthia Frobisher had been Head of English before being promoted to Deputy Head last term. And she never let Tess forget it. 'Honestly, she treats me like an incompetent teenager.'

'I wouldn't worry about it,' Jeff said. 'She treats us all like that.'

'I get it worse than you lot. She doesn't think anyone can run the English department the way she did. Except Marjorie Wheeler, of course, which is why she's so sick she didn't get the job.'

'Tess,' Helen interrupted her.

'I get fed up hearing how she used to do things,' Tess went on. 'Every time I come up with a new idea, she just looks down her nose at me and says—'

'Tess!' Helen shot a wary glance at the door. Tess didn't need to turn round to know Cynthia Frobisher was behind her. The hairs on the back of her neck were already standing on end.

Cynthia might only have been the Deputy Head but she was infinitely scarier than Eric Gant, the Headteacher. He was a kindly, white-haired old chap, who looked like he'd be more at home running the local bowls club than a big comprehensive. Mrs Frobisher, by contrast, looked as if she'd be happier running the Third Reich. She was in her fifties, hard-eyed and businesslike in a mannish trouser suit and flat shoes. Even her hairstyle was severe, falling in an uncompromising brown bob around her square face. She wore no make-up apart from a gash of alarmingly red matt lipstick that emphasised her mean mouth. She wasn't known as The Enforcer for nothing.

If she'd heard Tess' bitching, she gave no sign of it, as she swept in and dumped her armful of files on the coffee table. Tess eyed her nervously.

'Was there something you wanted, Cynthia?' The formidable Mrs Frobisher rarely ventured into the staff-room, preferring to keep to her office. But she still had an uncanny knack of knowing what they were all saying about her – thanks, no doubt, to her gossipy sidekick Marjorie Wheeler.

'Staff meeting.' She picked up the top file and flicked through it. 'Mr Gant has asked me to deal with this, as he's tied up with the Chair of Governors.'

'Kinky,' Jeff said.

'Hang on a minute.' Tess frowned. 'I didn't know anything about a staff meeting?'

'Didn't you? I sent all the Heads of Department an email about it this morning.' Mrs Frobisher's eyes glinted. 'Perhaps you accidentally deleted it? I know IT isn't your strong point.'

Cynthia accidentally hadn't sent it more like, Tess thought. She'd checked her mailbox at lunchtime and there was no sign of it then. 'I'm sure even I can spot an email,

Cynthia. Why didn't you mention it when I saw you earlier?'

'Really, I don't have the time to go running around the school checking up on people! I'm overstretched as it is. But if you're too busy, I'm sure we can struggle along without you?'

I bet, thought Tess. She could make all kinds of decisions behind her back, then run off to Eric Gant and tell him Tess wasn't doing her job properly. Wouldn't she just love that?

She smiled sweetly. 'I wouldn't dream of it, Cynthia. Just let me make a quick call.'

She slipped outside and phoned Dan from her mobile, asking him to put the casserole in the oven. He assured her he was doing his homework, but from the So Solid Crew track blaring in the background, she was sure he couldn't have been doing it very well.

When she got back, everyone was waiting for her. 'Phoning home, were you?' Cynthia asked, as if she hadn't been listening to every word. 'Family commitments can be such a worry, can't they? Especially in your situation. It must be hard for you to keep your mind on the job sometimes.'

Her voice dripped sympathy, but her eyes fooled no one, least of all Tess. She knew Cynthia didn't think she was up to the job and was just waiting for her to make a mistake. Which only made her more determined not to. 'Everything's fine, thank you,' she said tautly. 'Shall we get on with the meeting?'

Cynthia shuffled her papers. 'Mr Gant and the governors have been setting budgets for the coming year. They've looked at the resources available and at the areas with the greatest need, and they've come up with the following allocations for each department.' She handed round sheets of paper. Everyone grabbed theirs and scanned it eagerly.

'Great.' Jeff looked pleased. 'I can get that new equipment I wanted. The other stuff's falling to bits.'

All around there were sighs of relief or groans of dismay as the staff saw how much they had to spend. Tess said nothing. She couldn't bring herself to speak.

Finally she found her voice. 'There must be some mistake. My budget's been cut by twenty per cent.'

'That's right. Is there a problem?' Cynthia Frobisher looked innocent.

'But I asked for more money.'

'I don't see why. When I was running the English department I managed perfectly well on the amount you've been given. Less, in fact.'

Yes, and you only had to look in the stock cupboard to see why. 'But I need the money for new resources. I wanted to update the library, and buy some new texts—'

'What's wrong with the ones you have?' Mrs Frobisher looked frosty.

'They're a bit old-fashioned.' Everyone drew in their breath, sensing confrontation. Cynthia Frobisher had run the English department with ruthless efficiency for ten years. She wouldn't tolerate criticism, especially not from an upstart like Tess Doyle.

But Tess wasn't about to be put off. She'd stood up to bullies like Cynthia before. 'I just think the pupils should be aware that there have been books written in the last hundred years.'

'*Modern* texts, you mean?' Cynthia Frobisher's lip curled as if she'd just suggested they study *The Beano* for A Level. 'I'd call that dumbing down.'

'I'd hardly call Seamus Heaney and J.D. Salinger dumbing down, would you?'

Everyone looked at Cynthia. Tess suspected part of the reason she'd never updated the English resources was because she was out of her depth with anything other than the classics she'd studied at college. She was deeply suspicious of Tess' ideas because she was afraid of them. But Tess didn't want to make her feel threatened. She just wanted to do her job properly. Unfortunately, Cynthia's tight hold on the purse strings made that very difficult.

'Well, I'm afraid you'll just have to make do with mere Shakespeare,' she said. 'There's no money available.'

'There's money available for a new food tech room. And Jeff's equipment.'

Jeff bridled. 'You leave my equipment out of this!'

'That's necessary expenditure.'

'And learning about their own language isn't necessary?'

'As long as they can sign their name on a dole cheque they'll probably be able to cope,' Jeff sneered.

Tess shot him a furious look. 'I thought we were supposed to be raising standards?' she said.

'Raising standards yes. But not performing miracles,' he said. 'Let's face it, these kids will never achieve much.'

'They won't if they've got people like you teaching them.'

'You think it's all our fault? Look at the kind of homes they come from. Half their parents are in jail, the other half don't care what their kids get up to, as long as they're out of the house. Most of them are single parents living off the state—' He saw Tess' face and shut up. 'No offence,' he muttered.

'None taken,' Tess said. 'You can't help being a bigot.'

'There's nothing wrong with our GCSE English results,' Cynthia interrupted, silencing them both. 'They're perfectly competent.'

'There's more to life than GCSE results.' There was another indrawn breath from around the room. Not as far as Mrs Frobisher was concerned, there wasn't. She ruled her life by the school league tables. 'You do realise that once they've passed their exam most of these kids are never going to pick up a book again because we've put them off for life?'

'That's hardly our problem.' Mrs Frobisher closed her file with a snap. 'Anyway, as I've already said, there are no more resources available. So you'll just have to do the best with what you've got, won't you?' She smiled, seeing Tess' frustrated expression. 'You really mustn't take it so personally, Tess,' she said. 'You're still very inexperienced. You'll soon learn there are certain limitations to this job.'

Don't I know it, Tess thought. She sat in silence through the rest of the meeting, her eyes fixed on the wall calendar. Someone in IT had scanned Mrs Frobisher's head on to the busty body of a Page Three girl. For once it didn't make her laugh, not even when Cynthia tried to pretend she hadn't noticed it.

'Patronising cow,' she muttered, as they pulled on their coats to leave half an hour later.

'Try not to get too upset about it,' Helen said. 'All her meetings are like that.'

'I wish someone had told me that before I took this job,' Tess sighed. 'You'd think Cynthia would be encouraging the English department to do well, but I just get the feeling she wants me to fall flat on my face.'

'Of course she does. She wouldn't want you to make a better job of it than she did, would she?' Helen stared at her as if she was stupid. 'Besides, we all know she wanted her little pet Marjorie to get the job.'

'She would have been a disaster.'

'We all know that too. But at least Cynthia could have stayed in control. Marjorie would never have stood up to her the way you do.'

Tess took another pile of marking from her pigeonhole and stuffed it into her already bulging satchel. 'And there's me thinking I could make a difference.'

'At Haxsall Park?' Helen smiled. 'You've got more chance of having Mr Gant's love child.'

Tess zipped up her bag and hitched it over her shoulder. 'If I thought it might get me a few new textbooks, I might try it,' she said.

Chapter 2

It felt strange, walking into the new house. Everything looked familiar, but it still wasn't home. Even the furniture didn't seem right against the freshly painted magnolia walls.

Jack looked around. Maybe it would seem more homely when there were books back on the shelves, pictures on the walls and felt-tip stains on the pristine carpet.

Sophie was on one of the sofas with her three small cousins, glued to Sky One. Emily was stretched out on the other, her legs dangling over the arm, composing a text message on her mobile phone. Neither of them looked up when he walked in.

'Feet off the furniture, please.' He tapped Emily's trainers. She grudgingly slid them on to the floor. 'Where's Auntie Ros?'

Sophie turned her eyes from *The Simpsons* for a second. 'In the kitchen, unpacking.'

Jack listened. From beyond the door came the crash of pots, with an undercurrent of muted swearing. 'You two could have given her a hand.'

'I've been busy,' Emily said.

'On that thing, I suppose? Don't tell me you've been on it since you came home?'

'I've got a lot to say, haven't I? I mean, it's not like I see Katy at school any more. Not since we moved to this boring dump.'

'Hardly a dump, Em.' Jack looked out of the window at the crescent of brand-new executive homes, surrounded by neat lawns and flower beds. Each had a gleaming Audi or

BMW in the drive. He'd found out on their first weekend he was the only one who didn't turn out to wash his every Sunday morning.

'Still boring, though.'

Jack glanced at her. Her dark hair fell across her face as she bent over her phone. Somewhere under those baggy combats and stroppy manner she was turning into a real beauty. Soon she'd be fighting the boys off.

Another hurdle for him to look forward to. He felt as if he'd dealt with them all over the past nine months, from Emily's raging PMS to Sophie's embarrassing questions about exactly where babies came from.

He braced himself. 'Did you have a good day at school?'

'Okay,' Sophie said, turning her attention back to the TV. At seven years old, she was a lot easier to handle than her big sister. She couldn't have been more different to Emily. She was placid and sweet-faced, with a penchant for girly dresses and glitter. While Emily dressed like an off-duty commando, Sophie looked like she'd borrowed her wardrobe from backstage at a Shirley Bassey concert. But he knew it was only a matter of time before the hormone time bomb exploded. She'd already started eyeing up the bras in Tammy Girl.

'Boring,' Emily grumbled.

'Made any new friends yet?'

Emily sent him a scathing look. 'I don't want new friends. I liked my old ones.'

'Me too,' Sophie chimed in.

'You can still see them. Maybe you could invite them round, once we're more settled in?'

It was meant as a throwaway remark, but he might have known Emily would pick up on it. 'You mean like a party? Cool.'

'Hang on, I didn't mean—'

'Yeah, a party!' Sophie joined in excitedly. 'When can we have it? Can I have a new dress?'

Panic swept over him. 'We'll see.'

'You mean forget it.' Emily's shoulders slumped.

'I mean we'll see.' He hurried off to find Ros before Emily had a chance to nag him into doing something he might regret.

Ros was cross-legged on the floor, surrounded by kitchen paraphernalia. She was dressed for action in jeans and a T-shirt, her dark hair caught up in a bandanna.

'I can't believe you've been in this house three weeks and you still haven't got round to unpacking all this,' she said. 'Why did you have to bring all this stuff anyway? The only thing I've ever seen you use is the microwave. I mean, do you honestly know what to do with this?' She held up a complicated-looking piece of equipment.

'No idea. Miranda bought it.'

Ros put down the whatever-it-was. 'I'm sorry, Jack. I didn't think.'

'Silly, isn't it?' He looked around at the piles of boxes, each one clearly labelled 'Kitchen'. 'I move house to get away from the memories and end up bringing them all with me.'

'You'll always have them with you. Besides, you wouldn't want to forget her, would you?'

'No, but sometimes it hurts to remember.'

Ros got to her feet and came over to give him a hug. She might have been his big sister, but she barely came up to his shoulder.

'It'll get easier, bro,' she promised. 'It hasn't been that long, has it?'

'Nine months, three weeks and four days. Not that I'm counting.' He looked at the heap of pots and pans littering the worktops. 'You're right though. I don't need half this stuff. There's no room for it anyway.'

He hadn't realised how small this kitchen was compared to their old one. There was no room for the big pine table where they used to eat surrounded by the kids' school books, Miranda's paperwork and the Sunday supplements they never got round to reading. The work surface was spotless, unlike the old one, which bore the scars of when Jack had let a hot pan scorch it, and there was no greasy stain on the wall where Sophie had thrown her food from her high chair. She was a great aim, he recalled.

'I think the word you're looking for is compact.'

'And does that go for the garden, too?' Jack looked out of the window over the neat oblong of lawn.

'It's manageable.' Ros followed his gaze. 'Just right for you. You hate gardening, remember?'

'True. Miranda is — was — the green-fingered one.' He stared out at the featureless garden, veiled by rain. The old one would have been changing now, the leaves turning gold, the pyracanthus on fire with glowing amber and red berries. If he closed his eyes, he could almost hear Miranda making a fuss about raking up the endless piles of leaves while Sophie skipped in and out of them, spreading them around again.

'Have I done the right thing, coming here?' he said.

'You had your reasons.'

'Purely selfish ones.'

He'd tried to get over it; God knows, he'd spent the best part of a year trying. But he still couldn't bring himself to go on living in the house where they'd once been so happy. He couldn't face waking up in that same bed, that same room, without her every morning. Sitting down to eat in the kitchen, which had once been so full of life. Dozing off in front of *Newsnight* without her to tease him about getting old.

He'd only been back to the house a few times since Miranda died. The first was on the day of the funeral. It was a couple of days before Christmas and it had crucified him to see the brightly decorated Christmas tree, with everyone's presents wrapped and piled up underneath, as if she'd just nipped out to the shops.

He couldn't face going back after that. So when his mother had asked them to stay – 'just until you get back on your feet' – he'd accepted with gratitude. His mother had stepped in to Miranda's role, looking after the girls and taking care of the practical things while he nursed his grief. He could pretend he was a kid himself again, waking up in his old room every morning, listening to his dad grumbling at how there was never anything decent on telly every evening, and burying himself in his work to blot out the hours in between. But he knew it couldn't last.

In the end his mother had hinted that perhaps the time had come for him to start looking after himself and his family.

'Of course, your father and I love having you and the girls here, but I don't think it would be good for you to stay,' she'd said.

He could have remained there for ever, just functioning, never having to think again. But he had to accept she was right. He needed to start looking after the girls, taking responsibility.

And the first thing he did was put the house on the market and look for somewhere new.

He convinced himself he was doing it for the girls' sake. They'd be happier getting away from Leeds and making a fresh start. And the suburb of Haxsall, four miles out of York, seemed a good enough place. But he knew he wasn't fooling anyone. Least of all them.

'I've uprooted them from their school, their friends,' he said to Ros. 'Just because I'm too much of a coward to go back. It's probably the last thing they need. Especially Emily.'

'She'll survive. She's tough.'

'Is she?' He looked through the half-open door at the dark head, still bent over her phone. 'I'm worried about her.'

'It's you I'm worried about.' Ros was ever practical.

'Have you thought how you're going to manage? It's not as if you're just round the corner any more. Mum and I can't drop everything and turn up in five minutes whenever you need a babysitter.'

'Emily can babysit. She's old enough now.'

'But what about a childminder for Sophie? You need somewhere for her before and after school. Especially with you having such a long commute now.'

'I've got someone.' At least that was something in his chaotic personal life he'd managed to organise. 'She's just around the corner so I can drop Sophie off on the way to work.'

'And what about if you have to work late one night? Or if one of the girls is sick? What will you do then?'

'I don't know, do I? I'll cope somehow. I'm not the only person with kids in the world, you know. You've got three.'

'I know, but that's different. I'm used to it.'

'Are you saying I'm not?'

She sent him a sceptical look. 'Don't get me wrong, I think you're a great dad. But let's face it, Miranda did most of the childcare stuff.'

'I did my share.'

'I know you did. So does Greg, but he still has a panic attack if I threaten to leave him on his own with ours.'

'That's because they're all so tiny. I expect he's worried he'll lose them down the back of the sofa or something. Anyway, other people manage and so will I. I'll just have to be more organised. And if it all gets too much, I'll hire a housekeeper.'

'Ooh, get you, Mr Moneybags!' Ros rolled her eyes. 'Seriously, you might have to think about cutting back on your hours at work. You can't keep putting in twelve-hour days, housekeeper or no housekeeper.'

'I can see Humphrey Crawshaw going for that, can't you? Especially with the Westpoint project going on.'

'Not Westpoint again!' Ros groaned. 'It's all Greg goes on about at the moment.'

'I'm not surprised. If the Westpoint shopping mall gets planning permission, it will be worth a hell of a lot of money to Crawshaw and Finch.'

'I bet it won't do your partnership chances any harm either?'

'I take it Greg's been gossiping again?' Sometimes having a brother-in-law working for the same company had its drawbacks.

Ros looked innocent. 'He might have mentioned something. He says everyone's very impressed with your design.'

'Maybe.' Jack delved into the nearest box and pulled out a wooden spoon. 'Where shall I put this?'

Ros grinned. 'Don't tempt me!'

They unpacked for a while, filling drawers and cupboards with things Jack had no idea how to use, and probably never would. Then Ros said, 'You know what you really need?'

Jack blew the dust off a chipmunk-shaped biscuit barrel. 'A skip?'

'A woman.'

'Bloody hell, Ros, not again! I thought you were supposed to be a feminist.'

'I don't just mean to cook and clean. I mean for you. You need someone.'

'No, I don't. I've told you before, I'm a one-woman man. Anyway,' he went on briskly, 'I can just imagine what the girls would have to say about that!'

'They'd get used to the idea. You shouldn't be alone, Jack. It's not right. And Miranda wouldn't have wanted it.'

'Maybe not.' But that didn't mean he wanted it either. He tried to visualise another woman in the house, cooking in the kitchen with Miranda's pots and pans, curling up beside him on the sofa, sharing his bed . . .

His mind shrank away from the picture. No, he couldn't do it. No matter how much he told himself to look to the future, he knew another woman would never be part of it.

'I'm fine the way I am,' he said. 'Anyway, you don't have to worry about me, Ros. The girls and I will be okay.'

'Are you sure about that?'

'Of course. You'll see, in six months' time I'll have it all under control. The girls will be settled, I'll be a partner and – I'll have mastered every gadget in this kitchen.'

'Yeah, right!'

'I'm serious.' He looked around. 'I could be the next Jamie Oliver if I put my mind to it.'

Ros folded her arms and confronted him across the kitchen. 'Okay, Jamie, what are you cooking us all for supper then?'

'I don't know about you, but I really fancy fish and chips . . .'

Chapter 3

'I'm home!' Tess dumped her bag and umbrella in the hall.
'Dan?'

There was no sign of him. She sniffed the air. No sign of
that casserole either.

She went into the kitchen and touched the oven door. It
was stone cold. And there was the casserole dish, sitting on
the worktop where she'd left it that morning.

'Daniel Doyle!'

He was in his room, hunched over his computer with his
back to her, a pair of headphones clamped to his dark-blond
head. Tess crept up and clapped her hand on his shoulder.
He yelped with shock.

'Jesus! Mum!' He hit a key, blacking out the screen. 'Oh
no, the casserole!'

'Don't bother,' said Tess as he made a move. 'We'll be
eating at midnight if you put it in now. Honestly, Dan,
couldn't you just do one simple thing?'

'Sorry, Mum. I was going to do it but I sort of got carried
away.' He glanced back at the computer screen.

'So I see. I hope it was homework?'

'I finished that ages ago. This was – um – research.' He
looked shifty enough for Tess to be suspicious.

'Dan, I hope you weren't hacking into the college files
and changing your grades again? You know what they said
last time—'

'Calm down, of course I wasn't. I'm not that stupid.'

No, you're not, Tess thought. That was what worried
her. When it came to computers Dan was frighteningly

22

bright. She, on the other hand, could barely set the video. It troubled her to think what he could be up to and she wouldn't have a clue.

Fortunately for her, he was pretty sensible about it, although he did get carried away at times. What worried her more was the amount of time he spent glued to the screen. He had the excuse that he was studying computer science at sixth form college, but it was still an obsession with him.

She sighed. 'I suppose it's a takeaway again, is it?'

'I'll fetch it.'

'No thanks. I know what you're like. If you get on those arcade games at the chippie, I'll never get my supper.' She headed for the kitchen to pick up her car keys. Dan followed. He was using his wheelchair tonight. He preferred his sticks to get around college because they made him feel less conspicuous, but they tired him out after a few hours.

'Anything you want me to do?'

'You could put the kettle on. I'll have a cup of tea before I go out again.'

She stood aside as he wheeled past her to pick up the kettle, then headed for the sink. Tess automatically leaned over and turned the tap on for him. 'Mum!' Dan batted her out of the way. 'For heaven's sake, I can fill a kettle you know!'

'Sorry.' Tess watched, humbled, as he flicked the switch. 'Did you have a good day?'

'Not bad. Mostly revision. We've got a test on Friday.' He reached across to unhook the mugs from the mug tree. Tess forced herself not to do it for him, knowing how much he hated to be fussed over. Typical Dan, fiercely independent as always. He might have inherited his father's fair-haired looks, but he had her fighting spirit.

And God knows they'd both needed it. She'd been barely more than a child herself when Dan was first diagnosed with Spinal Muscular Atrophy. Luckily it was the mildest form and not life-threatening, but it still felt like the end of the world, knowing her precious baby would never walk or run or play football like the other boys, that his muscles would gradually give up, waste away, become useless.

At first she'd cried her heart out, but then she'd realised her tears were out of self-pity, and that she was doing Dan no favours by feeling sorry for herself. In spite of her own terror of what lay ahead, she owed it to him to give him the most normal life she could. But it turned out to be a hard struggle. Tess had never considered herself a loud or difficult person, but she soon found making a nuisance of herself was the only way to get things done. That, and refusing to take no for an answer. Before she even knew what was wrong, she'd practically camped outside her GP's surgery until he stopped dismissing her as a neurotic mother and finally referred Dan to hospital. Later, when he was older, she'd had a similar battle with the education authorities when they said the local school wasn't equipped to cope with her son's special needs. She'd written letters to councillors, organised petitions and finally even helped raise the money herself to put in the necessary ramps and disabled toilets.

She'd also encouraged Dan to join in with the other kids where he could. He'd gone to parties, sleepovers, on school outings. And when occasionally some mindless idiot teased or bullied him, Tess had been right in there too, sleeves rolled up, fighting back.

Sometimes she felt as if she'd spent most of her life fighting. She could cope with that, but it was other people's prejudice, their ignorance and stupidity she found hardest to deal with. Those who assumed that because Dan was in a wheelchair he was somehow mentally subnormal. Others who spoke to her as if he couldn't answer for himself, or didn't look at him at all because they were too embarrassed.

That was what made her mad these days. Why couldn't they see beyond the chair and realise what a confident, intelligent young man he was? If a little forgetful at times.

'There you go.' He put the mug down in front of her. 'What are you staring at?'

'You. I was just thinking how brilliant you are.'

'Mum!' The tips of his ears glowed fiery red with embarrassment. 'Just for making a cup of tea? Blimey, I'd hate to see you when I'm Head of Microsoft!'

It being Friday night, there was a queue at the chippie. The rain dripped off her short dark hair as she huddled inside her fleece, breathing in the glorious aroma of frying chips and vinegar and trying not to think about how starving she was.

There was the usual gang hanging around the arcade games. Tess recognised a few faces from Haxsall Park Comp, looking intimidating in their tracksuits and baseball caps. Not that she felt remotely threatened by them. They sent her uneasy looks, silently pleading with her not to acknowledge them in front of the older kids. It made her smile to think a word or a wave from her could destroy their street cred for ever.

Then she spotted Emily Tyler, hanging around the doorway. She looked different too, but just as awkward and leggy in baggy combat trousers and an oversized sweatshirt. For a moment Tess thought she might be with Leanne and Jordan, but then she noticed her father in the queue behind her. Now what was his name? John? James?

Jack. His name popped into her head a second before he saw her and smiled.

'It's Miss Doyle, isn't it?'

'Mr Tyler.' She slipped back in the queue to talk to him. 'How's the new house?'

'Chaos, I'm afraid. My sister's unearthing pots and pans as we speak. Hence the takeaway.'

'I don't have such a good excuse. My son just forgot to put the supper in the oven.'

'Your son?' His eyes flicked to her ringless left hand.

Tess changed the subject. 'How's Emily finding life at Haxsall Park?'

'I was just about to ask you the same question. Actually, I've been meaning to come in and see you, but what with the house move and work being so hectic I haven't had time.' He lowered his voice. 'I wondered if there were any problems I should know about?'

'Not that I'm aware of. I spoke to her today and she seemed okay. Why? Has she said anything to you?'

He shook his head. 'That's just it. She never tells me anything.'

'Typical fourteen-year-old. About as communicative as the Dead Sea Scrolls.' Tess grinned. 'Still, I don't think there's anything to worry about. She seems fine.' She didn't tell him about Leanne and Jordan. Hopefully that friendship would soon blow over once Emily found her feet.

'I'm glad to hear it.' He looked relieved. 'It's such a worry looking after Emily and her sister by myself.'

'Don't they have any contact with their mother?'

His smile disappeared. 'She died just before Christmas.'

'Oh, I'm sorry. I had no idea.' What an idiot, assuming he was a divorcee. Just because he didn't look old enough to be a widower. She should have known better, especially as she hated anyone jumping to conclusions about her and Dan.

Jack carried on. 'It's affected both of them badly, as you can imagine. Especially Emily. And then with the house move – it's been a lot for her to take in recently.'

'Of course.' And it wasn't just Emily and her sister who'd been affected by the last few months, she guessed. There were lines of strain around Jack Tyler's dark grey eyes that she was willing to bet hadn't been there a year ago.

Tess reached the front of the queue and gave her order.

As the woman behind the counter wrapped up her fish and chips, she turned to Jack. 'Try not to worry too much,' she said. 'Children are more adaptable than we give them credit for. I'm sure Emily will bounce back.'

He didn't return her smile. 'I wish I had your confidence,' he said.

Dan had warmed the plates and poured her a glass of wine when she got home. Tess put it down to him still feeling guilty about not putting the casserole in the oven.

Until they were sitting in front of *EastEnders*, their plates perched on their knees, when he suddenly said, 'Do you ever think about my dad?'

Tess took a hasty slug of wine to drown the chunk of haddock she'd just swallowed whole. 'Not often. Do you?'

'Sometimes.' He stared at the screen. Phil Mitchell was flinging a punter out of the Queen Vic. 'Don't suppose he ever thinks about me, though,' he said wistfully.

No, I don't suppose he does. Tess remembered the letters and photos that went unanswered until she gave up sending them. Phil had shown no interest in Dan before or after he was born, and probably hadn't given either of them a second thought since. 'What's brought all this on?'

'Nothing. I just wondered, that's all.' Dan kept his eyes fixed on the screen where Ian was having a row with Auntie Pauline. 'So you've no idea where he might be now?'

'The last I heard he went to university in London. Why? Are you going to look him up?'

She was joking when she said it. But a quick look at Dan's face told her he wasn't. 'I was thinking about it.'

She reached for the remote control and hit the mute button. Suddenly the goings-on in Albert Square seemed unimportant. 'You've never mentioned it before.'

'I'm mentioning it now.' He looked defensive. 'I'm just

curious, that's all. I've never met the man who was responsible for me being here.'

Responsible is hardly the word I'd use, Tess felt like saying. But she forced herself to stay quiet.

Dan glanced at her worriedly. 'You wouldn't mind, would you? I mean, you've always said if I wanted to find him you'd be okay about it.'

'Of course.' She toyed with her chips, which had suddenly lost their appeal. Talk about a shock! She'd always tried to be as open as possible with Dan about his father and the circumstances surrounding his birth. She'd also told him that if he ever wanted to trace him she wouldn't stand in his way. But saying something and meaning it were very different. And now it came down to it she realised she did mind. Very much.

'I shouldn't think he'd be that easy to track down,' she said. 'I know his parents moved away from here years ago. I don't have any other contacts for him.'

'There are loads of places I could look on the internet. It wouldn't be too difficult to find him.'

Of course. She might have known that wretched computer would come up with the answer. She stood up, gathering up their plates. 'Have you finished? I'd better get on with the washing up.'

Out in the kitchen, she plunged her hands into the hot soapy water and tried to get her thoughts together. She knew she was wrong to feel so angry, but she couldn't help it. Of course Dan had a right to know his father; it was naïve of her to imagine he wouldn't want to.

But at the same time, she couldn't help feeling it was deeply unfair. She was the one who'd taken care of Dan for seventeen extremely tough years. She was the one who'd struggled, made all the sacrifices. And now, out of nowhere, Dan had suddenly decided he wanted his dad.

Not that Phil had any right to claim that title. Not after the way he'd treated them.

He was her first serious boyfriend and she'd got pregnant the first time she slept with him. Looking back on it, she couldn't believe she'd been so stupid. If any of the girls in her Year 11 class had done that she would have been horrified. Although the girls in Year 11 were a lot more sophisticated than she was in those days.

But she'd had to grow up very quickly when the pregnancy test came back positive. After a sleepless night trying to get over the shock, the first person she'd told was Phil. His response wasn't exactly encouraging. While Tess was desperately anxious about her future, he was more worried about what his parents would say.

Even worse was telling her own mother. She didn't think she'd ever forget the disappointment on Margaret Doyle's face when she tearfully broke the news. Tess wished she would scream and shout, or even hit her. It would have hurt less.

Her mother was a strong, no-nonsense woman who'd brought up her two daughters on her own after their father died. She'd struggled to do her best for her girls, working long hours to provide for them. Her only wish was that they would grow up and make her proud.

She certainly wasn't proud of what Tess had done.

'And what does he have to say about it?' she'd asked.

'He said he'll marry me.' Tess sniffed back the tears, hoping it was the right thing to say.

'Very big of him, I'm sure.' She looked hard at Tess. 'Do you want to keep this baby?'

'I don't know.'

Margaret considered this. 'Right,' she said briskly. 'I think we should get this sorted out, don't you?'

She'd summoned a cowering Phil and his furious parents for a conference. One look at Daphne Purcell, hatchet-faced in a Country Casuals two-piece, and Tess had realised why he was so terrified of telling her. She was obviously the dominant one in the family and looked like she'd decided to dominate Tess and her mother too.

'You can forget about this ridiculous marriage idea for a start,' she'd said. 'You're both far too young.'

'If they're old enough to get themselves into trouble, they're old enough to take responsibility for it,' Margaret said.

Daphne looked her up and down, taking in the lined, unmade-up face, the threads of grey in her messy brown curls, the workworn hands that had never seen the inside of a manicurist's salon. In her eyes there was no doubt who was in control. 'That depends on what you mean by taking responsibility, doesn't it? Of course we're prepared to help. But I don't see why my son's life should be ruined over one mistake.'

'And what about my daughter's life? She's the one carrying this baby.'

'My Philip has a promising future ahead of him,' Daphne continued, ignoring her. 'He has a place at university and I'm not letting him throw all that away. He's very bright.'

'Not bright enough to take precautions, is he?'

'Neither is your daughter, apparently. Although it would hardly surprise me if she did this deliberately,' she muttered.

Margaret Doyle's face was expressionless. 'What's that supposed to mean?'

'Daphne, I really don't think—' Phil's father tried to interrupt, but his wife swatted him away like a troublesome fly.

'It stands to reason, doesn't it? My Philip would be a good catch for someone like your daughter.' Daphne looked around at the small but tidy council flat, her nose wrinkling. It hardly measured up to the Purcells' rambling Victorian pile on Fox Lane.

Tess saw her mother shift in her seat and for a terrible moment she thought she was going to knock Daphne out cold. Daphne must have seen the fighting glint in her eye too because she quickly said, 'But blaming each other isn't getting us anywhere. We need to decide what we're going to do about this mess. As I said, we're prepared to shoulder some responsibility. Meet some of the costs and so on.'

Margaret settled back in her chair. 'I'm glad to hear it.' But something in Mrs Purcell's face told Tess she wasn't talking about buying a pram.

'Now I'm sure you're as keen as we are to get this thing over and done with, so I've been making a few enquiries about clinics. Private, of course. We don't want to have to rely on the dreadful NHS for something as delicate as this—'

Tess watched her mother's expression change. 'You mean you want her to have an abortion?' she said slowly.

'Of course. Surely that's the only sensible option?' Daphne Purcell blinked.

'Sensible for you, you mean.'

'For everyone. You've said yourself we don't want our children's lives blighted by one mistake.'

Tess sat helplessly in the middle, watching them square up to each other. She looked at Phil, silently pleading with him to say something, but he wouldn't even meet her eye. He just stared at the floor like a ten-year-old who'd been caught with his hand in the biscuit tin.

Phil's father made another stab at joining in. 'Please, if we could just—'

'Shut up, Norman!' Daphne turned back to Margaret. 'You're not suggesting she should bring this unwanted child into the world?'

'Your son's child. And if he was half the man he pretends to be, he'd be taking care of my daughter instead of letting his mother fight his battles—'

'Will you both just shut up!' Margaret and Daphne turned to stare at Tess, who was on her feet between them. Phil was bug-eyed with terror.

She looked around, surprised at the silence. 'This is me we're talking about. When do I get a say in all this?' She

31

took a steadying breath. 'Right. First of all, I've got no intention of marrying Phil. Not because I don't want to ruin his future, but because I don't want to ruin my own.'

Daphne looked pleased. 'Very sensible. Now, what I thought was—'

'But I'm going to keep the baby,' Tess went on in a rush. 'It's my baby. And I want it.' She hadn't realised how much until she'd heard them talking about getting rid of it.

She glanced at Phil. He looked as if he was about to throw up with fear.

'I see. Well, in that case—' When Daphne reached into her bag Tess thought she was going to pull out a tissue and start crying, but instead she took out a leatherbound cheque book and gold pen. They all watched in fascinated silence as she scribbled a signature on the cheque, tore it out and handed it to Tess.

'What's this?'

'What does it look like? It's a cheque, for you and the – child.' Her face was pinched with disapproval. 'It should be enough to safeguard your future. On the strict understanding that Philip doesn't have to be involved. There will be no further communication, no more demands on my son. Is that understood?'

Tess didn't reply. She stared down at the cheque, her mind boggling at all the noughts in front of her. She'd never seen such a large amount.

She turned to Phil. 'Is that what you want?' He didn't answer, just gazed out of the window, a faraway look in his eyes, as if he just wanted to jump through it and run away.

'Of course it's what he wants,' his mother snapped.

'Fine.' Tess looked at the cheque for another moment, enjoying the brief feeling of having that much money in her hands. Then slowly, deliberately, she tore it up. 'If that's the way you feel, I don't need you or your money. Don't look so worried, I'm not going to be pestering your precious son. I don't want my baby growing up with a pathetic wimp for a father anyway!'

That had made Phil look at her. But by then it was too late. This time it was Tess who turned her back on him.

Her mother didn't say a word after they'd gone. She picked up the empty cups and carried them through to the kitchen in silence. Tess followed her, hardly daring to speak. Finally she steeled herself and said, 'Say something, for heaven's sake. Even if it's only, "Never darken my door again." '

'Doesn't seem like there's much to say, does it? You've already made your mind up.' She pursed her lips. 'That was a lot of money you threw away in there.'

Tess stared down at her hands miserably. 'I know.'

'It's no fun you know, bringing a child up on your own. Especially with nothing coming in.'

'I could get a job—'

'At sixteen? What kind of job do you think you'd get? You'd end up like me, no qualifications and having to take anything that's going just to make ends meet.'

Tess stared at the cracked lino on the kitchen floor. Her mother was right. She'd ruined her life and condemned herself and her baby to a lifetime of poverty, all because of one stupid, defiant act of pride.

There was a long silence. Her mother washed the cups, set them on the draining board, and reached for the towel to dry her hands. 'You did the right thing,' she said at last.

Tess felt hot, stupid tears of gratitude welling up in her eyes. 'But the money—'

'We don't need them, or their money. We'll get by. Heaven knows, I managed with you and your sister after your dad died.' She wagged her finger at Tess. 'But I meant what I said, you're not getting any dead-end job. You're going back to school to get yourself some proper qualifications. Baby or no baby, I want you to make something of yourself.' She smiled grimly. 'You were right about that lad being a spineless wimp. A man who can't stand up to his own mother is no use to you.' She gave Tess' hand a brief, reassuring pat. 'We'll manage, lass. Don't you worry.'

And they did. After Dan was born, her mother gave up her job in the local newsagents' to look after him while Tess went back to school. She took on a couple of evening cleaning jobs to bring in some money, while Tess found a Saturday job stacking shelves in the supermarket. Her older sister Frances chipped in too, once she'd left college and found a job as a secretary. Between them they took turns to work and look after the baby.

It was hard, and the months seemed to pass in a blur of exhaustion, but they got by. Tess never regretted her decision, or asked for sympathy, even when she was weeping over her A Level revision and having to cope with a screaming, teething baby who'd forgotten how to sleep.

She made herself promise not to contact Phil. But at the hospital, after Dan was born, she wrote to him in a weepy fit after seeing all the other new dads proudly holding their babies. She told herself he had a right to know he had a son, but deep down all she really wanted was to be like the other new mums, being fussed over by their partners. She'd never felt so lonely in her life.

She sent the letter to his parents as she didn't know where Phil was living in London. It went unanswered. She convinced herself they hadn't passed it on. Anything rather than admit the truth – that he didn't care.

She wrote again when Dan was two years old, after he was diagnosed with SMA. She kept it very businesslike, saying Phil had to know he was a carrier of the gene, just in case he ever wanted more children. His wife or girlfriend would have to be tested too, to make sure she wasn't a carrier, otherwise there was a good chance their baby could be born with it. What she didn't say was that she felt alone and frightened. She was only nineteen, she'd just started at teacher training college and finding she had a sick son who would need care for the rest of his life was all too much for her to cope with alone.

But still there was no reply. That was when it finally dawned on her that Phil really didn't care.

And now this. No matter how many times she told herself Dan had a right to know his own father, it still hurt. It wasn't as if he'd ever shown any curiosity before. They hardly ever talked about Phil, for heaven's sake. So why now, out of the blue?

Dan came in as she was finishing the washing up. She sensed him watching her from the doorway. 'Are you okay, Mum?'

'Of course.' She dredged up a smile. 'Why shouldn't I be?'

'It's just you've been washing that mug for five minutes. You'll scrub the pattern off if you're not careful.' He hesitated. 'I don't have to get in touch with him, you know. Not if it's going to upset you.'

Tess looked over her shoulder at him. It dawned on her how much he was beginning to look like Phil, with his unruly dark-blond hair and grey-green eyes. But she was the only one who knew that. Dan had never even seen a photo of his father. It wasn't fair to deprive him of such a large part of his past.

'I'm just being silly. Of course you've got a right to find him. I just didn't realise it was important to you, that's all.'

'I've been thinking about him quite a bit lately. He was about my age when you last saw him, wasn't he?'

Tess froze. She'd never thought about it before but Dan was exactly the same age Phil was when she got pregnant. She hadn't realised quite how young they were. No wonder his mother had been so protective of him.

And now it was her turn to be protective. Dan might be seventeen years old, but he was still her baby. She only hoped his search for his father wouldn't end up hurting him.

Chapter 4

Emily held the cigarette between shaking fingers and inhaled deeply. At first nothing happened, then suddenly a whoosh of hot, acrid smoke filled her mouth, her throat, her lungs. She felt as if she was drowning in burning tar. Gasping, she dropped the cigarette and fell back against the wall, coughing and choking, her eyes streaming.

'Muppet!' Leanne picked up the cigarette as it rolled towards the gutter. 'You've never tried it before, have you?'

'Bet that's not the only thing she hasn't tried!' one of the boys leered. Through a blur of watering eyes Emily caught their jeering expressions as they surrounded her.

She forced herself to laugh with them. These were supposed to be her friends, she reminded herself.

Luckily the boys lost interest and started kicking an empty can around the pot-holed playground. Leanne and Jordan sat on the wall, sharing a Silk Cut and pretending not to watch them. Emily sat and listened to them discussing last night's *Hollyoaks*, her mind elsewhere.

God, she was bored. All they ever talked about was who fancied who and who'd just been dumped by whom. If it wasn't boys, it was clothes and make-up. Emily reckoned Leanne and Jordan must know the entire contents of Miss Selfridge by heart. They'd seemed cool at first, and she was flattered when they singled her out on her first day to be their friend, but now she was beginning to wonder if they had a single brain cell between them.

She thought about her best friend Katy and the others

and what they'd be doing back at her old school in Leeds, and felt sick with longing. She really missed them all, especially Katy. They texted each other all the time, but it wasn't the same. Her old school was beginning to feel like a distant memory. Just like her old life.

The bell rang and they made their way slowly across the playground. Autumn had come rushing in with a vengeance after a few mild days. The cold wind stripped the leaves off the solitary beech tree in the playground and whipped at her new blazer. She hated her pristine uniform. It screamed 'new girl'.

She hated the new house, too. Sophie had felt the same at first but now she seemed to be getting used to it. She'd made friends at her school, and her new bedroom was bigger than the boxroom she used to have at the old house, with plenty of space for all her rubbish. She had an adoring childminder after school who bought her sweets and allowed her to watch endless TV. They even had a woman who did the cleaning so her dad wasn't so stressed all the time. Everyone seemed happier, more settled. Except her. She felt like the odd one out all round.

It was Chemistry first lesson. Emily would have liked to get straight to class, but she made herself loiter with Leanne and Jordan in the cloakroom while they faffed around putting on lipgloss. Everyone else had gone apart from Paris Malone.

She was a strange girl. Always on her own, never speaking to anyone. She didn't even make the effort to look like the other girls. Her sweatshirt had faded from red to deep pink with too much washing, and her skirt was too short. So was everyone else's, but from the way Paris kept pulling hers down over her knees Emily was sure it wasn't deliberate. Her fair hair was held back in a straggly ponytail, and her glasses slipped down her nose as she packed her books into her shabby holdall.

The door to her locker was open and Emily glimpsed a

flyer for an animal rights rally in Leeds pasted inside. She'd longed to go but her dad had insisted she was too young. She tried to catch Paris' eye to ask her about it but Leanne called her over to ask if she could borrow her hairbrush.

'You don't want to have anything to do with her,' she said loudly, running the brush through her streaked blonde hair. 'Everyone knows her mum's a right slag.'

Emily saw Paris' shoulders stiffen and waited for her to retaliate but she didn't. She went on sorting out her books, not looking up.

As Emily put the brush back into her bag, Mr Bunny stuck his balding head out of the side pocket. She made a grab for him but Jordan got there first.

'What's this?' She held it up by its tatty ear. 'See this, Lee? Emily's brought her ickle toy to school!'

'Give me that!' Emily snatched it out of her hand.

'Ooh, get her!' Leanne rolled her eyes. 'Wassamatter, worried we're going to pinch your ickle bunny wunny then?'

'Are you girls going to spend all day in here or what?' Fortunately Miss Doyle appeared in the doorway of the cloakroom, arms folded. She wasn't very tall but she was quite fierce when she wanted to be. 'Get a move on, you lot!'

Emily stuffed Mr Bunny into her bag and closed the zip. She felt silly, bringing him with her. Her mother had bought him when she was a baby. For years he'd gathered dust under her bed with all her other cuddly toys. But over the past few months he'd crept back on to her pillow. Emily didn't know why but she liked having him with her.

In Chemistry, Mr Kramer set them to doing an experiment to filter copper sulphate from sand. Emily had already done it in her old school, so she let Leanne and Jordan take charge and set up the experiment while she took notes. But her eyes kept straying to the far side of the classroom, where Paris was working on her own. Emily felt sorry for her, but sort of envied her too. At least she didn't have to listen to Leanne's non-stop commentary on the make-up habits of the rich and famous.

'. . . So I just thought it was a really good lipgloss, but my mum reckons no lipgloss is that bloody good and of course she's had the fat sucked out of her bum and put in her lips. Which is a bit gross, but if it makes you look as good as Liz Hurley – oh shit, when was I supposed to put the water in?'

But Emily wasn't listening. She was too transfixed by what was going on on the other side of the lab.

Jordan was heading across the room. It looked as if she was on her way to put something in the bin, but Emily could see her veering towards the bench where Paris was working. Paris was too busy writing up her notes to notice Jordan's silent approach, but as Emily watched in horror, she casually but deliberately nudged the test tube. It smashed to the floor, splashing its contents everywhere.

Paris swung round and Emily held her breath, just as Mr Kramer descended on them, his white coat flapping. 'What's going on?' he demanded.

Tell him, Emily willed silently. 'Don't know, Sir,' Paris muttered. 'Must have been an accident.'

'Clumsy girl! Don't just stand there. Get it cleaned up.'

'Yes, Sir.' As she trudged off to fetch a cloth, Emily saw Leanne and Jordan exchange knowing smiles.

'Serves her right for being such a swot!' Leanne sneered.

Outrage burned inside Emily until she felt as if the roots of her hair were going to burst into flames. She wanted to lash out at Leanne and wipe the grin off her smug little face. Before she knew what she was doing, she was out of her seat and heading across the room to where Paris was on her hands and knees.

Paris looked up, and Emily caught a flash of apprehension in her eyes, quickly masked by defiance. Emily got down on her knees beside her and began picking up the shards of glass.

Neither of them spoke. Paris wrapped up the pieces of glass and put them in the bin, while Emily fetched a cloth and mopped up the spilled water. She felt ashamed, even though it wasn't her fault. She wanted to say something but Paris didn't meet her eye. She didn't even thank her for her help, just gathered up her books at the end of the lesson and hurried off.

'See?' Leanne whispered, as they left the lab. 'Pig ignorant.'

But Emily was determined, and in the cafeteria at lunchtime she deliberately avoided the place at the table Leanne and Jordan had saved for her, and headed over to the corner where Paris sat alone, her nose buried in a book.

'Is this seat free?' She put her tray down without waiting for an answer.

Paris glanced up. 'I wouldn't sit there if I were you. Your mates won't like it.'

'I don't care.' Emily shot a defiant look over her shoulder. Leanne and Jordan were watching her. 'I can do what I like, can't I?'

'Please yourself.' Paris went back to her book. 'But don't blame me.'

A few minutes later, Emily began to wonder if she'd made the right decision. She'd expected Paris to be grateful, not ignore her.

'What are you reading?'

'*Of Mice and Men.*'

'Um – good, is it?'

'S'okay. Not his best.'

Meanwhile, Jordan and Leanne were sending her black looks from the other side of the cafeteria.

In the end she put down her knife and fork and said, 'Look, if you'd rather I sat somewhere else, you only have to say.'

'I'm doing it for your own good. Believe me, you really don't want those two giving you a hard time.'

'I told you, I don't care. I can look after myself.'

'Ooh, hard case.' Emily noticed the glimmer of a smile. Encouraged, she said, 'So why don't they like you?'

Paris put down her book and pretended to consider the question. 'It could be that they feel threatened by my intellectual superiority. But I think it's probably because my mum is a slapper and we live on the council estate. I expect that lot have filled you in on all the gory details already? Thought so,' she said, as Emily blushed. 'They never miss a chance.'

'They're hateful.'

'That's no way to talk about your best friends.'

'They're not my friends.'

'You seem pally enough. Anyway, you should consider yourself lucky. You've seen what they're like if they don't like someone.'

'Why don't you fight back?'

'What's the point? It's not going to change anything. Better to just ignore them and hope they get bored.' Close up she was very pretty, prettier than Leanne and Jordan, although she looked as if she was doing her best to hide it, with her shapeless clothes and hair drawn back off her face.

Emily looked around her. 'I hate this place.'

'Join the club.' Paris looked at her over the edge of her book. 'What was your last school like?'

'Better than this dump. If I'd had my way, I would have stayed there.'

'But your parents wanted to move, right?'

'My dad did. My mum's dead.'

'Oh.' Paris was silent for a moment. 'When did that happen?'

'Last year.'

'She wasn't very old, then?'

'Thirty-six.' Emily squirmed in her seat, hoping Paris wouldn't ask any more. She couldn't trust herself to talk about it.

41

Luckily, she changed the subject. 'It's tough, changing schools. I should know. This is my third since I was eleven.'

'Are you serious?' Emily stared at her. 'Why?'

Paris shrugged. 'We move around a lot. My mum has trouble settling down. Actually, what she really has trouble with is paying the rent. That's why we keep being evicted.' She smiled. She had a nice smile.

'And your dad doesn't live with you?'

'Hardly! I don't even know who he is. I don't think my mum does, either. She says she was drunk at the time.'

Emily stared at her. 'You're not serious?'

'Would I joke about something like that? She says I was called Paris because that's where I was conceived, but since she's never had a passport I don't think that's true somehow. Still, I suppose it's better than being christened Rowntree Park, isn't it?'

Emily giggled. 'You're lucky it didn't happen in a pub, or you might have been called Queen Victoria!'

They were still laughing when Leanne whisked past their table and knocked Paris' drink all over her lunch.

'Oops, silly me,' she trilled. 'I am clumsy, aren't I?'

Emily shot to her feet, but Paris held on to her. 'Leave her. She's not worth it.'

'You're not going to let her get away with it, are you?' Emily seethed, as Leanne sauntered back to her table.

'Like I said, it's better just to stay out of their way.'

'We'll see about that.' Before Paris could stop her, Emily made her way over to the table where Leanne and Jordan were sitting. As she brushed past the table, she nudged a bowl of chocolate ice cream into Leanne's lap.

'Oops, silly me,' she smiled sweetly. 'I am clumsy, aren't I?'

'You shouldn't have done that,' Paris whispered, as Leanne stalked off to the loos, followed by Jordan.

'Why not? She deserved it.'

'I know.' Paris glanced apprehensively over her shoulder. 'But I think you've just started World War Three.'

Chapter 5

'What do you mean, you've found him?'

It was just before eight in the morning and Tess was on her hands and knees searching through the cupboard for her shoes when Dan broke the news. She emerged, shoe in one hand, half a slice of toast in the other. 'How could you have found him already? You've only been looking a week!'

Dan looked sheepish. 'Actually, I'd sort of been looking for a while before I said anything to you.'

'I see.' So that explained all those late-night computer sessions. And she thought he'd been doing something innocent, like downloading porn. 'Why didn't you tell me?'

'I didn't want you to go mad.'

'Why should I go mad?'

'I don't know, but you're going a bit mad now.'

'I am not!'

'So why are you wearing odd shoes?' Tess looked down. In her agitation, she'd put on one black slingback and one brown one.

'The light's bad. We really need a new bulb in there.' She took off the brown shoe and threw it to the back of the cupboard.

'Anyway, I didn't think I'd find him so quickly,' Dan went on. 'But it turns out he wasn't that difficult to track down.'

Tess found the missing black shoe, stuffed the rest of her toast in her mouth and pulled it on while she took it all in. She was still in a state of shock. She thought she'd have time to get used to the idea of Dan tracing Phil. She actually hoped maybe he wouldn't be able to find him. But she'd reckoned without her son's determination and detective powers.

'How do you know you've got the right person? There must be hundreds of Philip Purcells in the country. Thousands, even—'

'Maybe. But the date and place of birth are the same. That would be too much of a coincidence, wouldn't it?' He paused, watching her. 'Don't you want to know where he is?'

Not really, Tess thought. She'd lived without knowing for seventeen years, her curiosity was unlikely to get the better of her now. But then she saw Dan's eager face. 'Go on, then. Where is he?' Too much to hope he was in jail.

'Down south. Near Basingstoke.'

Thank God for that. She was worried he'd turn out to be living in the next street. Although she hated herself for it, she couldn't help asking, 'Is he – um – married or anything?'

'Dunno. I've just got a name and address.'

Tess thought about it for a moment. 'So what happens now?' she asked.

'I'd really like to get in touch – if that's all right with you?'

She dodged the question. 'You're just going to ring him up? Out of the blue?'

'I thought about writing to him. It might be less of a shock that way.'

She nodded. Of course. Trust Dan to think of the careful, considered approach. If it was left to her, she would have jumped straight in there with both feet and probably ruined everything.

A thought occurred to her. 'Do you – er – want me to do it?'

'Do you want to?'

45

Absolutely not. As far as she was concerned, the swine didn't even deserve a Christmas card. But this wasn't about her, it was about Dan. 'If you think it will help.'

He must have seen the reluctance on her face. 'It's okay, Mum. I'd prefer to do it, if you don't mind?'

She nodded. Whoever wrote that letter, it would still be a hell of a thunderbolt for Phil. She wouldn't have minded being a fly on the wall when he opened it.

But what if he didn't open it? What if he ignored it, just like he had the letters she'd sent him all those years ago? After seventeen years of pretending his son didn't exist, she couldn't imagine him suddenly rushing forward to claim him. He'd probably got married, had a family of his own. Maybe he hadn't even told them about Dan? If that was the case, he wouldn't thank him for turning up out of nowhere.

She thought about it as she rushed around the house, gathering up her bags and coat and searching for her keys. She was so preoccupied she didn't even bother to protest when Dan retuned the car radio to Viking FM. By the time she pulled up outside his sixth form college she knew she had to say something.

'About your father. You won't expect too much, will you?'

He grinned. 'You mean he might turn out to be a sad old git who likes Pink Floyd?'

Tess smiled. 'That wasn't quite what I had in mind. He may have moved on with his life.' She chose her words carefully.

'And he might not want me to be part of it? It's okay, I've thought of that. I won't mind if he doesn't want to know. I just want to meet him, that's all. I don't want to mess up his life or anything.' Dan smiled, but his eyes were sad. He was already steeling himself for rejection, she could tell.

'How could you mess up anyone's life? You're my little

angel!' She enveloped him in a jokey hug, knowing it would drive him mad.

Dan pushed her away, blushing. 'Gerroff! People are looking.'

Tess grinned and waved as he headed towards the college building, making slow progress on his sticks. Her manic smile lasted until he'd turned the corner and disappeared out of sight. Then it was replaced by a scowl.

Bloody Phil. Wherever he was, whatever he was doing, she hoped he'd show his son more consideration than he'd ever shown her.

It was still on her mind at lunchtime, when she and Helen gathered with the others in the staffroom. Tess was standing at the copying machine, printing out some worksheets.

'I'm just worried Phil won't want to know him,' she said. 'It'll be like he's rejecting him all over again. Dan's been through a tough enough time, he doesn't need that.'

'He knows what he's doing.' Helen was her usual soothing self. 'Honestly, Tess, he's practically an adult. Old enough to look after himself.'

'Old habits die hard – oh, bugger!' Tess turned back to the photocopier, which had stopped chugging away and was now making an ominous whirring noise. 'What's wrong with this bloody thing now?'

'Try wiggling the tray. That usually works for me.'

Tess lifted the cover and peered inside. She punched a few buttons experimentally. Nothing happened.

'Must be a paper jam,' Helen said. 'It's always doing that.'

'Wretched machine. I'd be quicker doing this on a John Bull printing kit.' Tess crouched down and peered at the murky underside of the printer.

'Anyway, how do you know Phil will reject him?' Helen said. 'Maybe he's longing for the chance to get to know his son.'

'And maybe he's forgotten all about him.' Tess reached in and pulled out a handful of mangled paper. 'Let's face it, if he'd really wanted to come back and find us, it wouldn't have been that difficult, would it? I mean, it's not as if we've moved to the other side of the world and taken on a new identity. No, I expect he's got a family of his own by now. He's probably forgotten Dan even exists. That's what I'm really afraid of.'

'Are you sure about that?' Helen looked shrewdly at her.

'What do you mean?'

'If you ask me, you're more worried about what will happen if Phil doesn't reject him. Maybe you're feeling a teeny bit threatened? A bit possessive, maybe?'

'Rubbish!' Tess stood up and brushed the dust off her skirt. 'I've always said Dan has a right to find his father, if that's what he wants.'

'But admit it. You're secretly hoping he'll turn out to be a loser.'

Tess said nothing as she refilled the paper tray and pressed the Start button for the third time. 'Okay, so maybe I am. A bit,' she said reluctantly. 'But how would you feel if you'd brought a child up single-handed for seventeen years and then he suddenly turned round and announced he wanted his father? The father who'd abandoned him before he was even born?'

'I'd feel proud I'd brought up such a mature, sensible young man.'

'Cobblers. You'd be miffed as hell, and so am I. However you try to dress it up, it still feels like a kick in the teeth.'

'You know Dan doesn't see it like that. He loves you. He's just curious about his dad, that's all. This isn't a popularity contest, Tess.'

'Isn't it? That's what it feels like.' And Helen was right. Deep down she was secretly hoping Phil would turn out to be a god-awful nerd with appalling taste in clothes and

48

music. Preferably a Lada driver too. 'Damn!' She jabbed at the buttons as the photocopier ground to a noisy halt again. 'This thing is beyond a joke.'

'Try wiggling the tray again. What are you doing, anyway?'

'Copying some worksheets for my Year 8 class. I can't face those wretched grammar books again.'

'Worksheets?' Helen recoiled in mock horror. 'We know what Mrs Frobisher will have to say about that, don't we?'

'Mrs Frobisher can go and – oh no! Now look what's happened.' She pulled her arm out of the copier, her pristine white sleeves stained with dark smudges.

'It's a miracle,' Helen marvelled. 'That's the first time I've seen it print on anything. Shame it's your shirt, though.'

'What exactly are these?' Marjorie Wheeler looked down at the bundle of papers Tess had just given her with the same distaste as if she'd just slapped a decomposing mackerel in her hand.

'They're worksheets, Marjorie.'

'I can see that. What are we supposed to do with them?'

Tess bit back the suggestion that sprang immediately to mind. She could feel her enthusiasm beginning to crumble in the face of Marjorie's implacable resistance. Marjorie Wheeler was ten years older than Tess and had been her rival for the Department Head's job. As far as she was concerned, it was rightfully hers. Mrs Frobisher had spent five years grooming her as her successor until Tess whipped in and stole it. Now she saw it as her duty to uphold Mrs Frobisher's standards in the face of Tess' arrant sloppiness.

Tess understood her resentment and tried to make allowances. But sometimes it could be very wearing. 'I thought we could use them in class sometime. Maybe in conjunction with some free writing?'

'Free writing?' Marjorie looked so appalled Tess wondered if she'd misheard and thought she'd asked her to try some free love.

'Yes, you know – allow them to stretch their imagination?'

Still the same blank but horrified expression. How could she expect Marjorie to teach the kids anything about imagination, when her own was so shrivelled it would fit in a matchbox? In fact, everything about her seemed small and mean, from her tightly buttoned twinset to her permanently pursed mouth.

'Sounds like a good idea.' Tess could have hugged Stephen Kwarme, the newly qualified teacher, and not just because he was tall, muscular and looked like a younger and even more gorgeous Denzel Washington. 'It'll make a change from those grammar books, anyway.'

'There's nothing wrong with grammar,' Marjorie hissed. 'Grammar is one of the essential building blocks of the English language. Without grammar, there would be nothing but disorder, and chaos, and—'

'I agree,' Tess said hastily. 'But there's nothing wrong with trying something new, is there?'

Marjorie looked down at the paper in her hand. 'It seems rather unnecessary to me. Mrs Frobisher always said—'

'Yes, well, Mrs Frobisher isn't Head of Department any more, is she? I am.'

'More's the pity,' Marjorie muttered. Tess fought the urge to say something cutting. She was supposed to be motivating the staff, getting them on her side. Although nothing short of a white flag and total surrender would get Marjorie Wheeler to lower her guard. Which was a shame, because with the right amount of coaxing, Tess was sure she could be a good teacher.

'Look, it was just an idea. If you'd rather plan your own lessons—' She went to take the worksheets back but Marjorie clasped them to her chest.

'No,' she said. 'I'll – er – take these away and look at them.'

As they watched her scuttle out of the staffroom, Stephen said, 'You know where she's going, don't you?'

Tess nodded. 'Straight to show them to Mrs Frobisher. I expect they'll be working themselves into a lather of indignation and plotting my downfall over a plate of chocolate digestives within half an hour.'

'Doesn't it bother you?'

'I try not to let it. Hopefully I'll win her round one day.'

'I wouldn't bet on it. She seems very set in her ways.'

'And I'm very determined.' She looked at the box Stephen had just hauled into the staffroom. 'What's this lot?'

'Just some junk from my last teaching prac. I keep meaning to go through it, see if there's anything I want to keep that might be useful.'

Tess reached in and took out a photo. It was a team photo of some rather gorgeous-looking men in football kit. Stephen was at the front, nursing a trophy between his muscular thighs. 'I didn't know you played?'

He nodded. 'Our college won the championship last year.'

'You won't see many of them here. The last time Haxsall Park won a trophy for anything Abba had just won the Eurovision Song Contest. Come to think of it, that was about the same time Mrs Frobisher last bought a textbook.'

Stephen smiled. 'I know what you mean. Some of the books we've got were around when Noah took his GCSEs. And the library's even worse. Do you know, that woman only allows the kids to take out one book every month?'

'I know.' Tess had been having run-ins with Mrs Tate the librarian for ages. She ran the library with the same ruthless efficiency and lack of flair that Mrs Frobisher had used on the English department. Her idea of avant-garde modern literature were the Biggles books. But the real problem was she treated every book on the shelves as if it was her own. The last thing she wanted to do was let any of them fall into the clutches of some grubby teenager. 'I just wish I could do something to wake everyone up. Something that would grab the kids' attention, really get them interested. I don't suppose you've got any ideas?'

Stephen thought for a moment. 'Nude poetry readings?'

'Might be a bit chilly.' Tess looked back down at the photo in her hands. Although she wouldn't mind getting a better look at Stephen's fabulous physique . . .

She stuffed the photo back into the box before she broke into a sweat thinking about it, and quickly pulled out another. This was of a group of teenagers in old-fashioned costume, gathered on a stage. Stephen was standing next to a gawky-looking boy in a dress. 'So what's this? The college cross-dressing team?'

Stephen grinned. '*Charley's Aunt*,' he said. 'We had a very enthusiastic drama group in my old school.'

'It must have been enthusiastic to get a fifteen-year-old boy to wear a frock!' Tess tried to imagine persuading Jason Fothergill or Mark Nicholls that it would be a good idea to parade around in front of their peers in a shawl and bonnet.

And then it came to her.

'That's it,' she said. 'Stephen, you're a genius!'

'Why? What have I said?'

'I'll tell you later. After I've had a word with Cynthia.'

Chapter 6

That afternoon, Leanne and Jordan caught up with Emily on the way to PE. She was immediately on her guard, but they were surprisingly friendly.

'We don't want to fall out with you,' Leanne said. 'It's just *her* we can't stand.' She nodded to where Paris lingered behind them, watching and waiting.

'She's all right.'

'You don't know anything about her. Her mum's a slag. And she's been inside. Bet she didn't tell you that, did she?' Leanne smirked. 'Your mate Paris had to go into care. She's even got a social worker.'

Emily stuck out her chin. 'So?'

'And she's got loads of brothers and sisters, all by different dads. Sometimes her mum makes her stay off school to look after them, if she's too hungover or wants to go out nicking.'

Emily glanced over her shoulder. Paris had gone. 'At least she's not brain-dead,' she said. 'At least she can talk about something else but whether Posh Spice has had a sodding boob job!'

'Fine, if that's the way you feel.' Leanne shrugged. 'You stick with her. But don't say we didn't warn you.'

'Ooh, I'm scared.'

'You should be,' Leanne called back over her shoulder as she and Jordan headed off to the playing field.

She and Paris were the last to be picked for the team. As they stood shivering together on the touchline Paris said, 'Just so you know, I've only got two brothers.'

'What about the rest of it?'

'Mostly true.' Her face flashed defiance.

Emily looked up at the greying sky. 'I really hate hockey,' she said.

'At least we've got something in common.'

She ended up marking Jordan in defence. Luckily she was a bit of a wimp without Leanne to back her up, and apart from a couple of whacks in the shins when the teacher wasn't looking, Emily managed to escape unscathed.

They were getting changed after showers when she realised Mr Bunny was missing. Heart racing, she upended her bag, spilling books out on to the wet floor. But he was gone.

'Lost something?' Leanne asked innocently.

'What have you done with it?'

'I don't know what you're talking about.'

'No need to snap her head off, she was only asking if you'd lost anything,' Jordan said.

Emily held out her hand. 'Give it back.'

'Give what back, Em?'

'You know.' She felt the blush rising as silence fell around the changing room.

'You mean your bunny wunny? Thought you'd be a bit old for toys by now.'

'What's going on?' Paris stood behind her, drying her hair.

'And you can stay out of it, council kid.' Leanne thrust her face close to hers, so close she could almost count the freckles crowding her pudgy cheeks. 'Look, she's crying. Has Mummy's ickle baby lost her ickle toy, then?'

'Leave her alone,' Paris said. 'Her mum's dead.'

There was something about those piggy eyes and that screwed-up mouth so close to her face that made Emily snap. Before she knew what she was doing, she'd reached out and yanked a handful of frizzy blonde hair. Leanne screamed and twisted free, then flew at Emily, punching and clawing. A second later, they were circled by girls in various states of undress, all yelling. Their screams filled Emily's head as she went down, Leanne on top of her, pinning her to the hard wet floor. She hit out wildly, then felt a crunching pain as a fist made contact with her lip. Somewhere beyond the screams, she heard Paris' voice, pleading with them to stop. And then, 'What's going on?' The circle parted for Miss Wesley to come through.

Leanne immediately burst into tears. 'It was them, Miss,' she sobbed. 'They attacked me, the two of them.'

'That's right, Miss,' Jordan joined in. 'They just went for her.'

Miss Wesley turned to Emily. 'Is this true?'

Emily staggered to her feet, blood trickling from her lip. 'She started it.'

'And what exactly did she do to you?'

'She – she –' Her face flamed. She couldn't say it.

She looked around, waiting for someone to defend her. Blank faces stared back. They were all too scared of Leanne and Jordan to say anything.

'I see.' Miss Wesley folded her arms. 'Maybe you'd prefer to tell Mrs Frobisher? Go along to her office, the pair of you.'

'A school play?'

Tess and Cynthia Frobisher faced each other in the Deputy Head's office. Cynthia sat dominantly behind the desk, leaving Tess the low chair on the other side. It was impossible to assert oneself while sinking into its leathery depths.

'You want to put on a school play?' She made it sound as if Tess had suggested a nude revival of *Oh! Calcutta!*.

'Why not? It'll be fun.'

'It'll be a disaster.'

'How can you say that?'

'Because we've done it before and it's always been a

55

nightmare. The students simply aren't up to it. Let's face it, most of them have trouble remembering their own names, let alone lines. They're not interested.'

Tess held on to her temper with effort. Like it or not, she needed Cynthia's cooperation. She wasn't going to get anywhere without it. 'You're not giving them a chance.'

'Only because I know what they're capable of! And where would the money come from? We can barely cover lessons, let alone finance some lavish production.'

'It doesn't have to be lavish. We're talking about a school play here, not a remake of *Ben Hur*! Anyway, it would pay for itself once we start selling tickets.'

'Sell tickets?' Cynthia sat back, nostrils aquiver. 'You're not seriously expecting people to *pay* to see this debacle, are you?'

'Why not? Hopefully we'll even make a profit. We could buy some new books for the school library—'

'But that's tantamount to begging!'

'I wouldn't have to beg if you'd let me have more money.'

There was a tense pause while Cynthia weighed up the situation. Then she gave Tess her most patronising smile. 'Look, I know you mean well, but you simply don't have the experience to know when to use your judgement in these things. I'm sure in a few years you'll come to realise I'm right.'

That's if I haven't buried a hatchet in your head before then, Tess thought. She struggled to get out of her seat. 'Fine,' she said. 'I'll just go and tell Mr Gant you're not keen on the idea, shall I? Only he seemed to think it might work. But what does he know? I mean, he's only the Headteacher. He doesn't have your years of experience, does he?'

Cynthia paled. 'You've spoken to Eric?'

'Of course. I had to get his say-so before I approached you, didn't I?' Tess glanced at the phone, praying she wouldn't pick it up and call him. It would be too humiliating to be caught out telling such an outrageous lie.

Cynthia straightened the papers on her spotless desk, a sure sign she was annoyed. 'You should have come to me first, instead of bothering the Head. We're supposed to be working together.'

Funny how she never thought of that when she 'forgot' to send important emails and called staff meetings behind her back. Tess smiled beatifically. 'Of course we are, Cynthia. And I'm sure if we put our heads together, we can make this a huge success.'

But from the tight-lipped look on Cynthia's face, it was clear this play would take place over her dead body.

'It's so bloody unfair!' Emily complained, as they made their way up the stairs to Mrs Frobisher's office. 'Leanne's a lying cow!'

'She'll get away with it,' Paris shrugged. 'She always does.'

They headed off the main staircase and through the double doors. As they neared the door marked 'Deputy Head', Paris whispered, 'Try not to meet her eye. And whatever you do, don't answer back. She hates that.'

Miss Doyle was in Mrs Frobisher's office. 'Emily?' She looked up in surprise as the secretary showed them into the room. 'What are you doing here? What have you done to your face?'

'They were fighting in the girls' changing rooms,' the secretary announced behind them. 'Miss Wesley just called. Apparently they both set about Leanne Hooper.'

'Surely not?' Miss Doyle looked in bewilderment from one to the other. 'Paris, I can't believe you'd do something like that?'

Before Paris could answer, Mrs Frobisher said, 'I think I'd better talk to these two, Miss Doyle. We'll finish our little chat later, shall we?'

Miss Doyle didn't move. 'If you don't mind, Mrs Frobisher, these girls are in my form. I'm sure I can sort this out.'

Mrs Frobisher's smile became steely. 'Miss Wesley sent them to me.'

'But I know them.'

'Exactly. So your judgement is bound to be clouded, isn't it?'

For a second Emily thought Miss Doyle was going to lunge across the desk and grab a handful of hair just like she had Leanne's. But instead she got up and said, 'Fine. But I shall be talking to them myself later.'

'That's entirely up to you.'

Miss Doyle turned to Emily. 'I'd go to the medical room as soon as you're finished in here. That lip looks nasty.'

Emily's heart sank a little lower as the door closed behind her. She felt as if they'd just lost their only ally.

She turned to face Mrs Frobisher. She was ancient with a slash of vivid red lipstick on her thin mouth, a helmet of brown hair and eyes that lacked any sympathy.

Unnerved, she blurted out, 'It wasn't Paris. She had nothing to do with it.'

'I beg your pardon? I wasn't aware I'd invited you to speak?'

'I know, but I just wanted to tell you—'

'When I want you to say something I'll ask you. Now, just for that outburst we will all sit in silence for five minutes to give you time to reflect on your behaviour.'

The minutes stretched by. Emily tried to compose herself, anxious to get her story straight. But she was thrown off her guard when, as soon as five minutes had passed, Mrs Frobisher turned to her and said, 'Now, perhaps you could tell me what you think gives you the right to go around attacking other girls?'

'I didn't attack her!'

'Apparently there are witnesses who say you did.'

'Yes, but they're liars.'

'So everyone is lying except you?'

'Well – yes.' She heard Paris groan beside her.

'And you're saying you didn't lunge at her and pull her hair?'

'I did, but—'

'I'd call that attacking someone, wouldn't you?'

She was like a barrister on the telly, the way she twisted everything around. It was worse than being grilled by Anne Robinson. Emily was determined not to lose her cool. 'I'd call it retaliation,' she said.

Mrs Frobisher's eyes narrowed. 'Oh, you would, would you? And what exactly were you *retaliating* against?'

'She'd stolen something from me.'

'I see. And what had she stolen?'

Emily stared down at her hands. 'A toy rabbit,' she mumbled.

'Speak up, I can't hear you.'

'I said a toy rabbit.'

Mrs Frobisher's crimson lips stretched into a sneer. 'A toy rabbit? You beat a girl up because she stole your *toy*?'

'I didn't beat her up,' Emily said. 'She attacked me.'

'I don't blame her. If you go around pulling hair, what do you expect?' Mrs Frobisher turned to Paris, who'd been staring into space since they'd sat down. 'And you. What was your part in all this?'

'I told you, she didn't do—' Emily saw Mrs Frobisher's face and shut up.

'I wasn't asking you. Besides, knowing her background, I find that very hard to believe.'

Outrage flowed like heat through her veins. 'That's not fair!'

'I beg your pardon?'

'Don't,' Paris whispered, but Emily was too angry at the injustice to care.

59

'I said it's not fair. Why do you believe a cow like Leanne and not her?'

Mrs Frobisher looked about ready to explode. 'I realise you're new to this school and so your standards may be a little lower than we're used to.' Her eyes were like chips of granite. 'But I have to tell you that kind of behaviour simply won't be tolerated at Haxsall Park. You do not go around attacking other students, and you certainly don't speak to a senior member of staff the way you have just spoken to me.' She drew back in her seat and looked down at them. 'I was thinking of giving you the benefit of the doubt as it's your first term and you've obviously fallen under a bad influence . . .' Her eyes shot towards Paris. 'But after listening to your outburst I have to say I've changed my mind. You will both have an hour's detention tomorrow night.'

'But—' Emily began to protest, but Paris seized her arm and dragged her out of the office. 'That's so unfair!' she shouted, when they were safely out of earshot.

'Told you, didn't I?'

'But you didn't deserve it! If anyone does detention, it should be that lying bitch Leanne Hooper.'

'Let it go,' Paris said. 'Come on, we'll be late for French.'

'You go on, I'll catch you up. I've got to go to the medical room.'

'Do you want me to come with you?'

'No, it's okay. I'll catch you up.'

Paris looked wary. 'You're not going to do anything stupid, are you?'

'Like what?'

'I dunno. Do a runner, or something.'

'Don't you think I'm in enough trouble? Now, go on, you'll be late.' She gave her a push. Paris hesitated, then headed off, leaving Emily alone.

Don't cry, she warned herself, but she couldn't help it.

60

She'd wept a lot over the past year, but this time they were tears of rage and frustration.

She fled outside before anyone could see her. It was late afternoon and the sky was full of bruised purple clouds. The threat of rain hung in the air.

Emily hugged her arms around her, but she couldn't bring herself to go back inside. She never wanted to go back there. If she had to face Leanne Hooper, she'd do a lot worse than pull her hair.

The school gates lay ahead of her. Emily licked her swollen lip, tasting blood. Then she started walking. With every step she expected someone to call her back, but no one did. She was through the gates and out in the street before she even knew what she was doing.

Chapter 7

It was nearly two when Jack rushed into the glass and steel offices of Crawshaw and Finch, a Starbucks' Americano in one hand, Next carrier bag in the other.

His PA, Vicky, looked up from her keyboard. 'Not trouble with the washing machine again?'

'It's a nightmare. Thanks to Sophie's PE kit, all my shirts now have an interesting tie-dye effect.'

Vicky followed him into his office. 'You do know you're not supposed to put whites in with coloureds, don't you?'

'I do now.'

'Maybe you should try reading the instructions next time?'

'Have you ever tried reading an instruction manual written by a team of Japanese dyslexics?' He ripped the wrapping off his shirt. Vicky watched him with amusement.

'Anyway, I thought your cleaner did your washing and ironing these days?'

'So did I. Apparently that was something else I got wrong.'

Somehow, he'd ended up with the Jennifer Lopez of the cleaning world, a domestic diva who was prone to downing tools and going home if he accidentally bought the wrong brand of bathroom mousse.

He and Pauline differed wildly on what her domestic duties should be. He thought she should clean the house, stack and empty the dishwasher and do the occasional load of washing and ironing if he left it out for her. She thought she should drink coffee, watch *Trisha*, phone her friends and squirt some Pledge into the air five minutes before he walked in the door. He sometimes toyed with the fantasy of firing her, but they both knew he'd never have the nerve.

As he pulled the cardboard dressing from under the collar, a plastic clip pinged out from nowhere and narrowly missed his eye. 'Bugger! Why do these bloody things have so many pins and clips and bits of plastic?'

Vicky rolled her eyes. 'I'll leave you to it. Let me know if you can't manage the buttons on your own.'

He pulled off his shirt and tie and was just removing yet another pin he'd overlooked, when the door opened again. Without turning round, he said, 'It's all right, I am capable of dressing myself. I'm a big boy now.'

'So I see.'

He swung round. Charlotte Ferguson stood in the doorway. Like him, she was one of the senior planning consultants, thirty years old, tall and willowy with sleek auburn hair and challenging hazel eyes that could shrivel a man's gonads at fifty paces.

Those same eyes were now fixed appraisingly on his bare chest. Jack clutched his shirt protectively against him. 'Charlie! Can I help you?'

'I've brought that revised junction layout for you to look at.'

'Thanks. You can just leave it, if you like?'

'It's okay, I'm in no hurry.' She sat down, smiling mischievously. 'Besides, I'm enjoying the show.'

He turned away from her to button up his shirt, but he could still feel her eyes giving his rear the once-over. 'You realise I could probably do you for sexual harrassment?'

'I'm not the one parading around the office topless.'

For an instant as he turned his eyes dropped to her cleavage and then shot back up to meet her eyes. 'Right. Erm. Now, about that layout?'

'This is what I've come up with so far.' She came round to his side of the desk and spread the plans in front of him.

'You see the problem? I thought if we could just move this junction over to here –' As she leaned across, Jack caught a whiff of her sharp, sexy scent. He also realised she wasn't wearing anything under her black tailored Nicole Farhi jacket. 'That would ease the traffic build-up and take away some of the council's objections. What do you think? Jack?'

'What? Oh yes, right.' He averted his eyes from her plunging neckline. For heaven's sake, what was he thinking of? Charlie was a friend, a colleague. She was also not the kind of woman you treated lightly. Not if you valued your manhood, anyway. 'You're the traffic engineer. I'm just a humble architect, remember?'

'Not so humble from what I've heard.' Charlie rolled up the plans. 'Word is you're in line for the top job.'

'Me and everyone else.' It was no secret that Alec Finch was due to retire at the end of the year. For the past few months speculation had been raging over who would be offered his place in the partnership.

'Yes, but you're bound to get it. The others are all butt-kissing toads. They can't have a pee without emailing the boss about it.'

'What about you? You could be in the running.'

Charlie shook her head. 'I haven't been here long enough. But if Alec had decided to retire next year instead of this, I might have given you a run for your money.'

'I don't doubt it.' Charlie might be one of his nicer colleagues, but she was also one of the most ambitious. And she wasn't above using her sex appeal to get her way.

'Anyway, if I can't have the job myself I'd rather you did,' she said.

'Thanks. You're great at massaging egos.'

'I'm great at massaging all kinds of things.'

He was still wondering how to answer that when the door flew open and a man stormed in, followed by a breathless Vicky.

'Are you Mr Tyler?' he demanded. He was about sixty, stocky with thinning sandy hair.

'I tried to stop him,' Vicky said. I told him he needed an appointment—'

'It's okay, Vicky.' Jack stood up. He towered over the other man, although from the look of his flattened boxer's nose he still wouldn't have fancied taking him on. 'I'm Jack Tyler. And you are?'

'Sam Dobbs.' He ignored the hand Jack offered. 'I want to talk to you about this Westpoint thing.'

'I'll call security.' Charlie reached for the phone, but Jack stopped her.

'There's no need for that. What did you want to say, Mr Dobbs?'

Sam Dobbs looked taken aback. He'd obviously been expecting a fight. 'You can't let it go ahead. It would devastate the local community.'

'For heaven's sake!' Charlie snorted. 'We're building a shopping centre, not dropping an atom bomb!'

'You might as well be.' He turned to Jack. 'These shops are nothing to do with us. We don't even want them. It'll just mean more traffic clogging up the streets and less green space for the kids to play, not to mention all the local shops being put out of business.'

'As far as traffic goes, I think you'll find—' Charlie began to say, but Sam held up his hand.

'No offence, love, but I'm talking to the boss here.' He looked at Jack. 'You've got to stop this thing.'

Jack, who'd been trying not to smile at Charlie's outraged expression, pulled himself together. 'I'm sorry, Mr Dobbs, but you're talking to the wrong man.'

'You designed the thing, didn't you?'

'Yes, but we're only acting as consultants. If you want to object, you need to talk to the council. They give the final yes or no to the scheme.'

'Aye, and we all know what they're going to say, don't we? You lot are all in this together.'

Jack suppressed a sigh. Why did everyone always assume there was a big conspiracy going on? 'Actually, that's not quite true. There's going to be a public inquiry on Westpoint.'

The old man looked suspicious. 'Oh aye? And what's that when it's at home?'

'It's an independent inquiry, Mr Dobbs. A government-appointed planning inspector listens to all the arguments, then decides whether the project should go ahead. Like a court case.'

'I know all about court cases. The ones with the fanciest barristers always win.' He leaned forward across the desk, thrusting his face so close Jack could see the thread veins in his weatherbeaten cheeks. 'What chance do us ordinary people have against you lot, with all your money? I wouldn't be surprised if you were all in it together. You'll probably just give this inspector bloke one of your funny handshakes and the deal with be as good as done.'

'I wish it were that simple,' Jack muttered. 'Look, if you feel that strongly about it, why don't you try and muster some local support? Form an action group or something?'

'What's the point? No one wants to listen to us. No one cares what we think.'

'Perhaps they might, if you had a coherent argument to put across?'

Sam Dobbs' calloused hands balled into fists at his sides. Then the fight seemed to go out of him. 'I knew it was a waste of time coming here.' He looked from Jack to Charlie and back again. 'You're all the same, in your expensive suits and smart offices. It's all about profit with you lot. You don't care what's happening out there in the real world as long as you can drive around in your bloody Porsches!'

He was still mumbling to himself as Jack eased him out of his office and closed the door.

'What a rude little man,' Charlie said. 'You should have let me call security.'

'And give him the chance to go bleating to the local press? Westpoint is unpopular enough without attracting even more bad publicity.'

'I didn't realise it was that bad?'

'Bad?' He sat down and rubbed his eyes wearily. 'Sometimes I think it would be easier to build a bacon factory in Tel Aviv.'

He'd always known Westpoint was going to be a problem. A consortium of property developers had got together to build a major new retail park on an old airfield just outside the city. As planning consultants, it was Crawshaw and Finch's job to make sure the whole project went smoothly, from designing the buildings to making sure they obtained planning permission. But not surprisingly, the local residents weren't thrilled by the idea of several big department stores at the bottom of their gardens, and had kicked up so much fuss the whole thing had been referred to a public inquiry.

And contrary to what Sam Dobbs believed, it wasn't just a matter of 'funny handshakes'. If the inspector decided the locals had a case, he might recommend refusal. Which meant months of hard work down the drain, not to mention Jack's chances of securing the partnership.

Thanks to Mr Dobbs' unscheduled appearance, Jack was late for the Westpoint consortium meeting. As Westpoint were their most important clients, Crawshaw and Finch had wheeled out their biggest guns. Humphrey Crawshaw himself was chairing the meeting, surrounded by the heads of the legal, finance and environment departments. Jack's brother-in-law Greg, who was coordinating the project, sat beside him.

On the other side of the table were the suits from Westpoint, headed by Peter Jameson, a small man with sleek silver hair.

Jack nodded a greeting at everyone and took his seat at the far end of the table, next to Bernard Sweeting the environment expert, who was doodling trees on his A4 jotter.

Humphrey opened the meeting and passed it over to Greg, who consulted his notes for a moment.

'As you know, the council has given planning permission in principle for the Westpoint Centre to go ahead,' he began. 'But our plans have met with some local opposition. The residents aren't happy with the amount of disruption and extra traffic that may be generated by the scheme, and the city-centre retailers fear the centre will attract customers away from the city. Between them, they've managed to make enough noise for the local press to take an interest and have recently started a campaign to stop Westpoint going ahead.'

'We know that.' Peter Jameson looked irritable. 'We're all well aware of the problems. We hired you to get rid of them, not tell us what they are!'

'I'm coming to that.' There was a sheen of perspiration on Greg's upper lip as he flicked through his file. Not for the first time, Jack felt relieved he wasn't the one coordinating this project. Humphrey had approached him to do it, but he'd turned it down because Miranda had just died and he didn't feel he could handle it.

But he felt guilty as he watched Greg stumbling through his presentation. Jack had suggested him for the job but Ros had admitted he'd been having sleepless nights over it.

'We felt the best way forward was to launch a PR counter-offensive, to try and get public opinion on our side.' Greg found his place and carried on. 'We're about to produce a mailshot of our own, highlighting the positive benefits for the community. Greater retail opportunities, creation of local jobs, environmental benefits—'

'Environmental benefits?' Peter Jameson looked blank. 'Are there any?'

They all turned to Bernard Sweeting, who dropped his pen in panic. 'Well – um – we'll be planting fifty trees as part of the scheme.'

'Are we? That sounds good.' Peter nodded his approval.

'Unfortunately we're pulling down a hundred to build it.'

'Although obviously we won't be telling anyone that,' Greg put in. Jack noticed Peter Jameson's expression and cringed inwardly.

'Yes, but it doesn't take a genius to find out that kind of information, does it? The press will be on to us in five minutes.' He pinned Greg with a glacial stare. 'Frankly it seems a ridiculous idea to highlight the environmental benefits when any fool can see that at the end of the day there will be a few less acres of green space and a few extra roads.'

'Yes, but—'

'I'm afraid you're going to have to do better than that if you're going to stay in charge of this project.'

Greg looked crushed. He was a big, solid man with fair hair, merry blue eyes and the look of an overgrown, naughty schoolboy. In this case, a schoolboy who had been cornered by the playground bully.

'I think what Greg's trying to say is that we need to get the local authority on our side,' Jack stepped in quickly. Everyone turned to look at him. 'If they decide to take on board what the residents are saying, they could change their mind about granting us planning permission. Then we'd be in real trouble. We've got to give them a reason to get behind the Westpoint scheme. Show them they stand to gain by it going ahead. That's what you were coming to, wasn't it, Greg?'

Greg, who was still gathering his thoughts, stared at him blankly. 'What? Oh – er – yes.'

'You mean like a bribe?' Peter's eyes glittered.

'More like an . . . incentive. We thought we might offer them something they really need – like a new bus terminal. We could design it, give them the land and a bit towards the cost. And it would get around the problem of the increased traffic being generated by showing we're encouraging the use of public transport.'

There was a silence. Then Peter Jameson said. 'That seems like the most sensible suggestion anyone's come up with so far.'

'It's something we've been working on as a team for a while,' Jack said. 'Greg asked me to put something on paper a few days ago.' He looked down the table at his brother-in-law. 'I'm sorry I haven't managed to get back to you until now.'

'Er – no problem.' Greg shuffled his papers in front of him.

As the meeting closed, Humphrey Crawshaw cornered him. 'Excellent contribution as ever, Jack.'

'It was a team effort,' he insisted.

'Perhaps.' Humphrey sent him a shrewd look. 'It's just a pity you're not at the head of the team. I'm sure Jameson agrees.'

As he walked away, Jack noticed Greg standing there. From the look on his face, it was clear he'd heard every word.

'He's right,' he said. 'You should be the one in charge, not me.'

'Take no notice of them. You're doing a great job.'

'Yeah, right. That's why Jameson made such a fool of me in there. Face it, Jack, the man hates me.'

Jack wished there was something he could say. He hadn't realised Greg had taken it so much to heart. Usually he was always laughing, treating everything as a huge joke, including work. 'I work to live, not the other way round,' he always said, whenever Jack was burning the midnight oil over a drawing. 'Besides, there's only room for one rising star in this family.'

'Take no notice of Jameson, he's just a bully,' he said. 'You were always pretty good with bullies at school, as I recall?'

They'd been friends ever since they met at secondary school in Leeds. Back in those days, Greg had been his unofficial minder. Nobody messed with Jack Tyler when scrum half Greg Randall was around. 'Remember that time some kid stole my lunch money and you flushed his head down the toilet? What was his name?'

'Tony Jefferson.' Greg smiled reluctantly. 'Much as I'd like to, I think I'm a bit old to be stuffing Peter Jameson's head down the bog!'

'Nice thought though, isn't it?' Jack grinned.

They were still laughing at the idea when Vicky stuck her head round the door. 'Jack, I've got Emily's school on the phone.'

He sighed. 'Oh God, what's she done now?'

'That's just it, they don't know. They think she's run away!'

Chapter 8

Emily's bravado deserted her once she was outside the school gates. She stood shivering in the street, with no idea what to do next. She'd always fancied the idea of bunking off, but now she didn't feel clever at all. She felt like crying. Her school bag was still in the cloakroom, as was her coat. All she had were a few coins left over from her dinner money. It was too cold to wander the streets and she couldn't go home because she'd left her key in her bag.

She sat in the bus shelter, jingling the coins in her pocket. If she managed to con the driver into thinking she was a half fare, she could make it into the city centre. After that she wasn't sure what she would do.

A shadow fell over her. She looked up. There was Miss Doyle, holding Emily's coat and school bag.

'I thought you might be needing these.'

'Thanks.' Emily took them gingerly. 'How did you know where I'd be?'

'The bright ones always try to catch the first bus out of here. The others just go to the chippie and play on the arcade games. Although I have to say it wasn't exactly bright to walk out of school in the first place. Mind if I sit down?'

Emily shuffled along to make room for her. Miss Doyle sat down and they both stared up the empty road for a moment, looking for the bus that had so far failed to appear.

'Well,' Miss Doyle said. 'It's been quite a day for you, hasn't it?' Emily shrugged. 'So why did you run away? Was it because of Leanne and Jordan?'

'No! They don't scare me.'

'What, then?'

'I was just angry.' She explained what had happened in Mrs Frobisher's office. 'It wasn't fair,' she said. 'She shouldn't have taken it out on Paris. It was my fault, not hers.'

'If anyone was at fault, it was Leanne.'

'Yes, but they're not going to punish her, are they?'

'Probably not,' Miss Doyle agreed. 'But I'm a great believer in what goes around, comes around. And if it's any consolation, I bet one day Leanne and Jordan will get their come-uppance.'

'I'd like to be the one to give it to them.'

Miss Doyle smiled. 'I'll pretend I didn't hear that.' She stood up. 'We can't sit around here all day. I think it's going to rain any minute.'

Emily's defiance returned. 'I'm not going back to school.'

'I don't think there's much point, do you?' Miss Doyle looked at her watch. 'It's practically home time anyway. Why don't I give you a lift home? I've finished lessons for the day. Unless there's somewhere else you were planning to go?'

'Nowhere special.' Although there was somewhere. She'd been wanting to go for months.

Miss Doyle must have read her face, because she said, 'Look, if you need a lift anywhere, I'm happy to take you.'

Emily bit her lip. 'It's a long way.'

'I'm in no hurry. Like I said, I'm free for the rest of the day.'

She stared at her shoes, wondering whether to risk telling her. 'I'd like to go to the cemetery in Leeds. To see my mum.'

'Do you want me to take you there now?'

She looked up. 'Would you?'

'If that's what you want.'

Emily gazed down the road. There was no sign of the bus.

'Unless you'd prefer your dad to take you?'

'No chance! He won't go. He never goes to see Mum. I've asked him loads of times if he'd take us, but he always says no.'

'Maybe he's afraid it will upset you?'

'I'm not a kid!' Emily snapped. 'It's him who doesn't like being there, not me. He only thinks of himself. Just like when he moved here.'

Miss Doyle was silent for a moment. Then she said, 'In that case, I think we should go. We could buy some flowers on the way, if you like?'

'Are you sure?'

'Why not? I think school can manage without both of us, just this once. As long as we don't make a habit of it. But we'll have to let your dad know.'

'No!' Emily sat back down.

'Emily! The school will have contacted him by now. He'll probably be on his way home, worried sick. I've got to tell him.'

'I don't want him to know.'

'Fine. Then we're not going anywhere.' Emily stared at Miss Doyle, surprised. Adults had tiptoed around her so much since her mum died, it came as a shock to find someone who stood up to her.

'Okay,' she agreed reluctantly. 'But do you have to tell him exactly where we're going? He'll only be angry or try to stop me.'

'I can't believe that. Why should he try to stop you?'

'I told you, he doesn't want us to visit Mum. He wants us to forget all about her. You don't know him.'

Miss Doyle looked as if she might argue, then changed her mind. She pushed her glasses up her nose and thought for a moment. 'Tell you what, why don't I leave a message on your answer machine at home? I'll just tell him we've gone to Leeds but not exactly where we're going. How about that?'

Emily smiled. 'Deal.'

Miss Doyle's car was a wreck, but cool with it. It didn't look like a grown-up's car, not like her dad's boring BMW, or the Peugeot her mum used to drive. It didn't have a CD player or air conditioning. All it had was a radio cassette player, tied in place with a tatty bit of string. But she had some decent tapes, really good music like The Chemical Brothers instead of that sad old Phil Collins stuff her dad always played. And the glove compartment was stuffed with chocolate wrappers.

'It's my ecosystem,' Miss Doyle explained as she squeezed herself in behind the wheel. 'I've got everything I need to survive in here. Music, food – there's even some homework on the back seat, if I ever get bored in a traffic jam. Sorry, I've eaten all the chocolate, but I think there are still some jelly babies in the seat pocket next to you. I have put them out of reach otherwise I'd be hyperactive by the time I got to school.' She did an impression of a maniac, planted her foot on the accelerator and shot forward into the incoming traffic.

Emily giggled. She'd never seen a teacher out of school before, and she was shocked at how nice Miss Doyle was. She couldn't imagine any adult, let alone a teacher, listening to hardcore dance music and stuffing their face with jelly babies.

They passed the time on the way to Leeds with a discussion on the best way to eat them. Emily was all for nibbling the arms and legs off first, but Miss Doyle came down firmly on the side of decapitation. 'I don't know, it just seems kinder if they can't see what's happening to them,' she reasoned.

On the way, they stopped off and bought some flowers. Heavily scented cream roses tinged with pink, her mum's favourites. Miss Doyle paid for them. 'Pay me back some other time,' she said when Emily took out her meagre handful of coins.

It felt weird being back at the cemetery again after all this time. She'd thought she could handle it, but going through those wrought-iron gates brought it all flooding back. Coming through them in the back of the slow-moving black car, seeing everyone gathered by the grave. Then, as the car in front wheeled slowly round, getting her first glimpse of her mother's coffin in the back. It looked so small. Emily had tried to pretend it was nothing, just an empty box. She'd almost managed it too, until she saw the flowers. White carnations spelling out the word 'Mum'.

It was the same feeling she got now, looking at her mother's gravestone. The pale marble gleamed in the gathering dusk, the name picked out in black letters, 'Miranda Rachel Tyler'. Emily gulped in the cold air.

'I'm just going to have a look round,' Miss Doyle said. 'Come and get me when you want to leave.' Then she walked away, threading her way between the gravestones, leaving Emily to cry on her own.

Tess trudged up the path to the far end of the cemetery, her collar turned up against the cold spitting rain. The air smelt of freshly cut grass and rotting leaves. She sat on a bench under the dark canopy of a yew tree and watched Emily arranging the flowers on her mother's grave. Poor kid, she looked so young in her school uniform. Too young to have to cope with something so tragic.

She wished she could have made her first couple of weeks easier for her. She'd been furious when she found out Mrs Frobisher had given her and Paris detention.

'The girl's got to learn,' she'd said, when Tess argued with her about it. As if she hadn't had enough hard lessons in life already.

It was getting dark when Emily finished arranging the flowers and came to find her.

Tess smiled. 'Ready?'

Emily nodded. Her eyes were red-rimmed. 'Thanks.'

They walked back to the car in silence. Tess could tell there was something on Emily's mind, but she waited for her to speak.

Finally she said, 'Have you ever known anyone who died?'

'My dad. But it was a long time ago now. I was about your age.'

'And do you still miss him?'

Tess thought back to her father, Martin Doyle. A big man, always laughing. Even when he was angry there was always a twinkle in his eye. 'Very much,' she said. 'Although the pain does fade away a bit as time goes on, so you end up with just the good memories.'

Emily kicked at a pile of leaves. 'I don't think I'll ever have any good memories.'

'You might think that now, but wait and see.'

'You don't understand! I can't have good memories because—' she broke off.

'Because of what, Emily?'

'It doesn't matter.' She didn't say any more until they reached the car. Then, as Tess searched for her key, she blurted out, 'I was with her. When she died.'

'I didn't realise. How awful for you.'

'It was.' Her face was haunted. 'No one knows what it was like. No one knows what happened.'

'Do you want to tell me about it?'

She said nothing. They got into the car and Tess started it up, then joined the slow crawl of traffic heading out of Leeds.

'Why do they call it the rush hour, when no one's going anywhere?' she wondered aloud.

She was just reaching for the jelly babies when Emily suddenly said, 'We were out late-night Christmas shopping. She kept saying she had a headache, but I took no notice.'

Tess glanced sideways at her.

'I needed her to see the trainers I wanted for Christmas, to make sure she knew the right ones to get.' She stared straight ahead of her at the red tail lights of the car in front. 'We had a row about it, because she wouldn't go back to the shop. She just wanted to get home. I started getting angry, I told her I hated her, then she sort of – collapsed.' Like a dam breaking, her words came out in a rush, tumbling over each other. 'I didn't know, did I? I didn't know she was going to die.'

'Of course you didn't.'

'I would never have said it if I'd known. I didn't hate her, I didn't. But I never got the chance to tell her I didn't mean it.'

Tess swallowed the lump in her throat. 'Have you told your dad about this?'

'No! And I don't want you to tell him either.'

'Of course I won't, not if you don't want me to. But I think you should talk to him. He's worried about you.'

'How can I tell him I killed Mum? He'd hate me.'

'Emily, you didn't kill your mum.'

'How do you know? You weren't there. No one was. Except me.'

'I'm sure she could have collapsed at any time.'

Emily looked down at her bitten nails. 'That's what the doctors said at the hospital.'

'You see? So how could it have been your fault? Your dad could have been with her, or your sister. Or she might have been on her own.'

'No, it was me. If I hadn't shouted at her about those stupid trainers . . .' She fumbled in her pocket for a tissue. 'I wish I hadn't said those things. I wish I hadn't told her I hated her.'

'We all say things we don't mean,' Tess said. 'Your mum would have known that. She would have known how much you loved her.'

'Do you think so?' Emily sniffed back the tears.

'Of course. My son tells me he hates me every time I say he can't do something, but I know he doesn't mean it. Mothers know these things.'

They talked as they drove home, about music, school, Emily's friends back in Leeds. Tess wondered if Jack Tyler understood how much his daughter missed them.

As they turned off the A64 into the leafy suburbs of York, Emily said, 'I didn't know you had a son.'

'Where do you think the tapes come from?' Tess held up a cassette. 'Dan's studying for his A Levels at sixth form college.' She smiled at Emily's surprised expression. 'Go on, say it. You didn't think I was that old.'

'I didn't. You seem really young.'

'Everyone's parents are old, Emily. And old-fashioned. And not one of them knows what they're talking about.' That coaxed a smile out of her. 'Why don't you talk to your dad about what you've told me?'

'No!' Emily sank down in her seat and looked sullen. 'He wouldn't understand.'

'He might, if you gave him the chance. I'm sure he knows there's something on your mind.'

'He doesn't. He's too worried about himself to care how we feel. That's why he works all the time.'

'I expect he has a very demanding job.'

'It's not that. He just doesn't want to be with us.'

'Why ever not?'

'Because we remind him too much.' She looked at Tess, her eyes huge and desolate in her pale face. 'He wants to forget about everything. That's why we moved house. And that's why he never goes to the cemetery. He doesn't want anything to remind him of her.' A tear escaped down her cheek and she brushed it away. 'I think he'd move away from us if he could.'

'Oh, Emily! I'm sure that's not true. Your dad really

loves you. He wants what's best for you. Maybe he just doesn't know what that is yet.'

'Or he doesn't care,' Emily mumbled.

Following Emily's directions, Tess skirted the estate, past the parade of shops and headed out to the common. She was right, the Tylers did live in Hollywell Park. She'd seen the army of builders at work during the spring, but this was the first time she'd seen the 'executive development', as it called itself, in all its glory. It was certainly impressive, the gleaming new detached houses with their double garages and spreading lawns spaced out along wide, sweeping arcs of road. Not a burnt-out car or abandoned shopping trolley in sight. A bit different to her own modest two-bedroom bungalow just beyond the council estate.

As they neared the house, Emily chewed on her lower lip and said, 'Do we have to tell him where we've been?'

'I think he's going to want to know, don't you?'

'Couldn't we just say I had to come with you on an errand or something? He'll only get in a stress if I tell him the truth.'

Tess nodded ahead of her, where she'd spotted the silver BMW in the drive. 'I think it's a bit late for that, don't you?'

Chapter 9

He came rushing out of the house as Tess pulled up, still in his office clothes, his face as white as his shirt.

'Hello, Dad.' Emily looked sheepish.

'Emily.' He threw open the car door for her to get out. 'Where the hell have you been?'

'Didn't you get my message on your machine?' Tess asked, getting out of the car.

He swung round to face her. 'I did, thank you. It was waiting for me when I got home. After I'd spent an hour driving round the streets, looking for my daughter and going out of my mind.' His voice was icy with sarcasm. 'Do you mind telling me what you were thinking of, taking my daughter to Leeds without my permission?'

'She didn't take me, I wanted to go,' Emily protested, but he ignored her.

'Well?' he said. 'I'm waiting.'

Tess faced him unflinchingly. 'What was I supposed to do, let her roam the streets?'

'As a teacher, I would have thought it might have occurred to you to take her back to school.'

'She didn't want to go.'

'Oh, and that's all right with you, is it? A child doesn't want to go to school, so you don't make them? Is that how you treat truants, Miss Doyle? Take them for coffee at Harvey Nics?'

'Actually, we went to visit her mother's grave.'

She hadn't meant it to come out like that. Seeing his face now, she wished she'd kept her mouth shut.

'You did what?'

'I was going to tell you—' Emily tried to interrupt, but Jack turned his back on her. All his rage was directed at Tess.

'She wanted to go and see her mother,' Tess repeated.

'I see. And if she'd wanted to visit a methadone clinic, or the local cancer ward, I suppose you would have taken her there too?'

'Dad—'

'It's hardly the same thing,' Tess defended herself.

'Dad, please!'

'EMILY, GO TO YOUR ROOM!'

For a moment she stood her ground, fists tightening at her sides. Then, with a choked sob, she dashed off, leaving the front door quivering in its frame behind her.

Jack turned back to Tess. 'Now look what you've done.'

'Me?'

'I can't believe a teacher of all people would behave so irresponsibly. I suppose this is some kind of trendy educational theory, is it? To make children confront the harsh realities of life and death?'

'Now you're being ridiculous.'

'Ridiculous?' A muscle pounded in his cheek. 'Miss Doyle, I have spent the past nine months trying to help my daughters get over the trauma of their mother's death. Why do you think we've moved here, if not to get away from it? And now you go and stir it all up with your well-meaning, do-gooding—'

'Perhaps that's the problem?' Tess said.

'What?'

'I realise you're angry, and I'm not saying what I did was right. But what you're doing isn't right, either. You say you're helping them get over the trauma but you're not. All you're doing is burying it, trying to pretend it never happened.'

'Now just a minute—'

'Do you really think moving house will help Emily get over what happened? Do you seriously imagine she can forget something like that just by changing addresses? The pain hasn't gone away, Mr Tyler. And you won't make it go away by pretending it doesn't exist.'

'I'm not.'

'I'm sorry, but that's exactly what you're doing. Emily desperately wants to talk about her mother's death. She needs to talk about it. But she can't, because she knows you want to block it out.'

He looked rattled. 'That's nonsense. No one's trying to block anything out.'

'So why can't she tell you she wants to visit her mother's grave? Why does she feel she has to do it in secret? And why—' She stopped herself.

'Go on,' he said quietly.

'I can't. I promised Emily.'

The fact that he was trying to contain his anger only made him seem more threatening. 'So you're telling me my daughter can confide in you, a total stranger, but she can't talk to me, is that it?'

'Look, I'm not saying it's your fault—'

'Don't patronise me, Miss Doyle.'

'I'm not. I'm just trying to make you see that Emily needs to talk about what happened to her mother.'

'Don't you think she's been hurt enough, without me dragging it up every five minutes? You may not realise this, but Emily was with her mother when she died—'

'I know. She told me.'

He stopped. 'She told you? When?'

'When we were at the cemetery.'

'What exactly did she tell you?'

He looked so upset, she wished she could tell him. But she'd promised Emily and she couldn't break her word. 'I think you should ask her that. Unless you're the one who can't talk about it?'

'Don't try to psychoanalyse me, Miss Doyle. A five-minute conversation with my daughter hardly gives you an insight into me and my family.'

'I'm sorry, I didn't mean—'

'Emily's my daughter and I'll deal with this in my own way.' His voice was clipped with anger.

Tess stared at him in frustration. 'You know what? Emily was right about you. You don't want to listen, do you? No wonder she doesn't feel she can talk to you.' She headed to her car, then stopped and turned back. 'But shall I tell you something, Mr Tyler? Your daughter is a frightened, lonely little girl. So I suggest you deal with it very soon.'

She got into her car. Jack watched her, his mouth opening and closing in mute rage.

'I hope you don't think this is the end of the matter?' He finally found his voice as she started up the engine. 'What you did today was gross misconduct. I'll be speaking to your Headteacher about it!'

Emily pulled the pillow over her head to shut out the shouting. She heard the front door bang, followed by the sound of Miss Doyle's car backfiring down the road. Then footsteps came up the stairs, stopping outside her bedroom door.

'Em?'

'Go away.'

'Emily, we need to talk.'

'I said go away!'

She could sense him hesitating, then the door opened. 'Emily—'

'What did you have to shout at her like that for? She didn't do anything wrong!'

'Oh, I think she did.'

'No, she didn't. I was upset and I wanted to go and see Mum, so she took me. She was the only one who was nice to me in that whole stinking school, and now you've gone and ruined it all!'

The bed creaked under his weight as he sat down. 'Why didn't you tell me you wanted to see Mum's grave?' he said at last.

'I did, loads of times. You always said no.'

'I would have taken you, if you'd really wanted to go.'

'I did! Anyway, I don't need your permission!'

'You're right. You don't.' His breathing filled the silence. 'Look, Emily, if there's ever anything you want to talk about, you know I'll listen.'

'Yeah right. Just like you listened when we told you we didn't want to move here.'

'That was different. The thing is, I'm your father. If you've got anything on your mind, you should talk to me.' He hesitated. 'You've never really said what happened when Mum—'

'Stop it!' Emily pulled the pillow tighter over her head to block him out. 'I don't want to talk about it.'

'You talked to Miss Doyle.'

'So? She listened.'

'I'd listen, if you wanted me to. Em?'

Silence. She lay rigid, hardly breathing, waiting for him to give up. In the end he did.

'I'm sorry, I'm not very good at all this heart-to-heart stuff, am I? That was your mum's department. All I seem to do is cock it up.' He stood up. 'I'll go and get tea ready then, shall I? Microwave pizza okay for you?'

As he headed for the door, she thought about what Miss Doyle had said, about giving him a chance. 'Dad?' She rolled over, still hugging the pillow.

'Hmm?' The sadness in his face made her feel wretched. She desperately wanted to talk to him, but how could she? How could she drag up the memories he was doing his best to forget?

'Microwave pizza's fine,' she said.

To Emily's relief, Miss Doyle greeted her as if nothing had happened the following morning. Jordan and Leanne scowled as she took her seat at the back of the classroom. Leanne was sporting a bruised, puffy eye, inexpertly hidden under thick make-up. Emily wondered if she'd done it during their fight. She couldn't remember lashing out with her fists but she was pleased if she had.

She slid into the seat next to Paris. As usual, she had her nose in a book.

'I thought you might have gone on the run?' she said, not looking up.

'I nearly did.'

'Everyone was talking about it yesterday. You're a bit of a hero. It's not everyone who starts a fight and plays truant on the same day.'

Emily grinned. At least it was nice to be known as something other than the nerdy new girl.

'By the way, I've got something for you.' Paris put down her book and reached into her bag. 'He's a bit muddy, I'm afraid.'

In her hands was Mr Bunny. Emily gasped, 'Where did you get him?'

'Best you don't ask. As my mum always says, if you don't know nothing, the police can't do you for being an accessory.'

'What?'

Miss Doyle looked up. 'Can you keep it down at the back, I'm trying to do the register.' She pushed her glasses back up her nose. 'Leanne Hooper?'

'Here, Miss.' Leanne shot a look of loathing at Paris from her one good eye. Emily looked from one to the other and suddenly it dawned on her. 'You didn't?'

Paris gave one of her rare smiles. 'Like I said, best you don't ask,' she said, and went back to reading her book.

'Bloody hell, Tess, you took his daughter to a graveyard. What did you expect, a pat on the back?'

'I was only trying to help.'

'But you broke every rule in the book. Including aiding and abetting a truant. What were you thinking of?'

'I don't know, do I? It just seemed like the right thing to do at the time.' Tess spooned coffee into the mugs. The lesson before lunch break was her free period and she was supposed to be catching up on her marking for the afternoon. But with everything that had happened that morning she couldn't concentrate.

And of course Helen had followed her into the staffroom to catch up on the gossip. It wasn't just Emily's bunking off that was the talk of the school.

She hitched herself on to the desk, showing off a lot of smooth, tanned thigh under her netball skirt. 'So what else did Eric say to you?'

'What didn't he say?' Now she knew how the kids felt, being dragged up in front of the Headteacher. 'The way he went on about it you'd think I'd taken her to see a live sex show. He thinks Mr Tyler might remove Emily from the school.'

'Blimey, that's a bit of an overreaction, isn't it?'

'I don't know. I suppose I can't blame him. He's right, I should have talked to him first. For all I know, I could have scarred his daughter for life.'

They both turned as Jeff Kramer came into the staffroom, a pile of marking under his arm. He took one look at Tess and headed for the furthest corner of the room.

Tess sighed. 'There's someone who wouldn't be sorry to see me get sacked.'

'Take no notice of him. He's only sulking because Cynthia's told him he can't have his new equipment.'

'Yes, and whose fault is that?' She couldn't believe it when she got to work that morning and found out Cynthia Frobisher had called another staff meeting while she was in

Leeds and announced she was cutting everyone's budgets to cover the cost of the school play. It wasn't until she was snubbed in the staffroom that she realised they all blamed her, which was probably just what Cynthia intended.

'Don't let it get to you,' Helen advised. 'They'll get over it.'

'This isn't about the money. It's about Cynthia being vindictive. She didn't have to cut those budgets, she just did it so everyone would hate me.' Tess helped herself to a custard cream from the tin, even though lunchtime was only ten minutes away. 'Thank God she's not in this morning. If she found out about Emily Tyler, she'd be howling for my blood.' She crunched thoughtfully. 'It's at times like this I wonder if I'm really cut out to be a teacher.'

'Don't say that. You're brilliant.'

'The rest of the staff don't seem to think so. Besides, I let myself get too involved.'

'Okay, so you get a bit carried away sometimes. But that's only because you care.'

'Didn't care about my equipment though, did she?' Jeff Kramer grunted from the other side of the room. 'And I hope those biscuits are coming out of *your* budget,' he added, nodding at the ginger nut Tess had just taken from the tin.

She was just about to give him a suitably cutting reply when they were interrupted by Pam, the school secretary. 'Sorry to butt in, but Mr Tyler's here to see you, Tess.'

She looked at Helen. 'Oh God, what does he want?'

Helen grimaced. 'Your head on a plate, probably.'

He was waiting in reception, pretending to admire a photo of Eric Gant and not to notice the admin staff were all ogling him. Tess squared her shoulders and greeted him with her most professional smile. 'Mr Tyler. What can I do for you?'

'I think we need to talk, Miss Doyle.'

Tess glanced at the admin girls, all tapping at their keyboards while their ears strained to catch the gossip. 'Perhaps you'd like to come to my classroom?'

'Thank you.'

Tess wasn't sure which of them was feeling the effort of being polite the most. Him, probably. Had he come to tell her he'd decided to take Emily away? She couldn't bear to think the poor girl's life might be disrupted again because of her.

By the time they'd reached her classroom she knew she had to say something.

'Miss Doyle—'

'Look, Mr Tyler, I know you're angry and you have a right to be. I was in the wrong. I apologise.'

'Can I just—'

'Please. You had your say yesterday, and now it's time for mine. Like I said, I know I was in the wrong. But I don't think taking Emily away is the answer.'

'I don't think you understand—'

'I understand perfectly. You're upset and you're angry, but if you could just take a moment to reconsider—'

'Miss Doyle, I have no intention of removing Emily from this school.'

'Oh!' Tess stopped short. 'But Mr Gant said—'

'When I spoke to him last night I was angry. I wasn't thinking straight. I realise taking Emily away would be a bad idea.'

'I see. So what have you come to see me for?'

'I came to apologise. Or rather, I've been sent.' He didn't meet her eye. 'My daughter seems to think I overreacted.'

'Oh.' Was this the same man who'd phoned the Headteacher the previous evening demanding she be sacked?

The bell rang, followed a second later by the stampede of feet thundering past. 'Lunch,' Tess explained, seeing Jack's startled expression. She hesitated, then said, 'Look, I don't suppose you fancy joining me for something to eat? After the morning I've had I could really do with a break, and I don't think I can face the canteen.' She saw his quick frown. 'On second thoughts, forget I asked. It was a silly idea anyway—'

'I'd love to,' Jack said.

The Three Legged Mare, or the Wonky Donkey, as it was better known among the locals, was quiet at lunchtime. Over in one corner a couple of businessmen – sales reps, by the look of them – were grabbing a pint and a sandwich before heading back on the road. In the other were a group of Haxsall Park teachers, heads together around a table. Marjorie Wheeler was among them, Tess noticed. She didn't usually socialise with the rest of the staff. It was amazing what a bonding experience a good bitching session could be. She turned away quickly.

'What are you having?' Jack asked.

'Just an orange juice, please. I've got George Orwell with my GCSE lot this afternoon.'

'I think I'll risk a pint. I'm only designing a block of flats.' He looked over the top of her head. 'Why are those people staring at us?'

'They're from my school.' Tess waved in greeting. They all turned their backs on her and carried on talking.

'They don't seem very friendly.'

'No, well, I'm not exactly popular at the moment.'

'Why not?'

'I want to put on a school play.'

Jack's eyebrows rose. 'And is that such a crime?'

'It is if they're paying for it.' She explained briefly about Cynthia's *coup de grâce*.

'And this is the woman who gave Emily detention? She sounds a nightmare.'

'She is.' Tess glanced back at the group clustered around the table. 'Do you mind if we sit over there? I can't stand them watching us, waiting for me to choke on my baguette.'

They ordered their food and took their drinks to a window table overlooking the village green, as it was called. It was a picturesque name for little more than a grassy triangle with a clump of beech trees and a couple of swings, bordered on one side by the pub, and on the others by the Blockbuster video shop and the Haxsall Tandoori.

As their food arrived, Jack said, 'Emily tells me you've been very good to her.'

'I try. It can't have been easy for her, making a new start.'

'No.' He stared down at his pint. 'I hope I haven't made things even more difficult for her, losing my temper last night.'

'Of course not. Why would you?'

'She's worried you might hate her because of me.'

'Emily's a great kid. Nothing can change that.' She picked the lettuce out of her sandwich. 'Anyway, you had every right to be furious. What I did was stupid.'

He didn't argue with that, she noticed. 'It wasn't just that. I was jealous too.'

'Jealous?'

'I couldn't believe you'd managed to get through to Emily when I'd been trying for so long.' His voice was quiet. 'She's never told me what happened the day her mother died. Don't worry, I'm not asking you to tell me,' he said quickly. 'I'm just surprised, that's all.'

And hurt. Tess could see the unhappiness in his face. Poor man, he must have felt as if he'd failed. 'She probably just found it easier to talk to a stranger.'

'No, it's more than that. I arranged for her to see a grief counsellor after Miranda died. She wouldn't talk to her.'

'Maybe it was too soon?'

'Or maybe it was the wrong person.' His eyes were serious. 'You're right, I'm the one who should be talking to her. I should have tried harder to get through to her.'

'Get through to a fourteen-year-old girl? You'd stand more chance of communicating with aliens on another planet!'

'You managed it.'

'I've had a lot of practice.'

He pushed his salad around his plate, then gave up and put his fork down. 'I still should have tried harder. But I've been so wrapped up in my own feelings lately, I haven't given much thought to hers.'

'That's not surprising.'

'But I shouldn't be, should I? I'm all they've got. I should be there for them.'

'You're also human. You're bound to make mistakes.'

'Miranda didn't,' Jack said quietly. 'She had everything brilliantly organised. And she was great with the girls. She always seemed to know the right thing to do or say. I just keep putting my foot in it.' He looked rueful. 'Those children are a complete mystery, like the washing machine. They're noisy, unpredictable, and I never know when they're going to blow up.'

'Except unlike the washing machine they don't come with an instruction manual.'

'Even if they did, I probably wouldn't be able to understand it.' Jack sank his chin into his hands. 'That's what's so frustrating. In my job I know what I'm doing. I solve problems every day, and I'm good at it. But at home I'm faced with all these things I just don't know how to deal with. It's a scary feeling.' He turned his glass round in front of him. 'I think that's why I've been spending so long at the office. I keep saying it's pressure of work, but it isn't. It's just the only place I feel in control.'

'You're not the only one who gets scared, you know.'

'No?'

'Of course not. Most of us just muddle through, making it up as we go along.'

'Is that what you do?'

'Most of the time.'

'I bet you don't. I bet you're a brilliant mother.'

'I think Dan might disagree with you there!' she laughed.

'That's your son, is it? How old is he?'

'Seventeen.'

'Really?' He tried to hide it, but she could tell he was shocked. 'You must have been very young when he was born?'

'If you're asking was he an accident, then yes, he definitely was. I got pregnant on my sixteenth birthday. Some present!'

'So you weren't much older than Emily. I can't imagine her having a baby.'

'Neither could my mum, believe me.'

'Was she furious?'

'More upset than angry, I think. I was the brains of the family, you see. The one who was meant to do so well for herself.' She gazed into the depths of her glass.

'I'd say you've done pretty well for yourself.'

'Only because Mum stood by me. She was brilliant. I couldn't have coped without her.'

'What about Dan's father?'

'Not quite so supportive, I'm afraid.' Tess pushed her plate away from her. 'I thought we were serious about each other, but me getting pregnant was a bit too serious for him.'

'You mean he walked out on you?'

'I think ran is a better word. As fast as his legs could carry him.'

Jack smiled. 'I take it you don't see him any more?'

'It's funny you should ask that.' She told him about Dan tracking Phil down. 'I don't know if he's written to him yet, but I know he will. Dan can be very determined when he wants something.'

'Sounds like his mother.'

'No, I'm just pig-headed.'

They sat in silence for a while. Then Jack said, 'So how do you feel about seeing your ex again?'

'I try not to think about it. I don't even know if I will see him. Maybe he'll only want to see Dan. Or maybe—'

'Maybe he won't want anything to do with either of you?'

She nodded. 'Although I don't know which scares me more, him getting in touch or not getting in touch.' She took a sip of her orange juice. 'But you don't want to hear me droning on about my problems.'

'Why not? It makes a change from having to think about mine.'

They chatted for a while longer, until Tess noticed the rest of the staff heading for the door. 'Oops, I think that's my cue to leave.'

Jack glanced at his watch. 'I'd better make a move too. I've got a meeting in Leeds at two thirty.'

As they walked out to his car, he said, 'I don't suppose you'd like to come to a party, would you? As part of my penance for losing my temper, I've had to agree to Emily having a house-warming. She spent most of last night on the phone, fixing up for her friends from Leeds to come over.'

'In that case, I'd better not. I don't think Emily would appreciate her form teacher being there.'

'Probably not, but I could use the moral support. Please?'

'I'll check my diary.' She'd already made up her mind not to be there. She could just imagine Emily's face if she turned up. 'When is it?'

'The end of October. I'm putting it off for as long as possible.' They reached his car. 'Can I give you a lift back to school?' he asked.

Tess shook her head. 'I need the exercise. Well, thanks very much for lunch, Mr Tyler.'

He smiled. 'I think since I've invited you to a party you could get away with calling me Jack, don't you?'

Chapter 10

'Come on, Em, you'll be late!'

And she wouldn't be the only one. Jack glanced at his watch. It was almost eight. He had a site meeting with the council planners to discuss the Westpoint development at nine, and he hadn't even had a chance to look at their comments on his last set of revised drawings yet. He'd brought them home to work on but Emily had been having trouble with her maths homework and he'd spent the evening explaining the intricacies of trigonometry instead. By the time he'd made supper and stacked the dishwasher, then restacked it because it made funny noises, there wasn't much time for doing anything but dozing off in front of *Sex and the City*.

And then he'd been up in the night because Sophie felt ill. There was still a greenish tinge to her face as she stared into her bowl of Frosties.

'Get a move on, Sophie!'

She looked up at him. 'I don't feel well.'

He'd never dreaded that sentence before, but he was just beginning to realise what it meant. Those four words could plunge his well-ordered world into chaos.

'Are you sure?' He felt her forehead. Over the past month or so, he'd begun to realise there was a difference between a real 'I don't feel well' and a 'We've got double maths I don't feel well.'

'My throat hurts and I feel sick.'

'Maybe you shouldn't go to school today. I'll call the childminder.'

Emily came downstairs just as he was leafing through his address book. 'What are you looking for?'

'The childminder's number. Sophie's not going to school today.'

'Lucky pig.' Emily helped herself to cornflakes.

'Can anyone remember what the childminder's surname is?'

'You mean you can't?' Emily looked appalled. 'Well, that's great, isn't it? You leave us in the care of some stranger and you can't even remember her name. What if she abducted us? How would you know where to start looking?'

'If she abducted you two, I'd probably start looking in the local asylums – ah, here it is. Smith. No wonder I couldn't remember it.' He reached for the phone on the worktop and dialled the number. 'Try to eat something, Soph. It might make you feel better.'

The childminder made all the right soothing noises when she heard Sophie was feeling poorly, but her sympathy vanished when she realised Jack wanted to bring her round.

'What, all day?' she said. 'But my hours are before and after school during term-time. Those are the arrangements.'

'Well, yes – usually. But this is an exception, isn't it? I'll pay you, of course,' Jack offered quickly, but the childminder was having none of it.

'Sorry, I can't do it.' She raised her voice over the sound of the *Tweenies* in the background. 'I'm up to my ears in under-fives all day. Besides, what if she's got a bug? I don't want her spreading it round everyone else, do I? No, I reckon the best place for her is tucked up at home.'

I know how she feels, Jack thought as he put the phone down. Emily looked up from her cornflakes. 'I could stay off school and look after her, if you like?'

That was when Sophie dropped her spoon and threw up dramatically. Emily shot out of her seat in a second.

'Ugh, gross! On second thoughts, forget I said that. I'm

out of here.' She scooted into the hallway and a second later the door banged shut, leaving Jack and a forlorn-looking Sophie sitting at the kitchen table.

He mopped up the mess, got Sophie out of her school uniform and changed his own clothes, still wondering what the hell he could do.

Meanwhile the clock ticked on. Eight twenty-three. Even if he left now, he'd never make it to Leeds in time for that meeting.

He didn't realise he'd been muttering under his breath until Sophie emerged from her room in her *Simpsons* pyjamas. 'Sorry, Daddy,' she mumbled.

'That's okay, sweetheart, you can't help it.' Jack dredged a smile from somewhere. 'We'd better find someone to look after you.'

The first thing he heard when Ros picked up the phone was a blast of the *Tweenies*. Was that all anyone ever watched?

She sounded breathless. 'Jack, hi. How's it going?'

'Not very well, actually—' he started to tell her, but she cut him off.

'Look, can I call you back in a couple of hours? You just caught me. My next-door neighbour's come round to look after the kids and I'm sneaking out while they're distracted.'

'Oh.'

'Why? Is there anything wrong?'

'No – well, yes, as a matter of fact. Sophie's ill and—'

'What's wrong with her? Nothing serious?'

'I don't think so. She's just been sick. But the thing is—'

'Have you taken her to a doctor?'

'Well, no. She was only sick about ten minutes ago. But I just wanted—'

'Does she have any other symptoms? Headache? Stiff neck? Have you tried shining a light in her eyes?'

'Who do you think I am, the bloody Gestapo?' Jack was exasperated. 'She's fine, honestly. Just a tummy upset, that's all. But the thing is, I've got a really important meeting this morning and the childminder won't take her, so I wondered if I could drop her off at yours? Just until I get through with this meeting. It won't take long and I'd be really grateful,' he went on in a rush. 'I wouldn't ask you at such short notice but I'm desperate.'

Ros sighed. 'I'd love to help, Jack, but the thing is I've got a job interview at nine.'

'A job? You?' He forgot his own panic.

'Don't sound so surprised. I may have spent the last six years up to my elbows in Play-Doh and dirty nappies, but I do still have a few brain cells to rub together, you know. And now Ben's at school full-time I thought I should start using them again. I've got an interview at the library.'

'Good for you,' Jack said.

'But not for you. What about Mum? Can't she help?'

'I tried her. She'd already left for her yoga class.'

'Of course, it's Tuesday, isn't it? Isn't there anyone else? What about your cleaner? Or one of the mums from school?'

'It's Pauline's day off and I don't really know any mums. I'm afraid I'm a bit stuck.' He fought and failed to keep the self-pitying note from creeping into his voice.

He could hear Ros chewing her lip on the other end of the line. 'Look, why don't I just put off this interview? I'm sure if I rang the library—'

'Absolutely not. I won't hear of it. You go and get that job.'

'Well, I don't know about that!' Ros laughed shakily. 'I'm probably wasting my time anyway.'

'Rubbish. That library needs you.'

'Look, I'll call you when I get out, okay? Maybe I could come round to your office and pick Sophie up?'

'Fine. And good luck, Ros.'

'Thanks.' He put the phone down, and glanced at the

clock. There was nothing else for it. 'Get dressed, Sophie,' he called up the stairs. 'Daddy's taking you to work.'

There were raised eyebrows all round when he turned up at the airfield half an hour late and with Sophie in tow. Fortunately neither Peter Jameson nor Humphrey Crawshaw were there, though Greg and two men from the council's planning department were.

Greg left the two men and plodded across the field to greet him at the gate.

'Hello, Princess.' He bent down and scooped Sophie into his arms. 'What are you doing here?'

'She's not well enough for school. And I wouldn't do that if I were you. She threw up in the car,' he added, as Greg swung Sophie high in the air.

'Oops!' He put her down quickly. 'Don't you think she'd be better off at home if she's ill?'

'I didn't have much choice. It was either bring her or let everyone down. Anyway, she seems a lot better now.' He looked down at her. She'd lost her green colour and perked up tremendously since she'd been sick all over his upholstery.

'Poor sod, it must be a nightmare for you.' Greg looked sympathetic. 'Tell you what, why don't I keep her busy for a few minutes while you talk to the planning guys?'

'What about you? Shouldn't you be talking to them?'

'I've already had my grilling, thanks very much. It's you they want to talk to now.' Greg put his arm around Sophie. 'I'll show this young lady round the site and join you later, okay?'

In spite of Greg's help, the meeting didn't go well. Unfortunately the council planners had been over his drawings in the tiniest detail and asked all kinds of searching questions. Jack tried to bluff his way through and wished he'd spent more time preparing the night before, instead of doing Emily's homework. He could tell the planners weren't impressed.

By the time Greg joined them, he was floundering. Fortunately his brother-in-law had done his research this time and was able to fill in when Jack's mind went blank.

Finally the planners went away, apparently satisfied. Jack turned to Greg. 'Thanks for rescuing me. And for looking after Sophie.' He looked around the empty field. 'Where is she, by the way?'

'She got bored. Said she was going for a walk.' Greg scanned the horizon. 'Funny, I thought she'd be back by now.'

'Greg! You were meant to be keeping an eye on her.' Jack sprinted across the field. How could he lose both his children in the space of a week?

After five minutes of panic-stricken searching, he found her at the far end of the site. She was digging a hole with a stick, unconcerned that she'd nearly brought on a heart attack in her father.

'Sophie!' He doubled over, panting for breath. 'Why did you go wandering off like that?'

'Sorry. I was digging for treasure. Look what I've found.' She held her grubby fist out to him.

As the site was a former airfield, he was expecting a bit of old propeller, maybe a fragment of nose cone left over from a Second World War Lancaster. He wasn't expecting the earth-clotted lump Sophie dropped into his hand.

'What is it, Daddy?' she asked.

'I'm not sure.' He picked the earth off it. Underneath, it was long and smooth and jagged at the ends, as if it had shattered off a larger piece. 'It looks like a bit of bone to me.'

'Bone!' Sophie stared up at him, wide-eyed. 'Do you think there's a dead body down there?'

'More likely a dog's buried it.' Jack examined the chunk

of bone for a moment, then slipped it into his pocket. 'Come on, let's get back to the office.'

He'd left the car in a disused yard behind the airfield. As he rounded the corner, he spotted a youth in a baseball cap, squatting down beside one of the wheels.

Sophie saw him too. 'What's that boy doing?'

'Letting down my tyres. Oi, you!'

The young man looked up, saw him and sprinted off. Jack ran after him. He had a head start, but as he reached the rundown buildings on the far side of the field he caught his foot and went sprawling. Jack landed on top of him, knocking the wind out of them both.

'Let me go! You're breaking my arm!'

'I'll break your neck, you little—'

'You heard him. Let him go.'

Jack looked up as a shadow fell across them. Standing over him were three similar-looking youths in baseball caps and tracksuits, all armed with lethal-looking spanners.

And with them, looking even more menacing, was Sam Dobbs.

Chapter 11

'Let him go,' he said again. His voice was low and threatening.

Jack tightened his grip on the boy's collar. 'He was vandalising my car!'

'That's no reason to break his neck, is it?'

Jack looked around at the scowling faces. 'Call them off first.'

Sam turned to the youths. 'All right, lads. Show's over. Get back to work.'

'But Darren—'

'I said back to work!' Grumbling, they lumbered off back towards the rundown sheds. Sam looked at Jack. 'They didn't mean any harm.'

'So why were they carrying those spanners?'

'They're mechanics, you daft sod. They heard the shouting and came to find out what all the fuss was about, like me.' He nodded at the boy. 'Do you think you could get off our Darren? He seems to be going a funny colour.'

Jack got up and brushed off his trousers. Sam pulled Darren out of the mud and gave him a clip round the ear.

'You're here to fix cars, you silly bugger, not wreck 'em! Now go and get yourself cleaned up. Sorry about that,' he said, as Darren went off in the same direction as the others. 'Bit over-enthusiastic.'

'Is that what you call it?' Jack pulled out his phone. 'We'll see if the police agree with you, shall we?'

'You don't want to phone them.' Sam's smile disappeared.

'Why not?'

'Because the lad's in enough trouble with them as it is. Why do you think he's here?'

Before Jack could answer, Sophie came puffing across the field towards them.

'Daddyyyy! I need the toilet!'

'You can use ours,' Sam offered. 'Round the back, second door on the left. It's all right, she'll be quite safe,' he added, seeing Jack's frown.

Jack looked around. 'What exactly is this place?'

'You mean you don't know? I thought you were meant to be the architect?'

'They're just marked down as empty buildings on the plan.'

'They were empty, until we started renting them a couple of years back.' Sam extended his arms to sweep the yard. 'Welcome to Second Chance. I'll show you around, if you like.'

He led the way to a Portakabin office where a girl not much older than Emily was labouring over a computer keyboard. 'We've got visitors, Melanie,' Sam said. 'See if you can get us a couple of cups of tea out of that kettle, will you? Oh, and look after Mr Tyler's little girl when she comes out of the loo. I'm just going to give him the grand tour.'

Jack followed him into the yard. It was littered with rusting car parts, bits of broken toilet cistern and piles of wood. Surrounding it were a number of sheds and outbuildings, all in various states of disrepair. But Sam looked proudly around as if it were Blenheim Palace.

'Great, isn't it?' he said. 'That's the garage over there. You've already met the lads. And over there's the plumbing workshop and the carpentry shop. Oh, and that's the sparks department.' From the far end came the muted throb of a dance track. 'Music while you work,' Sam grinned.

'Upstairs is the kitchen. I expect they'll be serving up lunch soon, if you'd like to join us?'

'That's very kind of you.' Jack watched a pair of young men in hooded sweatshirts carrying a TV set across the yard. 'But what exactly is this place? Who are all these people?' And why do I feel as if I'm watching CCTV crime footage? he wondered.

'They're just kids,' Sam shrugged. 'Kids trying to straighten their lives out after being inside.'

'Inside? As in prison?'

'Young offenders' institutions, mostly. We aim to keep them out of prison. That's why we're here.'

'I didn't realise there was a difference,' Jack said, and wished he hadn't as Sam sent him a disdainful look.

'No, you wouldn't. I bet you've never even had a parking ticket, have you? Prison is for grown-ups, it's the hard-core stuff. Teenagers are mostly sent to young offenders' institutions. But that's not to say they won't end up in prison if they're not careful.' He picked up a plank of wood that had fallen down and stacked it against the wall with the rest. 'Some youngsters don't get a break once they've done time. They can't get a job because they've got a record, so they can't make a new start. Sometimes the only way they can get by is to start robbing again.' He raised his hand in greeting as the two lads came loping back across the yard. 'We try to help. We teach them some skills, give them a real job. We give them the chance to wipe the slate clean and get back some self-respect. Hence the name – Second Chance.'

He led the way to the garage. Inside it was hot and dark, and the air was tangy with oil fumes. The three boys working on a Vauxhall Vectra gave him dirty looks from under the bonnet.

'So how do you pay for all this?' Jack asked.

'We earn it, of course. Part of the money comes from fundraising, but the rest we make ourselves, repairing cars and electrical equipment, doing joinery and plumbing jobs, that kind of thing. We're practically self-supporting.'

Jack suppressed a shudder. He wouldn't like the idea of a couple of young thugs in his house, second chance or no second chance. God knows what they'd stuff in their pockets.

His distaste must have shown on his face because Sam said, 'Thank God some people are a bit more trusting than you.'

'You've got to admit, it is a bit risky.'

'So when you get a builder round to fix your guttering or you send that posh car of yours for a service, how do you know the person doing it hasn't been inside?'

'Well—'

'Exactly. You don't. At least we're honest about it.'

'Honest?' Jack laughed. 'That's hardly the word I'd choose.' He looked around. 'I appreciate what you're doing and all that, but do you really think these kids are going to change?'

'Why not? I did.'

Jack stared at him. 'You were in prison?'

'No, but I would have been if the police had caught me one more time. It was breaking and entering mostly. Oh, and I stole a couple of cars like yours, just for a laugh. I was a kid, I didn't know what I was doing. Just like this lot. There but for the grace of God and all that.'

'You really believe that?'

'I have to.' Sam pulled off his scarf and for the first time Jack noticed the dog collar peeping out from the fraying neck of his jumper. 'It goes with the job, you might say. Ah, it looks like Melanie's got the kettle working. Shall we go inside?'

The Portakabin was cosy after the October chill. Sophie was happily helping Melanie with some filing. Jack and Sam pulled their chairs up to the electric heater and drank their tea.

'So, what do you think?' Sam helped himself to a biscuit out of the tin.

'It's very admirable. And you say you're renting these buildings?'

'We were, until the Westpoint lot took away our lease. You know they own this bit of land?'

Of course he did. He'd put several thousand square metres of prime retail space right where they were sitting.

'We offered to buy it from them but they wouldn't hear of it,' Sam went on. 'Although to be honest I don't think we could afford the kind of money they're asking. So that's it for us. Unless you could have a word with them?' He looked hopeful.

'It's not my decision to make,' Jack said. 'I'm just the planning consultant. But I don't think Westpoint would want to give all this away, not when they can develop it and make a profit.'

'That's what it's all about, isn't it? Profit.' Sam crunched on his biscuit and stared out of the window.

'Couldn't you find new premises? There must be somewhere suitable?'

'Oh, there is. Lots of places. Trouble is, every time the locals get wind we're moving in, they get up a petition against us. Then the council refuses us planning permission, and we're back to square one.'

'I suppose you can understand that. I wouldn't want a load of ex young offenders on my doorstep.'

'And I don't want a bloody great shopping centre on mine, but it looks like I'm going to get one.'

'I'm sorry I can't help.'

'Are you?'

Jack put down his cup. He sensed he'd outstayed his welcome. 'Come on, Sophie, get your coat on. I'd better get back to the office before they wonder where I am.'

'Don't let me keep you. I expect you've got lots more lives to ruin before you go home for your tea.'

'Reverend Dobbs—' he began, then gave up. There was nothing he could say that Sam Dobbs wanted to hear. 'I'll see you at the public inquiry,' he muttered.

'I liked it there,' Sophie announced, as they headed back to the car.

'Me too.' He took a last look back at the place.

'Daddy, what's a bastard?' Sophie asked.

'What?'

'B-A-S-T-A-R-D. It's on the front of your car, look.'

Jack stared in disbelief at the spray-painted bonnet. Then he looked back at the Second Chance building. Three faces at the workshop window ducked out of sight.

On second thoughts, fuck them, he thought. The sooner this place is demolished, the better.

Vicky was waiting when he got back to the office. 'You took your time. I thought you'd be back ages ago.'

'So did I.' He slumped at his desk and stared at the pile of unanswered mail that had somehow sprouted. 'Anything interesting happen while I was out?'

'Depends whether you think Humphrey Crawshaw baying for your blood is interesting or not.' Vicky smiled at Sophie, who was perched on her father's knee. 'He's asked to see you in his office as soon as you get in.'

'Great. Just great.' Jack ran a distracted hand through his hair. 'I'd better go in and see him.' He looked up at Vicky. 'Could you keep an eye on Sophie for me?'

'Sure. We can raid the office biscuit tin.' Vicky winked at her.

Greg was already in Humphrey Crawshaw's office, looking tense and unhappy. He shot Jack a warning glance as he walked in.

'Come in, Jack.' Humphrey's smile didn't reach his eyes. 'Take a seat. Herbal tea?'

Jack eyed the murky khaki brew. 'It's a bit early for me, thanks.'

'Now, Jack, I thought we should have a chat.' Humphrey's friendly manner didn't fool Jack for a second. He leaned back against his desk, a tall, distinguished-looking man in his early sixties, with not a spare ounce of flesh on him, thanks to a combination of marathon running, rigorous gym workouts and a highly disciplined diet. Just looking at him made Jack feel like a slob. 'I hear the meeting with the planners didn't go too well this morning. I'm a little concerned as to why.'

'I expect you already know.'

'I wanted to hear it from you.'

'Okay, then. My daughter was ill and couldn't go to school, so I had to bring her along.'

'It was a one-off,' Greg, ever the peacemaker, put in.

Humphrey ignored him. 'The workplace is no place for a child, Jack.'

'I realise that. But I didn't exactly have a choice. The childminder couldn't take her, and—'

Humphrey held up a silencing hand. 'With respect, that's your problem, not ours. What I expect from you is one hundred and ten per cent commitment. And I have to say, I'm not getting it at the moment.'

'I thought the meeting went very well, under the circumstances,' Greg said quickly.

Jack met Humphrey's eye unflinchingly. 'In what way?'

'Sorry?'

'In what way aren't you getting commitment from me? I'm still meeting my deadlines, aren't I?'

'Well, yes—'

'And my work is of sufficient standard?'

'More than sufficient, you know that. But I'm just not seeing the effort any more. You're not putting in the hours you used to.'

'That's because I have two daughters at home who need

me.' Suppressed anger throbbed in his temple. 'I take my work home with me and if necessary I always make up any time I've lost. But I refuse to neglect my children because of some macho culture that says you have to be seen at your desk twelve hours a day just so you can earn brownie points from the boss.'

'Jack, please. I didn't mean to imply you weren't doing your job properly.' Humphrey backtracked wildly.

'I thought that's exactly what you were saying.'

'No one expects you to neglect your children. God knows, I've had kids myself, I know what it's like.' You also had a wife and a brace of nannies to look after them, Jack thought sourly. 'But we're a team and I see you as our top player. Our star striker, our David Beckham, if you like.'

'He's a midfielder,' Greg muttered.

'I rely on you,' Humphrey went on. 'I'm depending on you to bring this Westpoint project home. Don't let me down, will you?'

'My kids rely on me too,' Jack said, but Humphrey still wasn't listening.

'Now, I've organised a little get-together next week, just to oil the wheels with the Westpoint people. Stick it in your diary, will you? Kirsty can give you the details.'

'I'll see what I can do—' Jack began, then saw Humphrey's expression. 'I'll be there,' he said.

Greg followed him out of Humphrey's office. 'I'm really sorry about that,' he said. 'He was in a rage when I got back. God knows who told him.'

'I expect the planners called him to complain. I can't blame them, it was pretty unprofessional.'

'It was hardly your fault though, was it? You can't help Sophie being ill. Like you said, the girls have to come first.'

'Even if it costs me my job?' Jack's mouth twisted. 'I'm not much good if I can't provide for them, am I?'

'Come on, Jack. It won't come to that. You heard what

Humphrey said. You're his top man. Okay, so he might whinge a bit sometimes, but he can't do without you.' He grinned. 'You're his star striker!'

Jack smiled reluctantly. 'Let's hope I don't end up on the subs' bench.'

Sophie was waiting for them when they got back to his office. She was sitting on the edge of Vicky's desk, chomping happily on a ham and tomato roll.

'A man with a big basket of sandwiches came round,' she said, wide-eyed. 'Vicky said I could have whatever I liked.' She looked at Greg. 'Someone wrote bastard on Daddy's car.'

'Did they now?' Greg turned to Jack, eyebrows raised. 'Wasn't Humphrey Crawshaw by any chance, was it?'

'Very funny,' said Jack.

'I went digging up at the field,' Sophie went on. 'And I found treasure, didn't I, Daddy? Show Uncle Greg what I found.'

'If it's a winning lottery ticket, I want half,' Greg said, as Jack dug in his pocket and pulled out the piece of bone.

'Nothing so exciting, I'm afraid.'

'So I see. What the hell is it?'

'Daddy says it's a bit of bone. It could be a dinosaur, don't you think?'

'Could be, sweetheart.' Greg turned it over in his hand. 'Tell you what, why don't I send it to our special archaeology department to find out?'

'You don't have to do that,' Jack protested, but Sophie was already wildly excited at the prospect.

'Really? Do you think it's old?'

'Maybe. You never know, it might even be as old as Daddy.'

Chapter 12

A week later, Tess went to visit her mother. Margaret Doyle still lived in the same flat on the council estate where Tess and her sister had grown up. Apart from a smattering of new graffiti on the walls, the place hadn't changed much in thirty years. Children still chased each other on the grassy area at the front of the block, their bikes and skateboards abandoned around them. Washing fluttered like colourful bunting on makeshift lines stretched across the outside walkways that led to each front door.

Three women gossiping on the stairwell greeted Tess with nods and smiles as she puffed her way up to the third floor. Everyone knew Margaret Doyle and her daughters.

Her mother was waiting for her outside the flat. She hadn't changed much over the years either. There were a few more lines around her shrewd brown eyes and her dark hair was threaded with more grey than there used to be, but the brown skirt, beige cardigan and faded flowery slippers were just the same as when Tess had come home from school, dragging her bag behind her.

And she was still coming home from school now. Only this time it was someone else's homework she dragged with her.

Margaret greeted her with a nod, her arms folded. She wasn't the kind of mother who went in for big hugs and lots of kisses. Tess couldn't think of a time when she'd done either in the last ten years. But somehow that didn't matter. Other people might find her manner dour, but those close to her knew she would put herself out to help anyone in trouble. Although she'd probably give them a good talking-to and tell them to pull themselves together afterwards.

'This is a surprise,' she said. 'What's wrong?'

'Mum! Why does there have to be anything wrong? I just thought I'd pop round, that's all.'

She forced herself to meet her mother's eye, certain she must have guilt written all over her face. She never found it easy to lie to her. Margaret seemed to have an inbuilt truth radar.

Fortunately it wasn't working too well today. She sent her a suspicious look. 'You'd better come in, then. But watch yourself in the kitchen. I've got a man looking at my plumbing.'

The man in question was in his mid-sixties, tall with snowy hair and piercing blue eyes. He emerged from under the sink to give Tess a friendly smile.

'How do?' he said. 'You must be Teresa. I'm Ronnie. Your mum's told me all about you.'

'Really?' Tess turned questioning eyes to her mother.

'Ronnie's from the Over Sixties club. He's kindly offered to sort out my U-bend.' Was it her imagination, or did her mother look slightly flustered? 'I've been on to the council to do it but they take a year and a day to get round to anything.'

Ronnie came back out from under the sink, a wrench in his hand. 'That should do it.' He put down the wrench and wiped his hands on his overall. 'Try it now, Maggie.'

Maggie? Tess waited for her mother to point out that her name was Margaret, as she usually did, but she just leaned across and turned on the tap.

'Lovely.' She beamed as the water gurgled down the plughole. 'Thank you, Ronnie. How much do I owe you?'

'You know I'd never charge you anything. But a cup of tea might be nice?' Ronnie's blue eyes gleamed hopefully.

'It'll have to be some other time. Teresa's here now and we need to talk.'

'Oh, but I don't mind—' Tess began, but her mother was already hustling Ronnie towards the front door, barely giving him time to gather up his tools.

'Shall I see you on Friday? It's cribbage night,' he was saying as she closed the door in his face.

'He's a nice man, but he doesn't know when he's outstayed his welcome,' she said briskly. She turned the tap on again, allowing herself a small smile of satisfaction. 'But he's not a bad plumber, I'll say that for him.'

'He seems very nice,' Tess said.

'He's all right. Better than a lot of those old fools up there, always moaning about their aches and pains.'

Tess leaned back against the worktop and smiled teasingly. 'I didn't know you had a new man in your life.'

'I have no such thing!' Margaret looked outraged. 'There's nothing like that going on. Ronnie just offered to help me out with a few odd jobs, that's all.'

'He seemed very keen on you.'

'More fool him, then.' She flicked the switch on the kettle as it came up to boil. 'There'll never be anyone for me but your father.'

'Dad's been dead for twenty years.'

'What difference does that make?'

What indeed? Tess thought. The way her mother talked about him, anyone would think he'd died last week. Margaret was only forty when it happened, not much older than Tess was now. But since then she'd never known her mother even look at another man. She'd soon come to realise that it wasn't grief or guilt that stopped her, just the certain knowledge that she would never, ever find anyone she loved as much as Martin Doyle.

Tess envied her in a way. It must be wonderful to find one's soulmate like that. But so incredibly lonely to lose them.

She thought about Jack Tyler. Was that how he felt about his wife? Or would he eventually be able to move on, find happiness again? And if he did, would his children let him? Much as she welcomed the idea of her mother finding someone to keep her company now, she wasn't sure how she would have felt about it as a teenager.

Tess watched as Margaret poured a splash of boiling water into the pot, swished it around then tipped it out into the sink. 'You don't have to go to all that trouble,' she said. 'A teabag in a mug would do for me.'

'Aye, I daresay. But not for me. If you're going to do something, you might as well do it properly.'

That went for the rest of the flat too. It might be small and old-fashioned, but it was immaculately kept. The paintwork gleamed, the rugs were beaten to within an inch of their lives, and the air was scented with pine disinfectant and furniture polish. Tess knew without looking that there would be no dustballs or lost biros under the sofa, no crumbs lurking behind the microwave.

Not like her place. Tess also knew her slapdash attitude to domestic matters was a constant trial to her mother. She comforted herself that she was a working woman and therefore too busy to waste time worrying about limescale. But then she remembered Margaret had brought up two daughters single-handed, held down a job, looked after her grandson and still found time to buff up her bath taps.

But no matter how houseproud she was, Margaret still insisted they drink their tea around the kitchen table, the way they'd always done. The sitting room was for evenings and 'real' visitors, not for daughters dropping by.

So, apparently, were the custard creams. Tess looked around hopefully. 'No biscuits?'

'You'll spoil your tea.' Margaret pushed her cup across the table towards her. 'Well? Spit it out.'

Tess looked startled. 'What?'

'Whatever it is you've come to tell me.'

'I told you, I've just popped round for a visit.'

'And I'm Cilla Black! You don't just drop round out of

the blue unless you've got something you want to say. So let's hear it. And stop playing with that spoon. You're stirring your tea, not calling the faithful to prayer.' She put her cup down. 'You're not pregnant again, are you?'

'Mum!'

'What? The last time you had that look on your face that's what you told me.' She picked up her cup again. 'Whatever it is, it can't be as bad as that.'

Want to bet? Tess picked up her spoon then, seeing her mother's disapproving expression, quickly put it down again. 'Dan's been in touch with Phil.' She braced herself. Her mother said nothing. 'He found his address on the internet,' she hurried on. 'I wasn't sure if he'd write back, but he did.'

'I'm surprised he had the nerve,' Margaret said stonily. She looked at Tess. 'And you let Dan do it?'

'I couldn't very well stop him, could I?'

'You could have done something. You could have taken that computer away for a start.'

'He'd only use another one. He's seventeen, Mum, not seven. Besides, he has a right to know who his father is.'

'Father! Some father he's been all these years! Where was he when Dan was teething and you were up all night in the middle of your exams? Where was he when you were working all hours to make ends meet? Where was he when he should have been paying maintenance?' She stabbed her finger on the plastic tablecloth to make her point. She'd painted her nails a pale frosted pink, Tess noticed. She couldn't remember her ever doing that before. 'I don't suppose he thought much about his son then.'

'No, I don't suppose he did,' Tess said wearily. 'But that's all water under the bridge now, isn't it? The important thing is, Dan wanted to get in touch with him, and Phil seems keen. We should be pleased for him.'

It was the wrong thing to say. Margaret put her cup down with a clatter. 'Pleased? Pleased that he's deigned to talk to his own son after seventeen years? Anyway, I'm not surprised,' she sniffed. 'The hard work's all done now, isn't it? Dan's nearly an adult. Why shouldn't he just sweep in and take all the glory?'

They drank their tea in silence. She could feel the weight of her mother's disapproval. She knew what Margaret would have done under the circumstances; shouted, stomped around, and generally frightened Dan out of the very idea of looking for his father. It might have been an effective way of solving the problem, but Tess couldn't bring herself to do it.

Finally, Margaret said, 'Where is he now, anyway?'

'Somewhere down south, apparently. He works with computers.'

'Earns a fair bit, I suppose?'

'I expect so.' Tess narrowed her eyes. 'I'm not going to ask him for money, if that's what you're getting at.'

'Why not? Dan will be at university in a year. That's going to cost a bit.'

'I'll manage.'

'I daresay you will. But it'd be a lot easier if that useless article helped out.'

'Mum, I don't want anything from him! I've coped without his money for seventeen years and I'll cope now.'

'You're stubborn, do you know that?'

'And we all know where I get it from, don't we?'

Margaret got up and busied herself refilling the teapot, but not before Tess caught a rare smile. 'Happen you're right,' her mother said. 'You don't want to give him any excuse to come interfering in yours or Dan's life.'

Tess bit her lip. 'Actually—'

'I mean, living all that way away, he's not likely to hop on a bus and visit, is he?'

'Well—'

'Mind you, it's a pity he's not in Australia.'

'He's coming to dinner next Thursday.' Tess closed her

eyes as she said it, then opened them again to see Margaret staring at her, teapot suspended in mid-pour.

'Teresa, you're joking. Tell me you're joking?'

'Dan asked him,' Tess said helplessly. 'I didn't actually think he'd come, did I?'

'After what that man did to you, you're actually inviting him round?'

'Don't look at me like that. I'm not exactly happy about it either, you know.'

'Then tell him he can't come.'

'How can I? Dan's so excited about it, I don't want to disappoint him.'

'I know what I'd do.' Margaret shook her head. 'Honestly, Teresa, if you let that man over your doorstep, you're even dafter than I thought you were.'

'There's someone to see you, Jack.' Vicky looked uneasy, and Jack understood why when Sam Dobbs walked into his office, followed by one of the surly youths, who had a baseball cap and a pierced eyebrow.

'Hello, Mr Tyler.' Reverend Dobbs was dressed in his usual duffel coat and scarf, looking more like a *Big Issue* seller than a man of the cloth.

'You've got a bloody nerve, showing your face in here.'

'Now, before you start, just hear us out. Clint's got something he wants to say, haven't you, lad?' He snatched the baseball cap off the boy's head and shoved it into his hands. 'Well, come on. Let's have it.'

The boy lowered his shaven head. 'Sorry,' he mumbled. 'About your car.'

'It was you, was it?' Jack leaned back in his seat. 'Do you have any idea the kind of trouble you caused me? I didn't have a car for nearly a week. Not to mention all the insurance claims. I've got better things to do than fill out paperwork!'

'I said I'm sorry.' Clint stuck out his chin. A stud glinted on the end of it.

'I'm afraid that's not good enough. I should call the police.'

'You're not going to though, are you?' Sam stepped in. 'Look, the lad knows he did wrong and he's sorry for it.'

'Oh, really? And I don't suppose you had to drag him in here to apologise?'

'Of course I did. He's a kid, not bloody George Washington! But he's doing his best to make amends. It won't happen again.'

'Too right it won't. Next time I visit that site I'm coming by bus!'

'He just got a bit carried away, that's all. He was angry.'

'*He* was angry? How do you think I felt?'

'It was just a car, Mr Tyler. This is Clint's future you're taking away here. Without us, lads like him have got no chance of staying away from crime.'

'You mean like vandalising cars?'

Sam smiled. '*Touché*, Mr Tyler. But like I say, things are bad enough for these kids without you calling in the police. He'll pay for the damage, won't you, Clint?'

'It doesn't matter,' Jack said, as Clint's low brows sank even further. 'The company will pay for it.'

'Company car, eh? Nice.' Sam was impressed. 'All I get is a company bike. And even then I have to buy my own puncture repair kit!'

Jack laughed. He had to admit he liked Reverend Dobbs, in spite of his brusque manner and habit of hanging around with criminals.

'Tea?' he offered.

'No thanks, I'd better be getting back.' He looked at the drawings spread across the desk. 'No prizes for guessing what this is. Mind if I have a look?'

'Help yourself.' Jack pushed the papers across the desk at

him. 'These are the elevated plans of what the finished buildings will look like.'

'Very nice. You've done a great job, Mr Tyler.'

'Thanks.'

'No offence to your designs, but I'd still rather not see them happen.'

Before Jack had a chance to reply, Charlie walked in. She took one look at Sam and his thuggish-looking companion and said, 'Right, this time I'm definitely calling security.'

'It's all right, love, I'll save you the bother.' Sam pulled his hat further down over his ears. 'I'll see you, Mr Tyler. Hope you don't have any more car problems.'

'What did he mean by that?' Charlie demanded as soon as the door closed behind them. 'He wasn't threatening you, was he?'

'He's not that bad once you get to know him.'

'That's not what you said when they trashed your car.' Charlie folded her arms and looked at him shrewdly. 'You're not going soft, are you, Jack?'

'No, but I can understand why they did it.'

'Well, I still think the lot of them should be locked up for life,' Charlie said.

'For trashing a car? Blimey, I'd hate to have you on my jury!' Jack pulled the drawing towards him and studied it. 'I wonder if there is any way I can incorporate Second Chance into this scheme?'

'Don't even think about it,' Charlie warned. 'Peter Jameson would go mad.' She dumped a fat ringbound file on his desk. 'Here, this will take your mind off it. It's that traffic study you wanted.'

Jack lifted the file with both hands. 'Looks like light bedtime reading.'

'It'll certainly send you to sleep.' She paused. 'Talking of cures for insomnia, what time are you getting to Humphrey's party tomorrow night?'

'Oh God, is it tomorrow?' Jack groaned. He hadn't fixed

up a babysitter or anything. In fact he'd forgotten all about it. 'I think I might give it a miss.'

'But you can't!' Charlie sounded so dismayed Jack did a double-take. 'I mean – it's terribly important for your career. You know what Humphrey's like about people not coming to his soirées.'

'Maybe you're right.' He looked at the vast pile of work on his desk. 'I'll try to make it.'

She smiled. 'You'd better.'

'What do you think of this one?'

Charlie swished in front of the mirror, holding up a slip of black satin in front of her. Tom, her flatmate, barely glanced up from his copy of *What Car?*

'Are you sure you didn't try that one on ten minutes ago?'

'That one was long with thin straps. Pay attention, will you?' She turned back to the mirror. 'Do you think it's too tarty?'

'It's fine. If you're auditioning for *The Rocky Horror Show*.'

'Thanks. Your help is invaluable.' Charlie flung it down on the bed, where it joined Tom, Clive the cat, and a heap of other rejected outfits. Clive lifted his head and regarded her with sleepy yellow eyes. 'I don't even know why I'm asking you, anyway. You're hardly at the cutting edge of fashion yourself.' She looked disdainfully at his tatty trainers, ripped jeans and faded Spice Girls T-shirt.

'No, but I'm a man. And that's who you're trying to impress, isn't it?'

'Not at all. I'm just trying to decide what would look most professional for Humphrey Crawshaw's drinks party, that's all.'

'Fine. Then wear a nice, sensible suit. You can't get more professional than that, can you?' He flipped the page of his magazine. 'I take it Mr Perfect is going to be there?'

'I don't know who you mean.' She pulled an olive silk shift dress from the wardrobe and held it up against herself. Not bad. The colour brought out the green in her eyes, but it also added fire to her red hair, and she certainly didn't need that. She regarded it as her worst feature, especially having been teased over it for most of her life. Even though she was more drenched fox than belisha beacon, that didn't stop the kids at school calling her 'Ginge' and 'Carrot Top'.

At least the name-calling had stopped, but she still got tired of men sidling up and asking her if she was as fiery and passionate as her hair colour suggested. They usually found out when she gave them a stinging reply.

'You know. Him. Tom Cruise meets Christopher Wren.'

'You mean Jack Tyler? Yes, I think he might be there.' Who was she kidding? If he wasn't going, she wouldn't be going through these agonies. She would have worn her basic boring black and had done with it. And she certainly wouldn't have spent the best part of an hour blow-drying out the kinks in her stubbornly curly hair.

'What makes you think he's interested?' Tom asked from behind his magazine.

'What makes you think I am?'

'Hmm, let me think.' Tom pretended to consider. 'Could it be the way you mention his name every five minutes?'

'I do not!'

'No, you're right. It's more like every three. Or could it be the amount of time you spend getting ready for work every morning?'

'I have to look smart. We're not all scruffy computer geeks like you.'

'Just as well I am. There'd be no room in the bathroom for both of us in the morning.'

'You can always move out if you don't like it.'

'You don't mean that. You need me to help pay the

mortgage, remember? Besides, what would you do without me to keep your feet on the ground? If I wasn't here, you'd work even more ridiculously long hours and forget to have a life.'

'There speaks a man who spends his life in front of a computer and doesn't remember to eat unless I put a sandwich in front of him.'

Charlie smiled affectionately. Tom was right; they needed each other. They'd been soulmates ever since they'd met at university. Since Tom was the most gorgeous man on campus and she was considered to be the best-looking girl, everyone had assumed it would only be a matter of time before they got together. But apart from a little light-hearted flirting, they'd confounded them all by staying just good friends.

'I can always find someone to sleep with, but I can't always find a good mate,' Tom had said, and Charlie agreed. Which was why, when she decided to buy her horrendously expensive canal-side flat in Leeds, Tom was the one she chose to share it with.

The arrangement had worked well for the past two years, mainly because they understood each other so perfectly. They were both ambitious, both workaholics – despite the laidback, studenty image he cultivated, Tom ran his own very successful website design business – and most impor-tantly, neither of them was remotely interested in the other romantically. Tom had a string of beautiful, supermodel-like girlfriends and Charlie had Jack Tyler.

Or she would, if she got her way.

'So go on. What makes you think he's interested?' Tom asked again.

'Thanks for the vote of confidence!'

'I mean it. How long have you known him? Eighteen months? And he's never made a move on you, has he?'

'His wife died, remember? He's hardly likely to jump on me after that.'

She'd had a crush on Jack Tyler ever since she'd started at Crawshaw and Finch. He was the nicest and most approachable of her colleagues, as well as the best-looking. All the women in the office fancied him like mad. But Charlie had a strict hands-off policy when it came to married men – she'd been there before and it hadn't been a good experience. Certainly not one she'd like to repeat.

Not that she would have had the chance with Jack. As well as being one of the nicest men she knew, he was also the most faithful.

Charlie had met Miranda Tyler just once, at an office party shortly after she'd joined the company. She and Jack had made a striking couple, both tall, dark-haired and sophisticated. Charlie remembered watching her, so elegant and slender even after two children, and thinking how lucky she was to be married to someone like Jack.

A few months later, Miranda was dead. Overnight, Jack changed. He was like a zombie, in a total state of shock. Charlie felt deeply for him and longed to help, but it was as if he'd built up a wall around himself and hung a big 'Keep Out' sign on it. Despite being offered compassionate leave by Humphrey, he'd stunned them all by turning up at the office each day and working long, punishing hours. It was only the way he hid behind his office door and went for days without remembering to speak to anyone that gave away how he was really feeling.

He still worked long hours these days, but at least he talked more, although rarely about his wife or his family. Even though most of their conversations were frustratingly work-related, Charlie was sure she could be the one to help him through his heartache.

The only problem was she didn't know how Jack felt about her. She'd tried flirting a little, which hadn't had much effect, apart from making him slightly flustered. But was that embarrassed flustered or interested flustered? It was so difficult to tell with him. Sometimes she wondered if he'd even noticed.

But tonight would be the perfect opportunity to find out.

Chapter 13

'Where is it you're going?'

Jack looked up from struggling with his cufflink and caught Emily's eye in the mirror. She was lying on her stomach on his bed, chewing her pencil as she composed her party guest list. It was beginning to look frighteningly long.

'I told you, my boss is having drinks at his house.'

'Sounds boring.'

'Believe me, it will be.'

'So why are you going?'

'I have to. It's work.'

'But you're always working,' she complained.

'True.' It certainly felt like it, anyway.

'Who'll be there?'

'I don't know. A lot of clients, probably. People from work. Your Uncle Greg.'

She picked moodily at the corner of the duvet cover where the stitching was coming undone. 'Will there be any women there?'

'Possibly. Does Auntie Ros count?' he joked, but she didn't laugh. Jack turned to face her. 'Look, Emily, I don't want to go to this thing, believe me. I can think of better things to do.'

'Why are you going, then?'

'Because your Auntie Ros won't give me a minute's peace if I don't – oh, sod it!' He gave up with his cufflink and threw it down on the dressing table. 'I never could manage these things.'

'Let me do it.' Emily uncurled herself off the bed and picked up the cufflink. Jack looked at her dark head bent over his sleeve as she fixed it in place. She'd grown much taller over the past months. She was almost up to his shoulder now and she looked so much like Miranda it hurt.

Christ, he missed her at times like this. He hated going to parties without her. If he closed his eyes, he could almost smell her perfume as she flitted from the bedroom to the bathroom, emptying her wardrobe, pulling out outfits and rejecting them before declaring she had nothing remotely decent to wear. But within half an hour she would look stunning, her hair dark and glossy, make-up perfect, dressed in something gorgeous. He would look at her and feel like the proudest man in the world.

Missing her was like an ache deep inside him. I can't do it, he thought suddenly. I can't go.

'Dad?' Emily had finished fastening his cufflink and was looking at him curiously. 'Dad, are you all right?'

He pulled himself together. Mustn't lose it in front of the girls. 'Course I am. Come on, we'd better get to Gran's before Uncle Greg goes without me.'

By the time they got to Leeds, Ros and Greg were already there, their kids tucked away safely in his mother's spare bedroom. The girls were having Jack's old room, and Jack was sleeping on the sofa that night.

'There you are!' Ros said. 'We thought you'd bottled out.'

'I nearly did.'

'Why? Humphrey's parties aren't that bad,' Greg grinned. 'At least there's always plenty of booze.'

'There could be wall-to-wall lapdancers and I still wouldn't fancy it.'

'And you're not drinking, remember?' Ros tapped her husband on the chest. 'I refuse to drive again just so you can get drunk and make a fool of yourself.'

'Yes, my love. Anything you say.' Greg rolled his eyes at

Jack above his wife's head. Jack smiled back in sympathy. He'd lived with his big sister long enough to know what a bully she could be.

Sophie came into the room and wrapped herself around Greg's waist. 'Uncle Greg, did you find out anything about my treasure?'

Greg looked down at her. 'What treasure's that, sweetheart?'

'Her bone. You said you were going to send it to the laboratory,' Jack reminded him. 'She's been on about it for days.'

'Is it prehistoric?' Sophie asked hopefully.

'Oh, *that* treasure. No, sorry, Soph, I'm afraid your dad was right. It was just the remains of someone's Sunday lunch. A dog must have buried it there.'

Sophie looked disappointed. 'Can I have it back, then?'

'Sorry, love, I chucked it away. I didn't think you'd want it back.'

'Of course she doesn't,' Jack said quickly, as her lip jutted. 'What do you want with a manky old bone, Soph?'

'It might have been prehistoric,' Sophie muttered as she headed back to the kitchen. Greg watched her go.

'Oops, I think I've just lost my number one fan.'

'She'll get over it.' Jack turned to him. 'You didn't really send it to the lab, did you?'

'And make myself a laughing stock? What do you think?' Greg pulled a face. 'Peter Jameson thinks I'm a big enough idiot as it is.'

As they left, his mother and the girls were tucked up together on the sofa in front of a video, sharing a box of Maltesers. Jack wished he could stay in and watch it with them. He couldn't remember the last time he and the girls had enjoyed a night in.

'What are you watching?'

'Something with Julia Roberts.' No one lifted their eyes from the screen.

'Any good?'

'Don't know yet, we're still watching the trailers.'

Jack hesitated for a moment. Ros guessed what he was thinking and stepped in quickly.

'Oh no you don't. You're coming to this party. You never know, you might even enjoy yourself.'

He didn't enjoy himself. He stood with a drink in his hand, smiling and nodding while Peter Jameson cornered him about the new health club he'd just joined.

'The facilities are marvellous,' he droned on, as Jack stared into his empty glass with a glazed expression. 'Do you work out at all, Jack?'

'What? Oh no. No time these days.' He used to be a regular at the local gym. Now the only six packs he ever encountered were Sophie's favourite yoghurts.

'You should. The waiting list for mine is pretty long, but I'm sure I could pull a few strings and get you in.'

'Thanks. I'll – er – bear that in mind.' Once upon a time he would have jumped at the chance to earn some brownie points with an important client. Now he couldn't stop thinking about whether he'd forgotten to pack Sophie's teddy in her overnight bag. She couldn't go to sleep without it.

Just then Greg joined them and Jack allowed his jaw muscles to relax into his first genuine smile all evening.

'I'm sure my colleague here would be delighted to join your club, Peter.' He clapped his hand on Greg's bulky shoulder. 'He's gone to seed since he gave up playing rugby.'

'What are you talking about? I keep myself fit. I'll have you know I'm a keen follower of the Geri Halliwell workout video.'

'Yeah – from the sofa with a large whisky in your hand!'

'Why not? It's amazing how many calories leching burns off.'

Peter smiled thinly. 'I'm sure Graham wouldn't be interested in joining my club.'

There was an awkward moment where they both stared at their feet. Then Greg mumbled, 'The name's Greg.'

'What? Oh yes, of course. How could I forget?'

How indeed? It seemed unthinkable to Jack that the head of the Westpoint consortium could have forgotten the name of the man who was supposed to be coordinating the project. Either he had done it to be rude, or to underline how unimportant Greg was.

Whatever the reason, it must have hurt. Jack felt his brother-in-law's burning mortification as if it was his own.

He looked away, stared into the middle distance and longed for Miranda. At times like this, when things got really tedious, he could look across the room and see her there, charming someone, laughing at their jokes. She would catch his eye and smile, making it clear that even though she was with someone else, it was him she wanted. They would circle each other, silently flirting, until he was nearly mad with desire. Sometimes they'd barely get back to the car.

Suddenly there she was, smiling at him from the other side of the room. He blinked, then looked again, and realised with a shock that it wasn't Miranda. It was Charlie Ferguson.

A moment later she was by his side, looking stunning in bronze-coloured silk that clung to her well-toned curves and showed off her glorious autumnal colouring. Her hair was swept up in a loose, sexy style. The kind that only needed one tug of a pin to bring the whole lot tumbling down over her shoulders.

'Charlie!' Jack greeted her with relief. 'Do you know Peter Jameson?'

'We've met.' Charlie regarded him coolly, then said, 'You don't mind if I borrow Jack for a moment?'

'Of course.' Peter didn't meet her eye.

'Thanks,' Jack said, as they made their way swiftly through the crowd. 'Another five minutes of that and I would have run away screaming, partnership or no partnership.'

'You looked as if you needed rescuing.'

'I think poor Greg's the one who needs rescuing.' He glanced back to where Greg was desperately trying to talk to a disinterested Peter Jameson.

'He's a creepy little bastard.'

'Greg?'

'Jameson.' Charlie said it with such feeling that Jack turned to look at her in surprise. She was usually a fairly cool customer, good at hiding her emotions. But the look she gave Peter across the room was one of pure loathing.

'You sound as if you speak from experience?'

'Let's just say our paths have crossed before.'

Jack smiled. 'Now I'm intrigued.'

'Don't be. He doesn't deserve it.' She shrugged. 'It was just a boring case of sexual harrassment.'

'What?'

'Not me, you idiot. Christ, can you imagine me ever letting a little toad like that get the better of me?' Charlie laughed. 'No, it was a consultant at the planners where I used to work. We were doing some work on an apartment block he was developing and he seemed to think she was part of the package. She turned him down, so he got her thrown off the project.'

'Didn't she report him?'

'She tried, but the company hushed it all up. Didn't want to lose his valuable custom.' Charlie's mouth thinned with contempt. 'In the end, they gave her a nice fat pay cheque and sent her away. That was their idea of justice. Which is why I left.'

'You wouldn't have done the same?'

'Oh, I can understand why she did it. She knew she wasn't going to win, so she thought it was better to go with a pay-off and a decent reference than with nothing at all. But I would have stayed and fought, even if it cost me my job. There's no way I would have let him get away with it.'

'I can believe that.' Jack regarded her admiringly. He'd never had her down as the defenceless type. Charlie Ferguson might look fragile and feminine, but she was more than capable of taking care of herself.

Not like Greg. He glanced across the room to where his brother-in-law was still talking to Peter Jameson. At least he had his attention now. In fact, they looked to be quite deep in conversation.

He turned back to Charlie. 'Would you like a drink?'

'Please. Just a white wine spritzer. I'm driving.' She looked down at the empty glass in his hand. 'I take it you're not?'

He shook his head. 'I'm staying with my parents. They're looking after my daughters tonight.'

'How are they settling in to their new home?'

'Slowly, I think. Emily misses her social circle a bit more than Sophie, but at least she seems to be settling in at her new school. She's just auditioned for the school play.'

'Really?'

'And Sophie's made lots of friends at her new school. She's forever going round to other kids' houses for tea. I'm not quite sure of the etiquette, but I think I'm supposed to ask them back sometime.' He saw Charlie's glazed expression and stopped himself. 'I'm sorry, you should shut me up if I start droning on. I could bore for Britain on the subject of my daughters.'

'Not at all, it's fascinating.' She smiled brightly, a sure sign she hadn't listened to a word he'd said.

'Thanks, but I know there's nothing more tedious than listening to other people talk about their kids. Especially when you don't have any yourself.'

'Far from it.' She laid her hand across his wrist. 'You could never be tedious, Jack.'

Something about the husky way she said it confused him. She seemed to be standing a lot closer now, so close he could see the bronze flecks in her tawny eyes.

He gently extricated himself from her grasp. 'I'll – er – go and get those drinks.'

He was at the bar when Ros came up behind him.

'Who was that woman you were talking to?'

'Charlie Ferguson. She's one of our consultants.'

'So that's the famous Charlie, is it? Greg told me about her.' She glanced over her shoulder. 'He said she had the hots for you, but I didn't realise it was so obvious. Still, I suppose it would have to be, for Greg to notice.'

'What?' Jack laughed. 'Charlie? You've got to be joking.'

'Oh, come on, Jack. Even you can't be that thick. Anyone can see she was coming on to you. She homed in on you like a heat-seeking missile!'

'I think you've got the wrong idea. We're just friends, that's all. Not even that. More like work colleagues.'

'Then why was she flirting with you?'

'I hadn't noticed.'

'No, you wouldn't, would you? That's because you're a man. Trust me, she fancies you.'

Jack glanced across the room and caught Charlie's eye. She smiled and he looked away again sharply.

'You're blushing!' Ros laughed. 'Honestly, there's no need to be embarrassed about it, Jack. She's gorgeous. Isn't she, Greg?' She turned to her husband, who had just muscled his way through the crowd towards them, clutching a pint.

'What's that, my little Venus flytrap?'

'I was just saying how attractive Charlie is.'

'Oh God, yes. Absolutely stunning. Far too good for you, you lucky bastard.' He grinned at Jack. 'Not that I'm in any way envious,' he added, with a wary sidelong glance at his wife.

'What is this?' Jack looked from one to the other. 'I told you, there's nothing going on between me and Charlie.'

'That's all down to you, isn't it?' Greg said. 'Come on, Jack, everyone in the office knows she's after you. The only one who can't see it is you, apparently.'

'That's probably what she finds so attractive.' Ros nodded wisely. 'Women love a challenge.'

Jack looked from one to the other. It was as if they'd both started speaking Portuguese. 'Look, I don't know where you've got this idea from, but you're wrong. Charlie is no more interested in me than I am in Greg.'

'There you are.' Charlie edged her way in between them. 'I was wondering where you'd got to.'

Greg raised his eyebrows. 'You were saying?'

For the next twenty minutes Jack had to endure Ros' less than subtle interrogation of Charlie Ferguson. Why the poor woman didn't just walk away he had no idea. He felt like it, but sheer embarrassment kept him rooted to the spot as Ros probed into everything from Charlie's marital history – 'Not even a serious boyfriend? And you're how old?' – to her wardrobe – 'Manolo Blahniks, you say? They must have set you back a bit.' Charlie kept a fixed smile on her face but Jack could tell she was desperate to escape.

Finally, Greg rescued them both by fetching another round of drinks. 'So,' he said as he handed them out, 'how are the party preparations going, Jacko?'

'What party?' Charlie turned to him. 'You didn't tell me you were having a party.'

'It's not really my party. Emily – my daughter – is the one organising it.'

'Yes, but adults are invited too, aren't they?' Ros leapt in. 'We're going. You should come, Charlie. She could come, couldn't she, Jack? It's a week on Friday.'

Oh great. He could just imagine her bopping away to hard house garage funk or whatever they called it with

Emily's disreputable mates. 'I don't really think it's Charlie's thing—'

'I'd love to,' she interrupted him.

'But they'll all be teenagers. Teenagers with acne and bad attitudes, smuggling in cider and sneaking upstairs to snog under the coats.'

'It sounds like fun.'

'I doubt it.'

'Don't be such an old fogey, Jack,' Ros scolded him. 'Charlie's not that old herself. She'd probably love it, wouldn't you, Charlie?'

'It's okay. Jack's right, it doesn't really sound like my sort of thing.' Charlie's smile was even more fixed as she took her spritzer from Greg. 'If you'll excuse me, I really should circulate.'

'You utter cretin,' Ros snapped as Charlie pushed her way through the crowd. 'Now look what you've done. You've scared her off.'

'*I've* scared her off? What about you? "Have you got a serious boyfriend, Charlie? Do like you children, Charlie?" You'd make the Gestapo sound laidback.'

'Why did you have to put her off like that? You could tell she wanted to come to that party,' Ros went on, ignoring him. 'It would have been your chance to get off with her.'

'*Get off* with her? I'm thirty-six, not sixteen. I don't want to get off with anyone.'

'Yes, but—'

'Ros, listen to me. For the last time, I DO NOT WANT TO GET OFF WITH CHARLIE FERGUSON!'

Of course, at that moment everyone seemed to stop talking and an unnatural hush fell, so that the only sound filling the room was his voice. Jack looked around quickly. Charlie was at the far side of the room, talking to a small balding man. From the look she gave him it was obvious she'd heard every word.

As had everyone else in the room, and most of the kitchen staff.

'Idiot,' Ros hissed.

He went home shortly afterwards. The evening had been more than long enough for him, but since Ros and Greg were still enjoying themselves, he left them to it and decided to take a taxi back to his parents' house.

Humphrey lived on the smart outskirts of the city, hardly the place where cabs cruised, especially not when it was lashing with rain. Jack tried to call one from his mobile, only to find he'd forgotten to recharge it. He thought about going back to Humphrey's, but the thought of walking back into that crowded room filled him with dread. Deciding he might have better luck finding a taxi in the city centre, he began to trudge up the dark, deserted, tree-lined avenue, dodging spray from the passing cars. Cold rain dripped off his hair and down inside his collar.

He'd only been walking five minutes when a sporty Audi slowed up and pulled over to the kerb ahead of him. Jack recognised it instantly, his heart sinking.

Sure enough, as he drew level, the electric window purred down and Charlie stuck her head out.

'Need a lift?'

Jack looked up the empty, rain-washed street. 'I was planning to find a taxi.'

'At this time of night? You'll catch pneumonia before you catch a cab round here.' She reached over and opened the door. 'Come on, I'll give you a lift. Don't worry, I promise I won't force myself on you!' She smiled impishly.

Jack groaned. 'Look, I'm really sorry about that.'

'It's okay. Although I must say I've never been rejected quite so publicly before.' She looked up at him. 'Are you getting in or not?'

Inside the car was warm, dark and luxurious. The smell of rich leather mingled with Charlie's lingering perfume.

Jack sank back into the deep seat and let the soulful sound of Beverley Knight wash over him. It was the kind of car he and Miranda used to dream of owning, before real life took over and they had to swap looks and luxury for the practicality of washable upholstery and somewhere to stash comics and juice bottles.

'Can you tell me where I'm supposed to be going?' Charlie startled him out of his reverie.

'What? Oh, sorry.' He gave her directions to his parents' house. 'I was just indulging in a bit of car envy.'

Charlie smiled. 'I wondered why you had that big grin on your face. It is nice, isn't it? One of my many indulgences.'

'Lucky you, being able to indulge yourself.'

'Don't you?'

'Not these days.' He thought back wistfully to when he had time to himself. Spare hours to go to the gym, to lose himself in work, to go to a football match or watch the Grand Prix on TV. Now, if he was in front of the TV, he usually had the ironing board out.

Charlie smiled. 'Everyone needs to indulge themselves once in a while, Jack.'

They drove in silence. Charlie seemed fine, humming along to the CD as she manoeuvred the powerful car through the dark streets, but Jack still felt awkward about what had happened that evening. Finally, he said, 'Look, I am really sorry about what I said. I only said it to shut my sister up.'

Charlie smiled, not taking her eyes off the road. 'She is rather full-on, isn't she?'

'You'd noticed? She means well, but she's got this obsession with fixing me up with every single woman who comes along.' He glanced across at her. 'I'm sorry if she embarrassed you.'

'Sounds like you were the one who was embarrassed, not

me.' She paused while she negotiated a roundabout. 'I take it you're not interested in being fixed up?'

'Not by my sister.'

'But in principle?'

'I don't know. I can't really imagine it somehow.' He watched the rain running down the window. 'I know it's been nearly a year, but I can't help feeling if I was with anyone else it would seem like I was being unfaithful somehow. And I don't know if I could start again after being off the market for so many years. I wouldn't have a clue what to do.'

Charlie smiled. 'I don't think it's changed much.'

'No, but I have.'

They fell into silence again. Charlie said, 'I don't think I've ever taken a man back to his mum's before.'

'I know. Pathetic, isn't it?'

'I think it's quite sweet.'

Five minutes later they pulled up outside his parents' house. As he got out, Jack said, 'Look, about the party—'

'It's okay, I understand. You don't have to invite me if you don't want to.'

'I do want to. I'd like you to come. That is, if you don't mind being knee-deep in over-excited teenage boys?'

'It can't be any worse than being knee-deep in Humphrey Crawshaw's cronies!' She smiled. 'Remind me again on Monday and I'll check my diary.'

They said goodnight and she drove off. Jack watched her go, relieved there had been no awkward moment over a goodnight kiss. He'd been wondering whether he should give her a peck on the cheek or something, but while he was still psyching himself up for it she'd bid him a brisk goodnight and then gone.

Ros and Greg must surely have got it wrong, he decided. He and Charlie Ferguson were just good friends.

*

Charlie arrived home to find the flat in darkness. Funny, Tom hadn't said anything about going out. Maybe he'd got a last-minute invitation from one of his many female admirers.

She crashed around in the dark for a while, swearing and banging her shins on the furniture until she found the light. Clive the cat emerged sleepily from Tom's bedroom, outraged at being woken. He never slept on Tom's bed unless Tom was in it. Alone.

'Tom?' Charlie stood in the bedroom doorway, peering into the darkness. 'Tom, are you awake?'

'I am now.' He emerged grumpily from under the duvet. 'What time is it?'

'Nearly eleven.' She flicked on the light. Tom screwed up his face against the sudden brightness. His dark hair was spiked up on end. 'Why are you in bed? Are you sick or something?'

'I just fancied an early night. Not a crime, is it?' He struggled to sit up, pulling the duvet up around his bare chest. 'You're back early. Don't tell me Mr Perfect didn't show up?'

'As a matter of fact he did. I've just given him a lift home.'

'Oh dear, you must be slipping. I expected you two to fall in through the door, tearing each other's clothes off.'

'He had to get back to see to his kids.' She sat down on the bed, narrowly missing Tom's feet. 'He's kind of obsessed with them.'

'Don't sound so surprised. He's their father, isn't he?'

'I know. I just didn't expect him to be so – devoted.' His face had lit up when he talked about them, the way it used to light up when they were discussing a challenging new project.

'If he's that devoted, you're going to have to get to know them. You'd love that, wouldn't you?' Tom smirked.

'Actually, I'm going to. He's invited me to his daughter's party.'

'You? At some kid's party?' Tom laughed. 'I can just imagine you with jelly and ice cream all over your Armani, getting in a strop because you can't win Pass the Parcel!'

'Not that kind of party, dummy. It's the other daughter. The older one. I think she's fourteen. Or maybe fifteen.' She was sure Jack must have told her, but she'd tuned out somewhere in the middle of the conversation.

'Oh God. You at a teenage rave? Do you know what you're getting into here?'

'Don't be such an old git. I can be very cool when I want to be.'

'Charlie, no one over twenty-one is cool to a fifteen-year-old.'

'Thanks, but I do remember what it's like to be a teenage girl. Probably a lot better than you, come to think of it.'

Tom shook his head. 'I still think you're on dodgy ground here. You know nothing about children.'

'So? It can't be that difficult to learn, can it?' She smiled confidently. 'I'll wrap those daughters of his round my little finger. They'll love me.'

And so would Jack. She'd already made her mind up about that.

Chapter 14

Dan watched from the doorway as Tess rushed around the kitchen, still in her work clothes, clattering pots and pans.

'Shouldn't you be getting changed by now? He'll be here in twenty minutes.'

She stopped and looked down at herself. 'What's wrong with what I'm wearing?'

'Nothing. I just thought you might want to dress up a bit, that's all.'

'Dan, this is your father we're expecting, not a member of the royal family!' She lifted the lid on the nearest pan and gave the contents an exploratory poke. 'Anyway, it's you he's coming to see, not me.'

'All the same, you could put a bit of make-up on—'

'Excuse me?' Tess let the lid drop with a crash. 'Which is more important, me being dressed to the nines or me getting this dinner on time? Have you finished laying that table yet?'

Dan headed for the dining room, grumbling. Tess looked back down at her serviceable navy trousers and white blouse, now spattered with tiny dots of pasta sauce as well as smudges of ink where the photocopier had played up again. Maybe she should put on something a bit smarter. She didn't want to look as if she'd gone to any great effort just for Phil. But on the other hand, she didn't want to look as if she'd let herself go, either. There was a fine line between looking her best and looking as though she'd tried too hard, and she was afraid of crossing it. God forbid Phil should actually think she cared.

It was just one in a long line of fears and doubts that had plagued her ever since Dan announced his father was coming to dinner. With each day that passed she found it harder and harder to think of anything else. And now the big day was finally here. She'd felt sick with anxiety for hours, her emotions rebounding faster than a squash ball.

What if he'd changed beyond all recognition? What if he hadn't changed at all? What if he was married? What if he brought his wife and family with him? Tess wondered if the lasagne would stretch that far. Then fresh panic struck her. What if he was vegetarian? What if he, his wife and his ten children were all strict vegans who lived on nothing but wheatgrass and macrobiotic mung beans?

She took another gulp from the large glass of red wine she'd poured herself the moment she got home. Frankly, that was the least of her worries. What she was really scared about was seeing him again after all these years.

Dan had offered to let her read the letter Phil had sent, but she couldn't bring herself to do it. She told herself it was Dan's business and nothing to do with her, but now she began to wish she had read it. At least then she might have been prepared. As it was, she had no idea what kind of man would be standing there when she opened the door.

She could tell Dan was going through the same kind of apprehension, even though he did his best to hide it. He'd skipped a couple of lectures at college to come home early. Tess had come back from work to find him dressed in a relatively clean version of his usual uniform of oversized sweatshirt and jeans, his untidy fair hair combed. Even his bedroom was unusually tidy, with his CDs back in their rack and his computer paraphernalia put away instead of strewn everywhere. Part of her was touched that he'd gone to so much effort for his father. The other part was miffed that he never did it for her.

Dan came back in as she was tossing the salad. 'All done.'

'Thanks.' She slapped his hand as it strayed towards the

lemon meringue pie defrosting on the worktop. Then she noticed he was on his sticks. She'd been in such a rush when she came in, it hadn't registered. 'Aren't you using your chair today?'

He looked defensive. 'I don't need it all the time.'

'I know that. It's just you usually prefer it when you come home from college.'

'Well, I don't want it today. Okay?'

'Okay. No need to bite my head off.' She paused. 'Your father does know you're disabled, you know.'

He looked up sharply. 'How?'

'I wrote to him. When you were first diagnosed.'

'And he never wrote back?' Dan's expression was grim. 'Says a lot, doesn't it?' He gazed down at his sticks. 'That's probably why I haven't seen him since.'

'You know that's not true.'

'Do I?' She'd always taught him to ignore his disability, not to see it as an obstacle to anything he wanted to do. It shocked her to see him look so defeated.

Before she could answer there was a knock on the door. Tess and Dan stared at each other.

'That's him,' Dan said.

Tess glanced at the clock. 'It can't be, he's too early.' She took another gulp of wine. Suddenly she had the overwhelming urge to go to the loo.

Dan was already at the door before she'd made it out of the kitchen. Tess steeled herself as he opened the door. She came to the doorway, her smile fixed in place – and came face to face with her mother.

'Mum! What are you doing here?'

'That's a nice greeting, isn't it?' Margaret Doyle took off her headscarf, folded it carefully and put it in the pocket of her raincoat. 'And after I've waited nearly a quarter of an hour for the bus.'

'You do know Phil's coming round at any minute?'

'Oh, is it today? I had no idea.'

Tess gritted her teeth. 'I told you last week.'

'How am I supposed to remember everything you tell me?' Margaret pushed past her into the kitchen and dumped her handbag on the worktop. 'Shall I put the kettle on? Ooh, something smells nice. Is it foreign?'

Tess looked at Dan, who was making frantic eyebrow signals. But what could she do? Margaret Doyle was an unstoppable force when she wanted to be.

She hurried into the kitchen after her mother. 'Mum, I don't think you understand. Phil is coming round for dinner any minute now.'

'In that case, shouldn't you be getting ready?' She looked Tess up and down with a critical eye.

'But—'

'I'll keep an eye on the dinner, don't you worry. And you don't have to look at me like that. I'm not going to poison the man. No matter how much he deserves it,' she added.

'Mum!'

Margaret Doyle turned on her, hands on hips. 'Look, I'm just here to make sure he behaves himself, all right? I'm not going to make a scene or anything. I'm not even going to talk to him if I can help it.'

'Great. Just great.' As if this whole fiasco wasn't going to be awkward enough, she now had her mother's pointed silences to contend with.

She picked up the wine bottle to refill her glass. Margaret frowned. 'I hope you're not going to be half cut when he turns up? You're going to need your wits about you to deal with him, my girl.'

Strange, Tess thought. And there was me thinking the best way was to get so drunk I don't remember anything about it tomorrow morning. She left her mother poking at the lasagne as if it were some fascinating new breed of pond life she'd discovered, and went off to change.

Dan waylaid her on her way to her bedroom. 'What's

Gran doing here? She's not going to frighten him off or anything?'

'Of course not.' Tess hoped she sounded more reassuring than she felt. She had half an idea that Margaret might have bought herself a gun from one of the many dodgy characters on the estate and concealed it in that capacious handbag of hers. Nothing would surprise her about her mother.

She dithered for a long time over what to wear. She didn't want anything too sexy – although in a wardrobe full of jeans and sensible M&S suits, that wasn't very likely. She wanted something that said strong, independent, successful woman. Unfortunately, all that her wardrobe said was dowdy person who really should get out more. In the end she gave up and swapped her navy trousers for black and her shirt for a black top. She took off her pink fluffy slippers and put on a pair of heels, and was just touching up her lipstick when there was another knock on the door.

Oh Lord, this had to be him. She listened to the scuffle outside as Dan beat her mother to the front door. Then, with a last quick look in the mirror, she stood up and went to greet the man who'd changed her life and then walked out of it so many years ago.

Phil stood in the hall, half hidden behind an enormous bunch of chrysanthemums. He was flanked on one side by an excited-looking Dan, and on the other by a boot-faced Margaret.

As Tess emerged from her room, he turned to face her. Her first thought was that he looked the same. His face was a little older and craggier, and the fair hair was slightly receding, but those thickly lashed grey-green eyes hadn't changed. Or perhaps she only thought she recognised him because he looked so much like Dan.

'Tess.' And he still had the smile that had made her heart flip at sixteen years old. Except, she was pleased to note, it

144

no longer flipped at thirty-four. Although she couldn't deny he'd grown from a good-looking boy into a handsome man, all she could think was thank goodness he hadn't dressed up too much. His casual but smart chinos and Aran sweater were a lot less intimidating than the suit she'd been half expecting.

She was suddenly, uncomfortably aware that everyone had stopped speaking. Her mother was tight-lipped and frosty, and Dan was too busy staring at the father who had suddenly materialised in front of him. His sticks, Tess noticed, were pushed as far back as he could get them without falling down.

Everyone seemed to be expecting her to say something, so she looked at the flowers. 'Are those for me?'

'Oh, sorry. Yes.' He dumped them in her arms. 'I didn't know what else to bring you. Nothing seemed appropriate somehow.'

'Seventeen years' back maintenance money would have been a start,' her mother muttered.

Tess shot her a silencing look. 'They're lovely. I'll put them in some water.' She headed for the kitchen. 'Would you like a drink?'

'I'll get it,' Dan offered. 'What would you like?'

'Whisky, please. If you've got it.'

'Did you have a good journey?' Tess asked.

'Fine, thanks.' Phil edged past Margaret, who was barring his way into the kitchen. 'It feels weird, seeing you again.'

'Doesn't it? You haven't changed much.'

'Neither have you.'

'I'm sure that's not true.' Tess patted her hair. 'I must have aged about a hundred years.'

'Absolutely not. You still look just the same as you used to.' Margaret tutted loudly. Phil turned to her. 'You haven't changed either, Mrs Doyle. You're as lovely as ever.'

Tess cringed and quickly checked there were no sharp instruments within her mother's reach.

Phil looked confident enough, but she could tell by his drumming fingers that underneath he was as nervous as hell. She couldn't blame him. It must have taken a hell of a lot of courage to come here tonight.

'So – um – what have you been up to since I last saw you?' he joked feebly.

Tess smiled back, ignoring her mother's snort of disgust. 'Oh, you know, this and that.'

'Bringing up a child virtually single-handed,' Margaret put in.

Phil glanced uneasily at her, then turned back to Tess. 'Dan tells me you're a teacher now? Funny, I didn't have you down as that type.'

'I know. I surprised myself.' She put the flowers in the sink and began searching in the cupboards for a vase. 'Actually, I quite enjoy it. Most of the time.' She found a vase and blew the dust off. 'I hear you've done pretty well for yourself?'

'Oh, I wouldn't say that. I'm a fairly small fish really. But I do run my own software company.'

'It still sounds impressive, but then I don't know a CD-Rom from a sardine, I'm afraid. But Dan assures me it's all very high-powered and he really does know what he's talking about. He's obsessed with computers.'

'Must be genetic,' Phil said, which earned him a scowl from Margaret.

Tess could see she was brewing up to make another cutting comment, so she quickly said, 'Why don't you go in and talk to Dan? He must be dying to quiz you about gigabytes and hard drives and things.'

As soon as Phil had gone, she turned on her mother. 'Mum, what are you playing at?'

'What am I playing at? You're the one who's giggling and falling all over him.'

'I'm just being nice to him.'

'Yes, well, as long as you don't expect me to do the same.'

'I don't expect you to do anything. I didn't even expect you to be here, if you remember. Come to think of it, why did you come round? You still haven't said.'

Her mother gave her an old-fashioned look. 'Someone's got to keep an eye on you. Don't forget what happened the last time you two were alone together.'

'I was sixteen years old! I've grown up a bit since then.'

'So you say,' Margaret said darkly.

'Besides, you don't seriously expect him to ravish me over the microwave – oh, hello again.' She looked up as Phil appeared in the doorway, a glass in his hand.

'Sorry to interrupt. I've just come to get some ice.'

'Oh. Right. Help yourself.' Tess opened the fridge door and stepped aside. She felt her face flaming. 'Dinner will be ready in about ten minutes.'

'Great.' With a quick smile, he slipped out of the room. No sooner had the door closed than Margaret said, 'Hmm, I can see how much you've grown up. Every time he looks at you, you start blushing like a schoolgirl!'

'The only reason I'm blushing is because I'm embarrassed at you for being so vile to him!' Tess hissed back. 'Look, no one's asking you to welcome him into the family. Just try to put up with him for Dan's sake. This is what he wants, remember? The least we can do is go along with it.'

'I suppose so,' Margaret agreed grudgingly. Then, just as Tess was breathing an inward sigh of relief, she added, 'Just don't expect me to talk to the smarmy little so-and-so.'

In spite of everything, dinner turned out to be a far more relaxed affair than Tess had hoped for. Her mother may have sat at the end of the table with a face like a sucked lemon, but at least Dan and Phil chatted away like they'd known each other for years. They talked about computers, college, Dan's A Levels and his career plans. It was astonishing how much they had in common, right down to a lifelong and sometimes over-optimistic support of Leeds United.

If Phil was at all fazed by Dan's disability, he didn't show it. Tess was grateful for that. Far from being resentful that the two of them were getting on so well, she found she was pleased for her son. Helen was right, it wasn't a popularity contest. Just because Dan got on well with his father didn't mean he loved her any less.

Half a bottle of Rioja helped. Tess found herself relaxing and joining in with their conversation. She even managed to laugh a few times, even if it did earn her a scowl from her mother.

They talked about her job, and Phil's. Tess didn't understand a word, even when he'd explained it twice, but Dan seemed amazingly impressed. Apparently Phil had designed some high-powered business software, and some educational packages that Dan used at college. He was even more thrilled when Phil promised to come round with a sneak preview of some of the latest stuff his company had been working on.

'So you're planning to stay around, are you?' Margaret cut in.

'Actually, yes,' Phil replied calmly. 'I've managed to combine coming here with a couple of business meetings.'

Her mother pursed her lips. 'I might have known there'd be money in it.'

'I'm not doing it for the money. I'm doing it so I can spend some time getting to know my son.'

That silenced her. Tess pushed her chair back and stood up. 'I'll just take these away, shall I?' She began gathering up the plates.

'I'll help you.' Before she could stop him, Phil was on his feet too.

He followed her into the kitchen, his hands full of dishes. 'Nice to see your mum doesn't bear a grudge.'

'You can't blame her. She knows how tough it was for me after you left—' she stopped quickly. The last thing she wanted was to sound self-pitying.

'But you don't hate me?'

'My feelings don't come into it.' Tess turned away from him and began scraping leftovers into the bin. 'I'm doing this for Dan.'

'So you do hate me?'

She straightened up and slid the plates into the sink. 'I don't feel anything,' she answered honestly. 'Maybe I did hate you once. But it was all a long time ago. I'm too busy to hold on to a grudge.'

'I wouldn't blame you if you did, after what you must have been through.' Phil lowered his voice. 'I didn't realise he was so—'

'So what? Handsome? Intelligent? Or do you mean disabled? It's all right, Phil, you can say the word. I'm not going to burst into tears.' Tess looked back over her shoulder at him. 'I did write and tell you, if you remember? About fifteen years ago?'

He winced. 'I know. I'm sorry. It was just a hell of a shock, walking in and seeing him – like that. I'm still trying to take it in.'

How do you think I've felt all these years? she wanted to shout. 'And would you have still come if you'd known how bad it was?'

'Of course.' He looked genuinely shocked. 'What kind of man do you think I am?'

Tess smiled. 'Do you really want me to answer that?'

'I suppose I asked for that, didn't I?' Phil took the plate she'd just washed and reached for the teatowel. 'So what exactly is wrong with him?'

'Spinal Muscular Atrophy. It's a bit technical to explain, but basically it means the cells in his spinal cord that carry messages from his brain to the muscles are dying off.

149

Without the brain telling them what to do the muscles get weaker and weaker, until they stop working completely.'

Phil finished drying the plate and set it on the worktop. He seemed to be steeling himself. 'And will he die?'

'No, thank God. He actually has the mildest type, which isn't life threatening. We were lucky.'

'You call that lucky?'

Tess regarded him steadily. 'If you could see some of the babies who don't make it past their first birthday, you'd say we were lucky too.'

'So he was born like that?'

'He was certainly born with SMA, but we didn't notice the signs until he started to crawl. He just couldn't manage it the way the other babies did. But it took ages to get the doctor to admit something was wrong. He thought I was being neurotic.'

'You're not the neurotic type.' Phil picked up another plate from the draining board. 'It must have been a nightmare for you, bringing him up on your own.'

'I didn't have much choice, did I?'

'I'm sorry. If I'd known how bad things were—'

'You would have come back? I doubt that, don't you? Especially since you couldn't even bring yourself to answer my letter.'

'You're right.' He looked downcast. 'I probably would have left you to it. Just like I left you to it that night with my parents.'

The mention of his parents made her hackles rise. 'How are they, by the way? I don't suppose your mother was too pleased at Dan getting in touch?'

'She doesn't know. We kind of drifted apart after I went to university. I couldn't forgive them for what they'd done to you. What they'd made me do.'

'Nobody made you do anything. You didn't have to go along with it.'

'*You're* lecturing *me* on standing up to my mother?' Phil's eyebrows rose.

'Okay, maybe not,' Tess admitted. 'But there was nothing to stop you getting in touch later. We wouldn't have been too hard to track down.'

'I know. I was tempted a few times.'

'So what stopped you?'

'I didn't know how you'd feel about it. For all I knew you might have got married, had more kids. You might not have even told Dan about me.'

'I'd never lie to my son.'

'I know that now. But the longer I left it, the harder it was to get back in touch. In the end, I suppose I just took the coward's way out.'

'That sounds like you.'

Phil winced. 'I guess I deserved that.' He put the plate down and leaned back against the worktop. 'You didn't ever get married then?'

'No, I didn't. And you can stop looking at me like that, it wasn't because I've been pining for you all these years!'

'So why didn't you?'

'It just didn't happen.' She didn't want to point out that a single mother with a disabled son wasn't every man's idea of an ideal partner. 'What about you?'

'I was. We divorced three years ago.'

'Any children?'

'No. We split up because Angela couldn't have any.' His mouth twisted. 'Ironic, isn't it?'

Before Tess could answer, Margaret came barging into the kitchen with another armful of dirty dishes. By the way her narrowed gaze swept over them like a searchlight, she obviously expected them to be at it on the ceramic hob.

'Any chance of that lemon meringue pie?' she snapped.

The evening broke up fairly soon after that. Margaret refused Phil's offer of a lift home on the way back to his hotel.

'I promise I won't try any funny business,' he said solemnly.

'Where are you staying?' Tess asked, trying to stop herself smiling at her mother's outraged face.

'Middlethorpe Hall.'

'That's where all the rock stars and royalty stay, isn't it? Very posh. The software business must pay well.'

'It is pretty grand. Why don't you and Dan come over for dinner tomorrow night?'

'Well, I'm not sure—'

'That'd be great,' Dan leapt in while she was still thinking up a good excuse. 'You're always saying you never go out, Mum.'

Thanks for pointing that out, Tess thought. Fortunately Phil didn't seem to notice.

'I'll book us a table. About eight? And I'll drop that software round, okay?'

'He's very full of himself, I must say,' Margaret said as she prepared to go home.

'Why shouldn't he be? He's very successful.'

Margaret fiddled with the knot of her headscarf. 'Dan seemed very taken with him.'

'Yes, he did, didn't he?'

'That's not a good thing, you know. It will only lead to more hurt when he dumps him again.'

'What makes you think Phil's going to dump him?'

'He hasn't been interested for the past seventeen years, has he? No, you mark my words. As soon as he gets bored, he'll be off again and that's the last you'll see of him.'

I hope so, Tess thought. She'd enjoyed the evening, but she wasn't sure she could stand the idea of Phil popping round every five minutes. It would be a lot easier when he was safely back in London and Dan could arrange to visit a couple of times a year. That would suit her fine.

Dan was still on a high after her mother left. 'He was all right, wasn't he?'

'He seemed – okay.' Far better than she'd been expecting, actually.

'Didn't it feel weird, having him around? Almost – I dunno – like we were a proper family.'

'I wouldn't go that far.' Tess remembered what her mother had said and frowned. 'You do know this is just a visit, don't you, Dan?'

'Course I do. I'm not a kid.' He looked up at her slyly. 'Be nice if he did hang around though, wouldn't it?'

Chapter 15

The school hall stretched before them, empty and silent. Tess sat with her A4 pad on her lap, eyes fixed on the double doors at the far end, willing them to open. The only sounds were the tick of the clock measuring the painfully long, drawn-out seconds, punctuated by the rhythmic click of Mrs Frobisher's ballpoint beside her. Tess gritted her teeth. If she clicked that bloody thing once more, she'd strangle her.

On her other side, Stephen Kwarme shifted in his hard chair, his legs stretched out in front of him, and stared at his Patrick Cox loafers. He felt as uncomfortable as she did.

'Oh dear. It doesn't look as if anyone's coming, does it?' Cynthia could scarcely keep the satisfaction out of her voice.

'There's still time.'

'We've been here ten minutes and they haven't exactly beaten a path to the door, have they?'

'Perhaps they're still finishing lunch?'

'Or perhaps they aren't interested. I did try to warn you this wasn't a good idea.'

Tess looked down at the pad on her lap. At the top of the page she'd optimistically written 'Audition Notes'. Underneath she'd doodled a house.

Maybe she'd got the date wrong on the posters? Or perhaps she hadn't made them eye-catching enough?

Or perhaps she should just admit Cynthia was right and the whole thing was a disastrous mistake.

She slumped back in her seat and stared at the clock. It

would have been humiliating enough without Cynthia there to witness her utter defeat.

And of course, Cynthia had insisted on being there. Despite Tess' protests, she'd somehow convinced Mr Gant that she should be 'involved' in the production.

And she'd begun by laying down the law on exactly what the production should be.

'Maybe it's the thought of *Hamlet* that's put them off?' Tess ventured. 'Perhaps if we'd chosen something more suitable—'

'Nonsense, the Bard is always suitable. Besides, we've got all those doublets left over from the Jubilee pageant, we can't let them go to waste,' Cynthia said briskly. 'Not that it really matters anyway, since it's obvious no one is going to turn up.'

'Yes, but—'

'Excuse me a moment. I've just remembered something.' Stephen slid out of his seat beside Tess and hurried out of the hall.

'Like a rat deserting a sinking ship.' Cynthia voiced Tess' thoughts. Not that she blamed him. She felt like making a bolt for it too.

'He'll be back.'

'He'll be the only one.'

Five more excruciating minutes ticked by. Tess was just about to admit defeat when the double doors opened and Emily Tyler walked in.

She looked nervously around the empty hall. 'Am I too late for the auditions?'

'No!' Tess had to jam her backside into her seat to stop herself leaping up and hugging her. 'No, not at all, Emily. Come in.'

'Is it just me?'

'We're expecting a few more late arrivals,' Tess said firmly before Cynthia could interrupt. 'Why don't you read something for us while we're waiting?'

Emily was very nervous, but her voice was surprisingly strong and clear. Tess was thrilled. She didn't think she could have coped if she'd been dreadful. She glanced at Cynthia to see if she was similarly impressed. She wasn't. She hardly seemed to be listening. Her eyes were fixed on the clock in studied indifference, her thumb clicking her ballpoint, interrupting Emily's flow until finally the poor girl faltered to a stop.

'Thank you, Emily, that was very—'

'We'll let you know,' Cynthia cut her off rudely.

As she hurried out, Tess swung round in her seat. 'What did you do that for?'

'What? I only said we'd let her know. Isn't that what they usually say?'

'It wasn't just that. You were trying to put her off.'

'I most certainly wasn't!' Cynthia looked affronted. 'I can't help it if my attention wandered, can I? Her performance was hardly mesmerising.'

'I thought she was very good.'

'With respect, Tess, you don't have much to judge her against, do you? Anyway, since she's the only one who auditioned, it's rather irrelevant, don't you think? I mean, you can hardly have a school play with only one actor, can you?'

Suddenly it dawned on her, this was what Cynthia Frobisher had wanted and hoped for all along. Why else would she choose such a difficult play? She wanted to put everyone off so she could run back to Eric Gant and tell him how spectacularly Tess had failed. Just as she'd predicted she would.

She stood up, pushing her chair back. Cynthia looked up at her in surprise. 'Where are you going?'

'I won't be a minute.'

'Don't be too long, will you? I'd hate to get caught up in an unexpected rush.'

Tess ignored her. She pushed through the double doors

and looked up and down the corridor. Apart from a couple of Year 8s staggering up the corridor under the weight of a giant papier mâché camel, it was empty.

She caught up with Emily on her way back to the form room. The poor girl looked terrified when Tess came sliding round the corner behind her, red-faced and puffing like a steam train.

'Did you want me?'

'Yes – Emily – I – did.' Tess steadied herself against the wall and fought to get her breath back. 'Are the others – still in the form room?'

'I think so. Why?'

'Will – you give them a message – from me?' She put her hand to her chest where her heart was about to explode through it. 'Tell them I want them all at the auditions – now.'

Emily's mouth twisted. 'Yeah, right!'

'I'm serious. Tell them anyone who gets a part in the play will be excused English homework from now until Christmas.'

'Really? Cool.'

'Yes, it is, isn't it? Now hurry up and tell them.'

Emily headed for her form room, then stopped and turned round. 'But our next lesson's in ten minutes. We won't have time.'

Damn. Tess glanced at her watch. 'What is your next lesson?'

'PE.'

'Okay, leave it to me. I'll talk to Miss Wesley. She'll understand.' At least she hoped she would. 'Now get a move on!'

Cynthia was waiting impatiently when she got back to the hall. 'Where have you been?'

'Sorry, Cynthia, I had something important I had to do.'

'Haven't we all?' Cynthia stood up and began gathering up her things. 'I don't have time to hang around here waiting for something to happen. Besides, the lunch hour is almost over.'

'But there might be a last-minute rush.'

Cynthia raised a supercilious eyebrow. 'Tess, we've been sitting here for the last half hour. Somehow I don't think we're going to be trampled underfoot by a horde of would-be—'

She stopped, her head cocked towards the door. Tess heard it too. A sound like the low rumble of distant thunder. And it was heading their way.

'What the—?' Cynthia had barely reached the doors when they burst open and twenty Year 10s fought their way in, clamouring over each other to get to the front.

Tess smiled at Cynthia, plastered against the wall behind the door, hair askew.

'What were you saying about being trampled underfoot, Cynthia?'

Stephen crept back into the hall just as the auditions were ending. 'Did I miss something?'

'Only my utter vindication.' Tess grinned. 'You should have seen Cynthia's face when they all came rushing in.'

'They must have had a last-minute change of heart.'

'Or a last-minute bribe.' Tess told him about her plan. Stephen looked horrified.

'You didn't? Tell me you didn't?'

'Why not? Okay, I know it's not exactly orthodox, but half the time they don't do their homework anyway. At least this way they'll be absorbing some culture – why are you looking at me like that? Don't you think it's a good idea?'

'Brilliant,' Stephen agreed. 'Which is why I'd already thought of it. Where do you think I've been all this time?'

Now it was Tess' turn to look horrified. 'Oh God. You too?'

He nodded grimly. 'A fiver each for anyone who got a part.'

Tess took off her glasses and rubbed her eyes. 'Crafty little buggers. Oh well, at least it means we've got a cast. Now all we've got to do is wait and see how Cynthia tries to screw things up next.'

Jack stood in the middle of Saturday afternoon Tammy Girl Hell, waiting for Sophie to make her mind up between a pink spangled crop top and a blue one. He was jostled on all sides by determined ten-year-olds dressed like rock chicks, his brain scrambled by loud dance music. When he closed his eyes all he could see was glitter.

A young girl about Emily's age elbowed past him on her way to the changing room. As she passed, she dropped something from the pile of clothes in her arms. Jack bent down to pick it up.

'Excuse me,' he called after her. 'You dropped this.'

Everyone seemed to stop and look round at him as he stood there, dangling the maribou-trimmed thong from his finger. The girl went puce, grabbed the offending item and fled to the changing room. Everyone else stared at him as if he was a dirty old man. Including his daughter.

'Dad!' Sophie sounded more like her big sister than he'd ever thought possible. She rolled her eyes and headed for the changing room with a worryingly large armful of clothes.

Left alone, he felt even more like a pervert. A fairly conspicuous one, since he towered over all the other customers and most of the assistants. He didn't know where to put his eyes. If he looked one way, he was staring at a bra display. The other, he was gazing at a young assistant's bottom as she restocked the rails.

He shifted his gaze to the middle distance and found himself looking at the kind, bespectacled face of Tess Doyle.

She looked as harrassed as he felt, holding up two T-shirts. Relieved, he made his way through the throng to greet her.

'At last, a grown-up!'

Her smile lit up her face. 'Jack! What are you doing here?'

'Waiting for Sophie to finish trying on the contents of the shop.' He nodded towards the curtained cubicles. 'We've been here for the past hour and frankly I'm losing the will to live. I feel like handing over my credit card and telling her to buy the lot just so we can get out of this hell-hole.' He grinned at her. 'What's your excuse?'

'I'm trying to decide which of these to buy.' She held up the two tops. He squinted at them, his head on one side. One had 'Babe' emblazoned across the chest, the other 'Angel'.

'I would say you're more a Babe than an Angel,' he said at last.

Tess blushed. 'Thanks for the compliment, but it's for my niece, Lauren. She's ten on Wednesday.'

'Then I'd definitely go for the Babe. Although what do I know? I've already been told I have zero fashion sense.'

'You and me both.' She tucked them under her arm. 'The trouble is, she lives down south so I don't get to see her much. I'm not sure whether they'll even fit her.'

'I could get Sophie to try them on for you? God knows, she's tried on everything else.'

'No, it's okay. I'll take a chance.' She looked around. 'No Emily today?'

Jack grimaced. 'She took the money and ran, thank God. I don't think either of us could have coped with shopping together.'

Just then Sophie emerged from the changing room in a feather-trimmed halter top and a pair of jeans with glittery stars all over them. 'What do you think?'

Jack and Tess exchanged looks. 'It's hardly suitable for

winter, is it?' he ventured. 'Wouldn't you be better off with a nice jumper?'

'Dad! You know nothing about fashion!' Sophie declared, and flounced back into the cubicle.

He turned to Tess. 'See what I mean? Is it my imagination or do all seven-year-olds want to look like Hollywood hookers?'

'She's growing up.'

'Don't I know it? Soon I'll be completely redundant. My only function will be to hand over money and embarrass them in front of their friends. Speaking of which, are you still coming to the party on Saturday?'

'Ah yes.' Tess shuffled her feet. 'I meant to talk to you about that—'

'Don't tell me you can't come?'

'I'm still not sure it would be a good idea. I'm Emily's teacher. That makes me even less cool than you are. I'm probably the last person she'd want there.'

'But I want you there!' He was surprised at how much he meant it. 'Go on. Emily wouldn't even know you were there. We could hide in the kitchen and bitch about how young people don't know how to enjoy themselves.'

'Sounds like an offer I can't refuse!' Tess grinned. Jack suddenly realised how desperate he sounded.

'I'm sorry. I didn't mean to put pressure on you. If you're too busy—'

'I'll see what I can do.' She smiled. 'I could probably do with a night out. Anything to take my mind off this wretched school play.'

'Emily told me you'd got the go-ahead. How's it coming on?'

'It isn't. I'm beginning to wish I'd never come up with the idea.'

'Sounds a bit like this party.' A thought struck him. 'Why don't we have a quick coffee? Then we can commiserate with each other.'

'I'd love to, but I'm with my mum.' She glanced back over her shoulder. A frowning woman in a brown raincoat and a headscarf was bearing down on them.

'She could come too?'

Tess smiled. 'I don't think so. My mother has a deep suspicion of coffee shops. Why pay a fortune when you've got a perfectly good kettle at home is her motto.'

'It's a hell of a motto.'

'She's got a million of them.'

Tess' mother was a slightly taller, less smiling version of her daughter. She looked at Jack appraisingly, then said, 'Are you ready yet, Teresa?'

'I've just got to pay for this.' Tess looked regretfully at Jack. 'Some other time, maybe?'

'I'd like that.' Before he could suggest anything, Sophie appeared at his side, her arms still full of clothes. It didn't look as if she'd rejected anything.

'Who was that?' Margaret wanted to know, as soon as they were out of earshot.

'His name's Jack Tyler. His daughter's in my class at school.'

Margaret's eyes sharpened. 'So he's married?'

'Widowed. His wife died last year.' Tess reached the cash desk and handed over her Switch card.

'And so young, too. That's tragic.' Her mother looked back over her shoulder at him. 'Still, I expect someone will snap him up soon.'

'Mum!'

'What? He's a nice-looking man.'

'I know, but he's still grieving for his wife. I shouldn't think he's even thinking about finding someone else. Did you, after Dad died?'

'That's different. It's always much harder for a man, I think. They need a woman to look after them.' She turned back to Tess. 'Speaking of which, is that other one still making a nuisance of himself?'

'If you mean Phil, he came round last night.' She glanced at the assistant, who seemed to be taking far too long to put her card through the machine.

'That's three times this week. Looks like he's got his feet well and truly under your table.'

'He came to see Dan.'

'That's what you think.' Margaret's mouth pursed. 'If you ask me, he's after crawling back.'

'After seventeen years? I doubt it.'

'He seemed interested enough the other night. You two looked very cosy, chatting away in the kitchen.'

'I was just being polite. What was I supposed to do, ignore him completely?' Tess snatched the receipt and pen from the assistant, who'd now given up any pretence and was blatantly earwigging.

'No, but it doesn't pay to be too friendly either. You say he's divorced?' Tess nodded. 'Well, there you are, then. He'll be looking for someone else.'

'I'm sure he's got enough women to choose from without me.'

'How many are the mother of his son?' Margaret looked at her shrewdly. 'I expect that would be very nice for him, wouldn't it, stepping into a ready-made family.'

'You don't know what you're talking about. I told you, he's only interested in getting to know Dan. And I'm not going to stop him coming round if he wants to see his son. This is nothing to do with me.'

'That's what you think,' Margaret said.

Chapter 16

'For the last time, Emily, I'm not going out.'

'What's the matter? Don't you trust me or something?'

'Of course I trust you. It's everyone else I'm not sure about.'

'They're my friends, not a bunch of criminals.' Emily folded her arms across her chest. 'God, I knew it. This party's going to be a total disaster.'

Jack looked helplessly at Ros, who shrugged. 'Don't look at me. I'm only here to make the sandwiches.'

'You wait until your three are all teenagers.'

'Don't. I don't even want to think about it. I'm hoping they won't grow out of thinking Charlie Chalk's Fun Factory is the last word in party chic.'

'I might as well have my party there, the way *he's* going on.' Emily shot her father an evil look. 'Anyone would think we were going to have some mad sexy orgy the minute his back's turned.'

'What's an orgy?' Sophie asked.

Jack sighed and helped himself to one of the sausage rolls Ros had just taken out of the oven. Emily was already sulking because he'd refused to allow her to stock up on Bacardi Breezers at Sainsbury's.

'I know what teenage boys are like. I was one myself once.'

'Yeah, about a million years ago! They're not like that now.'

'I'm sorry? You mean they're not rampaging, hormonally crazed sex fiends?'

'Were you a rampaging, hormonally crazed sex fiend, Daddy?' Sophie asked.

'No,' Ros answered for him. 'Gran wouldn't allow it. He wore a tank top and ran the school stamp-collecting society.'

'That's a lie!' Jack protested. 'I had a haircut like that bloke from the Human League.'

'Only because you tried to do your own fringe and cut one side much shorter than the other.'

'I had my moments. And I never owned a tank top,' Jack insisted, but they were all laughing too much to hear him. At least it stopped Emily being furious with him, which was something.

'Anyway,' Ros said, 'your father can't go out. He's expecting someone, aren't you? Your friend Charlie, remember?'

'Oh God, I'd forgotten I'd even invited her.'

Emily stopped laughing. 'Who's Charlie?'

'Just someone from work,' Jack said dismissively. 'She probably won't even turn up.'

'Oh, she'll turn up. She seemed dead keen,' Ros smirked. It was too much to hope Emily hadn't noticed.

'Dead keen? Why is she dead keen?'

'Your Auntie Ros is just joking – again.' Jack glared at her. 'Haven't you got some vol-au-vents to check on, or something?'

Emily watched Auntie Ros taking another tray of sausage rolls out of the oven. There was no point asking her what was going on. She'd never tell.

And there was something going on, she was convinced of it. Why else would her dad look so shifty? He wasn't telling her everything.

She used to love secrets. A year ago they only meant good stuff – surprise outings, presents hidden on top of the wardrobe, that kind of thing. But a lot had changed since then. Her mum had died and now secrets were different, scarier. They meant whispered conversations that stopped when she walked into the room, tears behind closed doors, sudden house moves just when she thought she'd found her feet again.

These days, secrets meant change. And Emily had had enough of that to last a lifetime.

'You don't seriously expect me to go to this party, do you?' Dan asked.

'Why not? You'll have fun.'

'Fun? In a room full of giggling fourteen-year-old girlies?'

'Some boys your age would enjoy it.'

'Mother, some boys my age enjoy trainspotting, but that doesn't mean it's not pointless and laughable. Anyway, Phil said he might come round later.'

'Oh. Right.' That explains it, Tess thought. She might have known Dan would rather spend the evening with his father than with her. His wonderful, wealthy father, who knew all about computers and arrived laden down with state-of-the-art software and fabulous peripherals that made her carefully saved-for computer look like so much old hat. When the pair of them were together, they were like excited kids, talking in a language Tess couldn't understand, full of bits and bytes and binary codes. She was the only one in the house who couldn't converse in fluent Nerd.

Dan must have noticed her disappointment because he said, 'It's his last night. He's going back down south tomorrow.'

'I know.' Tess ruffled her son's hair. It was mean of her to begrudge Dan time with his father. But after seventeen years of having him to herself, she found it difficult to share him. 'You're not too upset about it, are you?'

'No way. He says he's coming back up to visit the first chance he gets.'

Don't hold your breath. Much as she hoped she was wrong, Tess couldn't help feeling her mother had a point. Once Phil was back at home and busy with work, it was likely Dan would slip into the background of his life, until he was reduced to a card at Christmas and a birthday gift when he remembered.

'I don't know why I'm going to this party myself,' she admitted, turning back to check her reflection in the mirror. 'Everyone will be half my age. Some of them will be in my class at school. How embarrassing is that?'

'Don't go, then. Stay here with me and Phil.'

That sounded even worse. Another evening of listening to them discussing gigabytes and megadrives and whether the X-Box would ever be as good as the Playstation, and she would go out of her mind with boredom.

'I can't. I promised I'd be there.' Although Jack Tyler had probably forgotten he'd even invited her.

It might have helped if she didn't feel so frumpy. Her black party dress was ages old, but since she only got to wear it once in a blue moon, it seemed extravagant to splash out on a new one. It still looked okay, but not exactly head-turning.

But whose head did she really want to turn anyway? Everyone was going to be under eighteen, apart from Jack. And she didn't think any woman was going to turn his head.

The party was in full swing by the time she got there. She could hear the thumping house beat halfway down the street. She wondered what the neighbours would make of it behind their discreetly drawn curtains.

There was a couple wrapped around each other in the front doorway. As Tess stepped past them to ring the bell, she caught a glimpse of the boy's profile in the porch light. It was Mark Nicholls, the troublemaker of 10A. Tess didn't recognise the blonde clamped to the rest of his face.

'Mark?'

'Bloody hell! Miss!'

Tess averted her gaze with a shudder. She didn't know who was most embarrassed – her, Mark or the blonde who was busy adjusting her clothing.

Sophie opened the door. Tess recognised her from Tammy Girl. She was wearing one of her purchases, a white sparkly shift dress with matching high-heeled mules.

'Daddy's hiding,' she announced. 'Me and my friends are dancing in my bedroom and Emily's friends are kissing everywhere else.'

She tripped off upstairs, leaving Tess alone. She followed the eardrum-crunching noise into the sitting room. Thirty pairs of hostile teenage eyes turned to look at her. What the hell are you doing here? they all said. Tess was beginning to wonder that herself. She had never felt so old or unwanted.

Thankfully, at that moment a dark-haired woman in a red dress appeared from the kitchen. 'You must be Tess? I'm Ros, Jack's sister. I'm afraid I don't know where my brother's got to,' she craned her neck to look around, 'but we're having civilised drinks in the kitchen, if you're interested?'

'Thanks. I brought this.' Tess handed over the bottle of Frascati she'd picked up from Oddbins on the way over.

'Great, I'll stick it in the fridge. Why don't you dump your coat upstairs with the others?'

All Tess really wanted to do was dive straight out of the door and go home. But the thought of meeting Mark Nicholls on the front porch again made her head upstairs.

The door to one of the bedrooms was open and she could see the coats piled on the bed. But as she reached the top of the stairs, a man's voice rang out from across the landing.

'Don't even think about sneaking into that room for a snog. I'm watching you.'

Tess swung round as Jack appeared in his bedroom doorway, a bottle in his hand. His frown disappeared when he saw her. 'Tess! Sorry, I thought you were one of those kids. You wouldn't believe how many I've turfed out from under those coats tonight.'

'So you're acting as bouncer, are you?'

'I've got no choice. Emily's banned me from the rest of the house. I don't suppose you noticed if they were wrecking the place, did you?'

'It all looked quite civilised to me.' Better not tell him about Mark Nicholls.

'That's only because I've confiscated all their booze.' He squinted at the label of the bottle he was holding. 'Have you ever had a Moscow Mule?'

'Can't say I have.'

'Don't bother, it's disgusting.' He swallowed the rest down in one gulp.

'Good to see you're putting them out of harm's way.'

'Someone's got to do it. I'm starting on the Bacardi Breezers next. Care to join me?'

Jack's bedroom was understated and masculine, in pale wood, dark blue and cream. A single photo of Emily and Sophie adorned his bedside table.

He reached down beside the bed and rummaged through the collection of bottles he'd stashed there. 'Lemon and Lime or Passion Fruit?'

'You choose. They both sound awful.'

'Passion Fruit it is, then.' He handed her a bottle and clinked it with his own. 'Cheers.'

Several bottles later, they'd come to the conclusion that a) they all tasted the same and b) they all tasted like bubble bath.

'And not even nice bubble bath,' Tess said. 'That cheap nasty stuff that comes in ten-gallon bottles and brings you out in a rash.'

Neither of them were in any hurry to join the party. They reclined on Jack's bed, chatting about life, work, children. The Bacardi Breezers must have been stronger than she thought, because by the end of the third bottle it seemed the most natural thing in the world to be lying on a king-sized bed next to a virtual stranger, confessing her innermost secrets.

'So how did you ever get to be a teacher?' Jack cracked the top from another bottle and handed it to her.

'It seemed like a good idea. Nice steady job, long holidays, hours that fitted in with Dan's school. Couldn't be better.' She took a swig from the bottle and grimaced. 'Ugh! What's this one?'

'Rhubarb and Red Cabbage, I think.' He rolled over and propped himself up on his elbow to face her. 'That doesn't sound like a very good way to choose a career.'

'It is when you've got a baby to think about.'

'So what did you want to do before he came along?'

Tess stared up at the ceiling. She could feel herself blushing. 'I don't want to tell you, it's too stupid.'

'Go on. It can't be any more stupid than what I wanted to do.'

She turned her head to look at him. 'What was that?'

'I wanted to fly Thunderbird Two. See? I told you it was stupid.'

'Why not Thunderbird One?'

He shook his head. 'Too flashy. If you watch the show carefully, you'll see it's Thunderbird Two that does the real work.' He looked so serious Tess could feel herself about to laugh. 'I was only seven years old at the time,' he protested. 'It's not like I went to the careers officer about it or anything. Although I did write an application letter to Mr Tracy asking to be considered if Virgil ever got too old for the job.'

'You didn't?' This time Tess couldn't stop herself laughing. She laughed so hard the bed shook.

'Come on, then,' Jack nudged her. 'What was your burning ambition?'

'If you must know, I wanted to be an actress.' She

170

stopped laughing and wiped her eyes. 'I was pretty good when I was younger. I went to classes and everything. I even had a walk-on part in *Emmerdale* when I was ten.'

'Very impressive.'

'Not really. You only saw the back of my head in the end, but it was something. I didn't realise at the time it was going to be the pinnacle of my career.' She smiled. 'I had it all planned. I was going to be a big star and take the world by storm.'

'So what happened?'

She sent him a wry look. 'I'll give you three guesses.'

'You could have still been an actress with a baby.'

'Not very practical though, was it? I couldn't very well leave Dan with my mum for months on end while I went on tour. Always assuming I ever found work in the first place. You have to cut your coat according to your cloth, my mum says. So that's what I did.'

'Very sensible.'

'That's me.' Sensible Tess. Sometimes she felt as if she'd spent her whole life being reasonable.

'Sounds as if you missed out.'

'I suppose I did. There were a lot of things I couldn't do because of Dan. I couldn't go clubbing every night because it wasn't fair on Mum. I couldn't take a year out after school to travel the world. I couldn't even go on a week's package holiday to Ibiza because I had to get a job during the summer break.' She sipped her drink. 'Sometimes I think I only had one moment of madness in my life, and that ended up with me having Dan.'

'Do you regret it?'

'I've never regretted having him. But sometimes I wish things could have been different.' She looked across at Jack. 'Dan's disabled.'

'Ah.' At least he didn't say he was sorry like most people did. That always made Tess feel frustrated. What did they have to be sorry about? It wasn't their fault her son couldn't walk.

He didn't look at her with pity, either. That was something else that got on her nerves.

'What's wrong with him?' he asked.

He listened carefully as Tess explained about Dan's disability. 'It must have been tough for you, bringing him up on your own,' he said, when she'd finished.

'No tougher than bringing up two daughters,' Tess said.

'I'll take your word for that.' He leaned back against the headboard. 'It's the emotional stuff that's really hard, isn't it?'

'You mean constantly worrying you're doing the right thing?'

He nodded. 'It's not so bad when there are two of you to make the decisions, because at least there's someone to back you up. And it's so exhausting having to set boundaries and stick to them all the time. Sometimes I come home from work and I'm so knackered I don't really care if Emily's done her homework or if Sophie's watching TV because I just want five minutes' peace and quiet.'

'I know what you mean. I used to send Dan to bed just because I was the one feeling tired.'

'You too?' he grinned. 'The girls think I'm the meanest man in the world when I do that.'

They sank into wistful silence for a moment, listening to the music shaking the floorboards beneath them. Then Jack said, 'Listen to us. We're meant to be having a good time, remember?' He reached down and produced a large bottle of lurid pink liquid. 'How about an Aftershock?'

'What the hell is that?'

'God knows. But it looks pretty lethal.'

'Do you think we should? It doesn't seem very responsible.'

'I don't know about you, but tonight I really don't feel

like being responsible.' Their eyes met. Tess looked away quickly.

She sat up, wrapped her arms around her knees and gazed around the room, so plain and lacking the personal touch of a woman. There was no stack of magazines on the bedside table, no jewellery or make-up on the dressing table. Just a solitary bottle of Eau Sauvage. Seeing it made her feel sad.

'What are you thinking?'

That you must be a very lonely man. She decided not to tell him what was really on her mind. 'I was just trying to remember the last time I was in a man's bedroom.'

'And when was it?'

'I can't even remember, it was so long ago. Isn't that tragic?'

'Nothing wrong with being choosy.'

'It's more a lack of opportunity than choice, I think.'

He nodded. 'Finding time for a relationship isn't easy when you've got kids.'

'Have you tried?'

'I don't think I'd know how any more.' He looked rueful. 'I expect the dating game's moved on a bit since I last did it.'

'You make yourself sound ancient!'

'Sometimes I feel it, believe me.' He drank his Aftershock without flinching. 'Anyway, it isn't just a lack of time for me. It's a lack of inclination too. I just don't feel ready for all that.'

'Don't you miss having a woman in your life?'

'I miss having *the* woman in my life.' He regarded her seriously. 'Sometimes I wonder if anyone will ever take Miranda's place.'

He sounded so intense, so full of unhappiness, Tess found she couldn't speak for a moment.

It was Jack who broke the silence. 'How about you? Have you had a serious relationship since Dan was born?'

'I've had boyfriends over the years. But they've always seemed to fizzle out before they got serious.'

'Because they couldn't handle you having a disabled son?'

'It's me who couldn't handle it.' She looked over her shoulder at him. 'Dan's always been my priority, ever since he was diagnosed. Everything takes second place to him. A lot of men find that difficult to accept.'

How many relationships had she backed out of as soon as she found them taking up too much of her time and energy? She couldn't make that final commitment, knowing Dan needed her more than any man she'd ever met.

'But he's getting older now, isn't he? Surely he doesn't need you as much?'

'Maybe. But that doesn't stop me worrying. If anything, I worry more because I know the day's coming when I can't look out for him the way I used to. He'll be on his own.' She suppressed a shudder at the thought.

'I think every parent feels like that. Emily's only fourteen and I'm already getting nervous about her getting hurt out there in the big bad world.'

'Believe me, the world seems a lot bigger and badder when your child's in a wheelchair. I've taught Dan to be independent and stand up for himself, but people can be so thoughtless. Do you know, we were out the other day and some horrible old man stared at us. Then he said, "Has your son always been retarded?"'

'What did you do?'

'I said, "No. Have you always been ignorant?"'

Jack laughed. 'I bet you're a wildcat when you're roused.'

'I've had to be.' She smiled. 'Trouble is, that doesn't make me every man's idea of the perfect partner.'

'Surely that depends on the man?'

He was so close she could see the dark rings around his

pewter eyes, as if someone had outlined them with a black felt-tip pen.

'Jack?' There was a flash of scarlet on the landing and a second later Ros appeared in the doorway. 'There you are! I – oh!' She stopped short when she saw Tess. 'I'm sorry.'

'I only came up here to dump my coat.' Tess slid off the bed and looked for her shoes. Ros turned to Jack.

'I just thought you'd want to know – Charlie's arrived.'

'Oh. Right. Thanks.' Jack didn't move.

'You could come down and say hello. She's come all this way especially for you.'

As Jack got off the bed and followed his sister to the door, Tess heard Ros hiss, 'Thanks for leaving me to look after everything, by the way.'

'Sorry. We just got chatting.'

'So I see. Just as well I didn't bring Charlie up here, wasn't it? You really would have blown your chances if she'd seen you sprawled out on your bed with another woman!'

Chapter 17

By the time she'd unearthed her shoes, he'd gone downstairs. Tess found him in the kitchen with a big fair-haired man and a willowy Nicole Kidman lookalike in a sexy cream dress.

No one noticed her as she slipped over to the makeshift bar by the sink and helped herself to a glass of mineral water.

'You don't have to stick to water, you know.' The fair-haired man appeared at her side. He was as tall as Jack, but not nearly so athletic-looking. His striped shirt didn't disguise his burgeoning paunch. 'We've got some hard stuff in the fridge. I just have to keep my eye on it so those little buggers don't get their hands on it.' He jerked his head towards the sound of the party in the next room. 'I'm Greg, by the way. Jack's brother-in-law.'

'Tess Doyle.'

He watched her add a handful of ice cubes to her glass. 'Are you sure you wouldn't prefer a glass of wine?'

'Water's fine.' Her head was already swimming, thanks to all the dodgy alcopops she and Jack had had. If she had any more, she might just keel over in the corner.

Not that anyone would notice. Tess glanced over to where Ros and Jack were engrossed with the glamorous redhead.

'Have you met Charlie?' Greg followed her gaze. 'She's a colleague of Jack's. Well, more than just a colleague, if you know what I mean?'

'I didn't know he was seeing anyone.'

'He isn't. Not yet, anyway. But he will be if my wife has anything to do with it. She's determined to throw them together,' he confided, his blue eyes twinkling.

I'm not surprised, Tess thought. They made a striking couple, both tall and good-looking, as if they'd stepped out of a Calvin Klein ad. Charlie's burnished beauty set off Jack's dark good looks perfectly. In fact, Charlie could have been a model. There wasn't a spare ounce of flesh on her elongated frame, and her legs seemed to go on for ever. Tess found herself unkindly hoping that perhaps she was a bit stupid or boring to make up for it.

'Let me introduce you,' Greg said.

'Oh no, I couldn't—' But he was already pushing her towards them, his guiding arm around her waist.

'Charlie, I'd like you to meet Tess. Tess, this is Charlie Ferguson, Crawshaw and Finch's fastest-rising star – apart from my brother-in-law, of course.'

'Greg! You're embarrassing me.' Close up she was even more gorgeous. Her creamy skin was flawless. She even had cheekbones – real ones, not put on with a splodge of blusher like Tess's. 'Ignore him,' she said. 'Except for the bit about Jack – that's true.' She turned to smile at him. Tess caught the adoring look in her eye and realised Ros wasn't the only one who was determined they should be together.

'Looks like my brother might have a rival soon.' Ros threaded her arm proudly through her husband's. 'Guess who we went out to dinner with last night? Peter Jameson!'

'Really?' Jack looked impressed, although Tess had no idea who they were talking about. 'How did that happen?'

'It's nothing, really.' Greg shrugged. 'He just invited us. Nothing special.'

'Excuse me? You call a posh restaurant nothing special?' Ros widened her eyes. 'I don't know what kind of social life you've been leading behind my back, but let me tell you it beats the hell out of fish fingers and beans with the kids!' She turned back to the others. 'He said he wanted to thank Greg for all the hard work he's been putting in on the Westpoint project. Seems he's finally noticed at last.'

'About time too.'

The four of them chatted about Peter Jameson and swapped office gossip while Tess nursed her mineral water and smiled blankly. She didn't want anyone to think she wasn't interested, but it was hard to follow a conversation peopled with characters she didn't know. And since everyone else seemed to know what they were talking about, she didn't like to halt the flow by asking questions. On top of which, her feet were beginning to hurt in her unfamiliar high heels. It had been such bliss to take them off on Jack's bed, she'd forgotten how uncomfortable they were.

She stifled a discreet yawn, but Charlie spotted it. 'Sorry, Tess. All this shop talk must be really boring for you.' Her smile lit up her tawny tiger eyes. 'I'm afraid that's what happens when we all get together.'

'I don't mind. It's – fascinating.'

'I wouldn't go that far!' She turned to face her. 'Tell us about yourself. What do you do for a living?'

'I'm a teacher.'

'Really? I bet you have some stories to tell.'

Why was it whenever people said that, her mind always went blank? Not that it would have mattered. They all seemed far too sophisticated to find life in the classroom enthralling.

'So where do you work?' Charlie asked.

'Haxsall Comp. I'm Head of English.'

'Tess is Emily's teacher,' Jack put in.

Charlie nodded in that thoughtful way people do when they're not quite sure what to say next. 'I have to say I absolutely hated English at school. It was my worst subject. Give me a quadrilateral equation any day!'

'I know what you mean,' Jack agreed. 'I could never tell my Aristophanes from my elbow either.'

They laughed. Tess fixed a smile. If she didn't sit down and get these wretched shoes off in one minute, her feet would be a bloody pulp.

She looked down at Charlie's shoes. Sandals with a fragile diamanté strap and tall, thin lethal heels like blades. So not only was she beautiful, intelligent and nice, she could also carry off killer shoes. Tess was beginning to develop an irrational dislike for her.

'Teachers get long holidays, though,' Greg said. 'Wouldn't mind a few of those myself.'

'You should have a word with your new friend Peter,' Jack teased. 'I'm sure he'd fly you out to his villa in the Algarve.'

Ros' eyes lit up. 'He's got a villa? I didn't know that.'

And then they were off again, talking about work. Tess shifted from one foot to the other and tried to keep the grimace off her face.

It was no good. She had to go. 'Would you excuse me a moment?' she said. No one noticed.

Outside in the garden, the cold night air penetrated the thin fabric of her dress. Tess sat down on the back step and eased her shoes off one foot, then the other. The light spilling from the kitchen window illuminated her mangled toes. She massaged them gingerly, wincing with pain.

What was she doing here when she could be at home in her nice comfy slippers? She'd turned up and done her bit. She'd even enjoyed it, more than she'd expected to anyway. But now it was time to leave.

She stood up to go back in. Her hand was on the door handle when she realised Jack and Charlie were alone in the kitchen. Ros and Greg must have sneaked off and left them to it.

She hesitated, watching them. Charlie suited Jack, she decided. But did he really need someone? His sister seemed to think he did, and she knew him better than anyone. But from talking to him, Tess could see it would take a very special woman to take his wife's place.

Maybe Charlie was that woman. She seemed to have all the right qualities. She was beautiful, intelligent, charming. And they obviously had masses in common.

Perhaps Ros was right. Not everyone was like her, destined to be alone.

At least that's what it felt like sometimes. For the first few years after Dan was born she hadn't had time to think about it. While most of her friends were getting into all kinds of romantic entanglements, dating men and dumping them and sharing weepy sessions over bottles of wine, Tess was too busy looking after her baby and keeping up with her college work. Then, when he'd been diagnosed with SMA, all her energies went into looking after him, making sure he got the right help and support and finding out all she could about the illness.

It was only in her mid-twenties that she started to think perhaps life and love had passed her by. All her friends were settling down, moving in with the men of their dreams, taking out mortgages and going on Sunday-afternoon trips to Ikea. Meanwhile Tess was moving in to her bungalow with Dan and worrying about getting the bathroom adapted. By the time he was older and she was ready for girly nights out at Café Rouge, her friends were holding couply dinner parties and heading off to antenatal classes together. Her whole adult life had been spent out of step with the rest of the world.

Not that she was short of offers from men. Being a single mother with a disabled son might have put some off, but there were others who were keen to stick around and even try to be a father to Dan. But sooner or later the relationship always ended.

As she'd told Jack, it was mostly her fault, not theirs. They were willing to commit, but she wasn't. Everything she had went into Dan. Not just looking after him – he was fairly independent these days – but worrying about him. She worried every time he caught a cold, in case it turned into a respiratory infection, or that he wasn't eating properly, or doing his physiotherapy. She worried that his spine would curve and he'd need surgery, that one day he would have to admit defeat and use a wheelchair permanently.

Mostly she worried about how he would cope when he was older. When he was living alone at college, when he had his first job. How would he fare when she wasn't there by his side to fight his battles for him, the way she always had been?

She was so preoccupied, she didn't have the space in her life to deal with anyone else's emotional demands. Worse than that, she'd forgotten how.

And then there was the fear. Dan's diagnosis had been a shock, and she knew that as a carrier of the gene there was a chance she might have another child with SMA. Next time it could be worse. The baby could be severely affected, or it could even die.

Or it could be perfect. Either way, she didn't think she could handle it. Irrational as it seemed, she knew having a 'normal' child would make her feel too guilty about what Dan had missed out on.

Which meant any man who came into her life would have to deal with her not wanting any more children. It was a lot to ask. Tess sometimes wondered if that was really why she backed off when things got too serious.

She looked back through the kitchen window. Jack was refilling Charlie's glass, laughing at something she'd said. Tess felt a stab of jealousy. Not for Jack, but for what he had. She felt like a kid outside a sweetshop, nose pressed against the glass, wanting all the goodies but knowing she could never have them.

★

'Where's Tess?' Jack looked around the kitchen. He hadn't noticed the room had emptied.

'I think she went home.'

'She didn't say goodbye.' He looked so disappointed Charlie felt wary.

'Is she a good friend of yours?'

'I told you, she's Emily's teacher.'

'Seems a bit odd, inviting her to this party. I would have died if my parents had invited any of my teachers to a party with my mates!'

'I needed moral support.' He helped himself to a sausage roll from what was left of the buffet. Charlie watched him carefully. He seemed very put out that Tess had gone home without telling him. A bit too put out, in fact.

'Is there something I should know about you two?' she asked lightly.

'In what way?'

'Are you an item or something?'

'You're joking? I hardly know her! Anyway, I'm not ready to be an item with anyone.'

Was that a warning? she wondered. If so, she wasn't about to be put off. She'd always enjoyed a challenge.

'Look, Jack—' They were interrupted by a little girl rushing in. She clutched a glass of Ribena, most of which had already gone down the front of her spangly white dress.

'Daddy, they're snogging in the spare room again!'

'Are they indeed?' Jack put down his glass. 'I'd better go and sort this out.'

Charlie put her glass down. 'I'll come with you—'

'No, you stay and talk to Sophie. I won't be a minute. Sophie, entertain Charlie.'

Great. Just great. She shot a sidelong glance at the small girl. In the uneasy silence, she could feel Sophie eyeing her up and down appraisingly while she stuffed a mushroom vol-au-vent in her mouth.

Finally she said, 'Why do they call you Charlie? It's a boy's name.'

'It's short for Charlotte.'

Sophie nodded, taking it in. 'I like your shoes.'

'Thanks.'

'Can I try them on?'

Charlie looked at her fingers, covered in greasy crumbs and sticky mushroom sauce, and winced. 'Why not?'

There was something slightly surreal about watching a seven-year-old girl clattering around in a pair of three-hundred-pound Gina slingbacks, slopping a glass of Ribena around at a dangerous angle. Charlie smiled tightly.

'Lovely,' she said. 'You should get your dad to buy you a pair.'

Sophie considered it. 'I might,' she said seriously. 'Do they do them in pink? That's my favourite colour.'

'I don't think so.'

Her lower lip jutted. 'Oh well, I've already got some pink shoes. My dad got them for me from BHS. They've got sparkly hearts on them.' She looked down at Charlie's sandals. 'Did yours come from BHS?'

'No, I bought them in London.'

'London!' Sophie looked impressed. 'I've got a lipstick from London. Mummy gave it to me. She's dead now, by the way.'

Charlie gulped. 'That's sad.'

'She had something wrong with her head.'

Seeing the troubled look in her eyes, Charlie quickly distracted her. 'What colour is your lipstick?'

'Pink, of course.' Sophie looked outraged, as if there was no other shade in the world. 'Do you want to see it?'

'I'd love to.'

Jack came back as Sophie raced past him and thudded upstairs. 'What did you say to her?'

'Girl talk. We've been discussing make-up and shoes.'

She leaned against the worktop to pull her sandals back on again.

'How did I guess?' he groaned. 'That's all she ever talks about. I'm afraid Emily and I aren't much good at that kind of conversation.'

'You mean Emily's not into shoes?'

'Only if they've got a Nike label on them. My eldest is not what you'd call a girly girl.' She could feel him watching her, admiring her legs. 'Speak of the devil.' He swung round as a tall, sulky-looking girl slouched in. 'This is Emily. Em, this is Charlie Ferguson.'

'Pleased to meet you.'

'Hi.' Jack was right, no one could have described her as a girly girl in those baggy black jeans and T-shirt. She wasn't exactly pretty, but there was a haunting beauty in those big dark eyes.

Eyes that regarded her with extreme suspicion, if not downright hostility.

Ignoring the look, she said, 'Are you enjoying your party?'

Emily shrugged one shoulder. 'S'okay.'

'It must be nice to see all your old friends again?'

Another shrug.

'She does string two words together sometimes.' Jack glared at her. Emily scowled back and brushed past them to fish a Coke from the sink full of ice.

'Someone's been sick outside,' she announced casually.

'Oh great. Who was it?'

'I don't know, do I? I wasn't exactly watching them.' She popped the can and turned round to face her father. 'Aren't you going to do something about it?'

'No, Emily, I'm not. As you can see, I'm talking to Charlie at the moment.'

Emily shot another hostile glance at her. 'So you're just going to leave it?'

'For the moment, yes. Unless you'd like to clean it up? I'm sure I can find you a mop and bucket.'

'Ugh, gross!' Emily looked as if she was about to tell her father exactly what he could do with his mop when Sophie rushed back in, her eyes brimming.

'It's gone!' she cried. 'Mummy's lipstick's gone. I went to the place where I keep it and it wasn't there.'

'Come on, sweetheart, don't cry.' Jack crouched down and put his arms around her. 'It'll turn up again, I'm sure.'

'But I put it in a safe place! I always keep it there.'

Charlie watched Jack hugging his daughter. Was everything always such a drama in this house? It was like living in a soap opera.

'Tell you what,' she reached for her bag. 'Why don't you borrow mine until yours turns up? I know it's not nearly as good as yours, but it's better than nothing.'

'Oh no, we couldn't—' Jack began, but Sophie had already snatched the Clarins lipstick and was trying it on the back of her hand.

'It's not the same as Mummy's,' she said in a disappointed voice, 'but I'll keep it anyway.'

'What do you say, young lady?'

'Thank you.' Sophie gave her a gap-toothed grin, her eyes still fixed on the lipstick as she twisted it up and down in its case.

'No problem.' Charlie's smile went a little rigid around the edges when she saw how Emily was glowering at her. What was wrong now? Was she jealous? Did she want a lipstick too? She was just about to offer her a rummage through her make-up bag when Emily slouched off again, followed by a jubilant Sophie, still swivelling her lipstick.

'You do realise you'll never see that again?' Jack said, when they'd gone.

'I don't mind.'

'All the same, it was very nice of you.'

'I can be nice when I want to be.'

'I'm sure you can.' She held her breath as he moved towards her, only to let it out again in a frustrated sigh when he took her glass and said, 'Do you want another drink?'

'Please.'

She watched as he reached into the fridge for the wine bottle. He was a very attractive man, but he didn't seem to realise it. Not like the posers she met at the gym, who spent their whole time admiring their muscles in the mirrors. Or the slickly groomed types who knew their way around the Clinique counter better than she did. Jack was naturally fit and athletically built, and he probably spent no more than five minutes in the shower every morning.

God, wouldn't she love to find out?

'Here you go.' She dragged her mind unwillingly back from the image of him stepping out of the shower, his dark hair dripping, and took the glass he held out to her. 'So, what did you think of the kids?'

It was the question she'd been dreading. Charlie racked her brain for the right words. 'They – um – keep you busy, don't they?'

Jack grinned. 'You could say that! There's never a minute's peace in this house.'

Tell me about it. Charlie stared at the brightly coloured painting stuck on the fridge of three stick figures holding hands outside a house. She was used to being able to utter a whole sentence without being interrupted by a whining child or a sullen teenager.

'I don't really know much about children,' she admitted. All she knew was that she'd never wanted any of her own. As an only child, she'd grown up in a household full of adults, without the rough and tumble of brothers and sisters around her. Her parents were in their forties when she was born and not the kind to build their lives around a child. Charlie had soon learned to adapt to them, rather than the other way round. By the age of five, she was sitting down to dinner with them – real food; her mother would never have tolerated chips or chicken nuggets – and talking and listening to the grown-ups around her. She had perfect table manners, never clamoured for attention or spoke with her mouth full, and would never have dreamed of talking to her father the way Sophie and Emily spoke to Jack.

But it wasn't just her upbringing. She wasn't remotely interested in babies. As a child she'd preferred her pony to dolls, and even now she couldn't work up more than a polite interest when one of the girls in the office came back from maternity leave with tons of baby photos.

But she sensed none of that was going to win Jack over, so she added quickly, 'But yours seem very sweet.'

'I don't know if I'd call Emily sweet!'

Neither would I, Charlie thought.

A squawk from upstairs distracted them. 'Sounds like Sophie and her friends are fighting again.' Jack sighed. 'I'd better sort it out.'

'Couldn't you just leave them?' Charlie pleaded.

'If I don't go now, someone will be coming down in a minute with a broken nose. You stay here, I won't be long.'

She was still waiting for Jack and wondering if she should just cut her losses and go home when Ros came into the kitchen for a refill.

'All on your own? Don't tell me he's disappeared again?'

'He's doing his bouncer bit, I think.'

Ros shook her head. 'He's an elusive one, my brother.'

'You're telling me,' Charlie muttered. 'Sometimes I wonder if he's trying to avoid me.'

'Of course not. He likes you. No really, he does,' Ros insisted, as Charlie looked sceptical. 'But you know what men are like. They're useless when it comes to expressing how they feel. Especially Jack.' She leaned in confidingly. 'I think he's out of practice.'

'In what way?'

'You know. Being married all those years, he's forgotten how to ask a woman out, that kind of thing. He's terrified of putting a foot wrong. And, of course, he's got the girls to think about. I'm sure that's why he hasn't made a move. But trust me, he does like you. A lot.'

Charlie was pretty sure Ros must have downed an awful lot of Chardonnay, otherwise she wouldn't be talking quite so frankly. But it was nice to know someone was on her side.

'So what do you suggest I do?' she asked.

'You could wait for him to make a move, but if I know my brother, you'll probably wait a long time. Or you could make the first move yourself. Or you could leave it up to me.'

'You?'

'Why not?' She rested her hand on Charlie's arm. 'You leave it to your Auntie Ros,' she said. 'I'll get you two together if it kills me!'

Chapter 18

It was nearly eleven when Tess limped home. She'd been looking forward to slipping out of her party clothes into her dressing gown and enjoying a blissful mug of cocoa in front of the last bit of *Newsnight*. So she was not amused to find Dan and Phil had taken over the sitting room and plugged the Playstation into the TV to play *Grand Theft Auto*.

'Hi, Mum.' Dan greeted her without taking his eyes off the screen. 'Good party?'

'Brilliant. If you like loud music and snogging teenagers.' Tess frowned at Phil. 'Are you still here? Haven't you got an early start tomorrow?'

'Not particularly.'

'Are you sure? I'd hate you to leave all that packing till the last minute.'

'But I don't have to be back down south until—' He caught her look. 'Sorry, you're right. I should be going.' He put down the games console. His car immediately spun off and crashed nose first into a street lamp.

'Do you have to?' Dan protested. 'Couldn't we have just one more game?'

'No, Dan, it's getting late. I should be making tracks.' Phil glanced at Tess as he said it. 'Besides, I don't want to be in your mum's way.'

'He's not in the way, is he, Mum?'

Tess looked from one to the other. Two extraordinarily similar pairs of green eyes looked back at her, silently appealing. She felt defeated.

189

'Do what you like,' she sighed. 'I'm going to put the kettle on.'

'Mine's a coffee. Milk, no sugar,' Phil called after her, picking up the console again. Tess' forthright reply was drowned out by the whine of car engines hurtling across the screen.

She flicked the switch on the kettle and stood staring out of the window at the night sky and the lights of the city twinkling on the horizon. She always looked forward to coming home to her little bungalow, but suddenly it didn't feel like her own any more. It had been invaded, taken over by a stranger.

And so, come to think of it, had her son. Dan had barely looked at her when she came in. Yet the moment it seemed Phil was leaving, he'd howled with protest.

It isn't fair! She'd never expected any thanks for bringing up Dan single-handed for seventeen years. But she hadn't expected to be cast aside like a battered old teddy when a brand-new toy came along either.

She was still silently fuming about it when Phil crept into the kitchen behind her. 'You know I was only kidding about the coffee, right?'

'All I want . . .' She swung round to face him, arms folded across her chest. 'All I want is to come home to my own space, soak my feet, enjoy my cocoa and watch *Newsnight* in peace. Is that too much to ask?'

'Not at all,' Phil said solemnly. 'I understand Naomi Campbell does exactly the same thing after a night out at the Met Bar.'

Tess felt her mouth twitching treacherously. 'Don't try to joke with me. I'm suffering a severe sense of humour failure,' she warned.

'I can tell.' He tilted his head sympathetically. 'Was the party that bad?'

She replayed the evening on fast forward through her head. 'Not really. I just wasn't in the mood, that's all. And my feet hurt.' She eased her shoes off and threw them into the corner. 'I am never, ever wearing those things again.'

'I'm not surprised. You look like you've walked barefoot through the Himalayas.'

'I feel like it, believe me.'

'Oh well, you know what they say. You have to suffer to be beautiful.'

'Stuff that. I'll stay plain and happy, thank you very much.'

'You could never be plain, Tess.'

The uncomfortable silence was broken by the pop of the kettle coming to the boil. Tess unhooked two mugs from the tree. 'You can have that coffee if you want.'

'No thanks. But there is something I can do for you before I go.'

'Oh yes? What's that?'

'A little trick I picked up from my ex-wife.' He winked at her. 'Come into the bedroom and I'll show you.'

'I beg your pardon?'

'Or we can do it on the sofa, if you prefer?'

Tess sighed heavily. 'Phil, I'm not in the mood for smutty innuendoes.'

'Who's being smutty? I'm only offering you a foot rub.'

'I don't think so.'

'Go on, you'll enjoy it.'

She finished making her cocoa and followed him reluctantly into the sitting room. 'I'm still not sure about this—'

'Stop moaning, woman. You'll enjoy it.'

'Enjoy what?' Dan turned away from the screen to look at them.

'I'm about to demonstrate some shiatsu on your mother.'

'Is that a good idea? She doesn't know any martial arts.'

'Shiatsu, Dan, not ju-jitsu. It's a form of Japanese massage.'

He knelt down in front of her. Tess jumped as he took

her left foot in his hands. 'I think you ought to know I'm extremely ticklish.'

'I remember. I'll be careful.'

'Phil, stop it!' But as he gently massaged her foot, working his way slowly from heel to toes, she was overcome by a rush of unbelievable bliss. 'My God, that's heavenly. Where did you learn to do that?'

'My ex-wife was a masseuse. You'd be amazed what talents I've picked up over the past seventeen years.'

'I'm sure I would.' She closed her eyes and allowed the sheer ecstasy to wash over her.

He went on massaging for a few more minutes, gently caressing each toe. 'I'm sorry if it seems like I've taken over your space a bit recently.'

'Dan's enjoyed having you here.' She opened one eye and looked around. 'Where is Dan?'

'He sneaked out a minute ago. Between you and me I think he found your groans of rapture a bit much.' He slid his thumb up her instep, easing away the tension. 'How about you? Have you enjoyed having me here?'

'If Dan's happy, I'm happy.'

'So you wouldn't mind if I came back sometime?'

'If you like.'

'Actually, I was thinking of the middle of November?'

Both eyes flew open. 'That's only two weeks away.'

'Is that a problem?'

'No. I'm surprised, that's all.'

'I've got some more business up here, a couple of meetings I couldn't manage to sort out this time around. And I'd like to see Dan again as soon as possible.' He stroked her toes thoughtfully. 'He's a great kid.'

Tess smiled. 'I know.'

'You've done a fantastic job bringing him up.' He put her foot down gently and picked up the other. 'I wish now that I could have done more to help.'

Tess didn't answer. She was too sleepy for an argument

and besides, there was nothing to argue about. She was beyond blame and recriminations. 'You're here now,' she said.

'I am, aren't I? It was really good of you to let me stick around. You always did have a big heart, Tess.'

'Like I said, if Dan's happy, so am I.'

He traced firm circles on the soles of her foot with his thumbs. 'So tell me about this party. Did anyone chat you up?'

'I don't think that's any of your business.'

Phil grinned. 'I take it that's a no, then? Otherwise you wouldn't have come home in such a foul mood.'

'Do you mind? I'll have you know I spent a great deal of this evening getting drunk in a man's bedroom.'

'On your own, or was he there too?'

'Funny!' Tess kicked out at him.

'Teresa Doyle, I'm ashamed of you.' Phil did a creditable impression of her mother. 'You of all people should know better than to get drunk in bedrooms at parties. Look what happened last time.'

It was too close to the knuckle to be funny, but Tess still couldn't help smiling ruefully. 'Watch it, you're on very thin ice. Anyway, for your information I wasn't drunk that night. I was—'

'In love?' Phil said.

'Incredibly stupid,' Tess finished firmly.

'You grew up a lot after that.'

'Someone had to, and I didn't see you volunteering.'

'I know.' He looked shame-faced. 'It took me a few more years than it did you. But I got there in the end, don't you think?'

His grey-green eyes met hers, full of appeal. Tess pulled a face. 'I suppose you didn't turn out too badly. In the end.'

Emily lay in bed, smiling up at the ceiling. Even though the house was silent, music still rang in her ears.

'Good party, wasn't it?' she said.

'Okay, I s'pose.' Her friend Katy sat cross-legged in her sleeping bag on the floor, rummaging through her over-night bag. Even in her tiger-print nightshirt she managed to look sophisticated. With all her slap on she looked about eighteen, which was how she'd managed to sneak into clubs so often. 'Shame there was no booze, though.'

'I know. I asked, but my dad wouldn't let me.' Emily sighed. The truth was, she wasn't that bothered. She couldn't see why everyone got so excited about alcohol. It always tasted horrible to her.

'Lucky I've brought my own then, isn't it?' Katy grinned wickedly and pulled a bottle out of her bag.

Emily stared at it in awe. 'What's that?'

'Vodka, dummy.' Katy unscrewed the top and took a swig, then offered it to her. 'Want some?'

'No thanks.'

'Suit yourself.' Katy put the top back on and stuck the bottle back in her bag. 'Not much talent, either. That Mark was fit, though.'

'He's all right.' This sleepover wasn't as much fun as she'd expected. She thought it would be a laugh to have Katy staying the night, so they could giggle and catch up with all the gossip. But all she wanted to do was talk about all the boys she fancied. She'd even tried to light up a cigarette, but Emily had stopped her. Her dad would go ballistic.

'Who was that girl you were talking to? The blonde one.'

'You mean Paris? She's really nice.'

'Looked like a bit of a dork to me,' Katy said dismissively. Emily thought Paris had looked anything but dorky, in a deep-pink dress that for once showed off her spectacular figure.

She was torn between defending her new friend and not upsetting Katy. She wondered if she was jealous. After all, they'd been best mates at school, she might not like the idea of being replaced by someone else.

'She's okay. We don't have a laugh like we used to, though,' she added quickly, but Katy wasn't listening.

'What about that woman your dad was with? The really glam one.' She hugged her knees. 'He was well into her, wasn't he?'

Emily knew exactly who she was talking about. 'She's just someone my dad works with.'

'Yeah, right! That's what he's told you!' Katy smiled knowingly. 'If you ask me, there's something going on there.'

'No, there isn't! He wouldn't do that.'

'Wouldn't tell you about it, you mean. Parents never tell their kids anything. Anyway, what's to stop him? It's not like he's still married or anything.'

Yes he is, Emily wanted to shout. He's married to my mum. And he always will be.

'And your mum's been dead nearly a year now,' Katy went on. 'He's bound to want a new girlfriend by now, if only for the sex.'

Emily squirmed down under the duvet and turned off the light. 'I don't want to talk about it.'

'I'm only saying, it's going to happen. You might as well face it. Emily?' Katy sighed in the darkness. 'You're not crying or anything, are you?'

'No.' Emily pulled the covers further over her head. Katy was wrong. There was nothing going on between her dad and that woman. He would have said something if there was. Wouldn't he?

Although, there was something about the way she'd looked at him that worried Emily. Her dad might not be interested, but Charlie definitely was. And then there was all that stuff Auntie Ros had said before the party . . .

'Anyway, if anything does happen, you'll probably be the last to know,' Katy said. 'I only found out about my mum and Roger when I came home from school and fell over his suitcases.'

'That's different. Your mum and dad are divorced.'

'So? He's not going to stay faithful to your mum for ever just because she's dead, is he?'

'I told you, I don't want to talk about it.'

'Suit yourself.' Katy burrowed down inside her sleeping bag. 'But don't be surprised if that one ends up being your new stepmother!'

Chapter 19

'Not going? What do you mean, you're not going? Dan, he's come all this way to see you!'

Tess stared at her son in exasperation. Why did he have to choose now, twenty minutes before she was due at a Parents' Evening, to do this to her?

'I know, but I've got this really important college assignment that's got to be finished by tomorrow. I haven't got time to go out tonight.'

'And this really important college assignment has just happened, has it? I mean, you couldn't have done it at the weekend when you were lying around watching TV?'

Dan blushed. 'Look, I'm sorry, okay?'

'It's not me you should be apologising to. You do realise your father has travelled three hundred miles to see you? Now it's a wasted journey.'

'He's around for a few days. I can see him any time.'

'And what about tonight? He thinks you're having dinner with him in,' she consulted her watch, 'less than an hour.'

Dan looked sheepishly at her. It was the kind of look he usually gave her when he was about to ask for some horrendously expensive but vital piece of hardware for his computer. 'I thought maybe you could go instead?'

'Me?' Tess' voice rose an octave. 'Dan, this Parents' Evening won't finish until eight. Then I've got a mountain of housework to do—'

'Why can't you leave that till tomorrow?'

'Why can't you leave your college assignment?' Tess

folded her arms. 'Anyway, your father's come all this way to see you. I'm sure he wouldn't want to spend the evening with me!'

'Oh, he doesn't mind,' Dan said quickly. 'And he says he can change the dinner reservation to eight-thirty, if that would help?' His voice trailed off under Tess' withering glare.

'You've already spoken to him?'

Dan hung his head. 'He's picking you up from the school at eight,' he mumbled.

'I see. Nice of you both to consult me first.' Tess sighed. 'Honestly, Dan, why did you have to go and do a thing like that? You've put us both in a really difficult position.'

'Sorry. He said he didn't mind.'

'I don't suppose the poor man felt he could refuse, with you putting pressure on him. And what about me? Didn't it occur to you that we might not have anything to say to each other?'

'You seem to be getting on pretty well to me.'

'We're only being polite.' She wasn't sure she could stand the strain of being pleasant for a whole evening. It was bad enough having to keep a smile on her face for the next two hours while she was harangued by parents wanting to know why their little darling was in the bottom set for English when anyone could see he was practically a genius.

And it would mean getting changed. Her trouser suit was sensible and businesslike for a Parents' Evening, but not smart enough for the posh restaurant Phil had booked. That would definitely need a skirt. Or a dress. Which in turn would mean tights. She wasn't even sure she still owned an unladdered pair, it was so long since she'd worn them. And then there was all the hassle of make-up, and contact lenses, and – oh Lord, why tonight?

Dan must have seen the despair on her face because he said, 'You'll be fine, Mum. Anyway,' he added, less reassuringly, 'Phil's probably used to you looking like a wreck by now.'

Tess grimaced. 'Thank you very much. That makes me feel so much better.'

'Has anyone seen my shirt?'

'Is this it?' Emily pulled a rag from behind a cushion and held it at arm's length without looking up from *Bliss* magazine.

'What's it doing there?' Jack took it from her. 'Oh no, look at it! It's full of creases. It's going to need ironing again.'

'Looks all right to me,' said Emily, still not looking up. 'Anyway, I don't know what you're making so much fuss about. It's only a stupid Parents' Evening.'

'I want to make a good impression. What happens at these things anyway?' Jack shrugged on his shirt. He was mortified to realise he'd never been to one before. Like everything else, he left that kind of thing to Miranda.

'You all take your clothes off and dance naked round a burning pile of exercise books,' Emily said. 'Dad, it's just a bunch of teachers sitting around. You're meant to talk to them about my progress. Oh, and if you're really unlucky you might have to look at some really sad display.' She glared over the top of her magazine. 'You will try not to say anything embarrassing, won't you?'

'Me? Embarrass you?' Jack smiled at her in the mirror as he knotted his tie. 'As if I could!'

The Parents' Evening was just as Emily had described it. Tables were set up around the hall, each with a harrassed-looking teacher behind it. Depending on their subject, queues snaked across the hall as parents waited for their turn to praise, complain or defend their offspring. Some looked worried, others smug. Along the other side of the hall, display boards had been set up to show off the children's artwork.

Jack scanned the tables and spotted Tess. It was a relief to see a friendly face. She was at a corner table, talking to an anxious-looking couple. He imagined her listening to their troubles. A queue was building up in front of her. Lots of people like him, all keen to talk to her. She seemed to attract them, not like some of the other teachers who sat stony-faced, staring into space.

She suddenly looked up and gave him a little wave. Jack smiled back and pretended to study the art display, embarrassed at being caught staring. Unfortunately, he turned around a bit too quickly and knocked a wonky-looking vase off its plinth. He caught it just before it hit the ground.

'Oops!' He grimaced at the people next to him, a hairy-looking couple in matching anoraks. 'Some little darling's masterpiece.'

'Ours, actually,' the man said. They walked off.

He glanced back over his shoulder. Tess was still deep in conversation with the couple. They looked as if they were telling her their marital troubles too.

He filled in the time by talking to the other teachers. He spoke to the German teacher, the History teacher, and the Design Technology teacher, but only because no one else was and he felt sorry for him. He heard enough to reassure himself that even if Emily wasn't top of the class, she tried hard, turned her homework in on time and didn't disappear behind the bike sheds with the fifth-form boys.

All the time he kept glancing across at Tess. She was now talking to a ferocious-looking woman in a Burberry raincoat. The woman kept jabbing her finger at Tess, who somehow managed to keep smiling.

Finally she finished making her point and moved on. Jack dived into the vacant seat just as Mr and Mrs Anorak were closing in.

'Another satisfied customer?' He jerked his head towards

the woman, who was now picking on the nervous-looking Head of RE.

'We aim to please.' Tess pushed her short dark hair off her face. She looked different tonight. She wasn't wearing her glasses for a start, and her brown eyes were fringed with thick dark lashes. 'How are you?'

'Great, thanks. Having a better time than you, by the look of it?'

'Oh God, do I look that bad?' She didn't. She looked very good. She was even wearing lipstick. And a flowery dress under her businesslike jacket. 'It's been a long day. And it isn't over yet.'

'Don't tell me you're going home to a pile of marking?'

'Not quite.' She gave him a funny little smile. She looked endearing with her glasses on, but he hadn't realised how pretty she was without them. 'How are things at home?'

'Oh, you know Em. She has her good days and bad days.' Like the rest of us, he thought. Except Emily could get away with slamming up to her room and crying on her bed while he had to get on with it.

'And how about you?'

Jack shrugged. 'I'm okay.' He looked around the crowded hall. 'I'm not sure I'm handling this very well, though.'

'In what way?'

'I don't think I'm asking the right questions. You know – intelligent ones.'

Tess laughed. 'You're not sitting an exam!'

'Are you kidding? Sometimes I feel as if I'm taking A Level child rearing, but I've missed most of the course and lost all my revision notes.'

Tess moved her hand and for a moment he thought she was going to reach out for him, then thought better of it. 'I'll let you into a secret, shall I? After two hours sitting here, your brain goes as numb as your backside. Most of us are just thinking of going home.'

'I'm sorry, I didn't mean to keep you—'

'Don't be silly, I wasn't talking about you. But I suppose we'd better get down to business.' She glanced over his shoulder at the hairy couple.

Tess quickly consulted her notes and they chatted about Emily's progress for a few minutes. Jack would have liked to go on talking, but Mr and Mrs Anorak were growing restive.

He got up and wandered aimlessly around the hall, pretending to look at the art. As the clock crept towards eight, the crowd of parents in the hall began to thin out and a few of the teachers started packing up to go home. Tess was one of them. Jack hurried over to her table as she was cramming her books into her satchel.

'Still here?' She looked up, surprised.

'I was so transfixed by your art display I completely lost track of time.'

'Year Eight's art tends to have that effect on people.'

He took a deep breath. 'I don't suppose you'd like a drink? We didn't get that coffee a couple of weeks ago and I just wondered if you'd prefer something stronger?'

He could already see the refusal forming on her face before he'd finished his sentence. 'I'm sorry, Jack, I can't. I'm afraid I already have plans for this evening.'

'Not your mother again?' He tried to hide his embarrassment behind a feeble joke.

'Not this time.' Tess glanced towards the doorway. A man had just walked in – tall, fair-haired, good-looking, in a tan suede jacket. He saw her, waved and made his way over.

'Hi, Tess.' Jack saw him swoop down to kiss her cheek and suddenly it all made sense. The dress, the make-up. She had a date.

He also realised how close he'd come to making a total fool of himself.

The man looked at Jack. 'Sorry, am I interrupting something?'

'No. Not at all.' Jack backed off. 'I was just going.' He turned to Tess. 'Have a nice evening, won't you?'

'Jack!' He stopped and looked over his shoulder. 'Some other night, maybe?'

He managed a smile. He'd already asked her twice and been turned down. He had no intention of making a fool of himself a third time.

'Who was that?' Phil asked, when he'd gone.

'Just a friend.' Tess kept her eyes fixed on the door.

'Are you sure about that? I could have sworn he was asking you out.'

'So? Friends can go out together, can't they? I'm going out with you.'

Phil smiled. 'Does that mean we're friends?'

'What else would we be?'

'I don't know. I got the distinct impression that as far as you were concerned I was only "Dan's father".' He imitated the slightly stroppy way she always said it. Tess gave him a not-so-friendly shove.

'Don't push it,' she warned. 'I might change my mind about going out with you at all.'

'What, and have me come all this way for nothing?'

Tess grew serious. 'I'm sorry about that. I could have killed Dan for letting you down. I hope you're not too disappointed he's not coming with us?'

Phil shrugged. 'Can't be helped. I'm glad to see he's taking his studies so seriously.'

'Hmm.' Tess had her suspicions about that. It wasn't like Dan to pass up the chance of a night out to stay in and finish an assignment. She had a vague feeling there was something else going on in her son's mind, but she hoped she was wrong. 'Anyway, we don't have to go out if you don't want to. I'm happy to cancel.'

She'd hoped he might agree so she could go home and tackle her mountain of ironing, but he didn't. 'It'd be a shame to waste a dinner reservation tonight. Especially when you've gone to so much effort.' He looked her up and down. 'You look great, by the way. I'd forgotten what gorgeous legs you have.'

'Phil!'

'Sorry. I didn't realise you were so touchy about compliments.' He spread his hands in a gesture of surrender. 'Look, I don't know about you, but I could do with a night out after the week I've had. Why don't we just enjoy ourselves for a few hours?'

Jack saw them emerge from the building and hunched down behind the steering wheel, but Tess didn't even look his way as she followed the fair-haired man to his car. A silver Porsche, of course. What else would a flash git like that drive?

He felt like a stalker, watching them. What did it matter to him what Tess did anyway? So she had a man. Big deal. He didn't know why he was so surprised. He didn't know why he was even interested. Just because everyone else had a life except him.

Sophie had gone to bed but Emily was waiting up for him when he got home. She was in the same position on the sofa, her feet up, still reading her magazine. Jack had the feeling she'd been staring at the same page since he left.

'Well?' she said.

'Well what?'

'How did it go? Am I going to be expelled? Did anyone notice your shirt? I hope you didn't say something stupid and make a complete fool of me?'

'No, you're not going to be expelled. No, no one noticed my shirt. And no, I didn't say anything stupid.' Apart from asking your teacher out when she blatantly wasn't interested. He poured himself a large drink.

'Good.' Emily sighed with relief.

'But I did snog your Geography teacher. That doesn't count, does it?'

'No, that's okay. Did his beard get in the way?'

'Not as much as Mrs Frobisher's.'

That made her giggle. It was a nice change from all the scowling and door slamming. He wished she'd try it more often.

Emily was in a surprisingly good mood. She even offered to make him a sandwich, something he could never remember her doing before. He hadn't even realised she knew where the kitchen was, from the amount of coffee cups that seemed to lose their way in her bedroom.

They were curled up companionably on the sofa watching *Taggart* when the phone rang. Jack reached for it, not taking his eyes off the screen. 'Hello?'

'Jack?' Charlie's voice on the other end made him sit up and reach for the remote control. He hit the mute button, much to Emily's disgust.

'I was watching that!'

'Shh!' He flagged her with his hand to be quiet and turned back to the phone. 'Charlie! This is a surprise.'

'Didn't you get my message?'

'What message?'

'I called earlier and spoke to Emily. I asked her to get you to call me back.'

'I expect she forgot.' Jack glared at Emily, who stared stony-faced at the silent screen. 'What can I do for you, anyway?'

'I just thought I'd warn you. Your sister's invited us both to dinner on Saturday.'

'Oh God.'

'I had pretty much that reaction too. I'm afraid she might be trying to fix us up.' She laughed. Jack didn't.

'I'll kill her when I see her,' he said. 'Look, Charlie, I'm really sorry. Ros is as subtle as a sledgehammer.'

'That's okay. You've got to admit, it's quite funny.'

'It's bloody embarrassing. I hope you told her where to go?'

'Of course not. I could hardly be rude, could I? Anyway, you never know. It might be fun.'

'I don't know about that.' Jack gritted his teeth. 'I'll call her and sort this out, okay?'

'Don't be too hard on her, Jack. I don't mind, honestly.'

'I do.'

He rang off, then dialled Ros' number.

'Oh, hi.' She sounded deceptively casual, a sure sign she was up to something. 'I was just about to call you.'

'I bet you were! What's all this about you inviting Charlie round to dinner?'

'Oh. You've spoken to her?'

'You bet I have. The poor woman was mortified, and so am I. Bloody hell, Ros, what made you do it?'

'I was only trying to help.'

'How? By making me look an idiot? By ruining my life?'

'For God's sake, Jack, calm down. You sound like you did when we were kids and I told everyone you had a thing about Sarah Greene.'

'Exactly. You embarrassed me then and you've embarrassed me now. For heaven's sake, Charlie's a work colleague!'

'But she likes you. And you like her.'

'Of course I like her!' He noticed Emily's ear cocked towards him and turned away. 'I like her as a friend.'

'So there's nothing wrong with coming to dinner with her as a friend, is there?'

'Except that's not what you had in mind.'

'I didn't have anything in mind. I just thought it might be a nice night out for you.' Ros sounded innocent. 'But of course if anything *did* happen—'

'Which it won't.'

'If you're so sure about that, what's the problem with spending an evening with her?'

Jack fumed silently. Ros had an annoying habit of running rings round him in an argument. She always had. 'You embarrassed Charlie,' he said again.

'She didn't sound embarrassed when I spoke to her. In fact she sounded dead keen.'

'She was just being polite.'

'And you're just being a coward. You'll thank me for this one day.'

'I doubt that.'

'You will. I mean, look how you were with Miranda. You would never have asked her out if I hadn't given you a push in the right direction. And that worked out all right, didn't it?'

'Charlie isn't Miranda,' Jack said sharply.

'I know.' Ros's voice was subdued. 'But she still seems like a nice woman. She's certainly very attractive, wouldn't you say?'

'I suppose so,' he conceded.

'And you've got masses in common.'

'I don't know about that—'

'Admit it, you do fancy her just a teeny bit?'

'Well—'

'So really I've done you a favour, haven't I?' Ros concluded brightly.

'Now, hang on—'

'Come on, Jack, I'm not asking you to marry her or anything. Just come round for dinner. It's not exactly a lifelong commitment, is it?' She took his silence for assent. 'Great. I'll see you on Saturday night. Oh, and don't worry about a babysitter for the girls. Mum says you can drop them off at hers with my lot.'

She rang off. Jack stared in frustration at the buzzing receiver. Maybe it was only dinner, but it was where it might end that worried him.

'What was that all about?' Emily asked, still not taking her eyes off the screen.

'Never mind that! Why didn't you tell me Charlie had rung?'

'I forgot.' There was something about the way she didn't meet his eye that made him suspicious. 'What did she want, anyway?'

'Auntie Ros has invited us to dinner on Saturday night.'

'All of us?'

'No, you're going to Gran's with your cousins.'

'Boring.' Emily made a face. 'So it's just you and that woman, is it?'

'I don't know. There might be some other people from work there.' He certainly hoped there would be.

'But it might be just the two of you?'

'Maybe.'

Emily frowned at the screen. 'Sounds like Auntie Ros is trying to fix you up with her.'

Jack sank wearily on to the sofa. 'Maybe she is.'

'And do you like her?'

He closed his eyes. He felt tired, his pleasant evening ruined. 'Emily, I don't really want to talk about this now.'

'Fine.' She jumped to her feet and stomped into the hall. A moment later she returned, shrugging on her denim jacket.

Jack looked up. 'Where are you going?'

'To see Paris. At least *she'll* talk to me!'

But Paris was too busy to talk when she got round to her flat. She was in the kitchen, cutting up slices of bread and jam. Her homework was spread out on the table. From the sitting room came the sound of two small boys squabbling over toys.

'Mum's gone out and those two haven't had their tea yet,' she explained, arranging the slices on a plate.

'Is that all they're having?'

'It's all we've got.' She picked up the plates. 'Put the kettle on, I won't be a minute.'

Emily followed her into the sitting room and watched as she calmly sorted out her brothers' argument and separated them to either end of the sofa with a plate each. Then she put on a *Star Wars* video and left them to it, with a stern warning not to make another sound.

'Do you have to do everything?' Emily asked, as they headed back into the kitchen.

'Only when Mum's out.'

'Where's she gone?'

'Out clubbing with her new boyfriend.' Paris fished two mugs out of the sink and rinsed them under the tap.

'What's he like?'

'Not bad. Better than the last one, anyway. He did a runner with the telly and Mum's child-benefit book.' She peered into the coffee jar. 'We're out of coffee. Will tea do?'

'Whatever.' Emily looked around. She'd never imagined Paris living in a place like this. Everything was so shabby and uncared-for. She took it for granted her home would always be clean and welcoming, and the food cupboards would always be full. It had never really dawned on her that anyone lived differently. How would she feel if she had to come home and take care of Sophie before she could get down to her homework every evening? She suppressed a shudder at the thought.

Paris must have guessed what she was thinking. She stiffened defensively. 'She's not out every night,' she said. 'And the only reason we don't have any food in the house is because she hasn't had time to go to the shops.'

'I'm not saying anything.'

'No, but that's what you're thinking.'

Emily blushed. She traced the chips on the rim of her mug with her finger. 'My dad's got a girlfriend,' she said. 'At least I think he has, anyway.'

She explained about the phone call. Paris listened, but didn't seem to grasp how shocking the news really was.

'So?' she said, when Emily had finished. 'Your dad's got a date. What's so wrong about that? Don't you want him to be happy?'

'Of course I do! It's just too soon, that's all.' Every step he took towards a new life was another he took away from his old one. Her mother's memory was like an old photo, fading more every day. Sometimes it felt to Emily as if she was the only one trying to hold on to it. 'My mum hasn't even been dead a year and he's looking for someone else.'

'Maybe he feels he needs someone.'

'Why? He's got us!' Emily blurted out. Paris gave her a look over her glasses.

'So you reckon he should forget all about women and dedicate his whole life to looking after you? Don't you think that's a bit selfish?'

Emily didn't answer. Maybe it was selfish, but it was the way she felt. She tried not to show it, but she felt very vulnerable. She'd already lost her mother and she was desperately worried about losing her father too. If this woman took him away, where would that leave her and Sophie?

She looked around the dingy flat. How long before she was in this position, taking care of her little sister while her dad hit the town with his new girlfriend?

Chapter 20

'To be or not to be, that is the – oh, sod it!'

Tess Doyle stared at the Year 10 art display on the hall wall and pretended not to hear as Neil Wallis scrabbled through his script, his finger moving down the lines.

'The question,' she said patiently. Neil nodded and ploughed on, his heavy brows drawn in concentration.

He could have been reciting the lines in Serbo-Croat for all the feeling he put into them. He was a hefty fifteen-year-old, the most feared midfielder in the Under-16s football league and the unlikeliest Hamlet since Dale Winton.

Casting him hadn't been her idea. Cynthia Frobisher had insisted on it.

'But he's terrible!' Tess had protested, but Cynthia had merely raised her eyebrows.

'Really, Tess, I'm surprised at you. I thought you of all people would have been pleased to give him a chance. Isn't that what all this is about? Waking some dormant love of literature?'

From the longing way he stared out of the windows at the school playing field, it wasn't working. Poor Neil. How could he be expected to carry the production? Being a spear carrier would be too taxing for him.

The rest of the cast were just as bad, thanks to Cynthia's interference. Mark Nicholls, who was a natural as the brooding Hamlet, had been relegated to playing Guilden-stern. And Emily Tyler, who Tess would have loved to cast as Ophelia, was filling up the background as one of the milling citizens of Elsinore. The fragile Ophelia was being played by Maeve Flaherty, a solid lump of a girl, who looked as if she could have floored Hamlet and probably half the Danish army. She sat at the side of the stage, chomping her way through a packet of Hobnobs as she waited for her cue.

The others were no better. As Hamlet stumbled through his lines, Claudius and Polonius sniggered in the background, while Queen Gertrude examined her split ends. She'd been dumped by Rosencrantz that morning and wasn't speaking to anyone.

'Not finished yet?' Mr Peake, the school caretaker stood in the doorway, tapping his watch.

'Not long now, Mr Peake.'

'It's all very well for you to say that, but I've got Weight Watchers in here at seven. I need to put the chairs out.'

'I'll make sure we're well out of your way by then.'

'And you'd better not leave a mess. I've got better things to do than tidy up after you lot. I hope you're not chewing gum?' He turned on Queen Gertrude. 'I'll have words with Mrs Frobisher if I find that on the stage.'

He shuffled off, mumbling. As if they didn't all have better things to do, Tess thought. She looked at her watch. Nearly six.

'Okay, let's call it a day, shall we?' She closed her book. 'Thanks everyone, you've all worked really hard.' But she was addressing an empty stage. As she looked out of the hall window, she could already see Neil Wallis sprinting across the playing field, leaping for imaginary headers and leaving a trail of script pages behind him.

The only one who hadn't disappeared was Emily. She took her time gathering up her things, dragging her feet as if she didn't really want to leave.

Tess watched her for a moment. She had a feeling she was waiting for her.

'Something on your mind, Emily?' she asked.

Emily lifted her shoulders in a half shrug. 'Not really.'

In other words there was, but she didn't want to come out and say it. Fine. Tess had too much to do to hang around trying to prise the problem out of her.

'You know where to find me if you want to talk, don't you?' She hiked her bag on to her shoulder and headed for the door.

Emily caught up with her in the car park. Tess heard her running foosteps behind her, but when she turned round Emily slowed down, dragging her feet again.

Tess stifled a sigh. 'Would you like a lift home?'

'S'pose.'

It took her five minutes of chatting about school, friends and family before Tess finally found out what was on her mind.

'Dad's got a girlfriend,' she said. 'That Charlie – you know, from the party?'

'How do you know?'

'I heard them talking on the phone. They're meeting up on Saturday.'

Blimey, that hadn't taken her long. 'And you're not happy about it?'

'It's not up to me, is it?' Emily stared out of the window. 'He doesn't care what Sophie and I think, so long as he's happy.'

'I'm sure that's not true.'

'It is! He never listens to us. Anyway, I think it's disgusting. He shouldn't have a girlfriend at his age.'

'He's hardly ancient!' Tess laughed, then saw Emily's face. 'Look, I know it can't be easy for you. But your dad was bound to meet someone sooner or later.'

'Why? Why does he have to meet someone?'

Tess searched her mind for a tactful answer, then gave up. It wasn't her place to explain any of this anyway. 'I think you should talk to your father about that.'

Emily looked down at her hands. Her nails were so

bitten down she'd started nibbling the cuticles, Tess noticed. 'Why can't things just stay the same?' she said quietly.

Tess looked at the dark hair falling over her face, hiding her expression. Poor Emily, she'd been through so much upheaval over the past year, no wonder she clung on to the little bit of security she had left.

'Not all change is bad,' she said. 'Sometimes things can change for the better.'

'Not for me.' Emily shook her head. 'First Mum died, then we had to move here. And just when I'm starting to get used to it, that cow comes along and it all gets changed again.'

'I know it's bound to feel a bit strange at first, having another woman around. But you never know, this Charlie could turn out to be really nice. You might even get to like her.'

'I'll never like her!' Emily said bitterly. 'She's got no right to take Mum's place!'

'I'm sure she's not trying to do that.'

'I bet she is!'

So that's what this is about, Tess thought. It wasn't just Charlie. Emily would have hated any woman who usurped her mother. 'Have you tried talking to your dad about this?'

'I can't. He wouldn't listen anyway.' Emily twisted around in her seat. 'He might listen to you, though.'

'Me? What am I supposed to say?'

'I don't know. Tell him you don't like her. Tell him she's no good for him or something.'

'But I don't know her. Anyway, why should he listen to me?'

'He will, I know he will. He likes you.' Emily's face was full of hope. 'You've got to do something!'

It would have been so easy to say yes, to get involved. Tess steeled herself. 'I'm sorry, Emily. I can't help you.'

'But you can! I told you, he'd listen to you—'

'Maybe, but it's not my problem!'

She hadn't meant for it to come out so sharply. The light faded from Emily's eyes. 'Fine,' she said shortly. 'Sorry.'

They were silent all the way back to Hollywell Park. When they reached her driveway, Emily slammed out of the car without a backward glance.

''Bye, Miss Doyle. Thanks for the lift,' Tess muttered. She wrestled the awkward gear stick into reverse, fuming quietly.

It wasn't her problem. She hadn't even asked to be involved. This was something Jack had to sort out, not her.

Correction – Charlie should be dealing with the sulks and the tantrums, not Tess. Charlie had the man, she should put up with the kids too.

'I'm a teacher, not a flaming agony aunt,' Tess said aloud as she sat at the junction, waiting to pull out on to the main road. A gap appeared but as she edged into it, a Volvo full of kids and Labradors with a harrassed woman behind the wheel moved forward and filled it, blocking her exit.

'Selfish cow!' Normally Tess would have sighed at her stupidity but she was so wound up she leaned on the horn. The woman turned around, startled, and made a helpless gesture of apology. Tess gestured back, less apologetically.

The lights changed and the traffic shifted forward. The Volvo shot off, relieved to escape. The Toyota behind it hung back, allowing Tess out. Tess caught the frightened eyes of the man driving. He obviously thought she was a deranged maniac. Tess pulled in front of him, scarcely bothering to acknowledge his kindness.

She was deranged, all right. But it had nothing to do with the Volvo, or even Emily. It was because of Jack Tyler.

When had she started fancying him? She wasn't even aware she had until Emily's revelations about Charlie. No matter how much she tried to put her darkening mood down to annoyance at being involved in someone else's problems, she had to admit it came down to something far more basic – she was jealous.

The lights changed to red as she approached, and for a mad moment Tess was tempted to jump them. She fidgeted in her seat, fingers drumming on the wheel, cursing at the hold up, even though she was in no hurry.

All the time, she thought about Jack and Charlie. When did they get together? It must have been at the party, after she'd left.

She thought back to that evening. Maybe if she'd played things differently, she could have been the one Jack ended up with? But at the time she hadn't realised the depth of her own feelings. And she'd underestimated Jack's. While she'd been so convinced he didn't want another woman, Charlie Ferguson had steamed in and nabbed him.

But would she ever have stood a chance against Charlie? You only had to look at them to see she and Jack were made for each other.

Besides, she didn't envy her. She might be gorgeous, with a great job, a designer wardrobe and the man she wanted, but she also had Emily to deal with. Tess suspected she was going to be in for a rough ride.

'Oh, no!' Ros opened the oven door and fanned away the cloud of smoke with her oven mitt. Jack stood in the doorway, watching her.

'Can I help?'

'Only if you know the number of a decent Chinese takeaway.' Ros poked at the charred lamb shanks in the roasting tin. 'Oh well, I'll just cover them in sauce and maybe no one will notice.' She looked up at him. 'For heaven's sake, Jack, crack open another bottle and stop standing there like a wet weekend! You're supposed to be enjoying yourself.'

Jack reached for the bottle opener and started to peel the

plastic wrapping from around the cork. 'I don't think this is a very good idea, that's all.'

'So you've said. About a million times.' Ros put the tin down on the worktop and closed the oven door with her foot.

'What if we don't get on? What if we've got nothing to talk about apart from work?'

'So? You can just say goodbye at the end of the evening and you've lost nothing.'

'Except my dignity,' Jack said gloomily. 'And a large chunk of my self-esteem.'

'But you'll never know if you don't try, will you?'

Laughter drifted from the other room as Greg dispensed the drinks generously to the other guests. Everyone was here.

Everyone except Charlie.

'She's late,' Jack said. 'I don't suppose she's coming.'

'Relax, she'll be here.'

'I expect she's decided not to bother.' She was probably on her way to a nightclub in Leeds right now, with some unencumbered, Porsche-driving twenty-something. That was the kind of man Charlie should go for, not a widower with two stroppy daughters and enough baggage to fill the hold of a jumbo jet.

He sipped his wine moodily. 'You do realise she knows this is a set-up?'

'How can she know? I've invited loads of people so it won't look obvious.'

'Obvious!' Jack spluttered into his glass. 'You couldn't be more obvious if you'd put a sign saying "Please Shag Me" round my neck.'

'That's Plan B.' Ros grinned. 'I just wanted to give you a helping hand since you're not getting anywhere by yourself.'

'Has it occurred to you I might not want to get anywhere?'

'Nonsense, I keep saying you need a woman in your life.'

'I've already got a woman in my life. In fact, I have two. And I don't suppose either of them would be too impressed at the idea of me seeing someone else so soon after their mother's death.'

He knew one of them wasn't. Emily had hardly spoken to him since Charlie's phone call three days earlier.

In the meantime, everyone kept telling him to go for it with Charlie. So what was stopping him? His old excuse, that it was too soon and he wasn't ready for another relationship, was beginning to wear thin. Miranda had been gone almost a year, and although the idea of sharing a bed with another woman still seemed strange, he'd started to think it might be nice to have someone to share his life with. If the right woman came along, he could even imagine himself falling in love again.

But he didn't know if Charlie was the right woman.

He said as much to Ros, who just laughed.

'What are you talking about? She's perfect for you. She's attractive, intelligent, and you've got so much in common.'

'Like what?'

'Well, you work together.'

'Great. We can discuss planning enquiries. I expect the long winter evenings will just fly by.'

'Look, she's interested in you. That's enough, isn't it?' Ros wiped her hands on a teatowel, picked up her glass, and put her arm through his. 'Come on, let's go and mingle with the guests. And for God's sake, try to look a bit more cheerful about it!'

Greg was handing round more drinks when they came in. Jack recognised Mike and Harry from work, plus their wives, one of whom was heavily pregnant.

He chatted with the other guests, but all the time he kept glancing at the door. He was painfully aware what everyone was thinking. They'd all totted up the numbers and worked out he must be the Spare Man. And where there was a

Spare Man, there was usually a Spare Woman. Except this time there wasn't, because she hadn't bothered to turn up. He didn't know which was worse, her standing him up or her coming. Either way he felt sick.

And then the doorbell rang.

'That'll be Charlie.' Ros sent him an 'I told you so' look and went to answer it. Jack listened to their voices in the hall with rising panic and excitement.

Ros could barely keep the smirk off her face as she walked in, followed by Charlie. She was wearing a gold silk dress, which managed to look classy and sexy at the same time. Her hair flowed in silky amber waves over her shoulders.

'Sorry I'm late, everyone.' Her gaze swept the room. 'I had some paperwork to finish.'

'At the weekend? Don't you ever stop working?' Mike asked.

'It needed to be done by Monday.'

'You know what they say, all work and no play—'

'Makes me a senior partner one of these days?' Her gaze came to rest on Jack, who felt himself blushing like a schoolboy.

Greg poured her a drink and they sat down to dinner shortly afterwards. Jack cringed as Ros shoved the other guests aside so he could sit next to Charlie.

'Now you two can chat,' she said.

Chance would be a fine thing, thought Jack. His tongue was glued to the roof of his mouth, and he knew he couldn't make small talk if his life depended on it.

This was crazy. He'd never had any trouble talking to her before. But then, he'd never really thought of her as a woman before. She was Charlie Ferguson, a work colleague, a mate. Now she was someone else entirely. And he wasn't sure he liked the change.

Fortunately Charlie saved him the trouble of talking too much. She chatted easily, mostly about work. But as she gossiped away about who was in line for Alec Finch's job, Jack was appalled to find himself stifling a yawn.

What was happening to him? A few months ago he would have been only too happy to delve into office politics. But now he found his attention wandering to the other end of the table, where Harry's wife Elaine was explaining the best way to remove Ribena stains from a non-colourfast T-shirt. It was the kind of problem that played on his mind these days, far more than who was going to secure the senior partnership.

Jack wasn't the only one feeling out of his depth. Charlie was beginning to wish she'd never come. She'd been looking forward to having Jack to herself but now he barely seemed to be listening to her. He was monopolised by Harry and Mike's boring wives, droning on about kids. As if that was the only thing he knew how to talk about these days. He must be bored to tears, she decided, although he seemed to be hiding it well.

And they were so patronising! The way they went on like he was some kind of hero, taking care of two children all alone. As if thousands of single mothers didn't do it every day.

She tried to say as much, but everyone just looked awkward. 'Yes, but it's different for women, isn't it?' Harry mumbled.

'It certainly is,' Charlie agreed hotly. 'They don't usually earn as much as men so they can't afford decent childcare for a start. Or cleaners, or housekeepers. Yet no one's sympathetic to them. They're treated like the scourge of modern society. It's hardly fair, is it?'

Silence fell. Charlie looked round at all of them. She had the bad feeling she'd said too much.

'You're absolutely right.' Jack smiled at her. 'Single fathers get all the sympathy and single mothers just get a hard time. Maybe it's because we look as if we need all the pity we can get?'

That got everyone talking again. As the conversation flowed, Charlie leaned over to Jack and said, 'I don't suppose I'll ever be invited to join the Mother's Union now.'

'Would you want to?'

'No thanks! Sorry if it sounded like I was picking on you, by the way,' she whispered. 'I just find it so bloody condescending. I mean, you're an intelligent man. How hard can looking after kids be?'

He smiled. 'I'm not going to bore you by telling you.'

'I don't know how you stand it.'

'I don't mind. I'll tell you what I really can't stand, though.'

'What's that?'

'My sister watching us like we're the last pair of mating pandas in captivity!'

Charlie glanced up to the other end of the table. Ros was smiling encouragingly back at her. She couldn't help laughing. 'I see what you mean. I hadn't noticed it before.'

'I have! What does she have to keep looking at us for? I mean, what's she expecting us to do?'

'I shudder to think!'

At least he was talking to her again. But before Charlie had a chance to make the most of it, he was hijacked by Elaine, wanting to know if Sophie had picked up head lice, as her youngest kept getting them and she'd tried everything to no avail.

Head lice! Charlie felt itchy just thinking about them. What kind of topic was that for sophisticated dinner conversation? She was horrified when Ros and Jack joined in enthusiastically, and the three of them went into a group bitching session about mothers who didn't inspect their children's heads regularly, and the trouble it caused for the rest of the class.

In desperation, she turned to Jo, who was picking at her cheese and biscuits.

'So what do you do?' she said.

Jo blinked up at her. 'Sorry? Do about what?'

'What do you do for a living?'

'Oh! I'm a solicitor. Employment law. Or at least I will be for the next three weeks. Then I'm off.' She smiled blissfully and patted her bump. 'No more uncomfortable chairs. No more commuting. No more feeling faint in meetings. I can't wait!'

'It sounds awful,' Charlie agreed. 'How long are you taking for maternity leave?'

'I'm not.'

'Oh!' Charlie gazed at her with new-found admiration. She'd read about those supermums who delivered their babies in their lunch hour and were back at their desks masterminding a corporate takeover by two. But somehow Jo didn't strike her as that type. 'You're going straight back?'

'I'm not going back at all.'

'You're kidding? But what will you do?'

'Look after my baby, of course.'

'But your career—'

'I can't think of a more satisfying career than being a mother,' Jo said piously. 'I don't hold with these women who shove their babies on to a childminder three weeks after they're born and rush back to work. I mean, what's the point of having children if you don't intend to spend time with them?'

And what's the point of spending all those years studying for a law qualification if you don't intend to use it? Charlie felt like asking. But Jo was looking far too pleased with herself to argue.

'It just seems like a waste to me,' she said.

Jo smiled. 'I used to be like you. I thought my career was the most important thing in the world. But you wait until you're pregnant yourself. I'm telling you, it puts all your ambitions into perspective.'

Not to mention shrinking your brain, Charlie thought. She didn't like the way Jo and Elaine were looking at her, as if there must be something wrong with her. Just because she wasn't obsessed with being pregnant and having babies. Just because there was more she wanted to do with her life.

Jo poked at the brie with her knife. 'Do you think this is unpasteurised?'

'I haven't a clue. Does it matter?'

'Jo's not allowed unpasteurised cheese in her condition,' Mike said.

'Or liver, or peanuts or anything with raw egg in it,' Jo added.

'Doesn't that drive you mad?' Charlie helped herself to a hunk of brie.

'Oh no, it's only for nine months. And when you think what's at the end of it – a tiny, new person.' Jo glowed with bovine complacency. All the women beamed except Charlie, who felt slightly sick.

'How long have you got to go?' Elaine asked.

'Only another two months. We can't wait, can we?' Jo reached for her husband's hand. 'Another few weeks and we'll be welcoming our new son or daughter into the world.'

'Better make the most of your freedom while it lasts, then,' Charlie muttered. She would have been heading for the nearest nightclub to dance the night away before she was condemned to a tedious round of nappy changing and 4 a.m. feeds.

'Is it your first?' Ros asked.

Jo nodded. 'I didn't want to wait too long to start a family. I know they say you should wait until you're in your thirties, but I can't think of anything worse than being a middle-aged mum.'

For some reason all eyes turned to Charlie.

'What about you, Charlie?' Elaine spoke for them all. 'Haven't you ever thought about having children?'

'I've thought about it,' Charlie said. 'But then I've thought about trekking in Nepal or bungee jumping off the Golden Gate Bridge. None of them really appeals to me.'

The men laughed. The women were silent. Charlie had the bad feeling she'd put her foot in it again.

Poor Charlie, Jack thought. She looked as if she'd rather be a million miles away. He knew how she felt.

'Are you planning to be there at the birth, Mike?' Harry broke the silence.

'Of course he is,' Jo butted in. 'Mike's going to video it, aren't you, darling?'

'Bloody hell!' Greg said. 'Remind me never to come round to your place. It's bad enough watching your own, without seeing anyone else's.'

'There speaks a man who passed out when they showed the birthing film in the antenatal class,' Ros smiled.

'I'm not surprised. It was like watching a slasher movie. I kept expecting Freddie Kruger to jump out at any moment,' Greg said. 'No, as far as I'm concerned, the best place for a man during the birth is in the nearest bar with a large whisky.'

'So how come you insisted on being there for all three of ours?' Ros asked.

'You wanted me there.'

'No, I didn't. You were no use at all. He sobbed his eyes out the whole way through,' she told the others. 'And when the first one was born, he was so overcome the midwife offered him gas and air.'

Everyone laughed. Then Mike said, 'What about you, Jack? Were you there when your daughters were born?'

He suddenly had a flashback of the labour room, of Miranda squeezing his hand so hard her nails drew blood. And then Emily arriving into the world, red and wrinkled and angry-looking, and all three of them crying. The pain flashed through him, exquisite and intense.

'Why don't you all go through to the sitting room?' Ros said hurriedly, shooting him a worried glance. 'I'll bring the coffee through.'

As they all got up, Jack hung back. 'I don't think I'll bother with the coffee, if you don't mind?'

'Are you sure? It won't take five minutes.'

'No, really, I'd better collect the girls from Mum's and head for home. It's getting late.'

'But it isn't even ten—' Ros started to say, then saw Jack's face and thought better of it. 'Well, if you're sure?'

He sat behind his steering wheel, staring into space. What an idiot. First mention of anything to do with Miranda and he'd fallen to pieces. How could he think he was ready for another relationship? He wasn't even ready to face civilised company.

A sharp rap on the window brought him to his senses. He looked up. Charlie was staring in at him, her face full of concern.

He buzzed the window down. 'Are you okay?' she asked.

'I'm fine.' He forced a smile. 'I just had to get away, that's all.'

'I know what you mean.' The wind whipped at her hair and she tucked it back behind her ear. 'Why don't we have that coffee at my place?'

'I don't know—' he looked at his watch.

'Just coffee, okay? I promise I won't pounce on you or anything.' She smiled. 'Not unless you want me to.'

Chapter 21

Charlie lived in a fabulously airy loft at the top of a converted warehouse overlooking the canal. Inside it was all high ceilings, big windows, wooden floors and white minimalist interiors. There was a high-tech kitchen area at one end of the vast living space, with an iron spiral staircase leading up to the bedrooms. It was the kind of place he might have liked to live in if he hadn't had to worry about sensible things like being near good schools and having space in the garden to play.

Not that you'd need a garden in this place. The girls could probably have a decent game of football in the space between the pale-cream sofas.

Charlie flicked on one of the halogen lamps, illuminating a fat ginger cat on the sofa. He blinked in the light, then tucked his head under his paws and went back to sleep.

Charlie dropped her coat over the back of one of the dining chairs. 'Make yourself comfortable. I'll get those drinks.'

Jack flopped down on the sofa next to the ginger cat. He put out a hand to stroke it. The cat opened one eye, then got up, stretched and moved pointedly to the far end of the sofa.

'I don't think your cat likes me,' he said, as Charlie returned from the kitchen area with a bottle of red wine in one hand, two glasses in the other.

'Don't be too upset about it. Clive doesn't like anyone except Tom. He's devoted to him.'

'Tom?'

'My flatmate.' She tipped Clive off the sofa and sat down next to Jack.

He looked at the bottle. 'I thought we were having coffee?'

'We were. But then I found this in the kitchen and I thought it would be so much nicer.'

'But I'm driving.'

'One glass won't hurt. You hardly had anything at dinner.' She handed him a glass. 'Anyway, you could always stay the night if you're over the limit. The sofa's very comfortable, so I'm told,' she added mischievously, before Jack could say anything.

He smiled back, admiring the way the low lamplight burnished her coppery hair. She really was beautiful, he thought. And bright and nice with it. What would be so wrong if he did stay the night? After all, it wasn't as if he had anyone waiting for him at home.

He gulped his drink, trying to drown the misery that welled up inside him.

'So where's your flatmate tonight?'

'No idea. Probably out with a woman. He's very popular with the ladies, is Tom.'

'How long have you known him?'

'For ever. We were at college together and we've been best friends ever since.'

'Just friends?'

She nodded. 'I love him to bits, but not in that way.'

'Very wise. It's not a good idea to get involved with your friends.'

'I didn't say that, did I?' She sent him a meaningful look and curled her long legs under her.

They talked about Ros' dinner party. They agreed it had been an excruciating evening, for all kinds of reasons.

'I'm really sorry Ros put you through that,' Jack apologised for the hundredth time.

'Don't be. I wanted to come. And I never do anything I

don't want to do, you should know that. Besides, I had to do something. I got tired of waiting for you to ask me out.'

He looked taken aback. 'Sorry?'

'Oh, come on, Jack. You must have noticed me flirting with you?' She smiled. 'And there was me thinking you just weren't interested.'

Thankfully she changed the subject. They chatted some more, swapping life stories. As they talked, Jack hardly noticed Charlie refilling his glass twice, until she held up the empty bottle and offered to fetch another.

'Did we drink all that? I must be right over the limit.' He squinted at the dregs of ruby liquid in his glass. 'I'd better phone for a taxi—'

'Or you could stay the night? I meant what I said about sleeping on the sofa. If you want to?'

He eyed her doubtfully. She knew as well as he did that if he stayed the night, it wouldn't be on the sofa. He could already feel himself slipping, falling under her spell. 'I don't know if that's a good idea. The girls—'

'—are quite safe with their grandmother,' Charlie finished. 'You could always call and let her know where you are, if you think she'll be worried? Although you're a big boy now. I'm sure she knows you can take care of yourself.'

Can I? he wondered, seconds before her mouth closed on his. He didn't seem to be making a good job of it at that moment. Her mouth was soft and warm and tasted of red wine. It hot-wired sensation down his spine into parts of his body that had been dormant for months.

He pulled away. 'I can't. It feels wrong.'

'Are you sure about that?' Her eyes were a deep green in the lamplight. He looked down at her soft mouth and knew he wanted to feel it against his again, in spite of everything. 'It didn't feel wrong to me, Jack.'

She kissed him again. This time he didn't pull away.

★

It took him a moment to remember where he was the following morning. Sunlight streamed between the slatted wooden blinds, casting bars of light across the rumpled white bed.

Jack looked across at Charlie, sleeping beside him, her coppery hair fanned out across the pillow. He watched her for a moment, taking in her creamy skin, the curl of her dark lashes against her cheek, the sensuous curve of her mouth. Even asleep she looked fabulous. How many men would love to be where he was now? He was the luckiest man alive.

Except he didn't feel very lucky. Truth be told, he felt wretched, and not just because of the incipient hangover or lack of sleep.

Last night had been great, sensational even. But it also felt wrong. It felt like a betrayal. As if the harsh light of the morning had caught him cheating in another woman's bed.

He crept out from between the covers so as not to wake Charlie, dressed quietly and headed downstairs.

A man, bare-chested and wearing faded jeans, sat cross-legged on the floor, leaning against the sofa, eating a bowl of cornflakes. The Sunday papers were spread out on the floor in front of him. From the way the ginger cat was curled in his lap Jack guessed this must be the famous flatmate.

'It's Tom, isn't it?' he greeted him. 'I'm Jack. A friend of Charlie's.'

'I guessed.' Tom didn't look up from the papers. 'Good night, was it?'

Jack blinked. 'Sorry?'

'Your dinner party?'

'Oh. Right. Not especially. We left early, as a matter of fact.'

Tom shot him a glance. 'Where's Charlie?'

'Still asleep.'

'I hope you weren't planning to sneak off without saying goodbye?'

Jack stared at him. 'Actually, I was going to make us both some coffee. Would you like some?'

'Mm, coffee. That sounds like an excellent idea.' Charlie appeared down the stairs, wrapped in a brown towelling bathrobe that showed off her long tanned legs. Her hair fell messily around her face but she still looked gorgeous. 'Morning, Jack.' She reached up to kiss him. Jack moved his head so her lips landed on his cheek. He was uncomfortably aware of Tom watching them.

Charlie didn't seem to notice his awkwardness. 'He makes coffee, Tom. Isn't he wonderful?' she purred.

'Terrific,' Tom muttered. 'Next you'll be telling me he can walk and talk at the same time.' He closed the paper, tipped the cat off his lap and stood up. 'I'm going for a shower. Excuse me, won't you?' With another look at Jack, he disappeared upstairs.

Jack watched him go. 'I don't think your flatmate likes me very much.'

'He's probably just nursing a sore head after last night.' Charlie curled her arm through his. 'Shall we take the coffee and the papers and go back to bed?'

'I can't.' Jack looked at his watch. 'I should pick the girls up soon.'

'Really?' Charlie pouted. 'I was hoping we could spend the day together. There's a nice pub a bit further along the canal. I know it's not exactly Venice, but it's scenic.'

'What about Emily and Sophie?'

'They could come too, I suppose. Or we could go shopping. Do you think they'd like that?'

He could just imagine what Emily would make of a trip to the shops with him and Charlie. 'It's a nice thought, but I really should be heading home. The girls are bound to have homework they need to finish, and I have to get their uniforms ready for school—'

'A woman's work is never done.' Charlie's smile didn't reach her eyes. 'I suppose you'd better make a move, then.'

There was something about the way she said it that gave Jack a twinge of guilt. He shouldn't be running away. Charlie deserved better than that.

He made himself stay long enough to finish his coffee. The silence lengthened, became embarrassing. He could feel Charlie's darkening mood. He couldn't blame her for feeling put out. She had a right to expect something other than a hasty brush-off after last night. He felt like a heel for not being able to give it to her. But it was all happening way too fast for him.

They said an awkward goodbye at the door. 'I'll call you, okay?'

'You do that.'

He hesitated. 'I would have liked to stay, I really would—'

'I know. Mustn't let the girls down, must you?'

She knew it was an excuse. And a feeble one, at that.

She was on the sofa, staring into space, her hands curled around her cooling cup of coffee, when Tom emerged from the shower ten minutes later, towelling his hair.

He looked around. 'Has he gone?'

'As if you didn't know. Don't tell me you weren't upstairs listening to every word.'

'I couldn't help overhearing.' Tom's expression softened. He slung the towel around his shoulders and headed towards her. 'I'm sorry, Charlie.'

'Sorry? What for?'

'Well – he's dumped you, hasn't he?'

'Dumped me?' She managed a brittle laugh. 'Don't be stupid, of course he hasn't dumped me. You heard him. He had to go and pick up his kids.'

'Yeah, right.' Tom nodded solemnly. 'Sorry, but that sounded a lot like dumping to me.'

'That's all you know, isn't it?' Nobody dumped Charlie Ferguson. Ever. It was always her sneaking off in the cold light of dawn, shoes in hand, her making vague promises to call . . .

'So when are you seeing him again?'

'I don't know, do I? Tomorrow, probably. At work.' Although she wasn't sure how she was going to handle coming face to face with him. More to the point, how was he going to handle it?

'So you haven't actually made any plans, then?'

She twisted round to face him. 'What exactly are you trying to say?'

'Nothing.' He backed off. 'Except it doesn't look very promising, does it? You sleep with him; he disappears into the dawn without asking to see you again.' He sucked his teeth. 'Not promising at all.'

'Like you're an expert.'

'I know when I've been dumped.'

'You would, wouldn't you? It's happened often enough.'

'No need to take it out on me, just because Mr Wonderful doesn't want to know.'

Charlie stood up, wrapping her robe tighter around her. 'I don't have to listen to this. I'm going to have a shower. I hope you haven't used all the hot water?'

'There's plenty left. Enough to drown your sorrows, anyway,' he called after her, as she stomped up the spiral staircase.

She washed her hair, scrubbing away at the roots with her fingers, as if she could wash all the negative thoughts out of her head.

She was angry with Jack for walking out on her and making her feel humiliated. But she was even angrier with herself for reading the situation so badly. For once her instincts had let her down. She should have known Jack was wary of getting involved. She should have taken it slowly, not rushed right in there and come on strong. Now she'd frightened him off.

She knew he wanted her, in spite of his doubts. He just wasn't ready to face it yet. He still had a few emotional hurdles to get over first. She had to back off a bit, give him time to come to terms with the idea.

She held the shower over her head and let the hot water rush through her hair, washing away all the soap.

It wasn't her usual style, to play the waiting game. But Jack Tyler was worth waiting for.

On Monday morning, Jack was in his office when a call came through from the council's environment department with a query about the Westpoint site. Jack, up to his eyes in his own work, was impatient.

'Can't you talk to Bernard Sweeting about it? That's his department, not mine.'

'I've tried calling and emailing him, but I've had no answer. I think he's out of the office this morning.'

'What about Greg? He's supposed to be coordinating the project.'

'Same story. Sorry Jack, I wouldn't ask but I really need those figure by lunchtime.'

Jack sighed. 'Okay, I'll go down there and see if I can find something. I'll call you back.'

Bernard wasn't in his cubby-hole office, but his door was open. Jack was scribbling a note on a Post-it when he noticed Bernard's Westpoint file on his desk. Thinking the figures he needed must be in there, he flipped it open and began to read.

'What are you doing?'

He was so startled he dropped the file. 'Bloody hell, Bernard! You frightened the life out of me.'

Bernard Sweeting's face was ashen against his shabby jumper as he stood in the doorway. 'What were you looking in there for?'

'Just some figures.' He explained about the call from the council. 'I thought it would be quicker if I looked them up myself.'

'Well, you won't find anything in there.' Bernard snatched the file out of his hands, put it into his office safe and slammed the door. 'I keep all that information on computer.' He unlocked his battered briefcase, took out a disk and slipped it into the machine. 'If you tell me what you want, I can email it through to you.'

'It's okay, I can wait—'

'I said I'll email it!' Seeing Jack's face, he lowered his voice. 'It might – er – take a minute or two to find.'

'Fine. I'll leave you to it. Just send it direct to the council's environment people when you're ready.' Jack tried to look over his shoulder, but Bernard moved his bulky body around, blocking his view. He glanced furtively back at Jack.

'Er – was there something else you wanted?'

'No, that's all, thanks.' Jack watched his hands trembling over the keyboard. 'Are you all right, Bernard?' he asked.

'Of course I'm all right. Why do you ask?'

'No reason. You just seem a bit edgy, that's all.'

'Edgy? I'm not edgy. Why would I be edgy?' Bernard gave a strangled laugh.

Why indeed? Jack thought, as he left Bernard's office. He'd never seen Bernard looking so stressed, not even when he'd accidentally felled a four-hundred-year-old tree with a preservation order and a history that went right back to Charles II.

And why lock that file in the safe? Why not just shove it in the desk drawer? After all, it wasn't as if it was classified information.

Unless there was something in there. Something Bernard didn't want anyone else to see.

He was still pondering it when he rounded the corner and crashed into Charlie by the photocopier.

'Hello, Jack.'

'Charlie.' Embarrassment rushed through him. 'I've – er – been meaning to call you. Are you free for lunch?'

'Lunch? Today?' She pushed her hair back off her face. 'Sorry, Jack, I'm afraid I'm busy.'

'Oh. Right. Tomorrow, then?'

'I'm not sure. Why don't I get my secretary to check the diary and get back to you? Maybe we could get together later in the week?'

'Okay. Thanks.' He scratched his head as he watched her go. What was that all about? She'd seemed so keen the other day. And to think he felt guilty about letting her down!

Charlie allowed herself a small smile of satisfaction as she watched him head back to his office. It would mean going out at lunchtime to avoid him instead of having a sandwich at her desk and catching up with work as she'd planned, but it was worth it. She could even head up to the Victoria Quarter and treat herself to something nice from Harvey Nicks. She'd need a new outfit for her lunch date later in the week.

She was glad she'd decided to back off. Now she could have the pleasure of reeling him in all over again.

Jack called in at Greg's office on the way back to his own. He was behind his desk, surrounded by teetering piles of papers as usual. His in-tray spilled over with unanswered mail and more unanswered emails blinked urgently on his computer screen. How he ever kept track of it all Jack had no idea. His secretary must be on the verge of a nervous breakdown.

He looked up and grinned when Jack walked in. 'Just the man I wanted to see. How did it go with the Ice Queen on Saturday? Did you get her to melt?'

'I don't know what you're talking about.'

'Don't play coy with me, Jacko. I know you spent the night there.'

'How did you know that?'

Greg shook his head pityingly. 'Tyler family grapevine, old son. Your mum rang Ros to say you didn't pick the girls up until Sunday morning.' He leered. 'Anyway, let's hear it. Is it true she wears chain-mail underwear? Tell me everything!'

'So you can report straight back to my sister? No chance.'

'Spoilsport.' Greg said good-naturedly. He leaned back in his chair. 'So if you didn't come to gossip, what did you want to see me about?'

'It's about Bernard Sweeting.'

Greg rolled his eyes. 'Oh Lord, what's he done now? Don't tell me he's gone down with Dutch elm disease?'

'No, but there's definitely something odd about him.' He explained about Bernard's reaction when he found him flicking through his file.

Greg frowned. 'And did you see anything in there?'

'I didn't have time. He snatched it out of my hands before I could look. Then he locked it in the office safe. Doesn't that seem a bit strange to you?'

'It does. But our Bernard's always been a bit strange anyway.' He grinned. 'Maybe he's got some dodgy photos he's downloaded from the internet?'

'I don't know. But I definitely think he's hiding something. Couldn't you check it out?'

'What do you expect me to do? I can't just march in there and insist he shows me the contents of his safe, can I?'

'I suppose not. But there must be some way you can find out?'

Greg sighed. 'If you're that worried about it, I'll think of something.' He wagged a warning finger at Jack. 'But if I accidentally get sight of a load of disturbing porn, I want you to know I'm holding you personally responsible!'

Chapter 22

'For heaven's sake, Neil, it's only a pair of tights. It's not like I'm asking you to wear a bra and thong!'

Neil Wallis folded his beefy arms across his chest and remained resolute. 'No way. No one said nothing about tights when I auditioned for this rotten play.'

The other boys all murmured agreement. Privately Tess agreed too, but there wasn't much she could do about it. It was another of Cynthia Frobisher's edicts from above; a wicker chest full of doublets and hose had been dragged out of the store room because, as Mr Peake explained, 'Mrs F reckoned they'd be suitable for costumes.' Apparently they were left over from the Haxsall Golden Jubilee pageant, when the lower school had inexplicably been dressed up as minstrels and maidens and made to cavort around a maypole on the village green. Quite what that had to do with the Queen's jubilee celebration Tess had no idea. But she was still left with several dozen manky pairs of tights, no costume budget and a mini rebellion on her hands.

'Why can't you lot just stop whingeing and flaming well get on with it?' Maeve Flaherty, aka Ophelia, bellowed from upstage, where she was passing the time giving herself a tattoo with the rusty nib of a fountain pen. She was desperate to get Neil Wallis in a clinch, so Tess had heard from Queen Gertrude. Poor Hamlet didn't stand a chance.

'It's all right for you,' Neil yelled back. 'You don't have to show your bleeding whatsits to the whole school.'

'That'll be a first if she doesn't,' Mark muttered.

'Oi, you, I heard that!' Maeve hitched herself off the box

she was sitting on and advanced on him menacingly. 'One more word out of you and I'll knock your teeth so far down your throat you'll be talking out of your—'

'Let's take five, shall we?' Tess clapped her hands for silence. Her temples were beginning to throb again. She'd got into the habit of downing a couple of Nurofen before each rehearsal, as a precaution.

In the middle of it all, Stephen walked in. 'How's it going?'

'Fine.' Tess gritted her teeth into a smile. 'Apart from the fact I've got half the cast threatening to walk out.' She noticed his glum face. 'What's wrong with you?'

'I've just been called in to see Mrs Frobisher.'

Tess covered her eyes with her hand. 'Oh God, what does she want now? No, don't tell me. She's had another brainwave. She wants us to do this production backwards. In Polish. With balaclavas.'

'No,' said Stephen. 'But she does want us to do it by Christmas.'

'What? We agreed the spring term.'

'I know. But apparently she's told Mr Gant it's all going so well we'll be able to put it on for the parents at the end of this term.'

'Going well? I've seen better organised war zones.' Tess looked around at the chaos. Hamlet had disappeared, the gravedigger was dribbling the skull around the stage, and Ophelia was challenging all-comers to an arm-wrestling contest. 'She'll just have to go back to Mr Gant and tell him she got it wrong, won't she? The way this lot are going, we'll be lucky if we're ready in four months, let alone four weeks.'

'I get the impression she'd like nothing better than to do just that,' Stephen said. 'I expect she'll also tell him the reason we're not ready is because you and I aren't up to the job. She might even talk him into letting her take over.'

'I'd like to see her try.' Tess watched grimly as Polonius

shuffled off the stage, clutching his wounded arm after being trounced by Ophelia. 'She'd probably just cancel the whole thing. Jason, will you stop kicking that skull around? I promised Mr Kramer we wouldn't let it come to any harm.'

She picked up her script wearily. 'Oh well, I suppose we'd better get this show on the road, hadn't we?' She looked around. 'Where's Hamlet? Has anyone seen Neil?'

There was a lot of feet shuffling and awkward looks. Then Jason piped up, 'Please, Miss. He's gone, Miss.'

'Gone? What do you mean, gone?'

'He's packed it in, Miss. Said he didn't want to be Hamlet any more.'

'I think it was the tights that did it, Miss,' Mark Nicholls sniggered.

'Great. Just great. So now I've got to do *Hamlet* with no Hamlet.' Her shoulders slumped. She felt like throwing down her script and following Neil Wallis' example.

Or maybe it was a blessing in disguise? Maybe Mrs Frobisher had done her a favour after all? 'Okay, we're going to have to adopt Plan B.' She turned to Mark. 'You can be Hamlet.'

'What?' He sat upright. 'I'm not wearing those tights.'

'Mark, no one is wearing the tights.' She picked up the offending pair and threw them over her shoulder. 'As of this moment, the tights are officially gone.'

A small cheer went up from the people on-stage. Stephen looked worried. 'But Mrs Frobisher—'

Tess swung round to face him. 'Do you know what? I don't really care what Mrs Frobisher thinks any more.' Stephen must have seen the wild glint in her eye because he backed away nervously. 'We haven't got time to argue. Let's just get this thing done, shall we? We'll try Act Three, Scene One, Hamlet and Ophelia. Don't worry about your lines, Mark. Just read from the script.' Everyone else is, she added silently. 'And Ophelia, remove that gum from your mouth. We'll take it from after the soliloquy.'

'The what?' Maeve stretched a long string of pink gum from between her teeth.

'From where you come in.' Give me strength, Tess thought.

The scene went quite well, considering Hamlet didn't know his lines and Ophelia had all the fragile grace of a New Zealand All Black. Tess was even beginning to feel quite hopeful until Mark put his script down and said, 'None of this makes sense.'

'It's not supposed to make sense, Mark. He's supposed to be ranting like a madman, remember?'

'I know that. But the rest of it doesn't make sense either. I mean this bit: "The power of beauty will sooner transform honesty from what it is to a bawd than the force of honesty can translate beauty to his likeness." What's that all about?'

'Much as I'd love to discuss the many interpretations of Shakespearean verse with you, Mark, I'm afraid we simply don't have time. So just say the lines, would you?'

'How can I say the lines if I don't understand what they mean?'

'What do you mean you don't understand? Are you thick or what?' Maeve snarled.

They carried on for another five minutes. Then Mark's script went down again. 'Why's he telling her to go to a nunnery?'

'He's telling her she might as well become a nun because all men are worthless liars,' Tess explained.

'He's right there,' Maeve muttered.

'Oh, and you'd know, wouldn't you? You've had enough of them.'

'What did you say? You take that back, Mark Nicholls!'

'Children, please—'

'Make me.'

'I will as well!'

'Ooh, I'm scared.'

'You flaming well ought to be. 'Cos I'm going to tell my brother and he'll come down and murder you.'

Tess turned to her sharply. 'What did you say?'

'Nothing, Miss.' Maeve turned red. 'I didn't say anything.'

'She said she'd get her brother on to Mark, Miss.' Queen Gertrude, ever ready with the gossip, stepped forward. 'He's a squaddie, up at Catterick.'

'He's just come back from Afghanistan,' Maeve added. She turned to Mark. 'He'd sort you out, no problem.'

'That's it!' Tess shouted. They both looked at her, baffled.

'Miss?' Maeve frowned. 'I was only kidding, our Lee wouldn't really murder anyone—'

'I don't mean that.' Tess beamed at them both. 'Look, let's call it a day, shall we? Why don't you all go home? And don't bother taking your scripts with you, you won't be needing them after today.'

They left with backward looks over their shoulders, as if they couldn't make their minds up whether Tess had flipped or not. Stephen didn't seem too sure either.

'What are you playing at? None of them know their lines.'

'That doesn't matter.' She flicked through the script. 'Mark's right, none of this is relevant. That's why they can't learn it. It means nothing to them.'

'So?'

'So I'm going to make it mean something.' She plonked down on the edge of the stage next to him. 'Maeve saying that about her brother gave me the idea. It was just like Ophelia in the play. Her brother was a soldier and ended up sorting out her love life, didn't he?' Stephen went on looking at her blankly. 'So, why not retell this story in a way the kids will understand? Make it modern-day?'

Stephen's expression slowly transformed from blank to horrified. 'You mean you're going to rewrite Shakespeare?'

'Only a bit. It'll be the same story, but just a bit – tweaked. I'm sure the kids will find it easier to remember the lines.'

Stephen shook his head. 'Mrs Frobisher's not going to like it.'

'Mrs Frobisher's not going to know, is she?' She smiled at his stunned expression. 'Don't worry, Stephen. I'm sure it will be a lovely surprise for her on opening night!'

Charlie was fifteen minutes late for lunch. Jack ordered a bottle of wine and chewed nervously on a breadstick as he waited for her.

Finally she arrived. All eyes swivelled to follow the tall, sexy redhead in the black trouser suit and spiked heels as she made her way through the crowded restaurant to his table.

'Sorry I'm late. Something came up.' She slid into the seat opposite. Ignoring the open bottle of Frascati on the table, she summoned the waiter and ordered a mineral water.

'So,' she said. 'What did you want to see me about?'

Jack stared at her blankly. Had he got it wrong? The way she was acting, it was as if Saturday night had never happened.

Her coolness unnerved him. 'It – it's about the other morning,' he stammered. 'I just wanted to say I'm sorry for rushing off like that.'

'It's fine, no problem.'

'It's not that I didn't want to spend time with you, but I had to collect the girls.'

'So you said.'

The waiter arrived and took their order. As he walked away, Jack said, 'I would have stayed if I could. But I'd already said I'd be home the night before, I didn't want them to worry . . .' He toyed with his knife and ended up dropping it on the floor. When he came up, Charlie was watching him, a slight smile curving her lips.

'I told you, it's absolutely fine. Look, I'm a big girl now, you don't have to fob me off with excuses.' She shrugged. 'It was a one-night stand, simple as that. We both knew what we were doing. It was fun, but it's over. End of story.'

'I'm not the kind of person who has one-night stands.'

'And you think I am?'

'I'm not saying that.'

'So what are you saying, Jack?' Her eyes were challenging and direct.

He only wished he knew. He'd been trying to work it out for the past three days, ever since he fled from her flat.

In the end the only thing he could think of was to be totally honest. 'That night . . .' His voice faltered. 'You were the first woman I'd been with – since Miranda died.'

Her expression softened a fraction.

'It felt like I was being unfaithful. That's why I panicked and ran. It was nothing to do with you.'

'Why didn't you tell me?'

'I don't know. But it was wrong of me to run away like that. I'm sorry.'

'I can't say it didn't hurt.' Charlie topped up her glass, this time from the wine bottle. 'Do you think you'll ever feel like you're not cheating?'

'I don't know.'

The waiter arrived with their food. A Caesar salad for her, sea bass for him. Neither of them touched it.

'How do you think your wife would have felt about all this? Would she have wanted you to spend the rest of your life alone?'

'Probably not.' They'd actually talked about it once, in the half joking way people did when they were young and thought they had their whole lives ahead of them. Miranda said she'd like to think of there being someone to take care of Jack and the girls after she'd gone. He said if another man

243

so much as looked at her he would come back and haunt them both.

Thinking about it made him feel heavy with sadness. 'I don't know what Miranda would have made of it,' he said. 'But even if she did give her blessing, I'm still not sure I'm ready for another relationship yet.'

'Who said anything about a relationship?'

Jack frowned. 'I'm sorry, I just assumed—'

'That I'd be trying to trap you into making a commitment? Do I look that desperate?' Charlie picked up her fork. 'If I'd wanted to find a man and settle down, I could have done it a long time ago. At the moment I just want to have fun.'

'Fun?' Jack looked rueful. 'I think I've forgotten what that is.'

'Then I'm just going to have to remind you.' Charlie reached across the table and covered his hand with hers. 'We're both grown-ups, Jack. What's wrong with us getting together and enjoying each other's company? No promises, no pressure. We'll just see what happens.'

'What about the girls?'

She withdrew her hand slightly. 'What about them?'

'They come as part of the package. Do you think you can handle that?'

'I don't see why not. They seem like very sweet kids.' Jack grinned. 'We are talking about Emily and Sophie, aren't we?'

'Like you said, they come as part of the package. As long as I get you to myself occasionally, I'm sure we'll get along fine.'

He didn't share her optimism. 'It might be a bit difficult at first. Particularly with Emily. She took her mother's death especially hard. I don't know how she'll take to the idea of me with someone else.'

'We'll find out, won't we?' Was it his imagination, or did Charlie's smile seem a little fixed as she attacked her salad?

'Oh no!' Tess tapped frantically on her laptop keyboard. 'Where's it gone? Where's it gone?'

Phil and Dan looked over from where they were watching *Star Trek*. 'What have you done now?'

'Deleted all my notes, that's all. Everything I'd done so far. Bloody stupid computer!' She bashed the Return key a few more times in sheer panic.

'Can I help you?' Phil strolled over. 'What seems to be the problem?'

'If I knew that, I'd fix it, wouldn't I?' She hit the Return key again. Nothing happened.

'Calm down. Bashing the thing won't help, will it?'

'No, but it makes me feel a hell of a lot better!'

'She's hopeless with computers,' Dan called over from the sofa.

Tess shot him an evil look. 'Thank you, Dan,' she said. 'I think even I can spot when the wretched thing doesn't work.'

Phil sat down beside her at the table and pulled her keyboard towards him before she could do any more damage. 'Let's have a look, shall we? I'm sure it can't be too bad.'

Tess' shoulders relaxed. She understood why his clients loved him. She could have put a hatchet through the damn thing and he would have made it sound like a temporary blip. Whatever it was, Phil could fix it.

Or so she thought. His brows gradually lowered in a frown as he tapped a couple of keys, then a few more. Then he wiggled the connection cord in its socket. Always a bad sign. Tess only did that when she was truly desperate.

Finally, he said, 'What exactly did you do to it?'

'I didn't do anything. It's got a grudge against me. It's never liked me.'

'It isn't a person, Tess. It doesn't have feelings.'

'Want to bet? If that thing could talk, the first thing it would say would be "I hate your guts".'

'If that thing could talk, the first thing it would say would be "Get some IT lessons, woman, and stop being such a dinosaur," ' Dan said.

Phil straightened up, his eyes still on the blank screen. 'Well, I think I know what you've done to it.'

'Do you?'

'It's what we in techno-speak call well and truly buggered.' He grinned at her. 'But don't worry, I'm sure it's fixable. I'll take it away and tinker with it, if I may?'

'Would you? Thanks.'

'No problem. What were you working on, anyway?'

'*Hamlet*.'

He frowned. 'I hate to tell you this, but it's already been done.'

'Very funny,' Tess said. 'I need it for rehearsals on Friday, if that's possible?'

Phil sucked on his teeth like a builder who's about to tell someone their house is subsiding. 'Two days? That doesn't give me much time. But I'll do my best.'

'Thanks, Phil.'

He stayed for another glass of wine then headed home, earlier than they'd expected. 'I'd better make a start on your mother's computer,' he told a disappointed Dan. 'Looks like it might be an all-night job.'

'I feel sorry for him, having to go back to that hotel,' Dan said as they waved him off.

'All that luxury? I don't.' She could have done with a few days of pampering herself. Life was very pressured at the moment, with the mock GCSEs, Stephen and Marjorie both away on courses and, of course, the wretched school play. With the first night less than four weeks away Tess was beginning to realise just how much she'd taken on. She hadn't even finished writing it yet. 'It must be bliss to pick up the phone and order room service instead of going to all the hassle of cooking.'

'It's a bit impersonal, though. And it must be costing him

a bomb.' Tess could see the way Dan's mind was working moments before he said, 'Why don't we ask him to stay here?'

'For a start, we only have two bedrooms. Where's he going to sleep?'

'On the sofa?'

'Oh, he'd love that. Why would he give up a nice comfortable hotel room for our sofa?'

'He wouldn't mind. At least he wouldn't have to keep going backwards and forwards all the time. And it would be nice to have him here,' he added wistfully.

Nice for whom? Tess wondered. Dan might be besotted by his new dad, but she couldn't imagine anything worse than sharing a house with Phil. Not because she disliked him or anything, but she was used to having her own space. The thought of meeting him bleary-eyed over the cornflakes every morning wasn't appealing.

Dan seemed to read her thoughts. 'You do like him, don't you?'

'I wouldn't go that far.'

'But you've got to admit he's a nice guy?'

'He's okay. He could be a lot worse. But that doesn't mean I want to live with him.'

'I thought you two seemed to be getting on really well?' Dan sounded casual, but he didn't fool Tess.

'What's that supposed to mean?'

'Nothing. Just commenting, that's all.'

'Dan!' Tess gave him a warning glare. 'I know what you're up to and I'm telling you now it's not going to work.'

'I don't know what you're talking about.'

'Really? So all this sneaking off and leaving us alone together isn't part of some great plan? What about dropping out at the last moment so we have to go out to dinner without you?'

'I told you, I had a college assignment.' Dan averted his face, but she could see he was blushing.

'You seem to have a lot of those at the moment. Usually when your father's coming round.' Tess folded her arms. 'There's no point in denying it. I know you're trying to set us up.'

'As if!' Dan looked indignant. 'Why should I care who you go out with?'

'Good question,' Tess said.

They lapsed into silence for a moment. Then he said, 'But what's so wrong about it anyway? Phil's an okay bloke, you said so yourself. And I like him.'

'Oh, so that makes it all right, does it? It doesn't matter what I think, as long as you like him.' Tess turned on him furiously. 'Dan, I don't need you to organise my love life for me!'

'Someone's got to. You're not making a very good job of it yourself.'

'Thanks a lot!'

'Okay, then. When was the last time you had a boyfriend?'

'I don't know, do I?'

'See what I mean? You're thirty-four, Mum. You're not getting any younger. You should find someone before it's too late.'

'You make me sound like a mangy old dog at the RSPCA no one wants! The only reason I don't have a man is because I'm too busy.'

'Doing what?'

'Looking after you, for a start!' As soon as she'd said it she wished she could bite the words back. She'd always been careful not to make Dan feel as if he was any kind of burden to her, because he really wasn't. And now she'd just gone and blurted out something like that. 'I'm sorry, I didn't mean that—'

'I know. But the thing is I can look after myself these

days. It's you I'm worried about. This time next year I could be away at college if I get accepted. Then you'll be all on your own. I don't want to think of you like that.'

'I won't be on my own. I'll have my work and my friends. And I'll have Gran.'

'Great. You can go to the Over Sixties club together!' Dan smiled wryly. 'Seriously though, Mum, I don't like to think of you by yourself. I couldn't handle the guilt of you growing old alone and being eaten by your cats.'

'I don't have a cat. I don't even like cats.'

'You know what I mean.'

Tess smiled. How strange to think that all the time she'd been worrying about how Dan was going to cope when he left home, he'd been thinking the same about her.

'So you reckon I should grab your father while I can, so I don't end up alone and desperate. Is that it?'

'You could do a lot worse. And it's nice having him around, isn't it? Almost like we're a real family.'

'I thought we were a real family?'

'We are. But having Phil here sort of makes it more real. Now I know how all the other kids felt when they talked about their mums and dads.'

A lump rose in her throat. She'd never realised Dan felt the loss so badly. She'd done her best over the years to be mother and father to him, and it looked as if she'd failed.

He must have read her forlorn expression, because he said, 'I didn't mean that the way it sounded. You've been great, you really have. I didn't even think about Phil for years. Not until he was here. Now, I don't know – it feels right. I just wish we could make it permanent, that's all.'

'And how does your father feel about this? Or doesn't he get a vote either?'

'I'm sure he'd have you. And wouldn't it be nice for you to have someone to take care of you?'

'I can take care of myself, thank you very much!'

'Yes, but it'd be nice not to have to, wouldn't it?'

Yes, it would be nice, Tess thought, after Dan had gone to bed. It would be nice to have someone to share her worries with, to talk to at the end of a miserable, frustrating day. Another person to take some of the pressure off, to shout down the phone at repairmen to get them to turn up on time, to help carry the suitcases when they went on holiday and take the photos. All their holiday snaps were of either her or Dan, very rarely of them together, because one of them had to hold the camera.

It would also be nice to have someone to share the good times with, to laugh with, to get all soppy with on Valentine's Day.

But she knew Phil wasn't that someone. It sounded like Dan had got it all neatly sewn up in his mind. She and Phil would get together, he would have the two parents he'd apparently always wanted, and Tess wouldn't have to be lonely.

But surely you could be just as lonely with the wrong person as you could be on your own? And Phil was definitely the wrong person. They got on together, far better than she'd imagined they would. But she knew it could never go further than that. If it hadn't been for her getting pregnant, they would probably have split up anyway.

Sorry, Dan, she thought. Much as she would have done anything for her son, she couldn't make herself fall in love with someone.

Chapter 23

Emily was very surprised when her father suggested a shopping trip to Leeds. He hated shopping, especially with her. They'd both agreed early on that the best way to avoid killing each other was for him to give her a wodge of cash and let her get on with it. But here he was, bundling them into the car, apparently looking forward to spending some quality time together.

Sophie was madly excited, of course, but Emily couldn't help wondering what he was up to. She sat beside him in the front seat, listening to him hum tunelessly to boring old Eric Clapton. He seemed in such a good mood. Too good for a Saturday-afternoon shopping trip anyway.

Then she found out why. He'd headed straight for Next, saying he needed to look for a new shirt. After browsing listlessly in the Womenswear department for a few minutes, Emily had returned to find he still hadn't bought anything.

'Haven't you finished yet?'

'Hang on, I'm still deciding.'

That wasn't like him either. He usually dashed in and bought the first thing that came to hand. Most of the time he didn't even look at it until he'd got home. Now he stood there, a blue shirt in one hand, lemon in the other, as if his life depended on his choice.

'Buy the blue one.'

'What's wrong with the yellow?'

'Nothing, if you don't mind looking gay.' Emily stifled a yawn. 'Why don't you just buy them both? Come on, I'm starving.'

'Just a minute.' He kept looking around, craning over the heads of the milling shoppers. Emily frowned.

'Who are you looking for? The fashion police?'

'Jack! What a surprise.'

Emily swung round. There was Charlie, carrier bags in hand, her dark-red hair swinging glossily around her made-up face. She wore a cream sweater, high-heeled boots and chocolate leather jeans that looked as if they must have cost a fortune.

She watched Charlie move in to kiss her father. She was heading for the lips, but he averted his face at the last minute so she caught his cheek instead.

'Hi, Charlie. Fancy seeing you here.' Jack turned to Emily and Sophie. 'You remember Charlie, don't you, girls?'

Charlie beamed at them. Emily glowered back. Did they think she was stupid, or something? His surprised act didn't fool her for a second. This was a set-up. Why else would he be so keen to take them to Leeds? And why else would he be hanging around, dithering over a shirt?

And why, come to think of it, would Charlie Ferguson be in the men's department?

'I was just looking for a new shirt.' Jack held them both up. 'What do you think?'

Charlie considered them for a moment. 'The lemon one, definitely,' she said. 'It's very you.'

'Do you think so? Emily thinks it might be a bit much.'

'Nonsense, you could do with livening up your image. Don't you think so, Emily?' She turned her dazzling fake smile on to her.

'Don't ask me,' Emily shrugged, then added under her breath, 'Who cares what I think anyway?'

But no one heard her. They were already on their way to the cash desk, Sophie skipping happily behind them. With the hideous yellow shirt.

She'd hoped Charlie might disappear after that, but then

her father said, 'We were just on our way to lunch in McDonald's. Would you like to join us?'

'I'd love to,' Charlie said. 'But you'll have to tell me what to order, I've never been there before.'

'Never been to McDonald's?' Sophie looked shocked. 'What, never ever?'

Charlie shook her head. 'Never ever.'

'Then you've missed one of the culinary treats of the century,' her father said. 'But don't worry. We'll look after you, won't we, girls?'

Sophie nodded enthusiastically. Emily rolled her eyes in disgust. This was supposed to be their day out, just the three of them. Now Charlie had hijacked it. Why couldn't she just butt out? They spent precious little time alone with him as it was, without her turning up and ruining everything.

Not that Sophie seemed to mind. She was already cuddled up next to Charlie in the queue, pointing things out in the illuminated overhead menu. Charlie was looking apprehensive.

'Don't they do salad?' she asked. Emily watched the way her father grinned at her. Almost lovingly, she thought. Her stomach flipped with anxiety. He couldn't. He just couldn't. It was like all her worst fears were coming true.

Charlie monopolised him all the way through lunch, talking about boring stuff to do with work. Even her father looked glazed, listening to her. Emily watched her pick at her fries – she'd refused even to consider a burger – and wished she'd choke on them. At least it might shut her up.

Why couldn't he see how fake she was, with her big smiles and pretending to be charmed by everything? And the way she looked at him, like he was Brad Pitt and Tom Cruise all rolled into one. It made her feel sick, but she couldn't stop watching them. Any second now Charlie was going to lean over and kiss him and then it really would be goodbye, Big Mac.

Sophie seemed to be won over. She stared up at her with

an awed expression. Emily knew she was probably taking in every detail of her hair and make-up so she could copy them at home later. She was like a pathetic little puppy dog, admiring her shoes, her hair, her perfume.

'I like your trousers.' She stroked them with ketchupy fingers. Emily smiled as Charlie squirmed and tried not to look disgusted. 'Did you get them from London?'

'Actually, I got them from Milan.'

'Milan!' Sophie looked impressed.

'As if you even know where that is,' Emily said disgustedly.

'I do!'

'Go on, then. Where is it? She probably thinks it's the other side of Leeds.' She saw Charlie smiling and shut up. How dare she think she was making a joke for her benefit! 'I think wearing leather and fur is cruel,' she added loudly, to put her in her place. 'Animals die just so people can wear their skins. It's barbaric.'

'Some might think that burger you've eaten is pretty barbaric too,' Charlie pointed out coolly.

Emily looked down at the half-eaten Big Mac in her hand. It was difficult to square her belief in animal rights with her love of burgers and bacon sandwiches, but she couldn't give them up. She knew she was on dodgy moral ground, but Charlie had no right to point it out. 'That's different,' she muttered.

'Why? Because it's you and not me?'

'People need to eat. They don't need to wear leather.'

'They don't need to eat meat, either, but they do because they enjoy it. And it might interest you to know that the intensive cattle farming needed for those burgers causes a massive depletion in the Amazonian rainforest. They cut down areas the size of this country every day just to make room for the cows. How do you feel about that?'

Emily met her cool, challenging gaze across the table. She could feel her face burning with rage and humiliation.

'Would anyone like a McFlurry?' Her father tried to break the tension, but it was too late.

After lunch they headed for Top Shop, Charlie still trailing along with them. Why didn't she take the hint and go? Emily watched her trying on bandannas and belts with Sophie, as if she was remotely interested in them. Fake, fake, fake. Normally it would be her Sophie was pestering to try glittery eyeshadows on the back of her hand, but she'd forgotten all about her, she was so enchanted by her new best friend.

Emily sloped off to the other end of the shop and began trying on shoes, just for something to do. She tried on a pair of strappy wedge-heeled mules just for a laugh. They were hideous tart's shoes, about a million miles away from the trainers she usually wore.

'Very nice.' She looked up. Charlie was standing over her. For God's sake, couldn't she get away from that woman? 'You ought to get your dad to buy them for you. They make your legs look amazing.'

'I can make my own mind up, thanks.' Emily shook off the shoes as if they were infected and stuffed her feet back into her tatty trainers.

'Suit yourself. But they did look good.'

What would you know? Emily thought. She was ancient, thirty at least. As she stood up, Charlie said, 'Sophie's thinking of buying a T-shirt. She wants your advice.'

'What does she want my advice for? She's got you.' Emily elbowed past her and headed for where her father was loitering by the door, looking bored as usual. 'I want to go shopping on my own,' she announced flatly.

'Why? I thought this was meant to be a family trip?'

Emily shot a meaningful glance at Charlie. 'So did I,' she said.

'Well, I think that went rather well,' Charlie said wryly, as they watched Emily slope out of the shop.

'Take no notice of her. She's always like that. It's her hormones.'

'I don't think so. Not this time.' Charlie shook her head. 'I told you it wasn't a good idea to spring this surprise thing on them. She wasn't fooled for a minute.' At the time she'd allowed herself to be persuaded because it seemed a lot easier than facing them in a formal meeting. Now she was beginning to wish she'd just got it over with. She suspected she'd made an enemy for life.

And an enemy like Emily could make it even more difficult for her to get close to Jack.

'You've certainly won Sophie over.'

Charlie smiled. Sophie was sweet, if a little demanding. But there was only so long she could discuss the relative merits of pearly versus glittery nail polish without her brain exploding with boredom.

At least Sophie wasn't as sulky as Emily. The way she'd looked at her in that awful burger place! All she'd done was try to have a reasoned argument with her. Emily demanded to be treated like an adult, but she couldn't handle it.

Was it always going to be this hard? she wondered.

She looked at Jack. Being with him made up for it. Or so she hoped. They'd only actually been out together once, and that was only a rushed drink after work because he had to get back for some concert at Sophie's school.

She threaded her arm through his. 'As I've been such a good girl, do I get my reward?'

He grinned. 'Don't tell me you want that rhinestone tiara you and Sophie were trying on?'

'Not quite. I was thinking more of dinner tonight?'

'Tonight?' His face fell. 'Sorry, I can't. Sophie's got a friend coming to sleep over.'

When am I going to be invited to sleep over? she wondered. 'Couldn't you leave them with a babysitter?'

'I could – if I could find one with nerves of steel. No, I'd better be there in case they run riot. You know what kids are like.'

Charlie forced a smile. No, she didn't. But she was beginning to find out.

Two days later, Jack had to go up to the Westpoint site again, to meet the council's highways officers about a possible change to the traffic access. It was late afternoon by the time they'd finished. The trees at the edge of the site spread their skeletal branches against the darkening sky. The air had the November smell of burning leaves, mingled with the metallic tang of the factories' fumes. A sparrow hawk skimmed and dodged overhead. Jack watched it wheeling through the sky before it plunged like a missile towards the ground after its prey.

Beyond the trees, huddled behind a barbed-wire fence, he could make out the ramshackle shapes of the Second Chance buildings. He wondered if the barbed wire was to keep intruders out, or the workers in.

He trudged around the perimeter of the site, trying to imagine how it might all look with thousands of square metres of shops on it. All that activity, all those people. Cars streaming in and out, a complex network of roads and roundabouts cutting across the field, the still night air illuminated like daylight by the brightly lit shops, everyone coming to buy, to browse, to gawp at the spectacle. Piped muzak replacing the exuberant chatter of the starlings high in the trees . . .

Usually he was pretty good at visualising how things might look – that was part of his job, after all – but this time the picture jarred.

He turned away from the scene and headed back to his car. As he approached the gap in the fence, he disturbed a couple of blackbirds pulling at the ground. They rose into the sky with indignant, clattering cries. As Jack drew nearer he could see why they were so furious at being disturbed.

They'd found a patch of ground where the earth had recently been turned over, making it a feasting ground for hungry birds.

He wouldn't have noticed it in the gathering darkness, but now he could see the blunt edges of where a spade had been. Whoever had dug the hole had obviously tried to cover their tracks; bits of turf had been hastily laid over the mound to disguise it. But they hadn't done a very good job. The shape was still clearly visible. A dark patch, roughly the size and shape of a grave . . .

'What you doing?'

He swung round and found himself blinded by a torchbeam aimed straight at his eyes. He lifted his hand to shield the light. 'What the—'

'Oh, it's you.' Sam Dobbs lowered the torch. He was in his usual grubby duffel coat, his face grim under his knitted hat. 'What do you want? Come to dig it up, have you?'

'Dig what up?'

'I dunno. Whatever's buried down there.'

Jack took a step back from the mound. 'What makes you think there's anything buried down there?'

'Look at it, son.' Sam gestured towards the ground with his torch. 'It'd have to be a mole the size of a carthorse to do that kind of damage. And I don't think anyone would come all the way up here to make mud pies, do you?' He shook his head. 'No, there's definitely something down there. Question is – what is it?'

Jack looked at the dark, shapeless mound and felt his heart quicken. He knew what he thought it was. He just didn't like to say it out loud.

'Are you going to dig it up and find out, or shall I?'

He caught the amused glint in Sam's eye. 'Do you know anything about this?'

'Got nowt to do with me.' Sam was infuriatingly enigmatic. 'See nowt, say nowt, that's my motto.'

'I'm sure that comes in very useful in your line of work.'

'Being a vicar, you mean? I s'pose it does.'

'I was thinking more of your sideline as a latter-day Fagin.'

'Now hang about!' Sam advanced on him. 'Exactly what are you suggesting?'

'It seems a bit funny, that's all. This – thing – appears here, with your lot living next door.'

'So you think one of my lot, as you put it, has done someone in and buried them here? Is that what you're saying?'

'Maybe. Or it could be stolen goods or loot from a post office robbery. You tell me.'

They stared at each other for a moment. Then Sam threw back his head and laughed.

'Loot? Loot? You've been watching too many films, I reckon.' He wiped a tear from his eye with the sleeve of his coat. 'You're priceless, son, you know that? Those lads wouldn't know how to rob a post office. And they're about as likely to do a murder as you or me. They're strictly small time. And if they did do anything like that, most of them have got the good sense not to bury the evidence in their own back yard!' He shook his head. 'No, I reckon you want to look for your culprit a bit closer to home, before you go flinging your accusations around.'

Jack's eyes narrowed. 'Meaning?'

'Meaning the fella I saw up here with a spade wasn't one of my lot. He was one of yours.'

'You saw someone?'

'Course I did. I keep my eyes open and my wits about me, lad. Not like some people.' He tapped his temple. 'Loot, indeed! You're a funny one.'

Jack ignored him. 'So who was it? The man you saw?'

'How should I know? All I know is I've seen him hanging around with your bunch. The last time you were up here, as a matter of fact. Little bloke, round glasses. Bit like Himmler.'

'Bernard Sweeting?'

'Is that his name? I wouldn't know.'

Jack looked around. It made sense. Bernard was their environmental expert. He was probably just taking some soil samples or something.

He turned back to the mound. But that was one hell of a soil sample. It looked as if he'd dug up a wheelbarrow load.

'And you definitely saw him burying something?'

'Now I couldn't swear to that. But he looked a bit shifty when I came up and spoke to him.'

'You spoke to him? What did he say?'

'Nothing much. He wasn't too friendly, as a matter of fact. Told me in no uncertain terms that this wasn't my land or my business and I had no right poking about in it, either.'

Bernard had a point there, Jack admitted silently. And Sam Dobbs could seem a threatening character, with his squashed-in prizefighter's face and gruff manner. He was probably just trying to defend himself.

But something still didn't add up. Why would Bernard be taking more soil samples now? Unless there was something he wasn't telling anyone.

'So when was this?' he asked.

Sam shrugged. 'Not long. About a week ago. Maybe a bit longer. It was after you came up here with your little girl, anyway. How is she, by the way?'

'She's fine,' Jack answered absently, his thoughts racing.

'She's a lovely little kid. Still got that treasure of hers, has she?'

'Treasure?'

'That bone. The way she was clutching it you'd think it was the crown jewels.' Sam smiled fondly.

Jack didn't answer him. He looked around. Come to think of it, Sophie had dug it up somewhere around here . . .

Then he spotted it, sticking out of the ground, about ten

yards away. The piece of stick Sophie had been digging with.

Fragments of disconnected thought rushed around in his brain. He tried to put them all together, to make sense of them. But it was difficult, like doing a jigsaw with half the pieces missing.

'Are you all right, son?' Sam watched him with a look of concern.

'I'm fine.' Jack thought for a moment. 'Sam, what do you know about cracking safes?'

Sam sighed. 'I already told you, my boys are all strictly petty crime—'

'What about you?'

'Who have you been talking to?'

There was something about the sharp way he said it that made Jack suddenly realise that maybe Sam Dobbs' shady criminal past hadn't been as small time as he liked to make out.

'Forget it,' he said. 'I shouldn't have asked you. I'll think of some other way of finding out what I need to know. Be seeing you, Sam.'

He started to walk away, but Sam called him back. 'This thing you need to know – there wouldn't be any mischief behind it, would there?'

'I don't know. That's what I'm trying to find out.'

'So it wouldn't be like you were trying to steal anything?'

He shook his head. 'I think someone's hiding something and I want to find out what it is.'

Sam scratched his stubbly chin for a moment. 'In that case, I don't suppose it would do any harm to give you a few tips, would it? Just in case you decided to have a go yourself, like?'

Jack smiled. 'I think the Almighty might overlook it, just this once.'

'I hope so, lad. He's overlooked enough in my life already, I'd hate to go blotting my copybook with Him all over again.' He looked back at the mound thoughtfully. 'You don't really think there's a body buried there, do you?'

'I don't know,' Jack said. 'But I've got a bad feeling about this place.'

Chapter 24

'Where's Ophelia? Has anyone seen her yet?'

Stephen looked up from helping a soldier on with his boots. 'She's still at the rugby match. Helen says she'll drive her straight over as soon as the game's finished.'

'She'd better get a move on. The curtain goes up in ten minutes!'

Tess threaded her way amid the backstage chaos, tripping over strewn clothing and discarded props. Out in the front of house, the school orchestra was struggling through *Happy Days Are Here Again*.

'Not exactly appropriate for *Hamlet*, is it?' Stephen grimaced.

'I don't know. They're certainly murdering it.' Tess winced as the horn section tried and failed to hit a top C. It wasn't what she would have chosen, but Mr Herriman the music teacher had insisted it was the only thing he could manage. And since he was already on Prozac and heading for his second nervous breakdown, Tess had thought it wiser and kinder not to argue.

He wasn't the only one suffering with his nerves. Tess peered through a crack in the heavy velvet curtains. The audience was filling up as parents shuffled into their seats, each clutching their photocopied programmes. In the front row she spotted the Chair of Governors, flanked by Eric Gant on one side and Cynthia Frobisher on the other. Seeing her there made Tess feel sick with anxiety.

'Maybe this wasn't such a good idea after all,' she said to Stephen.

'Are you kidding? The kids love it.' He nodded to where Rosencrantz and Guildenstern were running through their lines behind the black curtain that screened the wings from the main stage. He was right. Her jazzed-up modern-day version had certainly captured their imaginations. The cast had not only turned up regularly for rehearsals, they'd even volunteered for extra sessions to make sure they were word perfect. For the last two weeks, Tess kept stumbling across little knots of them in corridors, corners of the school playground and even the toilets, testing each other on their lines.

'I just hope Cynthia feels the same.' Tess glanced back at her through the curtains. She was picking up her programme from under her seat, looking at the cover. Tess steeled herself. Any moment now she would open it, read the blurb and realise exactly what was going on.

But then Marjorie Wheeler arrived and Cynthia tucked the programme back under her seat without reading it. Tess watched them talking, their heads close together. Bitching about her, probably. They'd have plenty to bitch about by the interval.

She looked up and spotted Jack Tyler on the fifth row. Charlie Ferguson was beside him, dressed in a grey trouser suit that would have been mannish on anyone else but looked stunning on her. Jack was still in his work clothes. They must have come straight from the office.

She leant over and whispered something to Jack. He laughed, gazing straight back into her eyes. Tess imagined them driving up from Leeds together, discussing something high-powered that had happened at the office. And what had she been doing all day? Making cardboard swords.

She was just about to drag herself away from the curtain when she saw Helen Wesley come into the back of the hall, still in her ultra-short PE kit, blonde hair caught up in a girlish ponytail. She looked around, then hurried down to the stage, oblivious to the admiring stares of countless fathers that followed her.

'Psst!' Tess beckoned her over from between the curtains. 'Where the hell have you been?'

'I've just come from the hospital. There's been an accident.'

Tess' blood ran like ice through her veins. 'What kind of accident? Where's Maeve?'

'She was badly tackled during the match. Sorry, Tess, she's got a broken ankle.'

Tess reached out from between the curtains and dragged Helen through them. 'So where is she? Couldn't you just bring her anyway? She could have limped a bit, for God's sake. No one would have noticed.'

'No, but they might have noticed the two black eyes.'

Tess leant back against the lighting pillar. She suddenly felt very weak. 'Well, that's it, isn't it? It's over. We can't go on without an Ophelia.'

'Haven't you got an understudy or something?'

'Do me a favour! I had enough trouble finding one Ophelia, let alone two!'

'Excuse me?' Emily coughed behind them.

'Not now, Emily. Can't you see I'm having a crisis?' Tess said irritably. 'Why did you have to make her play in that stupid rugby match?' she asked Helen.

'Don't blame me!'

'Why not? You're the reason she's got a broken ankle!'

'Miss Doyle?'

Tess rolled her eyes and turned to face her. 'Yes, Emily? What is it?'

'I can do it.'

'I beg your pardon?'

'I can do Ophelia. I mean, I know all her lines.' Emily looked from one to the other and blushed to the roots of her hair.

'How come?'

'Never mind that!' Helen interrupted. 'She's the answer to all your prayers.'

But Tess wasn't used to having her prayers answered. It was too easy. 'Are you sure you can do this? It's a big role.'

'I think so.'

'Does it matter?' Helen said. 'For God's sake, get her in that costume before she changes her mind!'

For once it did seem as if God might be on her side. Emily turned out to be word perfect, and so was everyone else.

As the house lights dimmed and the soldiers – modern-day versions in fatigues 'borrowed' from Maeve's brother's barracks – took their places on the stage, Tess hung back in the wings to watch the audience's reaction.

Or more to the point, Cynthia Frobisher's reaction. While the parents' faces changed from glazed boredom to delight when they realised they were being treated to a shortened version of the story in modern language, Cynthia's grew rigid with displeasure. The lights were low but Tess was sure she could see steam rising from her ears.

In the interval, when she saw Cynthia rise from her seat and make her way purposefully towards the stage, flanked by an equally outraged-looking Marjorie Wheeler, she quickly dived down the back stairs, out into the corridor and outside before they could catch her.

The night was cold but clear. Beyond the dark ridge of the science block she could hear the whine of traffic on the bypass. The playground was illuminated by pools of sulphurous light from the street lamps.

She turned the corner and nearly fell over Jack Tyler sitting on the steps of the science block, smoking.

He jumped and dropped his cigarette when he saw her. Tess smiled. 'Shouldn't you be doing that behind the bike sheds?'

He looked ruefully at the cigarette he'd just ground

under his heel. 'Stupid, isn't it? Old habits die hard in these places.'

'Do you mind if I join you?'

'Please.' He shifted along the step to make room for her. 'Where's Charlie?'

'Queuing for the ladies'. I just came out to get some air.' Tess sat down beside him. 'I didn't know you smoked?'

'I don't. Only when I'm nervous.'

'What are you nervous about?'

'What do you think? My little girl's up there on that stage.' He took another cigarette out of the packet and lit it. 'She never told me she had a main part.'

'She didn't. Not until an hour ago.'

'You're joking?'

Tess shook her head. 'She took over when Ophelia dropped out. She's pretty good, isn't she?'

'Good? She's bloody amazing.' He took a drag on his cigarette and watched the smoke ring drift up into the night sky. 'I didn't realise how grown up she was until I saw her up there. Her mother would have been proud of her,' he said quietly.

He covered his eyes with his hand. It took a moment before Tess realised he was crying, his broad shoulders shaking with emotion.

Without thinking, she put her arms around him. He didn't resist. He let her pull him closer, hold him against her. She could feel his hair bristling against her cheek. He smelt of soap and freshly washed shirt.

After a few moments he pulled away from her. 'I'm sorry,' he said gruffly. 'I don't know what came over me.'

'Here,' she took a tissue out of her bag and handed it to him. 'It's crumpled but clean.'

'Thanks. God, I feel silly.' He wiped his eyes. 'You must think I'm an idiot.'

'Of course not.'

'Charlie will, if she sees me like this.' He stood up and

brushed himself down. 'I'd better get back inside, before she thinks I've done a bunk.' He darted a quick glance at her. 'Thanks,' he said.

And then he was gone.

Tess watched him hurrying back to the school hall. She felt desperately sorry for him. What kind of relationship must he have with Charlie Ferguson if he couldn't let her see him cry?

She didn't go back inside for the second half. She stayed on the steps, hugging herself to keep the cold out and wishing she'd had the sense to grab her cardie before she made her escape. A thin shirt was no match for the biting December air. But she was too afraid to go back inside for it in case Cynthia was still prowling around backstage, looking for her.

She didn't know how long she sat there, her muscles seizing up with cold and cramp. But she still jumped when Stephen came round the corner.

'So this is where you're hiding! Everyone's looking for you.'

'I bet they are!' Tess' teeth chattered. 'And I expect Cynthia's leading them with my P45 in her hand.'

'Don't be so dramatic! They love it. Can't you hear them?'

Tess strained her ears. Sure enough, over the traffic noise, she could hear the muffled sound of applause.

'Aren't you going to take your bow?'

'I'd rather not.'

'Tough. You're coming.' Stephen dragged her to her feet and led her, protesting, back into the building and along the corridor to the side of the stage. The applause grew louder as they drew closer. By the time they reached the wings it was positively thunderous.

Tess peeped out at the cast, lined up on the stage. A few were bowing, others bobbed nervously, while the rest just looked dazed. Watching them, she suddenly felt a swell of maternal pride.

'Look at them.' Her voice was choked. 'Don't they look—'

She didn't have time to finish the sentence. Stephen shoved her in the small of her back towards the stage. She tripped over a trailing curtain cord and stumbled into the blinding glare of the footlights.

She stared out at the sea of faces. People were on their feet – clapping, not making for the doors in search of refreshments. Among them were the Chair of Governors and Eric Gant. Cynthia was still sitting down, and looked to be baring her teeth. Or was she? Tess risked another look. No, she was smiling. Tess looked away, unnerved, and found herself staring at Jack Tyler. He gave her the thumbs up. She grinned stupidly back.

She'd done it. They'd done it. In spite of all Cynthia's scheming and all the setbacks, it had happened. The faces blurred into a fog as her eyes filled with tears.

Afterwards there were drinks for the audience, provided by the PTA. Tess was so overcome by nerves she didn't want to go, but Stephen and Helen manhandled her into the crowded hall.

'You've worked hard for this, you deserve a bit of praise,' Helen told her firmly. 'If you don't go, Cynthia will only take all the credit.'

Not that there was much praise coming her way. Tess huddled in the corner, a plastic cup of warm Liebfraumilch in one hand, a bowl of peanuts in the other, while everyone milled past her. On the other side of the room, Cynthia was holding forth to a group of parents. Telling them all about her hard work, Tess guessed. She didn't care. She was just relieved it was all over and she'd escaped with her job.

She crammed a handful of peanuts into her mouth. She'd been too nervous to eat before the performance and now she was ravenous.

'Tess?' She turned round, mouth full of peanuts.

'Oh, hello, Jack.' She wiped her mouth with her sleeve. 'Sorry, I haven't had a chance to eat yet.'

'Don't let me stop you.' His grey eyes crinkled at the corners as he looked down at her. 'You did a great job tonight. How do you feel?'

'Like going home and sleeping for a week!'

'I just wanted to say how sorry I am about earlier. I don't make a habit of crying on people's shoulders, believe me.'

'At least you didn't do it in front of an audience.' She blushed to think how she'd burst into tears and had to be led away by a sniggering Polonius.

'I thought it was very touching.'

'You mean I made a complete idiot of myself!'

'I don't think anyone noticed.'

'Of course not. That photographer from the *Evening Press* was probably just taking pictures of the scenery.' She looked rueful. 'Anyway, you've got nothing to apologise for. It's been an emotional evening.'

'An emotional year, you mean.' Jack's face was bleak. 'Next week it'll be exactly a year since Miranda died.'

No wonder he was so upset. Tess regarded him sympathetically. 'How are you coping?'

'It depends. I thought I was doing okay, but I've had trouble sleeping lately. I can't stop thinking about it, going over it all in my head. Wondering what it would have been like if none of this had happened.'

'That's not surprising. Have you thought about seeing a doctor?'

'What could he do? Give me pills to make me forget?' Jack's mouth twisted. 'What really worries me is Christmas. It's only two weeks away and I don't know how we're going to manage.'

'What did you do last year?'

'Strangely enough it wasn't so bad. I think we were all too numb to feel anything, and the rest of the family rallied around to help. But my sister's going to visit her in-laws this year and my parents are off on a coach holiday to the Highlands.'

'I'm sure they'd cancel if you really wanted them to.'

'I expect they would. But they were meant to go last year and they put it off because of Miranda's death. I can't ask them to do it again.' He looked grim. 'It's my own fault. I've been going around telling everyone how brilliantly we're all coping, and they've started to believe me.'

'But you're not?'

'Most of the time we are, but it always seems worse at times like this.'

Tess nodded. She could still remember the first Christmas after her father died. Her mother had gone to so much trouble to make it as special as it always was. They had a tree, turkey, loads of presents. It had been a disaster. No one was in the mood to enjoy it. Everything they did reminded them someone important was missing. Tess had felt too guilty to play with her new toys, she and Frances had bickered all day and later they'd found their mother in the kitchen crying quietly as she made the stuffing.

'If I were you, I'd do something completely different,' she advised. 'Don't stay in the house, because you'll only get morbid. You should go out and make some new memories, instead of dwelling on the old ones.'

'What do you suggest?'

'I don't know.' She searched her mind for ideas. 'Couldn't you go on holiday? Somewhere hot and exotic?'

'I thought of that, but everything's fully booked. I can't even get a place on my parents' coach to the Cairngorms!'

'What about Charlie? Couldn't you spend Christmas with her?'

Jack frowned. 'Not a good idea. Emily hasn't exactly taken to her.' His look spoke volumes. 'I think spending Christmas together would ruffle a few too many feathers.'

Emily's or Charlie's? Tess wondered. She pondered the problem for a moment, then it came to her. 'Why don't you come round to ours?'

Jack shook his head. 'We couldn't impose on you—'

'You wouldn't be. My mum's going to spend Christmas with my sister in London, so it'll just be Dan and me. We could pool our resources. It'll be fun. That is, if you want to?'

'I'd love to. And I'm sure the girls would too.' He looked doubtful. 'But wouldn't your boyfriend mind?'

'I'm sure he would, if I had one. But since I don't that's not a problem, is it?'

'What about that man at the Parents' Evening?'

'You mean Phil? He's not my boyfriend. Well, not for the past seventeen years, anyway. He's Dan's father,' she explained.

'That's him, is it? So Dan got in touch with him, then?'

'I couldn't stop him! Actually, it's worked out quite well. He's not the monster I thought he would be.'

'You seemed to be getting on well when I saw you.'

'Not as well as my son would like us to,' Tess said.

'Really? Why's that?'

Before she could reply Charlie drifted up, a cup of wine in each hand.

'Here you are, darling. Sorry I've been so long, but I got collared by some strange little man over by the refreshments – oh, hello. It's Tess, isn't it?' Her smile widened. 'Great play. I thought I'd be bored senseless, but I loved every minute.'

'Thank you.' Why did she have to be so nice? It didn't give Tess a chance to hate her. 'Emily was very good, wasn't she?'

'Very. Although since she's such a drama queen that's hardly surprising!'

Tess glanced at Jack. Either he hadn't heard, or he'd stopped reacting.

They made small talk for a while, but Jack seemed less talkative when Charlie was around. As for Charlie, it was obvious, in spite of her niceness, that she wanted Jack all to herself.

In the end Tess decided to leave them to it. 'Oh well, I suppose I'd better go and mingle.'

Charlie made a brave stab at looking disappointed. 'It was nice meeting you again, Tess.'

'And you.' She turned to Jack. 'Let me know about Christmas, won't you? We can make some arrangements.'

'What arrangements, Jack?' she heard Charlie say as she walked away. Oops. Tess ducked quickly into the crowd.

'So I said to Miss Doyle, what we really need is something more modern, more on their wavelength,' Cynthia was telling the Chair of Governors as she hurried past. Tess didn't stop to set them straight. She was more worried about the conversation that was going on on the other side of the room.

Or rather, the lack of it. Charlie and Jack were half turned away, jaws set, eyes looking everywhere but at each other.

Chapter 25

Charlie was still simmering in the car on the way back to Jack's. She knew she was being childish but she couldn't help it.

What made it worse was that Jack couldn't see why she was so angry.

'It's not as if we made any plans together,' he said. 'You're going skiing without me.'

'I asked you to come.'

'What about the girls?'

'They could have come too,' she said, less convincingly.

'I bet your friends would have loved that!'

'Or you could have left them with someone.'

'They're children, Charlie, not a pair of Labradors. I can't just dump them in boarding kennels whenever I feel like it.'

More's the pity, Charlie thought. She glanced in the wing mirror. Emily was hunched on the back seat, pretending to listen to her CD player. But Charlie knew she could hear every word they said. And was probably loving every minute.

Naturally she'd been very enthusiastic about the idea of spending the day with Tess. Especially when she saw how wound up Charlie was about it.

It wasn't just the thought of him not being with her that irked her. It was the thought of him being with Tess. Charlie wasn't sure about her. She had a feeling Tess had a crush on Jack. She wasn't seriously worried about her as a rival, but who knew what could happen if he was left alone with her on Christmas Day? Christmas was an emotional time, it could do strange things to people. As could copious amounts of champagne and cooking sherry.

'You should have talked to me first,' she insisted. 'We're supposed to be a couple.'

Jack didn't reply, but his frown gave his feelings away. It wasn't what they'd agreed. They were supposed to be keeping their relationship casual, but she wanted more. She wanted the dreaded C word. Commitment. The word she didn't dare utter to Jack.

She knew she was falling for him. She'd never felt like this. She was usually in control of her emotions, but for once she could feel them running away with her. She was even starting to feel jealous, something she'd always dismissed as a waste of time.

She glanced across at Jack's unsmiling profile as he concentrated on the road ahead. She was sure he could feel the same too, if only he'd allow himself to let go of the past.

And if it wasn't for another couple of small problems . . .

Her favourite REM track came on the CD and Charlie leaned forward to adjust the volume. Emily immediately snatched the headphones off her head. 'Do you mind? I can't hear my music.'

'No, but we can.' The tinny 'tsch tsch' of Emily's CD player had been driving her mad ever since they left school. 'Do you have to have it so loud? God knows what it's doing to your ears.'

'They're my ears,' Emily snapped back. She turned up the volume so the tinny beat filled the car.

'That's enough, Emily.' Jack warned. Emily clamped her headphones back on and retreated into angry silence.

Charlie stared at him. Was that it? If she had been rude at that age to an adult, her father would have given her a reprimand she wouldn't forget in a hurry. But somehow Emily was allowed to get away with murder. Jack didn't seem to care how awful she was to Charlie. As long as his precious baby wasn't too traumatised.

They were silent until they got back to Jack's house. He reversed his car on to the drive beside hers and turned off the engine. 'Are you coming in for coffee?'

'Are you sure you haven't made other plans?' she asked shrewishly.

Jack sighed. 'Obviously I haven't, or I wouldn't be asking.'

Charlie thought about refusing. If any other man had treated her like that she would have slammed the car door in his face and told him never to call her again. But she had a horrible feeling Jack wouldn't call her anyway. Hating herself for her lack of pride, she meekly said, 'Okay.'

Ros was babysitting. She was snuggled up with Sophie, watching *Friends* and flicking through a magazine. She smiled wearily when they came in.

'How was the play?'

'Great.' Charlie took off her coat, draped it over the back of the sofa and sat down. Ros immediately closed her magazine and tapped Sophie on the backside with it.

'Come on, little minx, it's time you were in bed. And me.' She yawned and stretched her arms wide.

'Aren't you going to stay for coffee?' Jack asked.

'No thanks. I'm working at the library tomorrow morning, and it's quite a drive back to Leeds.' She was already struggling into her coat. She reached up and kissed her brother on the cheek. 'Night, Jack, night, Em. Night, Charlie,' she added as an afterthought.

'Goodnight,' Charlie said, but she was already gone. It was very strange. After trying so hard to throw them together, Ros had seemed cool towards her since the dinner party. Charlie wondered if she'd said or done anything to upset her.

Probably because she hadn't said she was dying to have a baby or acted fascinated enough in the conversation about headlice, she decided.

Jack saw Ros to the door, then went upstairs to supervise

Sophie's teeth-cleaning, leaving Charlie and Emily to sit in frozen silence. She'd been hoping for some time alone with Jack, but it didn't look as if it was going to happen. Emily seemed as if she was there for the rest of the night, stretched out on the sofa, the remote control in her hand.

'Shouldn't you be in bed by now?' she hinted.

'Dad always lets me stay up on a Friday.' Emily pointed the remote at the screen and flicked through the channels.

I bet he does, she thought. Emily was turning into a wilful little brat and Jack was doing nothing to stop her. But there was no point talking to him about it. He wouldn't hear a word said against her.

And Charlie didn't feel it was her place to tell Emily off, much as she felt like it. So all she could do was put up with her rudeness and tantrums, or try to ignore them. Neither of which came easily to her.

Jack came back downstairs and went straight into the kitchen to make the coffee. Charlie followed him.

'Is Emily going to sit there all night?' she asked.

'It's Friday. She always stays up on a Friday.'

'So she said. I just feel a bit uncomfortable with her watching us all the time.'

'It is her home.'

'It would be nice to have some time to ourselves, don't you think?'

'I know. But it's difficult. We have to be discreet.'

You're telling me, Charlie thought. Spending the night together had to be planned like a covert military operation, involving babysitters, clandestine phone calls and the smuggling of toothbrushes. It always had to be at her place, never his, and even then he left in the early hours so he could be home before the girls woke up. They'd been seeing each other for a month, and apart from that first night they'd never woken up in the same bed.

'Discreet? Bloody hell, I'm barely allowed to hold your hand as it is. What do you suggest, we become pen pals?'

'Now isn't the time. It's coming up to the anniversary of their mother's death. It's an upsetting time for them.'

For them, or for you? Charlie watched him as he made the coffee. She sometimes wondered if the real reason why he kept her at arm's length was because he still felt guilty about their relationship, not because he was worried about upsetting the children.

'Emily's fourteen years old. And she's not stupid. If she hasn't worked out we're sleeping together by now—'

'Shh! Keep your voice down, she'll hear you.'

'So what? The sooner she gets used to the idea, the better. Then maybe she'll stop looking at me like I'm some kind of nasty lab experiment.' She cuddled up against him. 'Still, we won't have any chaperones when we go away for the weekend, will we? I'll have you all to myself.'

'You make it sound like a dirty weekend.'

'That's up to you, isn't it?'

Jack grinned. 'We are talking about Crawshaw and Finch's team-building weekend in the Lakes, aren't we? The only chance we'll have to get dirty is when we're face down in mud being trampled underfoot by a bunch of gung-ho accountants.'

'Oh, I don't know. I could let you share my sleeping bag.' As Charlie lifted her face to kiss him, Emily walked in.

'Ugh! Don't mind me.' She pushed past them and headed for the fridge.

'For heaven's sake!' Charlie couldn't stop herself snapping. 'Don't you ever knock?'

'Don't you ever stop slobbering over my dad?'

'You see what I mean?' Charlie turned to Jack. 'At least we won't have to put up with this when we're away.'

She hadn't meant to say it; she knew Jack hadn't told Emily about the team-building weekend. He was still waiting for the right moment to break it to her, he said.

Well, she knew now. And she didn't look too pleased about it.

'Who's going away?'

'It's just a work thing,' Jack said quickly. 'And it's not until January. Not for another month.'

'Nice of you to tell me,' Emily muttered.

'He's telling you now, isn't he?' Charlie said. Although she hadn't meant to blurt it out, she couldn't help feeling an unworthy twinge of satisfaction that Emily was the one being put out for once.

But her triumph disappeared when Emily slammed out of the room and Jack turned on her. 'Thanks a lot,' he said.

'It's not my fault. I thought you would have said something by now.'

'I told you, I hadn't found the right time.'

'And when would that be? As you're on your way out of the door? For God's sake, Jack, you can't go on protecting her for ever. Sooner or later she's got to learn that you're a grown man and you've got your own life to lead.'

'I've also got two daughters who need me.'

'I know what she needs!'

She saw the look on his face and knew she'd said the wrong thing. He put down his coffee cup and headed for the door.

'Where are you going?'

'To see my daughter.'

'But we need to – talk,' she said, as the door slammed.

Charlie tipped her coffee down the sink. She held the cup in her hand for a moment, then turned around and hurled it at the wall in sheery fury.

She stormed out and sat in her car for a few minutes, waiting to calm down. Secretly she was also hoping Jack would come out and beg her to stay, but he didn't. The lights in the upstairs windows blazed. As she watched, Jack's silhouette appeared at one of them and pulled the curtains closed. He didn't even look down into the street.

Charlie turned the key in the ignition and sped off, furious as hell.

Tess, meanwhile, was still struggling to deal with the enormity of what she'd done. Less than two weeks until Christmas, and she'd invited three people she barely knew to join them. This meant her low-key Christmas with Dan had suddenly turned into a full bells-and-whistles affair.

Dan wasn't too pleased about it either. 'Who are these people, anyway?'

'Jack's just a friend. His daughter's in my class at school.'

'Since when did you start inviting kids from school round for Christmas?'

'Her mother died a year ago. I felt sorry for them.'

Dan grunted. 'I don't know why you don't just turn this place into a soup kitchen and have done with it.'

'Stop it, Dan. I've got enough on my mind without you giving me a hard time.' She ticked off the list on her fingers. 'I'm going to have to buy some presents for them, although God knows what they'd like. And we'll need a bigger turkey. How big will it have to be to feed five, do you think?'

'Six,' Dan said quietly. 'I've invited Phil.'

'What?' Tess sank down on to the sofa. 'When did this happen?'

'He rang the other night. We got talking about Christmas, he said he wasn't doing anything so I invited him.'

'Thanks for telling me!'

'Sorry. I didn't think you'd mind.'

Tess took it all in. Six people. She'd never cooked a huge Christmas dinner before. A horrible image of herself wrestling with a giant turkey formed in her mind.

But it wasn't just that. For reasons she couldn't fathom, the idea of Jack and Phil sitting around the dinner table together filled her with unease.

'I wish you hadn't invited him, Dan. This makes things very awkward. I don't even know if we've got enough chairs, for a start.'

'So call your friends and tell them they can't come.'

'I can't do that! They'll be so disappointed.'

'So will Phil.' Dan looked stubborn. 'Besides, I think he has more right to be here than that lot.'

'He could come on Boxing Day instead?' Tess suggested hopefully.

'No chance,' Dan said. 'This is the first Christmas I've ever had with my father. I'm not missing out on it for anyone.'

He had a point, Tess thought. Much as she hated to admit it.

She thought about phoning Jack to cancel. She actually got as far as dialling his number, but her nerve failed her when he picked the phone up.

'Tess. Thank God it's you.' He sounded weary. 'I thought it might be Charlie and I haven't got the strength to deal with her at the moment.'

'Have you two had a row?'

'You could say that. Actually, she and Emily had the row; I got caught in the crossfire as usual.' He sighed heavily. 'I don't blame Charlie for being pissed off. Emily was being stroppy with her and I didn't do much to help. But it's so difficult not to take sides, I always end up upsetting someone.' He brightened up. 'Anyway, I'm glad you called. I wanted to talk to you about Christmas.'

'Ah yes, I'm glad you mentioned that.'

'Thanks so much for inviting us. The girls are really looking forward to it and so am I. I can't tell you what this means to me,' he said quietly.

'Actually, that's what I was calling about.' Tess bit her lip. She couldn't bring herself to do it. 'I – um – just wondered if you could bring a couple of spare chairs with you?'

Chapter 26

It was noon on Christmas Day, and Tess was at the kitchen sink humming tunelessly along to the carol service on the radio while she tackled the potato mountain. Apart from the veg, which had yet to be peeled, everything was suspiciously under control. The monstrous turkey was cooking nicely, having been in the oven since the crack of dawn. She'd had a bath and washed her hair, using the posh Aveda stuff her sister had sent, treated herself to a Clinique face pack – a present from Dan – and dressed in the black trousers and bronze sparkly top she'd bought for the staff Christmas party. She'd cracked open her first bottle of champagne an hour ago and toasted herself with a Buck's Fizz to celebrate her brilliant organisational skills.

The only thing spoiling her good mood was Dan. He was in his room – playing on his computer so he said, although Tess suspected he was sulking because Phil had called to say he'd had a water main burst outside his home and he couldn't leave in case his house got flooded. From the way Dan was acting, anyone would think Tess had deliberately burst the flaming thing herself.

He ignored the doorbell when Jack and the girls arrived. Tutting, Tess went to the door, wiping her hands on a teatowel.

'Merry Christmas!' Jack waved a bottle of Bollinger at her. Emily and Sophie stood behind him, their arms full of presents.

'Thanks. I've already opened a bottle.'

'Is there any left?'

'Cheek! Do I look as if I've been face down in the broccoli?'

She stepped aside to let them into the narrow hallway. 'Dan!' she called. 'Our guests are here.' No answer. 'He's probably got his headphones on,' she said, knowing full well he was in the middle of a major strop.

She led them into the sitting room. 'Nice place,' Jack commented, shrugging off his black leather jacket. He was wearing black jeans and a chunky grey sweater that matched his eyes.

'Thanks. It's not quite as grand as yours, but we like it. Ah, here's Dan.' She smiled brightly as Dan wheeled in. 'Dan, this is Jack, Emily and Sophie.'

'Hi,' Dan grunted. 'Have you seen my Eminem CD?' he asked Tess.

'I imagine it's in your room.'

'Well, I can't find it.'

'Perhaps if you tidied up in there occasionally, you might be able to find things?' Tess was tight-lipped.

'Perhaps if you didn't tidy up, I might know where I'd left them?' He spun the wheelchair round and headed back to his room.

Jack's eyes twinkled. 'It feels like home already!'

They chatted for a while, then Tess prised Dan out of his room to hand out the presents she'd bought for Jack and the girls. After much thought, she'd settled on some glittery make-up and hair accessories for Sophie and a CD for Emily.

'I hope it's okay?' She watched her face as she unwrapped it. 'I'm afraid I don't know one band from another, but Dan assures me they're the latest thing.'

'It's brilliant, thanks.'

'My turn.' Jack picked up the large, gift-wrapped box in front of him and shook it gently. 'It's big enough. Are you sure it's mine?'

'I can't think of anyone else who'd want it. I hope you

like it,' Tess said shyly. She'd been so certain he would when she spotted it in the Discovery Store. But suddenly she wasn't so sure. What if he didn't understand? What if he didn't get the joke?

But he did. He ripped off the paper and his face broke into a grin. 'I don't believe it,' he said. 'Where did you find this?'

'What is it?' Sophie and Emily clamoured to see. 'It's a toy rocket!' Sophie looked disappointed.

'Not just any old rocket. This is Thunderbird Two.' He gazed at it lovingly.

'It has lots of features, apparently,' Tess said. 'Almost as good as the real thing, the boy in the shop said.' She blushed. 'I hope you don't think it's too silly?'

'It's just what I always wanted,' he said.

'Open yours now.' Sophie, eager to move on to the next diversion, handed her and Dan their gifts. Dan's was a computer game; hers was a bottle of *Trésor*.

'How did you know this was my favourite?' she asked.

'I just recognised it.'

'Liar!' Emily said. 'He went round Fenwicks three times sniffing everything before he found out which one it was!'

Tess laughed, flattered. 'I didn't realise it was that memorable.'

'I'd know it anywhere.'

She turned to her son. 'What about yours, Dan? You wanted that game, didn't you?' He grunted. 'I'm amazed you found one he didn't have,' she said quickly, to cover his sullen response.

Tess went off to check on dinner and Jack followed, leaving Sophie playing with the new Barbie she'd got from her grandparents, and Emily and Dan in awkward silence in front of the TV.

He flicked channels. 'Anything you want to watch?'

'Not bothered.' Emily hardly dared speak to him, he was

so rude. As if it was her fault they were here. His mum had invited them.

At the same time, she couldn't take her eyes off his wheelchair. She kept sneaking sideways glances at it. She had no idea Miss Doyle's son was disabled.

'You can try it out, if you're that interested?' he said, not looking round.

'What?'

'The wheelchair. You're obviously fascinated by it.'

Emily averted her eyes back to the screen. 'Sorry,' she mumbled.

'S'okay. Everyone stares. Why should you be any different?'

She hesitated. 'Were you in an accident or something?'

He nodded. 'I did a bungee jump and the rope broke.'

'Really?'

'No, I just said it to be interesting. I was actually born like this.'

'Oh. Right.' She couldn't think of anything else to say. 'So – um – do you mind being in a wheelchair?'

'No, I love it. I love that I can't go into shops because they've got steps outside. I love that I can't get my money out of the bank because I can't reach the cashpoint. Most of all I love that people like you talk to me as if I'm retarded!'

'I don't know, do I? I've never met anyone like you before!'

'Well, I've met lots of people like you, believe me.'

They sat in silence, both glaring at the TV screen. Sophie pulled Barbie's party dress off, revealing a pair of unsexy big white knickers.

'You would have thought she'd wear a thong, wouldn't you?' she said, disappointed.

Dan grinned. So did Emily. 'Sorry,' he said. 'Take no notice of me. I'm just a bit pissed off at the moment.'

'Because we're here?'

'Because my dad isn't.' He picked up the TV remote

control and hit the Off button. 'Stuff this,' he said. 'I don't suppose you fancy a game on the computer?'

'They sound as if they're getting on okay,' Tess listened from the kitchen a few minutes later. 'I'm sorry, I don't know what's got into my son today. He isn't usually such a Kevin.'

'Don't apologise. Believe me, it's nice to know I'm not the only one with a surly teenager.'

'Like I said, he isn't usually that bad.' Tess opened the oven and pulled out the roasting tin to turn the potatoes. A whoosh of heat rose up, melting what was left of her make-up.

'Emily is. She's been even worse since I started seeing Charlie.'

It doesn't take a genius to work out why, Tess thought. 'How are things between you at the moment? Have you made it up?'

'We're speaking, but she's being a bit frosty.' Jack took the champagne bottle out of the fridge and refilled their glasses. 'I don't know what to do for the best. It always seems to be me having to take sides. I just wish she and Emily would get on with each other. She doesn't seem to have any trouble with Sophie.'

'That's because she's not at an awkward age. Emily's bound to be wary of anyone new,' Tess said.

'You try explaining that to Charlie. She thinks I should be a bit more heavy-handed. But the way I see it, that will only make Emily resent her more.' He sipped his drink. 'I'm not going to drive my daughter away, especially when I'm not sure if Charlie and I even have a future together.'

'You're not?' Tess came up so fast she nearly hit her head on the oven door. 'I thought you liked her?'

'I do. That's the problem. I don't want to hurt her, but I don't know if I can give her what she really wants.'

'Which is?'

'Commitment. She wants us to start making plans for the future as a couple. It's not unreasonable, I suppose. But I'm not ready for all that.'

'Because you're still in love with Miranda?'

'Because I'm not in love with Charlie.' He sent her a level look over the rim of his glass. 'I'm not saying I couldn't fall for someone. But she's not the woman I want.'

They looked at each other and a flash of heat rose in her face that had nothing to do with the oven.

The doorbell rang, breaking the tension. Tess heard Dan rush to answer it. 'Dad's here!' he yelled.

'I left the water board sorting out the burst main and drove straight up.' Phil stood in the hall, smartly dressed in a cream shirt and charcoal-grey trousers, his floppy fair hair brushed back off his face. 'Dan sounded so disappointed on the phone I thought I couldn't let him down.'

His smile faded when he saw Jack. 'Oh, hello. We've met, haven't we? At the Parents' Evening?'

'This is Jack,' Tess said. 'Jack, this is Phil, Dan's father.'

They shook hands. Neither of them looked terribly pleased to see the other.

'Sorry, I didn't know you were expecting anyone else,' Phil said.

Jack frowned. 'Neither did I.' They both looked at Tess.

'I'll just go and check on the potatoes again,' she said, and ducked back into the kitchen.

By the time she got back Phil was unloading Dan's present from the boot of his Porsche. Judging by the size of the box, there was no surprise about what it was.

'A new motherboard!' Dan gazed at what looked to Tess like the gubbins from the back of an old TV set. 'I've been wanting one of these for ages. And it's got dual BIOS, a twelve-volt connector and an optical S/PDIF output.'

'Sounds marvellous.' Tess smiled. For all she knew about

computers, he could have told her it was a 2.5 GHz camel with USB ports, Athlon socket and an optional third hump.

'And it's got onboard RAID for faster hard disk drive arrays,' Phil pointed out. 'You'll have to update your software to take account of the increased memory, of course. But I can let you have a lot of that stuff. We've just got the new version lying around the office, straight from the States. It's not available in this country yet.'

'Actually, Mum's already bought me some for Christmas.' Dan gave her a shy, sideways glance.

'Oh. Right.' Phil had the grace to look embarrassed. 'Well, the existing version's just as good, of course. Even better, in some ways.'

Tess knew she was being placated. She also knew she'd just wasted nearly a hundred quid on something Phil had 'lying around' the office.

She wasn't going to throw a tantrum about it. The atmosphere was fraught enough already.

'Dinner's nearly ready,' she announced. 'Get your father a drink, Dan. We'll be eating in ten minutes.'

It was hardly the jolly affair she'd planned. There were long, tense silences, punctuated by awkward small talk. Dan ignored everyone else and chatted to Phil about motherboard installation and the relative merits of the dual CPU system. Tess played with her food and gazed at Jack, marooned at the other end of the table. She would have liked to talk to him but Dan had manoeuvred her as far away as possible, next to Phil.

Jack was trying to keep up a show of good spirits for the girls, but he'd gone quiet since Phil arrived. And yet she felt there was still so much to say. Especially after what had happened in the kitchen.

It was no surprise to her when, shortly after lunch, Jack announced he was going home.

'But you haven't been here long!' Tess protested. 'At least stay and have another drink?'

'No, I'd better be going. You'll want some family time.' He looked across at Dan and Phil, who'd cleared the dining-room table and were engrossed in dismantling Dan's computer on it.

He leaned forward and pecked her awkwardly on the cheek. 'Thanks for a lovely day, Tess. And for the presents.'

'You're welcome. Thanks for mine.'

She watched them go, burning with frustration. Family time, indeed!

She went back inside and slammed the door. Phil looked up vaguely from the instruction manual. 'Have they gone?'

Tess was too angry to answer him. 'I hope you're not going to leave all this stuff here? It's meant to be a dining room, not the head office of Microsoft!'

'Oops,' Phil whispered. 'Someone's in a bad mood.'

'Yes, I am. And do you want to know why? Because you two made my friends feel so uncomfortable they've gone home.'

'Hang on a minute! I haven't done anything.'

'You didn't help. Whispering in corners like a pair of schoolkids, sharing your little private jokes. Even I felt as if I didn't belong and I live here! And as for you—' She squared up to Dan, hands on hips. 'I was ashamed of the way you behaved. Sulking and snapping at Jack whenever he tried to talk to you. I've never brought you up to be rude to people.'

Dan stuck out his chin defiantly. 'I never asked him to come, did I?'

'No, but I did. They were my friends, Dan. And you made them feel unwelcome.' She took a deep breath, trying to contain her anger. 'I think you should call him and apologise.'

'No way!'

'Dan!'

'I didn't want him here. He can get stuffed for all I care!'

'Daniel Doyle! You come back here this minute!' But

he'd already slammed out of the room. Phil and Tess stared at each other.

'Would it help if I left too?' he asked.

'I don't think things can get much worse, do you?' She sat down at the table, all the fight gone out of her.

This had started off as such a good day. Everything had gone so well, she'd had so much to look forward to. Now it was all ruined.

Phil came round the table to sit beside her and handed her what was left of his champagne. 'I wouldn't have come if I'd known it was going to be awkward,' he said.

'It's not your fault. It's Dan I'm really angry at.'

'He can't help being a moody teenager.'

'It's not just that. It's what he's trying to do that annoys me.'

'What's that?'

'You mean you don't know he's trying to push us together?'

Phil looked taken aback. 'What? I hadn't noticed.'

'Then you must be blind. Think about it. All those times he's managed to work it so we're left alone together? Like that night we went out to dinner?'

'You mean he didn't have a college assignment?'

'I don't know. But it seems a bit strange that he's suddenly become so keen on keeping up with his homework.'

Phil shook his head. 'Why would he want to do that?'

'Because he wants a happy ending. He wants you and me to walk off into the sunset and give him the perfect nuclear family he's apparently always wanted.' She couldn't keep the bitterness out of her voice.

Phil regarded her carefully. 'And don't you believe in happy endings?'

Tess thought about the mess that today had turned out to be. She thought about Jack, heading for home with the girls when she so badly wanted him to stay.

'Not today,' she said bitterly.

It looked as if it was about to snow. The sky had a threatening, yellowish-grey tinge to it, and the raw wind whipped at them as they trudged homewards towards Hollywell Park.

'Why did we have to go?' Sophie trailed along behind them, her arms full of half-naked Barbies. 'I was having a nice time. I wanted to stay.'

'I know, but Tess had another guest. We would have been in the way.'

He didn't want to stay and watch Phil worm his way back into Tess' affections anyway. It was fairly obvious that was what he was after.

'Do you think Tess will get back with Dan's father?' Emily surprised him by asking the question that had been going through his mind.

'I don't know. She might.'

'I think she should. She needs someone.'

'She wouldn't thank you for saying that!'

'It's true, though. That's what Dan says, anyway.'

'How do you know that?'

'He told me. While we were playing on the computer. He wants his dad to marry his mum so they'll stay together. He says he's always wanted two parents.' She looked wistful for a moment. 'I think they'll get together.'

So do I, Jack thought. He was amazed how glum the idea made him feel.

'What are we going to eat when we get home?' Sophie demanded, as they turned off the main road and into the wide, sweeping avenues of Hollywell Park. The streets were deserted, apart from a gaggle of small boys trying out their new bikes around the cul-de-sac. Lights blazed in every window. Jack could imagine all kinds of merriment going on behind those closed doors, with families getting together to enjoy the festivities. It made him feel achingly lonely.

He summoned a smile for Sophie's benefit. 'You've just had a big dinner. Haven't you eaten enough?'

'Yes, but I might want turkey sandwiches later. We always have turkey sandwiches on Christmas night.' She looked subdued, remembering.

'Maybe we could have festive beans on toast instead?' he suggested.

Sophie shook her head. 'It's not the same. I bet Tess has got turkey sandwiches,' she said.

As they turned the corner, it was Sophie who spotted her first. 'Charlie!' She ran towards the sporty Audi TT parked beside Jack's BMW on the drive.

Charlie got out of the car. She was wearing a long cream coat, her hair tucked up inside a pale fur hat. She smiled wanly at Jack. 'Surprise!'

'I thought you were meant to be skiing?'

'I was, but I came home. I missed you.' She moved into his arms for a hug. Jack held her briefly, then made a show of rummaging in his pocket for his key.

As he unlocked the door, she said, 'I'd better get the presents out of the car.'

'Presents!' Sophie jumped up and down.

'Don't get too excited. I didn't have much time to shop so I got them at the Duty Free.'

'So it's a bottle of Glenfiddich for me and a couple of hundred cigarettes each for the girls, is it?' Jack said.

'Not quite that bad. I do have some imagination, you know.' Jack opened the door and the girls rushed inside. He went to follow them, but Charlie held him back.

'Sorry I've been such a bitch,' she said. 'I should be more understanding about the children. I know how important they are to you. It's just I wanted to feel I was important to you too.'

Jack instantly felt a twinge of guilt. 'I'm sorry I didn't

back you up more with Emily. I realise she can be a nightmare at times.'

'I'm just not very used to dealing with kids, I'm afraid.' She smiled shakily. 'I've always assumed they were like little adults, but they're not, are they?'

'Sadly no.' Jack looked rueful. 'And you can't just ignore them when you've had enough either.'

They laughed. It almost felt like old times, when they were friends, before all this complicated stuff began.

'I will try with the girls, honestly,' she promised.

And I'll try with you, Jack thought. It must have taken a hell of a lot for her to come here, he decided. Emily had been a monster to her, yet she still had the guts to come back. And to interrupt her skiing holiday. That must mean something.

He gazed into her tawny green eyes. He'd been so negative about their relationship, he hadn't really given her a chance. But he was lucky to have her. Charlie Ferguson could have had any man she wanted, yet she'd chosen him. The least he could do was try to make a go of it.

Once inside, he poured them both a glass of wine and they sat down to open the presents. Sophie was thrilled with her grown-up bottle of perfume, and Jack liked his leather briefcase.

'Sorry it's nothing more exciting,' Charlie said. Leaning closer, she added, 'I'm wearing your other present. I picked up some La Perla underwear in Val d'Isère.'

Jack smiled tightly and glanced around to make sure Emily and Sophie hadn't heard. He could feel himself blushing to the roots of his hair. He quickly handed Charlie her present, a businesslike Palm Pilot. She looked pleased, but he sensed she would have preferred something more personal. He'd meant to buy her something special, until he realised he had no idea what kind of jewellery she liked, or even if she ever wore any. He was also dismayed to realise that he could recognise Tess' perfume across a crowded room, but not hers.

Charlie had bought Emily a CD. Unfortunately, it was the same one Tess had got her.

'Oh well, I can always change it,' Charlie said brightly. 'Or I might keep it for myself and buy you another one. Who knows, I might even get to like garage music!'

Jack waited tensely for Emily's sarcastic reply. Her lip curled but thankfully she said nothing.

'I'm surprised you came home so early,' Charlie said, when all the gift-wrapping paper had been cleared away and they were relaxing with their wine. 'What happened? Did Tess burn the turkey?'

'No, but her ex turned up.' He explained about Phil. Charlie listened, wide-eyed.

'Really? How interesting. Do you think they'll get back together?'

'How should I know?' He felt subdued and changed the subject. 'Why don't we all have a game of something, to pass the time?'

Charlie looked as if she could think of better ways of passing the time, but she smiled brightly and said, 'Why not? I haven't played a board game for years. What shall we play?'

They finally settled on Monopoly, as it was the only game Charlie could remember. It turned out to be a bad choice. Monopoly was one of those games that brought out the worst instincts in people anyway. But with Charlie and Emily pitted against each other it was a definite needle match.

It began when Jack handed over the deeds of Old Kent Road and Whitechapel to Sophie.

'Why has she got those?' Charlie asked. 'We haven't started playing yet.'

'We like to give her a head start,' Jack explained.

Charlie wasn't happy, although she was trying not to show it. 'That's hardly fair, is it?' she said with a fixed smile.

'It's only a game!' Emily rolled her eyes. 'It's not like she's got Park Lane or anything.'

They finally began to play, but Jack could see Charlie was getting more and more wound up that Emily was buying the properties she wanted.

'What do you need Leicester Square for?' she demanded. 'You know I've got Piccadilly and Coventry Street.'

Emily shrugged. 'That's the game.'

'Yes, but I can't build any houses or hotels if I don't own them all.'

'So?'

'So they're not doing you any good, are they? You can't build anything either!'

Jack caught the glint in Emily's eye. That wasn't the point as far as she was concerned, he guessed. The point was to wind Charlie up until she exploded.

'Let's calm down, shall we?' he pleaded. 'Who really cares about winning anyway?'

Charlie sent him a perplexed look. 'What's the point of playing if you don't care who wins?'

Later, she retaliated by nabbing Mayfair before Emily could land on it.

'But I've got Park Lane!' Emily protested.

Charlie smiled maddeningly. 'So?'

Jack could see Emily about to reach boiling point and stepped in quickly. 'Come on, you two. Let's not fall out over a daft game.'

'Tell her that,' Emily jabbed an accusing finger. 'Anyone would think it was the Olympics, the way she's going on!'

'Just because you're a bad loser.'

Emily stood up, knocking the board and upsetting all the pieces. As she stomped off, slamming the door behind her, Jack wearily got to his feet. But Charlie stopped him.

'No,' she said. 'I'll go.'

'You?'

'Don't panic, I'm not going to start a row.' Charlie glanced at the door. 'But I think it's about time your daughter and I had a little heart to heart.'

She tapped on Emily's door. There was no answer, but she walked in anyway.

The bedroom was in darkness and the first thing Charlie did was trip over a pile of clothes strewn on the floor. She kicked them to one side and looked around. In the faint light from the street lamp outside she could make out posters stuck haphazardly all over the walls, and a dressing table overcrowded with books, CDs without their covers and rows of empty mugs. Charlie suppressed a shudder. If Emily was her child, she'd never stand for that kind of mess in her home.

But if Emily was hers, she would probably have left home a long time ago.

Emily was in bed, a huddled shape under the duvet, a pillow pulled over her head.

Typical, Charlie thought. She starts World War Three then runs away to hide. 'Emily?'

'Go away!' Her voice was muffled by the pillow.

'That's the point. I'm not going anywhere.' She sat down on the edge of the bed.

'I hate you! You're a horrible old cow!'

'To be honest, I'm not that keen on you, either. But since we're stuck with each other I think we should try to make this work, don't you?' Emily didn't reply. 'Not for my sake, of course. Frankly, you can be as big a nightmare as you like and you still won't beat me. I'm thinking about your father.' She shifted a little further down the bed. 'He feels he can't love us both because you're making him choose.'

'He doesn't love you!' Emily spat. 'He only sleeps with you! He'll never love you.'

'That's where you're wrong.' Charlie searched for the right words. 'Look, I'm not very good at talking to kids, so I'm just going to say this straight. I know you're pissed off because your dad's going out with me, but that's just the way it is. I'm sorry things have worked out this way. I'm sorry your mum's dead. But you hating me won't bring her back, will it?'

Silence. Charlie waited a moment, then gave up.

'Fine. If that's the way you want it.' She stood up. 'I've tried talking to you like an adult, but I can see I'm wasting my time. You're just a spoilt little kid who can't deal with the truth. But I'm telling you this, Emily. If you think you can get rid of me, you've got another thing coming.'

Jack was waiting anxiously for her when she got downstairs. 'How did it go?'

'How do you think?'

'Maybe you didn't handle it right?'

Or maybe she's just a manipulative little cow, Charlie thought. 'To tell you the truth, I'm sick of trying to handle it. Now it's your turn.' She grabbed her coat from the banisters. 'You sort it out, Jack, and let me know when you've done it. I'll be waiting.'

Chapter 27

Emily sat in her Maths class, staring at the clock. Nearly ten past two. Her dad would be in the Lakes by now.

Would Charlie be with him? Stupid question. She never left him alone these days. At least she and Emily had given up pretending to be nice to each other. Now they just tried to stay out of each other's way. Not that it was easy, as Charlie seemed to be around more and more. How long before she moved in permanently? Emily wondered.

She'd tried to talk to her dad about it, but he just laughed. 'Why on earth would she want to move in with us when she's got a fabulous flat of her own in Leeds?' he said. He could be very naïve sometimes. Emily knew Charlie was slowly getting her claws into him, even if he couldn't see it. And she also knew she and Sophie weren't part of the package.

She was too afraid to mention it to her dad, but it was clear Charlie didn't like them being around. Even Sophie, who adored her. And now she had their father to herself for a whole weekend. All weekend to show him how wonderful and easy life could be without children cluttering it up. How long would it take her to make him see he'd be better off without them?

Maybe even as she sat there, pretending to tackle her trigonometry test, Charlie was sweet-talking him into letting them go and live with Auntie Ros while he moved into her fabulous flat. He might not take much convincing; if he could forget their mum, he wouldn't have much trouble abandoning them.

And Emily had played right into her hands by being such a stroppy cow. She'd been so insecure about everything, she'd turned into a monster to live with. Her dad would probably jump at the chance to be rid of her.

At least she was spending the weekend with Katy in Leeds rather than going to Gran's with Sophie. It was her reward for not kicking up a fuss about him going on this team-building weekend. She couldn't wait. Katy was so wise and grown-up, she'd know what to do. She'd probably come up with a million plans to get rid of evil Charlie.

Katy met her from the station. She looked even older than Emily remembered from the party in November. She was dressed in tight jeans, strappy sandals and a skimpy T-shirt, even though an icy January wind was blowing. Emily felt very young in her sensible coat and trainers.

After much squealing, jumping up and down and hugging each other, Katy announced they were going to McDonald's for tea.

'It's okay, I'm paying,' she said.

'But won't your mum be expecting us?'

'Where do you think I got the money from, dummy?' Katy laughed. 'Besides, Mum never cooks. She's crap at it. Mostly we just microwave stuff out of the freezer.'

It came as a shock to Emily. Her dad might not be the best cook in the world, but at least he tried.

Katy lived in the same area Emily once had. As they approached the terrace of tall Victorian villas, she felt an unexpected stab of panic. She found it hard to breathe, as if her lungs were squashed against her ribs.

Katy stared at her worriedly. 'Are you feeling all right? You're not going to be sick or anything?'

'I'm fine.' She took a deep, steadying breath, and the moment passed.

Did her dad ever feel like that? she wondered. If he did,

she could almost understand why he'd been so desperate to move.

As Katy put her key in the door, her mother appeared in the hall, a glass of wine in her hand.

'Alan? Oh, it's you.' Her look of disappointment was quickly masked when she saw Emily. 'And you've brought a little friend with you. How nice.'

'This is Emily. I told you she was coming, remember?'

'Did you? You know I can't remember everything you tell me, darling.' Her voice was slurred. 'Well, come in, anyway. Welcome to the mad house.'

'Thank you, Mrs Jefferson.'

Katy's mother smiled. 'Call me Vanessa, darling, every-one does.' There was a shriek of laughter from the sitting room. Vanessa glanced over her shoulder. 'I've got some friends round, so—'

'Don't worry, we won't get in your way.' Katy dumped her school bag in the hall and pushed Emily in the direction of the kitchen.

'The coven,' she explained. 'Mum's cronies. They always come round to get pissed and sympathise when my stepfather's working late again.'

'My dad's always doing that.'

'Yeah, right!' Katy snorted. 'You don't get it, do you? Working late means he's probably shagging his secretary in some hotel.' She threw open the fridge door. 'Do you want anything to drink? I expect that lot have had all the wine, but we've got beer.'

'Won't you get told off?' Emily glanced back at the door.

'Do you really think they take any notice of what I do? They're too busy screwing up their own lives.' There was a bitter edge to Katy's voice as she helped herself to a can of Stella. She popped it open and handed it to Emily. 'Don't tell me you don't drink either?'

Emily steeled herself and took a swig, gagging as it hit the back of her throat. How did adults drink that stuff and not throw up?

'You get used to it,' Katy grinned. 'Anyway, you drink it for the effect, not the taste.'

There was another shriek from the sitting room. 'Listen to them.' Her voice was full of contempt. 'In a couple of hours they'll all be crying and wondering why they've never managed to stay married for more than five minutes. Come on, let's go up to my room.'

The attic had been converted into a bedsit for Katy. It had everything – TV, computer, stereo, video, telephone, even her own bathroom. Emily looked around in admiration. 'You're so lucky.'

Katy shrugged. 'It's okay, I s'pose. They mainly give me all this stuff to keep me out of their way.' She sorted through her video collection. 'What do you want to watch? I've got some good horror movies.'

Emily would rather have watched something funny, or romantic. But she shrugged and said, 'You choose.' After all, how scary could it be?

Forty blood-curdling minutes later, she found out. She was huddled in the dark on Katy's bed, watching the film from behind a cushion and wondering why the stupid heroine had gone into the empty school at midnight, as it was obvious the hideously deformed, hook-handed psycho-path was prowling the corridors, when the front door suddenly banged.

Katy's shoulders stiffened and her head went up. 'He's home,' she said. 'They'll start in a minute.'

Sure enough, a moment later, Emily heard raised voices in the hall below, followed by the coven making their escape. The voices grew louder until they reached scream-ing pitch. Katy's mum seemed to be doing most of the screaming.

Emily glanced anxiously at Katy, but she just picked up the remote and cranked up the volume.

The row went on long after they'd gone to bed. Emily lay in her sleeping bag, listening. She didn't know which terrified her more, the thought of the hook-handed psychopath lurking in the darkness, or the screeching coming from downstairs.

She couldn't remember her parents ever fighting like that, but Katy seemed used to it. She even managed to go to sleep, while Emily stared at the unfamiliar shadows and wished she were back in the safety of her own bed. She'd never missed home so much in her life.

Home. When had she started to think of it as that? If anyone asked her, she would have vehemently insisted that Leeds was still her home. But now it felt unreal, unwelcoming. As if she didn't belong. Her real home was back in Haxsall, with her dad and Sophie.

She dozed fitfully and woke in the grey early dawn. She uncurled her cold, stiff limbs and listened. At least the house was quiet. She was ragingly thirsty, but she didn't like to venture downstairs on her own in case she found a couple of bodies with kitchen knives sticking out of them.

It was hours until Katy woke up and they went downstairs. There were no bodies, but there was a man in the kitchen, slumped at the table. He looked as if he'd had even less sleep than Emily.

'Hi, babe,' he greeted Katy with a weary smile. 'Be an angel and put the kettle on, would you?'

'Where is she?' Katy flicked the switch. 'Still in bed, I suppose?'

'Your mother has a headache this morning.'

'A hangover, you mean.' Katy opened the nearest cupboard and looked inside. 'We're out of bread.'

'Are we? Oh dear. I suppose your mother must have forgotten to buy it.'

'Typical. I bet there's no bloody cereal, either.'

Emily held her breath and waited for her stepfather to

give her a lecture on language, but he just cradled his head in his hands and groaned, 'Not so loud, sweetheart.'

'We'll just have to get something when we're out.' Katy went to her mother's handbag and helped herself to a handful of notes out of her purse. 'We're going.'

'Fine.' He didn't ask where, or how long they'd be. Emily had often wondered what it would be like to have so much freedom. Now she wasn't sure she liked it.

'Won't your mum mind?' she asked, as they left the house.

Katy looked wistful. 'I shouldn't think she'll even notice.'

They caught the bus into the city and wandered around for a couple of hours, browsing through the CDs in Virgin Megastore and trying on clothes in Miss Selfridge. It was boring when she didn't have any money to spend. Katy offered to share hers, but that didn't feel right either.

'Your mum will be expecting it back, won't she?'

'I wish you'd stop going on about my mum,' Katy snapped. 'She doesn't watch my every move, you know. What do you think of these jeans?'

They went back to McDonald's at lunchtime. From the way Katy flirted with the spotty boys behind the counter, Emily thought she must go there an awful lot. It was a wonder she wasn't twenty-five stone and covered in acne.

They sat side by side in the window, watching the shoppers in Briggate. While they ate their burgers, Emily tried to tell Katy about her problem with Charlie. She kept having to repeat herself because Katy was distracted by the boys deliberately clearing tables close by them. After Emily had been through the whole thing for the third time, Katy shrugged and said, 'So? I told you it would happen, didn't I?'

'But what am I going to do about it?'

'Not much you can do. If he likes her, he's going to go

on seeing her whatever you do or say.' She bit into a chip. 'Look at my lot. I don't remember any of them ever asking how I felt.'

'How long has your mum been married to your stepdad?'

'Too long.'

'Have they always argued like that?'

'Suppose so. They wind each other up all the time. My mum's always drinking, so Alan stays out late and sleeps around. And because he's out shagging around, my mum drinks. It's a vicious circle really.'

'Don't you get sick of it?'

'I've got used to it. At least he's better than the last bloke she went out with. He used to lech all over me.'

'Ugh, gross!'

'It was. Very. Anyway, when they're on at each other, they leave me alone, so it has its good points.' She finished her milkshake and slid from her stool. 'Come on, I need to do some serious shopping.'

'What about your dad?' Emily ran to keep up with Katy's long strides as she crossed the street.

'What about him?'

'Do you still see him?'

'Sometimes. Although my mum doesn't like it. She can't stand him because he left her in the lurch with me and married a blonde bimbo. And the bimbo doesn't like it because she wants him all to herself. Her and the new baby,' she added bitterly.

She hurried on ahead, leaving Emily trailing behind.

Poor Katy, she thought. And to think she had always envied her for being so cool.

Could her life turn out like that? What if her dad moved in with Charlie and they had a baby? She and Sophie would definitely get pushed out then. Except when they needed a babysitter. She felt sick at the thought. No way would she want anything to do with Charlie's kid!

And what if it all went wrong? What if her dad ended up

like Katy's mum, hitting the bottle and brooding about the terrible mistake he'd made? The thought of listening to those earth-shattering rows night after night made her feel ill too.

Her dad was all she had. That was why she was so afraid of Charlie coming between them. It was different for Katy. She still had two parents, even if they were both useless. Emily only had one. If he was taken away from her, she would be all alone. And alone meant vulnerable.

They wandered into various shops and Emily watched as Katy treated herself to a pair of jeans and a couple of new tops with her mum's money. The last place they visited sold accessories – cheap hairslides and bobbles, bangles and brightly coloured plastic things. They had some fun trying on the jewellery and nail polishes. Then Emily spotted a belt she liked.

'Have it,' Katy said.

'Dur, I don't have any money, remember?'

'So?'

'So what do you expect me to do, just walk out with it?'

'Why not?'

She saw the look in Katy's eyes and realised she was serious. 'I couldn't!'

'I do it all the time. It's fun.'

'But it's stealing! What if you get caught?'

'That's part of the buzz, dummy. Anyway, no one's ever caught me, have they?'

'No, but—'

'Look, it's easy. You just have to be really cool about it. Act natural.'

Emily wondered how she could act natural when she already felt as if she had the word 'Thief' emblazoned in neon across her face.

'Very natural,' Katy said sarcastically, as Emily stood rigid with fear, her eyes bulging. 'Why don't you just go up to that girl there and tell her you're going to nick something?'

She tutted. 'Honestly, it's easy. I'll stand behind you, so they don't see what you're doing. Then just slip it in your bag.'

'But what if I get caught?' Emily's tongue was already stuck to the roof of her mouth.

'You won't. No one's going to chase you up the road for something worth a couple of quid, are they? Especially not this lot.' She looked around at the dull-eyed assistants picking at their nail varnish. 'Look, I'll do it if you're scared. Just stand behind me and I'll slip the belt to you, okay? Then get ready to run.'

She didn't think she could run anywhere. Her legs had turned to the consistency of custard. 'I don't want—' she began, but Katy was already in front of her. The next second she felt something being pushed into her bag.

It all happened very fast after that. Emily saw one of the assistants moving towards her across the shop, forcing her way past the girls trying out eyeshadows.

'Leg it!' Katy bolted for the door. Emily tried to follow, but she cannoned into a jewellery display. As earrings showered down around her, she suddenly felt a rush of adrenaline to her legs and sprinted to the door. She made it and briefly felt the daylight on her face before a hand descended on her shoulder and a voice said, 'Excuse me, Miss. Do you mind showing me what's in your bag?'

Chapter 28

Margaret Doyle was very big on honesty. She didn't believe in make-up to conceal her ageing face, and wouldn't give house room to underwear designed to conceal her various lumps and bumps.

But she was looking decidedly shifty when Tess confronted her that Saturday morning.

'What do you mean, where did I spend Christmas? You know where I went. Down to your sister's in London.'

'But you told me you weren't coming back until Saturday. And I've just spoken to Frances and she mentioned you left on Wednesday. I just wondered where you'd been for those three days?'

'Does it matter where I went?' Margaret bristled defensively. 'Honestly, Teresa, I'm sixty-five years old. Anyone would think I was a child, the way you're checking up on me!'

'I'm not checking up. I'm just curious, that's all.' It wasn't like her mother to disappear off the radar for seventy-two hours. After Frances happened to mention it on the phone, she'd come straight round to find out what was going on.

She'd found her mother in the kitchen as usual, tackling some hand-washing at the sink. She did it the old-fashioned way, scrubbing on the stubborn stains with soap and a hard brush.

'Don't trust machines. Hand-washing is the only way to get them really clean,' she always said when she saw Tess piling her laundry willy-nilly into the washer-dryer. Tess sometimes wondered if her mother was born in the wrong century. She'd be much more at home down on the banks of the Ouse, beating her whites with a stone.

She seemed to be scrubbing particularly hard in her agitation. 'Yes, well, if you must know, I decided to have a couple of days in London. That's not a crime, is it?'

'Not at all.' Tess was taken aback. 'Were you on your own?'

'No, I was with my fancy man! There. Are you satisfied now?'

Tess smiled. The idea of her mother with any man, let alone a fancy one, was too ridiculous to be true.

Then Margaret held up the garment she was washing against the light to inspect it for stains, and Tess suddenly saw what it was. 'Mum – is that a man's shirt?'

'Happen it is.' Margaret plunged it quickly back into the bowl of soapy water. 'I'm doing them for Ronnie. His machine's broken down, and since he's been good enough to do a few odd jobs for me, I offered to return the favour. Although it comes to something when you can't even rinse through a few shirts without getting the third degree,' she grumbled.

Tess was still pondering this when her mobile rang. It was Phil.

'Where are you?' he asked.

'At my mum's.'

'Is Dan with you?' She could hear from the rush of traffic in the background that he was in his car.

'No, he's at home. Phil, what's all this about?'

'I'll tell you when I see you. Where can we meet?'

'Can't you just come round to our place?' Tess glanced up. Her mother was wielding the scrubbing-brush like a piston, her spine stiff with disapproval.

'I'd rather not. This is between you and me.'

Tess thought for a moment. 'Well, I'm supposed to be off to the supermarket after I leave here—'

'Give me directions and I'll meet you there.'

She pressed the Off button and looked up. 'It's all right, you can spare me the lecture.'

Margaret blinked. 'What lecture?'

'The one about me not getting too friendly with Phil.'

'It's nothing to do with me,' Margaret said. 'Your private life is your own concern.'

Tess stared at her. Now she really was convinced there was something wrong with her mother.

Phil was at the supermarket before her, waiting in the customer car park, his gleaming Porsche standing out among the everyday Volvos and Fords.

'What's all this about? I thought you weren't coming up until Monday?' she said, steering her trolley in through the automatic doors. Phil followed her.

'I needed to talk to you before then. It's about Dan.'

'What about him?'

Phil looked troubled. 'I don't know if I should be telling you. I promised Dan I wouldn't, but you've got to know sometime.'

Tess stopped dead. Several trolleys cannoned into the back of her. 'Know what? What's going on?'

'He's decided he doesn't want to go to university.'

Her first thought was, Is that all? Phil looked so grave she'd suddenly had the wild idea that Dan was seriously ill and hadn't told her. Then she realised this was serious. This was about Dan's future.

And he hadn't told her.

'Don't be ridiculous,' she said. 'He's got to go to university. It's all planned. He's got all the prospectuses and everything. We've been looking through them for months.'

'Apparently he's changed his mind. He wants to get a job working with computers instead. He says that'll teach him more than three years at uni.'

She pushed her trolley round the fruit and veg department, throwing in apples and carrots at random, her mind elsewhere.

'How long have you known about this?' she demanded.

'He told me when I came up at Christmas.'

'Christmas!' She stopped again. There was a lot of tutting as everyone manoeuvred their trolleys around her. 'You've known since Christmas and you're only telling me now?'

'Dan asked me not to.'

'But I'm his mother!' She'd been sorting out his problems since he was a baby. Every time he hurt himself, she was there with a plaster and a kiss to make it better. Every time someone was cruel to him, she was the one who crashed heads together. And now he'd made one of the biggest decisions of his life and he'd turned to Phil, not her. Phil, whom he'd only known five minutes.

She stared at the artichoke she'd picked up by mistake. 'I'm his mother,' she repeated.

Phil must have noticed her hurt and confusion. 'I had to prise it out of him,' he said quickly. 'He didn't want to tell either of us.'

'I'm not surprised. He probably knew I wouldn't allow it.' She did a three-point turn with the trolley and headed up the next aisle.

'I don't think you've got much say in the matter.'

'Of course I've got a say! Do you think I'm just going to stand by and let him make the biggest mistake of his life?' She pitched a can of beans into the trolley, crushing a packet of chocolate digestives.

'It's his life,' Phil said quietly.

'He's seventeen years old! How's he supposed to make those kind of decisions at that age? He's far too young to know what he wants.'

'You were that age when he was born. I seem to remember you knew exactly what you wanted.'

Tess ignored him. She charged into frozen foods,

randomly helping herself from the freezer cabinets. 'It's ridiculous,' she muttered. 'I'm going straight home to talk some sense into him—'

'Hang on a minute.' Phil held her back as she cut a swathe through the microwaveable ready meals like Boadicea slicing through the Roman army. 'And you wonder why he didn't feel he could talk to you? You can't just rush in there and start laying down the law. He wants to handle this himself.'

Tess looked shaken. 'But he needs me!'

'Not this time.' Phil's voice was gentle, reasonable. All the things Tess wasn't feeling at that moment. 'He's almost grown up, Tess. You've got to let him think for himself.'

Tess looked around at the supermarket shelves, slightly dazed. If Dan didn't need her, she'd lost her purpose in life. She'd been his champion, his protector for so long she wasn't sure she knew how to do anything else.

Phil put his finger under her chin and turned her forlorn face up to meet his. 'You look like you could do with a drink.'

They paid for the shopping and headed for the pub. Tess was still in a state of shock but Phil steered her to a seat and put a brandy in front of her.

She looked down at it. 'Ugh, I hate brandy.'

'Drink it, it'll make you feel better. It's good for shock.'

'I haven't had a shock.'

'Want to bet? You haven't seen your face.'

She glanced at her reflection in the mirror. Come to think of it, she did look a bit wan.

They talked about Dan, and his future. 'He's so young,' Tess wailed.

'He's nearly eighteen.'

'But what if all this turns out to be a horrible mistake?'

'Then he can go back to college and start again. Anyway, it's the only way he's going to get on in life, by making mistakes and learning from them. You can't take that away from him.'

'I'm not trying to take anything away from him.' All she wanted to do was to protect him, just as she'd always done.

Phil managed to calm her down. He was good at that, Tess thought. But then he could afford to be detached. He wasn't as close to Dan as she was.

She said as much to Phil, who looked hurt. 'Just because I haven't known him long doesn't mean I don't love him,' he said.

'I know that.' Tess was instantly contrite. 'But you don't feel for him the way I do. We've been together so long, just the two of us. I know what he's thinking, how he's feeling.' Or she thought she did. Now she wasn't so sure.

'Then maybe it's time you both had some space?'

'Are you trying to say I want him to depend on me?' Tess snapped. 'I've spent seventeen years fighting for just the opposite.'

'And you've done a great job,' Phil said. 'But you've got to let go now. He'll never learn to cope on his own while you're around to fight his battles for him.' He sipped his beer. 'He's willing to give it a go. Why can't you?'

Because I don't know how, she wanted to wail. She stared disconsolately into her drink. It was awful not to feel needed any more.

Phil seemed to understand. 'Maybe it's time you stopped being Dan's mum and started being yourself?' he suggested gently.

'Oh yes? And what do you suggest I do? Take up yoga? Write a novel? Find myself a man?'

'Why not, if that's what you want?'

She smiled. 'And have you anyone in mind, oh great and wise one?'

Phil's face was serious. 'Me,' he said.

Her mobile rang before she had time to take in what he'd said. Tess fell on it, punching the buttons.

'Yes? Hello? Yes, this is Tess Doyle. What? You're joking? Oh my God, when did this happen? Have you contacted her father? Oh, I see. Yes, well, tell her not to worry. I'll see what I can do.'

She pressed the Off switch and turned to Phil. 'That was the police. They've arrested Emily Tyler for shoplifting.'

He frowned. 'Who?'

'You remember, she came round to my place at Christmas?'

'Oh, right.' His face clouded. 'So why are they calling you? Where's her father?'

'Away on some business trip. And Emily's refusing to give the police her surname or a contact number for him. The only number she'd give is mine.'

She gulped down her drink and stood up. Phil watched her. 'I suppose you're going to race down there and help her? Take on the local constabulary if you have to?'

'Of course. What else can I do?'

'What else indeed?' Phil pulled a wry face. 'Another helpless soul with a problem to solve and you can't resist jumping in to help.'

'That's unkind, Phil.'

'It's true, though. Good old Tess Doyle, always doing and fixing. But when are you going to do something about your own life?'

'We're not charging her, because we've nothing to charge her with,' the duty sergeant explained. 'According to the shop assistant, it was her mate who actually pinched the thing. Not that we've got any chance of catching her.' He looked at Tess hopefully.

'Sorry, I can't help you. I don't know any of her friends in Leeds.'

'Anyway, we might have got all this cleared up a long time ago, if she'd been more cooperative.' The sergeant looked grumpy. 'Are you sure you don't have a contact number for her father?'

'I'm afraid not,' Tess lied, hoping her blushing face wouldn't give her away.

'Well, at least you've given us a name and address. We'll send someone round tomorrow to have a word with him.'

'You do that.' By which time, hopefully, she would have managed to calm him down. 'Sergeant, Emily's not usually like this.'

'Hmm.' The police officer looked unconvinced. 'Wait here, I'll get her for you.'

Tess sat in the grim waiting room, staring at the posters telling people to mark their property and lock their valuables away in their cars, and tried to work up some indignation. She'd broken every speed limit to get here, but now her panic had subsided, she realised Phil was right, it was none of her business. Jack should be here sorting this out, instead of playing soldiers in the woods with Charlie.

But any shred of anger disappeared the moment the door opened and Emily came out beside the police officer, pale-faced, her eyes huge with apprehension. When she saw Tess she burst into tears and rushed into her arms. They hugged each other for a moment, then Tess whispered, 'Come on, let's get out of here.'

'Thanks for coming,' Emily mumbled as they got into the car. 'I couldn't think of who else to ring.'

'Why not your dad?'

'I didn't want him to know.'

'He's got to find out sometime. The police will tell him, even if you don't.'

'I know.' She chewed her thumbnail. Tears rolled down her cheeks. Tess fished in her bag for a tissue and handed it to her.

'It's okay,' she said. 'We'll think of something. It's not as if it was your fault, was it?' Emily said nothing. 'I suppose your mate Katy was behind it? It's all right, I'm not going to go back in there and tell them.'

'I was so scared,' Emily sobbed. 'I thought they were going to lock me up. They kept asking me all these questions. I didn't know what to do.'

'It's over now.' Tess put her arm around her. 'Come on, let's get you home.'

'Where can I go?' Emily pulled away from her. 'I can't go home until Dad gets back, and I – I don't want to go back to where I was staying.' Her voice trailed off.

'What about your Gran's? Sophie's there, isn't she?'

Emily shook her head. 'I can't face it. They're bound to ask all kinds of questions and I wouldn't know what to say.' She looked at Tess, biting her lip.

She sighed. 'In that case I suppose there's only one place we can go, isn't there?'

'Where's that?'

Tess started up the car. 'My place,' she said.

Chapter 29

Jack stuck his head out of the bushes and ducked back again as a paint pellet whizzed past his ear and splatted on the tree trunk behind him. He sat down and pulled off his helmet. He was cold and wet, he ached all over, and he was sick to the teeth of squelching around a muddy field being shot at by a bunch of overgrown kids. He wanted to go home.

So much for team-building. In the past twenty-four hours, he'd been drenched after his team's hastily constructed raft fell to bits halfway downriver, he and Greg had nearly come to blows in the rain when their tent collapsed in the middle of the night, and he'd been dangled off a bridge on the end of a piece of abseiling rope by a sadistic bunch of bastards from Accounts.

And now those same sadistic bastards were stalking him through the woods. He was fed up with being yelled at and shot at, and most of all he was fed up with wearing bloody silly army fatigues like Action Man.

He desperately missed his kids. He'd already sneaked out of base camp the previous night to call his mother and speak to Sophie, only to have his mobile confiscated by the over-enthusiastic platoon leader.

'No phoning home!' he'd barked.

'But my family—'

'Sorry, soldier. Your team is your family now.'

How he'd resisted the urge to knock his teeth down his throat Jack didn't know. But he did know that if he met him in the field now he'd probably ram the butt of his paintgun somewhere the sun didn't shine.

The team didn't feel like his family. Not any more. Not since he'd seen what was in Bernard Sweeting's Westpoint file.

Cracking the safe had been easy, thanks to Sam Dobbs' instructions. But now he was beginning to wish he hadn't done it.

Running footsteps crashed through the undergrowth a few yards from where he crouched. Jack ducked down and waited for them to pass. This wasn't a game any more. Since reading that file, he'd begun to wonder who was really on his side.

He'd watched them all last night, gathered around the camp fire, laughing over their barbecue in the rain. Who else knew? he wondered. Who was in on it? He felt as if he couldn't trust anyone any more.

He'd been tempted to talk to Greg about it last night, when they were alone in their tent. His brother-in-law had guessed something was wrong.

'Anything on your mind, Jacko?' he'd said. 'You've been very quiet all evening.'

Jack thought about telling him. But in the end he couldn't bring himself to do it.

'Just thinking about the kids,' he'd said.

There was a rustle in the bushes. Jack couldn't even be bothered to pick up his gun. He didn't care any more. Let them shoot him. At least it would put him out of his misery.

The undergrowth parted and Charlie appeared, looking lean and menacing, like Lara Croft in her fatigues, her paintgun braced at her hip.

'Jack!' She let her gun barrel drop. 'Are you injured?'

'No.'

'Then why aren't you out there in the field, fighting with the others?' God, she was beginning to sound like something out of *Saving Private Ryan*.

'Because I can't be bothered.'

She looked shocked. 'But your team needs you. We're

317

already a man down, thanks to Rav catching a pellet in his backside.'

'I don't care.'

She stared at him. 'But we can't let Accounts beat us!'

'Why not? What does it really matter if they do beat us? I mean, it's not as if we're actually at war, is it? What are they going to do, tie us to chairs and force us to listen to the basics of double-entry bookkeeping?'

'That's not the point.'

'Then what is? What does any of this crap really matter?'

'It's a team-building exercise.'

'Team? Don't make me laugh. We're not a team. Teams don't keep secrets. And they don't lie to each other.'

Charlie frowned. 'What are you talking about?'

He thought about telling her, then decided against it. It was bad enough he knew, without burdening her with it too.

'Nothing. Just battle fatigue, that's all.' He rubbed a weary hand over his eyes. 'Or maybe I've just realised how utterly pointless my job really is.'

'You can't say that! You're the best in the company.'

'The best at what? At designing buildings no one wants? At putting profits before people?'

'I don't know why you're talking like this.' Charlie said. 'It isn't like you.'

'That's just it. It *is* like me. You just don't realise it.'

He stood up. She looked up at him in alarm. 'Where are you going?'

'Out there.' He strapped his gun to his back.

'You're going back to fight?'

'No, I'm going to pack.'

'You're not leaving? You can't. It's against the rules.'

'Maybe I'm tired of playing by other people's rules.'

'What shall I tell Humphrey?'

'Tell him I've gone AWOL.'

He stood up. A paint pellet whizzed past him, narrowly missing his ear.

'Jack?'

He turned. The crack of gunfire was followed by a split second of pain between his eyes, which sent him reeling backwards.

'Bloody hell!' He clapped his hand to his forehead, expecting to see blood. But all he saw was a splodge of bright-yellow paint in the palm of his hand. 'Jesus, what did you do that for?'

She glared at him. 'For being a fucking deserter.'

By the time he got back to the tent he was spattered in so much neon paint he looked like the Berlin Wall. He peeled off his fatigues and tossed them into a corner. He was just pulling on his jeans when Charlie walked in, her combats pristine.

'You survived, then?'

'Of course. And I brought down a whole battalion of bought-ledger clerks single-handed.' She tossed her forage cap on the bed and shook out her red hair. 'I pinned them down in a foxhole. They were begging for mercy by the time I'd finished with them.'

'I bet they were. So does this mean war's over?'

She nodded. 'Everyone's gone to the mess hall to get cleaned up. We won, by the way, in case you're interested?'

'I'm not.'

She watched him throwing his things into his bag. 'You're really going?'

'Looks like it.'

'Can I ask why?'

'I told you, I'm tired of playing games.' He sniffed his sweater, which smelt of musty damp, then flung it into his bag.

'You do realise, if you walk away now, you can kiss goodbye to that senior partnership?'

'To be honest, I don't really care.' The sooner he got out of Crawshaw and Finch the better.

'And are you walking out on me too?' He didn't answer. 'I'll take that as a yes then, shall I?'

'I'm sorry, Charlie.'

There was a long silence. 'Is it because of the girls?' She looked down at her hands, but he could hear in her voice that she was fighting back tears. 'Is it because I didn't try hard enough with them?'

'Maybe it's because you had to try.' He sat down on the camp bed beside her. 'You did everything you could and I'm grateful for that. But it wasn't you, was it? You were always putting it on, having to make an effort.'

'I didn't mind.'

'Not now, maybe. But you would have, sooner or later.' He reached for her hand. 'We don't fit into your life, Charlie. And you don't fit into ours. No matter how hard we both tried, sooner or later we would have ended up resenting each other.'

She snatched her hand away. 'So you're doing this for my benefit, is that what you're saying?'

'No. But I hope one day you'll see why I had to do it.'

'Oh, don't worry. I can see it now!' Her voice spat venom. 'I've had a lucky escape from you, Jack. A bloody lucky escape. You're not the man I thought you were!'

'You're probably right.' He stood up, stuffed the last of his clothes into his holdall and zipped it up. 'I'll be seeing you, then.'

'Don't count on it. I don't waste my time with losers!'

He turned and walked out. As he pushed through the tent flap a boot whizzed through the air, narrowly missing him.

He could still hear her crying when he reached the gate. His heart contracted with pity, but he kept on walking.

★

Charlie lay under the camouflage netting on the assault course and wept. Tears ran down her cheeks and dropped into the mud. She didn't need this. She didn't need to be face down in filth, she didn't need the cold and wet seeping through her combats. And most of all, she didn't need that prick of a platoon leader standing over her, yelling in her ear.

'Move it, soldier!' He prodded her with the butt of his pretend rifle. 'You're letting your team down. They're already twenty seconds behind thanks to you! This is not time to stop and put your make-up on!'

She found the strength and edged forward, propelling herself through the freezing ooze with her elbows. She kept herself going by thinking of all the choice things she was going to say to him when she got out of this wretched hell-hole.

It wasn't just the fact that Jack had walked out that upset her. It was the fact that she'd been dumped so humiliatingly. Everyone knew they were supposed to be an item, and Charlie found it very hard to hold it together when people kept giving her sidelong looks and asking her in hushed tones if she was all right.

In the end she couldn't stand it any more and had phoned the only person she could think of who could make her feel better.

'Well, if it isn't Rambo!' Tom laughed when he answered the phone. 'And what have you been doing today? Fashioning rabbit traps out of your underwear?'

The sound of his voice, so cheerful and welcoming, had been enough to make her burst into tears. Tom was instantly all concern.

It took her ten minutes to tell him everything, because she had to keep breaking off to sob and blow her nose. Tom was the only person she would ever have cried in front of. She didn't have to put on a front, pretend to be Charlie Ferguson the go-getting, hard-nosed bitch. He'd lived with her, seen her at her best and at her worst. He was absolutely her best friend.

Being her best friend, he was full of outraged vehemence about Jack's desertion and called him some choice expletives, which made her feel a lot better. He also gave her a pep talk that wouldn't have disgraced the evil platoon leader.

'Now look here,' he said in his best Colonel Blimp voice. 'You're in the army now, soldier. So you'd better bloody well get on with it. You didn't see me blubbing like a girl when I lost a leg in El Alamein, did you?'

Charlie smiled, wiped her tears. Trust Tom to cheer her up.

'What are you smirking about, soldier? This is no laughing matter, you know!' Another prod with the rifle butt. Charlie inched forward and at last emerged from the netting – only to be faced by a towering wall.

'Don't just stand there! Start climbing!'

'Who do you think I am? Spiderman?' Charlie craned her neck to look up. There didn't seem to be any visible footholds. Feeling the platoon leader bearing down on her, she pushed herself forwards and started climbing.

Somehow she managed to scramble up to the top – and froze. She clung on to the rough timber, looking down at the sea of faces looking up at her, and wondered what the hell she was doing there. She was a planning consultant, not a bloody commando. What the hell did this have to do with putting together traffic-impact assessments?

Rebellion boiled inside her. She began to think Jack Tyler had the right idea walking out, even if he was a treacherous bastard.

'What are you doing up there? Get down immediately!' The platoon leader's red, stubbly face appeared beneath her. As did the ground, which seemed to be coming up to meet her.

'How do you suggest I do that without a parachute?'

'Don't be such a fucking wimp! Get down here now!'

Angry tears sprang into her eyes. 'Don't you call me a fucking wimp! I've just broken a fucking nail, and I'm not prepared to break my fucking neck too!'

The platoon leader opened his mouth, but his yell of rage was drowned out by another sound. The triumphant, stirring sounds of *Ride of the Valkyries*, just like *Apocalypse Now*. Everyone turned to see where it was coming from. Charlie, still clinging to her narrow perch, risked a look. She half expected to see a fleet of American helicopters throbbing across the sky, spraying them all with bullets.

The music grew louder until it was deafening. Then, out of the trees crashed a battered old Volkswagen Beetle, music blaring from the boom box in the back, Tom grimly hanging on behind the wheel.

Charlie laughed so hard she nearly fell off the wall. Tom brought the car to a halt and got out.

'What are you doing up there? Don't jump, you silly cow, he's not worth it!' he called up.

Still laughing, she managed to slither to the ground, not caring that she scraped most of the skin off her hands and shins as she did. By the time she reached solid ground, Tom was in the middle of an altercation with the platoon leader.

'What the hell are you doing here? You can't bring that car in here. This is private property!'

'I'm from Military Intelligence.' Tom flashed a card at him. 'This young lady is needed for a special mission. A matter of national importance. All very hush hush. Strictly need-to-know basis.' He tapped the side of his nose.

'What the—'

'Sorry, old boy. No questions.' He bundled Charlie into the passenger seat and closed the door. 'If I tell you any more, I'd have to kill you.'

They drove off, leaving the platoon leader speechless behind them. Charlie could see him in the wing mirror, watching them, his mouth hanging open.

'You're an idiot, do you know that?' she laughed, as they sped out of the compound and on to the open road. 'And I've left all my stuff back in my tent.'

'We can always go back for it.' Tom stepped on the brake.

'No! They'll probably have the military police out looking for me. Besides, I can't face eating another meal out of a bloody billycan.' She relaxed back against the seat. 'I couldn't believe that bullying bastard's face when you suddenly appeared out of nowhere! What was that card you showed him?'

'My library card. He seemed quite impressed, don't you think?'

Charlie giggled. 'Fool!'

'At least it brought a smile to your face,' Tom commented.

'True.'

'So does this mean you're over Mr Wonderful?'

She thought about it for a moment as she watched the scenery flash past. 'I wouldn't say that. But now I think about it, I suppose Jack had a point. I don't think I'm cut out to be anyone's stepmother.'

'Only in the evil Cinderella and Snow White sense,' Tom agreed.

'I wasn't that bad!' She prodded him in the shoulder. 'But I never realised how much kids restrict you. Just think, I'll be able to go to pubs and not sit outside in the freezing cold to be near the swings. And I'll be able to eat in restaurants that don't have laminated kids' menus.' She smiled blissfully. 'I can't wait. Talking of which, where shall we eat tonight?'

'I told you, we're on a special mission.'

'If it involves eating out of a billycan, count me out.'

'Where's your sense of adventure?' Tom grinned.

'I left it on top of that wretched wall. Along with half a

set of acrylic nails.' She examined her hands. 'So go on, what's this special mission?'

'At eighteen hundred hours we're due to rendezvous at this rather nice little country hotel I spotted in a village on the way here. We will proceed to the bathroom where you will take a shower. Between you and me, you're not smelling your best.'

'Thanks very much! And then?'

'Then at twenty hundred hours we will make a pincer attack on the restaurant. And having successfully completed our mission we will retreat to the bedroom where I will make love to you for the rest of the night.'

Charlie laughed. 'Yeah, right!'

Tom's eyes twinkled. 'You think I'm joking?'

Chapter 30

'What do you mean, she's not here?'

'She's gone home. That's what she said, didn't she, Katy?'

'S'right.' Katy scuffed her boot against the front door mat. When Emily did that, it was a sure sign she was lying.

'And you just let her go, knowing there was no one there?'

'What did you expect me to do? Tie her to the bed?' Jack caught a faint whiff of alcohol on Vanessa Jefferson's breath. 'Anyway, I didn't see her leave. As a matter of fact, her things are still upstairs. I thought you'd come to collect them.'

'You're telling me she's disappeared without taking her stuff with her, and you didn't ring the police?' Sweat broke out all over Jack's body. He glanced back at the car where Sophie was waiting, reassuring himself she was still safe, at least.

'Of course not. Look, don't worry about it. Katy wanders off all the time, don't you, darling? They always turn up in the end.'

'Your daughter might, but mine doesn't.' Jack looked at Katy. 'Are you sure you don't know where she's gone?'

'I told you, didn't I?' Katy couldn't meet his eye.

'I hope you're not calling my daughter a liar?'

Jack looked back at Vanessa, clinging to the doorframe. 'That's exactly what I'm saying. Now she can either tell me what she knows, or she can tell the police. It's her choice.'

'Not the police!' They both turned to face Katy, who looked panic-stricken. 'It wasn't my fault,' she whimpered.

'What wasn't your fault?'

Katy stared at the ground. 'I think Emily might have been arrested.'

And then it all came out. Jack felt the blood drain to his feet, leaving him light-headed as Katy explained what had happened.

'It was her idea, not mine!' she said. 'I didn't want to nick anything, but she thought it would be a laugh. I'm telling the truth this time,' she insisted, as Jack looked sceptical.

'Why should I believe you?'

'*My* daughter isn't the one in the police station,' Vanessa Jefferson said with asperity.

No, but she should be, Jack thought, and held on to his temper. 'Do you know where they took her?' Katy shook her head. 'So you just ran off and left her, is that it?'

'I don't blame her. The poor child must have been frightened to death.' Vanessa put a protective arm around Katy's shoulders. 'If I were you, I'd stop interrogating my daughter and try to track down your own. Oh, and you'd better take her things with you,' she added, as Jack turned to leave. 'I don't want her here any more, leading my Katy astray.'

Jack caught Katy's sly look. 'I think it's a bit late for that,' he muttered.

It took him two frustrating hours before he finally tracked down the police station where Emily had been taken, only to find that she'd been released without charge. Even more bizarrely, it had been Tess Doyle who'd taken her. What the hell was going on?

The duty sergeant must have sensed he was close to breaking point, because he offered him a cup of coffee while he explained what had happened. But Jack still left feeling dazed.

Why hadn't Tess called to tell him what was going on?

Didn't she think he had a right to know if his own daughter had been arrested? Didn't she stop to wonder how it would make him feel, knowing she'd gone through all that and he wasn't there?

'Daddy, slow down!' Sophie pleaded from the seat beside him. Jack glanced at the speedometer. He hadn't realised he was doing well over ninety, his fingers white on the wheel. He eased his foot off the accelerator and forced himself to calm down. This time it was anger, not fear, making his heart race.

His mobile rang just as he reached the turn-off to York. It was Tess.

'Where are you?' she said.

'On my way home.'

'Thank God for that. Listen, Jack—'

'If it's about Emily, I already know.'

'You do? How?'

'Never mind that! Why the hell didn't you tell the police to phone me?'

She sounded taken aback. 'Emily wouldn't give them your number.'

'But you could.'

'She didn't want me to.'

'So what? I'm her father, for Christ's sake! Don't you think I have a right to know if my daughter's locked up in a prison cell?'

'I didn't want to interfere.'

'Fucking hell, Tess!' He was so angry he didn't think of toning down his language for Sophie's sake. 'You bailed my daughter out of jail without telling me! If that's not interfering, what is?'

'What should I have done, left her in there?'

'You know what I mean. Why didn't you pick up the phone and let me know?'

'What do you think I'm doing now?'

Her calmness made the blood sing in his ears. 'We'll talk

about this later,' he threatened and hung up. The second he pressed the button he realised he hadn't even asked how Emily was.

Shit, shit, shit! He banged his hands on the steering wheel. Sophie gave him an old-fashioned look.

'You nearly hit that blue car,' she said.

By the time he got to Tess' bungalow, he was so eaten up with tension and anger he was ready to explode.

'Where is she?' he demanded as soon as she opened the door.

'In Dan's room, listening to CDs. I thought we should talk first.'

'Oh, did you? Since when did you start making the decisions in my family?'

Tess flinched. 'I just wanted to give you the chance to calm down before you said something you might regret, that's all. Look, I realise you must be angry—'

'No, Tess, I don't think you can even imagine how angry I am right now.' The muscles in his jaw ached from where he'd been clenching them for the past hour. 'Let me ask you something. What if it was your son caught shoplifting and I didn't tell you? How would you feel?'

'As pissed off as you, probably. But of course I was going to tell you—'

'When? When were you going to tell me?'

Her confidence faltered in the face of his blazing anger. 'When I felt the time was right.'

'What gives you the right to decide that? I'm Emily's father. I should have been the first to know, not the last! How do you think I felt, going round to pick her up and finding she'd disappeared off the face of the planet?'

'I didn't know you were coming home early, did I?'

'Just as well I did, isn't it? Otherwise I might not have found out at all.'

'What's that supposed to mean?'

'Well, it makes sense, doesn't it? My daughter's arrested

and you're the first person she calls. Then you rush off and collect her and don't bother to tell me. How do I know this wasn't going to be a little secret between the two of you?'

'Now you're being ridiculous.'

'What's ridiculous about it? She obviously feels far closer to you than she does to me—' He broke off, furious at himself for letting his hurt show.

Tess' expression softened. 'Look, why don't you have a drink or something? You look like you need it.'

'No, thank you. I'd like to take my daughter home, please. If it's all right with you?' he added sarcastically.

'Of course. I'll call her.' Tess stiffened. As she headed for the door, she said, 'And you wonder why Emily didn't want the police to call you.'

'What's that supposed to mean?'

'You're hardly the easiest person in the world to talk to, are you?'

He opened his mouth to answer, but she was already gone.

'He didn't sound too happy,' Dan remarked after they'd left.

'He wasn't.' Tess watched them through the window as they drove off. 'Poor Em. I don't think I made a very good job of calming him down.'

'A lifetime's supply of Prozac wouldn't have calmed him down, the mood he was in.'

'Maybe I should go round there, try to explain—'

'Are you mad?' Dan stared at her. 'He'd only bite your head off again. No, I reckon you'd better stay well out of this one, Mum.'

'How can I? Besides, he's right. I should have told him as soon as I found out. I'd be furious if it happened to you.'

'Not much chance of that, with the disabled access in most of the shops around here. Besides, glittery belts aren't really my thing.'

'It's not funny, Dan.'

She went on looking up the empty street through the window until Dan said, 'You're going to do it, aren't you? You're going to go round there?'

'I can't leave it like this.'

'Why are you so bothered? No one's asking you to get involved.'

'I know. But I can't help caring, can I?'

Dan looked at her shrewdly. 'About her or about him?'

She decided to leave him to calm down before she went round. She was having a glass of wine and mindlessly watching *Blind Date* when Phil arrived.

'Sorry, Dan's round at a friend's,' she said as she opened the door. 'I can call him, if you like?'

'It's you I came to see.'

'In that case, you'd better come in.'

He shrugged off his suede jacket. 'How's that girl? The one you rescued.'

'Emily's fine, I think. Can't say the same about her father, though.' She poured him a glass of wine and told him about her confrontation with Jack.

Phil gave her an 'I told you so' look. 'After you went all that way to help her? Don't know why you bothered.'

'Because I can't resist a helpless soul with a problem to solve?' Tess parroted back at him. 'And since my son no longer needs me, I'm forced to inflict myself on strangers.'

Phil smiled. 'I didn't mean to be so harsh. Have you talked to Dan?'

'No, and I'm not going to. I'll wait for him to tell me, if he wants to. I won't push it.'

'Very sensible.'

'But that doesn't mean it's not killing me,' she went on. 'As you may have gathered, patience isn't my strong point.'

'That's why you need me.'

'Excuse me? I wasn't aware I needed anyone.'

He didn't reply. He got up and went over to look at the photos ranged on the mantelpiece. He picked up one of Dan and studied it for a long time.

'He's a great kid, isn't he?'

'The best. But then I am biased.'

'I've really enjoyed spending time with him, more than I ever thought I would.' He put down the photo and picked up another. 'I never really thought about what it would be like to be a father. When Angela and I found out we couldn't have kids, I wasn't that bothered. I couldn't imagine wanting that kind of responsibility.'

Tell me about it, Tess thought bitterly. He'd been quick enough to run away when he found out she was expecting Dan.

'But things have changed now. I've realised what I've been missing all these years. I don't want to lose that.'

'How could you? Dan's part of your life now.'

'I wish he could be a more permanent part.'

Tess laughed. 'You're his father. What could be more permanent than that?'

He put the photo back. It was a picture of her, she noticed. She suddenly had a spooky premonition about what he was going to say, seconds before he turned round and said, 'We could get married?'

She was too shocked to speak for a moment. Finally she asked, 'What's brought this on?'

'I've been thinking about it for a while. I want to be a more permanent part of Dan's life. And yours.'

'Phil, has Dan put you up to this?'

'No! I haven't even spoken to him about it. It was you who made me think, when you said he was trying to bring us together. At first I thought it was a joke, like you. But then I got to thinking some more and I thought, Why not? We make a great team, Tess. We could be good for each other. We're both alone, we're both lonely and—'

'Who said I'm lonely?' Tess interrupted him.

'Aren't you?'

She shook her head. 'Just because I'm alone doesn't mean I'm lonely.'

'Maybe it's just me, then.' He looked wistful.

'So you thought you could pick up where you left off with me?' Tess said. 'A nice ready-made family for you to walk in to?'

He looked uncomfortable. 'That's part of the reason, yes.'

'I see. You split up with your wife and you're feeling as if you've missed out. Then we come along and suddenly you're a family man. You've got a wife to look after you, and a grown-up son you can be proud of, without any of the hassles that go with bringing up kids.'

'If that's what you think, then you don't know me at all!' Phil's eyes blazed. 'All right, I'll admit I'm lonely, but I don't need anyone to look after me. And as for not having the hassles of bringing Dan up, don't you think I'd turn the clock back if I could? I'd give anything to have those years back and for you not to have to go through all that alone.'

Tess stared at the drink in her hand.

'I'm sorry.' He put his glass down on the coffee table and sat down beside her. 'I know I can't make up for the past, but I can share your future. I can make things easy for you, Tess. You and Dan can have the life you should have had.'

Tess bristled. 'Our life has been absolutely fine, thank you,' she snapped. 'We don't need you to come along and make everything okay for us!'

'That's not what I meant at all.' Phil was instantly contrite. 'Of course you've done a brilliant job, you only have to look at Dan to see that. I'm just saying I want to share it. I want to be part of your lives, instead of always feeling like I'm a visitor, on the outside looking in.'

'You can be part of Dan's life without me.'

'But I want you too.'

She regarded him suspiciously. His face was open, sincere, as if he really meant it. It would be so tempting to take him up on his offer. He was a funny, kind, attractive man and they didn't come along every day. They got on well and she knew now that he would be a good husband and father. But still . . .

She smiled. 'You're a lovely man, Phil—'

'Why do I sense a but?'

'But . . . you're doing this for all the wrong reasons. You don't really want me. You've just talked yourself into it because you feel guilty for abandoning us and you think it's the right thing to do.'

'That's not true!'

'Okay, then. Answer me one thing.' She looked him squarely in the eye. 'Do you love me?'

She saw his gaze flicker away, just for a fraction of a second, but it was enough. 'Yes,' he said.

'Sorry, I don't believe you.'

'I do love you,' he insisted. 'I'm just not – in love with you. Not yet. But it could happen,' he added hopefully.

Tess shook her head. 'It wouldn't work.'

'Why not? We're friends, aren't we? Good friends. Isn't that enough?'

'Not for me.'

'So that's it, then?'

'You know it isn't. There'll always be a place for you in Dan's life.'

'But not in yours?'

She shook her head sadly.

They finished their wine in near silence. There wasn't a lot more either of them could say. She asked Phil if he wanted to stay and wait for Dan, but she was relieved when he refused.

They said goodbye at the door. 'I don't suppose there's any chance you might change your mind?' he said. Tess shook her head. 'At least think about it for a couple of days, won't you?'

'I will.' But she already knew her answer would be the same if she thought about it for the next thousand years.

It was just as well Phil didn't stay. Twenty minutes later, Dan called to say he was staying overnight at his friend's. Tess instantly went into Mother mode, checking he'd remembered everything he needed.

'For God's sake, Mum! Stop fussing! I can take care of myself, you know!'

'Of course you can.' She remembered what Phil had told her that morning and checked herself. He was right. Dan was nearly eighteen. But old habits die hard.

She had a bath while she psyched herself up to see Jack. But as she was about to get dressed, the doorbell rang.

Jack looked more exhausted than angry now. The strain of the day was etched into every line of his face.

'Sorry for calling so late,' he said. 'Only I felt we needed to clear the air.'

'Of course. Come in.' She stepped aside. 'I was going to come round myself but I thought I'd give you some time first.'

'Time to calm down, you mean?'

'Something like that.' She led the way into the sitting room. 'Would you like a glass of wine? I think there's some left in the bottle.'

'Drinking alone? That's not a good sign.'

'Not quite. Phil came round.'

He looked from the bottle to her dressing gown. 'I see.'

'How's Emily?'

'In bed. She was worn out after everything that's happened today.'

'I'm not surprised. I guess you must be too?'

'You could say that.' He took the glass she handed him and sank on to the sofa beside her.

Tess chose her next words carefully. 'I wanted to see you, to say I'm sorry. You were right, I should have given the police your number or phoned you straight away. I had no right to interfere like that. I don't blame you for being furious.'

'That was supposed to be my line! I'm the one who should be apologising. You were only doing what you thought was best. But I was in such a state of shock, I hardly knew what I was saying.' He leaned back against the sofa cushion and stared at the ceiling. 'It's not every day your fourteen-year-old daughter gets arrested for shoplifting.'

Tess twisted her glass around in her hands. 'I've been thinking about what you said – about me keeping it a secret. I really would have told you, you know. There's no way I would have kept something like that from you.'

'I know. Like I said, I wasn't thinking too clearly.'

'It's not that Emily feels closer to me than she does to you. If anything, it's because she feels too close to you that she didn't want you to know.'

He turned to look at her. 'How do you work that out?'

'Think about it. The reason she didn't call you is because she didn't want you to see her in that situation. She felt ashamed and didn't want to hurt you. Would she do that if she didn't care?'

He ran his hand through his hair. 'I don't know. I'd like to think you're right.'

'I'm always right.'

At least that coaxed a reluctant smile from him. 'I just wish I wasn't always wrong.'

'You're not.' Impulsively she reached over and covered his hand with hers. Their eyes met and suddenly it felt like the most intimate gesture in the world.

Gingerly she pulled her fingers away and wrapped them around her glass. 'I'm sorry if it spoilt your team-building weekend.'

'That was already over as far as I was concerned.'

'Is that why you came home early?'

He nodded. 'I'd had enough of playing soldiers.' He took a deep breath. 'I've finished with Charlie.'

She suddenly felt light-headed, and it was nothing to do with the wine. 'How did she react?'

'She shot me.'

'What?'

'I made the mistake of telling her when she had a paintgun in her hands.'

'Lucky for you it wasn't a real one.'

'I don't think that would have stopped her.'

He smiled ruefully. A smile that played havoc with her self-control. She held on to her glass even tighter. 'I'm sorry. I liked her.'

'So did I. I still do. But we were never cut out to be a couple.'

'So why did you go out with her?'

'I don't know. Everyone kept telling me it was a good idea, and in the end I believed them. As I said, I like her as a friend. Although whether she'll still be a friend after today I don't know.'

'Maybe you're not ready for another relationship?'

'Oh, I think I am.' His eyes held hers. 'I just don't think Charlie was the right woman.'

The air tingled with anticipation. Tess' gaze shifted from his eyes to his mouth and back again, knowing with absolute certainty that he was going to kiss her.

Then he seemed to change his mind, suddenly turning cool again.

'So what did your ex want?' he asked.

'Sorry?' It took her a moment to drag her thoughts away from her utter disappointment. 'Oh, you mean Phil? Actually he asked me to marry him.'

She waited for him to laugh, but he didn't. 'What did you say?'

'I told him I'd think about it. But he already knows what my answer will be.'

He sipped his drink and thought about it for a long time. 'It might be a good idea,' he said at last.

Her heart plummeted. 'What makes you say that?'

'It makes sense, doesn't it? He's a nice man and he obviously cares about you. And you've already said Dan would like the two of you to get together.'

'And that's a good enough reason, is it?' Frustration made her snap.

'Isn't it?'

'I've spent the last seventeen years putting my son first. Don't you think it's time I thought about what *I* want?'

'And what do you want?'

You, she wanted to shout. But what was the point when he obviously didn't feel the same way?

They finished their drinks and Jack left. Tess watched him walk to his car, still hoping that he might turn around. But he didn't even look back at her.

So that was it. At least she knew where she stood with him now. Absolutely nowhere.

She went back into the sitting room and picked up the empty glasses. She was carrying them back to the kitchen when the doorbell rang again.

Sighing, she dumped the glasses in the sink and went to answer it.

'Don't do it,' Jack said.

'Sorry?'

'Don't marry him.'

'But—'

But she never managed to get the rest out because the next second he'd gathered her into his arms and kissed her.

Chapter 31

He pulled away. 'I'm sorry, I shouldn't have done that.'

Tess didn't answer. Her heart was thundering like the Grand National winner heading for Becher's Brook.

'I've got no right to barge my way into your life like this,' Jack went on. 'It's selfish. And it's ridiculous.'

'Jack—'

'I mean, I'm probably the last man you'd want to get involved with, right? What have I got to offer, apart from two stroppy kids and a lifetime of emotional baggage?'

'Jack, listen—'

'You're right. You're a free agent now. You could probably have anyone you wanted—'

'Jack Tyler! Will you shut up?'

Before he could react she trapped his face between her hands and kissed him. Then she took his hand. 'You'd better come inside before the neighbours start talking.'

They cracked open another bottle of red wine as Jack talked.

'I didn't just come round to apologise,' he said. 'I came round because I needed to see you. That's partly why I split up with Charlie. I realised she wasn't the woman I wanted to be with. It's you I want.'

Tess stared into the ruby depths of her glass. 'When did you work that out?'

'I don't know. It kind of crept up on me. But by the time I'd plucked up the courage to ask you out your ex had got there first.'

'There was nothing going on with me and Phil.'

'I didn't know that at the time, did I? I was jealous as hell when he turned up at that Parents' Evening.'

'Ah yes, the Parents' Evening.' Tess smiled. 'I really did want to go out for that drink with you. But you never asked me again.'

'There didn't seem to be much point. That was when I gave in and started seeing Charlie. I didn't think I had much choice.'

'That wasn't very fair on her.'

'Why do you think I finished it? It wasn't just that I didn't think we were suited. I couldn't stop comparing her to you.'

Tess felt herself blushing. 'I'm not sure we'd bear much comparison. She's so beautiful.'

'Not as beautiful as you.' He laced his fingers between hers. 'At Christmas I realised you were the woman I'd been looking for.'

'It must have been the enticing aroma of turkey giblets that did it!' Tess joked feebly, to cover her raging nerves. 'But if you felt like that, why did you do a disappearing act?'

'Because I couldn't handle seeing you and Phil together. I could see how well you got on and I knew Dan wanted you to be together, so I decided to back off. But it was hell,' he admitted gruffly. 'I spent the rest of the day thinking about the two of you here, alone.'

'And all the time I was thinking about you,' Tess admitted quietly. 'How stupid are we?'

'Very.'

He took her hands in his, pulling her closer to him. It all felt so unreal, as if all her daydreams had come true. Tess was almost afraid to speak.

'So where do we go from here?' she whispered.

He gazed down at her, his eyes warm with desire. 'I know where I'd like to go,' he said.

Somehow they made it to the bedroom. Her body was already molten with longing as they fell on the bed, clothes discarded, mouths fused together.

This was how she'd always imagined it would be, but never thought it would happen. She kept wondering if she was dreaming and had to keep reassuring herself by touching him. But as her fingers moved over every inch of him, feeling the silken skin, the taut sinews, the hard play of muscles under her hands, she still couldn't believe it was real.

But if it was a dream, she wanted to remember every perfect, sexy, delicious moment. She closed her eyes, trying to imprint it all on her memory – his clean scent, his tongue making tantalising circles on her bare skin, the touch of his strong fingers stroking her, sending exquisite sensations shimmering through her body. How perfectly they moved together, his body against hers. It had never felt so right, so perfect. She wanted it to go on for ever.

But finally it was all too much and raw, explosive pleasure took over, blanking out her mind to everything else as their sweat-drenched bodies moved together, harder and faster, spiralling towards oblivion.

Afterwards they lay amid the tangled sheets. Tess was almost afraid to move, worried that the slightest shift would make the blissful illusion disappear.

'Are you okay? You're very quiet.' Jack looked at her, his eyes full of concern.

'I was just worried I might have imagined all this,' she admitted.

He lifted himself up on to his elbow and looked down at her. 'We could always try it again and find out?'

'That sounds tempting.' She smiled up at him. 'Are you sure you're up to it?'

'That sounds like a challenge, Miss Doyle. And you know I can never resist a challenge.' The glint in his eyes sent a tingle of anticipation down her spine, followed seconds later by genuine surprise and pleasure as his lips began to trail over her shoulder, her breasts, and down over the curved planes of her stomach.

God, but he was good at this. She tried to blank out the thought of him practising on Charlie, of her slender, perfect, elongated limbs. What did he make of her in comparison, with her less-than-perfect body?

The thought made her arch away from him. He came up, looking surprised. 'What is it? Don't you like it? Do you want me to stop?'

'It's not that . . .' What could she say? 'I was just – being stupid, that's all. Thinking about Charlie.'

His face darkened. 'What about her?'

'She's so gorgeous and everything, I'm not nearly as beautiful as her. I bet she was really good in bed, too,' she said lamely. She could feel herself blushing.

Jack shifted back up the bed until his face was level with hers. 'Yes, she was. Very good,' he said shortly. 'She gave a virtuoso performance every time.'

'Great.' Tess retreated under the covers and pulled them up to her chin.

'In fact, if sex was an Olympic event, I reckon she would have brought home the gold.'

'All right, you don't have to rub it in!'

'But that's not what it's about, is it? It isn't about pushing the right buttons and hitting the jackpot.'

'Isn't it?'

'No, it isn't. Or at least, it shouldn't be.' He reached out and brushed a damp strand of hair off her face. 'It's about chemistry, being with the right person. I don't suppose you'll believe me when I tell you this, but I never felt as close to Charlie as I did to you when we ended up on my bed during Emily's party.'

'Really?'

He nodded. 'Really. That's when I realised how much I wanted you. Even if you aren't nearly as beautiful as her.'

342

She caught the teasing look in his eyes. 'Bastard!' She reached for a pillow but he was too quick for her. He rolled on top of her, pinning her to the bed, his hard body crushing hers.

He looked down at her. 'Well, Miss Doyle?' he said. 'How about we try for that Olympic gold?'

By the time he left in the early hours, they must have achieved medals in a whole pentathlon at least.

'Do you have to go?' Tess pleaded as she watched him dress in the shadowy darkness.

'I'm afraid so. I meant to leave ages ago, but you kept dragging me back to bed.'

'Excuse me? I don't seem to remember you putting up much resistance.'

'I didn't, did I?' He stood up, pulling on his jeans. Tess lay back against the pillows and admired the sculpted muscles in his broad shoulders, tapering down to the flat stomach. She felt herself go weak with longing again. Now she knew what he was like, would she ever stop lusting after him? she wondered.

'So what happens now?' she whispered.

'I suppose we just go back to our own lives and forget this ever happened. Joke,' he said, as Tess' face fell. 'What do you think happens? Do you seriously think that I'm going to let you go now we've finally got together?'

Put like that, it did sound a bit unlikely. But Tess still couldn't believe her luck. 'What about the girls?'

'What about them?'

'Are you going to say anything to them – about us?'

'What do you suggest? "Guess what, girls? I've just spent the night making mad passionate love to Miss Doyle"?'

Tess blushed. 'You know what I mean.'

'Of course I'm going to tell them. Why shouldn't I?'

'They might not like the idea.'

'Then they'll just have to get used to it, won't they?'

'Like they did with Charlie? That didn't turn out too well, did it?'

'That was different. They never liked Charlie. They love you.'

Not for long, Tess thought. 'Only because I'm not a threat. Emily might feel differently if she knows we're – you know.'

He frowned. 'So what do you suggest? Do you want me to lie to them?'

'No! Of course not. I just don't know how to handle this.' Tess sat up and hugged her knees. 'Maybe we should slow things down a bit – give them a chance to get used to me being around before we make any big declarations?'

'Like an old-fashioned courtship, you mean?' He considered it. 'It might be fun. As long as I can still come round and ravish you every night, of course!' His eyes gleamed.

Tess smiled enigmatically. 'We'll see.'

After he'd gone, Tess lay back amid the sheets, her body still aching pleasurably. What a night. She couldn't remember when she'd ever been made love to so expertly, so thoroughly – or so frequently.

It was all perfect. Too perfect, in a way. Pragmatist that she was, in the back of her mind she couldn't help feeling that something had to happen to spoil it.

And she was pretty sure she knew what that something was. A stroppy fourteen-year-old called Emily.

That was why she was so keen to take things slowly. She didn't want to upset Emily or Sophie. They'd been through enough upheaval already, she didn't want to create any more for them to cope with.

But she knew that if she and Jack were going to make this work, they had to be very, very careful.

It was a few days before Dan finally confided in her about his plans. Tess, mindlessly working her way through a pile of ironing, forced herself not to pitch in straight away with advice.

'So what do you want to do?' she asked, when he'd finished telling her.

Dan eyed her warily. 'Are you feeling all right, Mum?'

'I'm fine. Why shouldn't I be?'

'No reason. It's just I thought you'd try to talk me out of it.'

Tess hid a smile. 'Do you want me to?'

'No.'

She could feel him watching her, still waiting for her to explode. 'It's your life, Dan.'

'So you're not disappointed or anything?'

'Well, of course I would have liked you to go to university. You're a bright boy.' She chose her words carefully. 'But if you really feel you'd be better off getting some hands-on experience—' And you can always go back to college if it doesn't work out, she added silently.

'I do,' said Dan. 'It's not just because I can't face another three years at school. I don't really need a degree for the kind of work I want to do.'

Tess attacked the collar of a blouse with the tip of the iron. 'Jobs aren't that easy to come by, Dan. You might find you need those extra qualifications.'

'I've already got a job. I'm going to work for Phil.'

Tess let the iron drop. 'You're what? Since when?'

'I talked it over with him a couple of days ago. It makes sense, doesn't it? I want to work in computers and he owns his own software business. He says I can go down to Basingstoke and learn the ropes. Then he might think about opening a new office up here. That would be great, wouldn't it?'

But Tess wasn't listening. 'So you two have got it all sewn up, have you? Thanks for talking to me about it! Or doesn't my opinion count for anything any more?'

'Of course it does,' Dan said quietly. 'I just wanted to get it all sorted out before I told you, that's all.'

'You mean you wanted to make sure I couldn't object! Well, I'm sorry, Dan, but I think it's a lousy idea. You and your father haven't thought it through at all.' She picked up the iron and flung the blouse back on to the pile. 'Where are you going to live while all this is going on?'

'With Phil.'

'And his place is suitable, is it? It's all specially adapted?'

'No, but he can easily get that sorted out.'

'Of course he can! Your father's brilliant, he can do anything!' Tess saw him wince, but she didn't care. 'Whatever the problem is, he can wave a magic wand and everything will be perfect! Shame he wasn't here seventeen years ago, then maybe you wouldn't have needed me at all!'

Dan stared at her. 'I thought you'd be happy for me. What's your problem?'

'My problem? My problem is no one seems to care how I feel any more.' Her voice was choked. 'Everyone's doing such a great job, sorting their lives out, and I'm just expected to go along with it.'

'Like you said, it is my life,' Dan pointed out quietly.

'And I'm expected to stand aside and watch you ruin it?'

She hadn't meant it to sound like that. Dan gave her a look of reproach and then left the room, closing the door behind him.

Tess picked up the next item on the ironing pile and slung it on to the board. It was one of Dan's T-shirts. Typical. She wasn't good enough to discuss her own son's future, but she was allowed to do his ironing for him. Maybe she shouldn't bother doing it? Maybe she should stick them all in a bag and pack them off to Phil to do, since he seemed to be calling the shots these days.

She propped the iron up on its stand, covered her face with her hands and allowed the tears to flow. Stupid, stupid, stupid.

She was more angry with Phil than Dan. How dare he take over her son's life without even consulting her! Didn't he think she had a right to have a say in his future? Maybe he'd planned it all, talked Dan out of going to college so he could take him away from her.

But she was even angrier at herself for being so selfish and needy. She'd spent so many years teaching Dan to be independent, but the moment he was, she tried to snatch it all away from him.

She could feel the beginnings of a headache nagging at her temples. She unplugged the iron and went to lie down before it took hold.

She must have fallen asleep because half an hour later she woke up to find Dan reaching over to put a cup of tea on her bedside table.

'I thought you might be needing this,' he said.

'Thanks.' She sat up, rubbing her eyes. 'What time is it?'

'Nearly seven. I've finished the ironing, by the way.'

'Really?' She'd never known him do that before. She didn't even think he knew what the iron was for. As far as he was concerned, clothes just appeared in his wardrobe, flattened as if by magic.

Dan watched her sip her tea. 'I'm sorry,' he mumbled. 'I didn't mean to upset you.'

'And I didn't mean to upset you, either.' Tess gave him a watery smile. 'Take no notice of me, I'm being stupid and selfish. I just can't bear the thought of my little baby leaving, that's all.'

'Mum!' Dan hesitated a moment. 'It doesn't have to be like this. You could come too?'

'What would I do in Basingstoke?' Tess laughed.

'You could find a job. I'm sure they have teachers down there. We could all be together.'

She sighed. 'We've been through all this, Dan. I already told you, it won't work. Your father and I will always be friends, but it can't be any more than that. That's not how relationships work.'

'I only want you to be happy.'

'I'm fine, honestly.'

'And you're sure you don't mind about me going?'

She swallowed hard. Of course she minded. After so long together she couldn't imagine an hour going by when she wouldn't miss him. But she had to let him go.

'I think it's a very good idea,' she said bravely.

It seemed enough for him. He swung his chair round, but as he headed for the door he turned and said, 'Anyway, I don't suppose I'll have to worry about you being lonely, will I? Not now you've got Jack.'

Tess spluttered into her tea. 'How did you know about Jack?'

'Come on, Mum, I might be in a wheelchair but I'm not blind! Someone's put a smile on your face the last few days.' He grinned. 'So how long's it been going on?'

'None of your business! You're not the only one who can have secrets, you know!'

Chapter 32

Jack turned up on Sunday morning with an armful of Sunday papers. The day was cold, grey and wet, and rain dripped off his hair. He was wearing faded Levis, a white shirt and black leather jacket, and Tess felt herself melting with lust.

'Where are the girls?' she asked, after she'd kissed him.

'Sophie's back at the house with her gran. Emily's gone into York shopping with Paris. I thought we could go back to bed with these?' He held up the newspapers. 'Unless, of course, you have any better ideas on how to pass the time?'

'I'd love to, but Dan's here.' Tess glanced over her shoulder. He might be fine about her seeing Jack, but she didn't feel very comfortable about disappearing into her bedroom with him, much as she wanted to.

'In that case, why don't we forget the papers and go out for a walk?'

'A walk?'

'Apparently it's what people used to do before cars came along.'

'Very funny. Why would you want to walk in this weather?'

'Because it's romantic. And it's the only way we're likely to get any time alone. And I do want to be alone with you. Very badly.'

The look in his eyes made her catch her breath. 'In that case, I'll get my umbrella.'

She quickly changed into a skirt and put her contact lenses in. It was crazy, because Jack had seen her in jeans and specs a million times, but it was a long time since she'd had anyone to make an effort for and she wanted to make the most of it.

They made their way up to Haxsall Common. As it was so grey and wet, they had the place virtually to themselves, apart from a few determined dog walkers.

They talked as they trudged through the mulch of mud and wet leaves. Tess could tell Jack had something on his mind. He finally admitted it was a work problem, but wouldn't tell her any more.

'It's something I've got to sort out for myself,' he said grimly, then changed the subject. 'How are the preparations for the Basingstoke move going?'

'Anyone would think he was going next week, the way he's carrying on,' Tess grumbled. 'Actually, if he had his way, he probably would be going next week.' But she'd insisted he stay on at the sixth-form college to finish his A Levels. Tess had been adamant about that and Phil had agreed, much to Dan's chagrin.

'I suppose he can't wait to get out in the big bad world and start earning money?'

'Can't wait to get away from me, more like.' Tess kicked at a stone in her path.

'I'm sure that's not true.'

'Isn't it? You haven't heard him. It's "Phil says this, Phil says that." Apparently Phil is having the ground floor of his house specially adapted into a flat for him so he can have his own space.' She grimaced.

'You should feel flattered,' Jack said. 'It's a sign you've brought him up well if he's that confident. He obviously feels he can cope on his own.'

'I never thought of it like that. Maybe I've got it wrong. Maybe it's just me who can't cope on my own.'

'Then it's lucky you've got me, isn't it?'

He grabbed her, pushed her back against a tree and kissed her long and hard.

Tess came up for air, breathless and laughing. 'Jack! Someone might see!'

'I don't know if you've noticed, but it's pouring with rain and we're the only ones stupid enough to be out in it. Besides, who's going to care?'

'Someone from school? They might tell Emily.'

'So what?' Jack's face clouded. 'I don't like lying to my children. They deserve better than that, and so do you.' He traced the line of her jaw with his finger. 'I don't want this to be some kind of dirty secret. I want the whole world to know about us. Starting with the girls.'

'Are you sure about that?' Tess looked wary. 'I don't like lying to them either. But I don't want them to get hurt. Especially Emily.'

'They'll have to get used to it. Because there's no way I'm giving you up.'

He kissed her again, pushing her back against the tree, his body pressed against hers, their mouths merging together with pent-up desire.

Emily and Paris trailed back from the bus stop, their collars turned up against the rain.

'Well, that was a waste of time,' Emily grumbled. 'All the way to town to buy you a pair of shoes and you leave your purse at home.'

'I said I was sorry, didn't I?' Paris replied tetchily.

They walked in silence for a moment. 'What do you want to do now?' Emily asked.

'You could come back to my place?'

'Why don't you come back to mine instead?' She was secretly a bit unnerved by Paris' mum and her boyfriend, with their pierced eyebrows, noserings and tattoos.

'If you like.' They turned and retraced their steps up the road towards the common, which in turn led to Hollywell Park.

'Bet you're happy now your dad's split up with his girlfriend?' Paris said.

Emily thrust her hands into her pockets, her shoulders hunched against the cold rain. 'It wasn't my fault they split up.'

'You didn't help, did you?'

She shrugged. 'He's much happier now, anyway.' Really happy, in fact. Happier than she'd seen him in ages. And knowing she had nothing to fear made her happier too. She couldn't remember when the house had been so harmonious.

As they reached the road that skirted the common, a small terrier shot out of the undergrowth, narrowly missing the wheels of a passing lorry. The driver slammed on the brakes and yelled something to Emily about keeping her bleeding dog under control.

'He's not mine,' she shouted back. She gathered the shivering animal up in her arms. 'Poor little thing. Look at him, he's terrified.'

'I'm not surprised.' Paris came up behind her. 'Put him down, Em. You don't know where he's been.'

'But he's all cold and wet.' She pressed the dirty, bedraggled fur against her cheek.

'He's not the only one. Can we get home, please? Before I catch pneumonia.'

'What shall I do with him?'

'I don't know. Just put him down and let him run back to his owner.'

'What if he hasn't got one?' She felt under the damp fur. 'He hasn't got a collar. He might be a stray.'

'Well, I'm not taking him home. We're in enough trouble with the landlord.'

Emily peered into the dense undergrowth. 'We should see if we can find his owner.'

'I've got a better idea. Why don't we just let him go?'

But Emily had already set off through the long damp grass. With a long-suffering sigh, Paris followed her.

It was only lunchtime, but the trees overhead blocked out what little light there was, making everything grey and murky as twilight.

'Did you ever see that film, *The Blair Witch Project*?'

'What about it?'

'That was set in a place like this. These three students kept going round and round in circles, getting more and more lost. And all the time this unseen horror was trailing them—'

'Snowy!' someone shrieked from the trees. Emily screamed with fright, and the dog leapt from her arms and bolted towards the undergrowth.

'You naughty dog!' A woman in a grey anorak appeared, a lead in her hand. 'Fancy slipping your collar like that!'

'We found her on the main road. She nearly got run over,' Emily explained. The woman ignored her. She bent down and slipped the collar over the dog's head. Then, with a last dirty look in their direction, she gathered Snowy up in her arms and marched off the way she'd come.

'Charming!' Emily said. 'Did you see that look? Anyone would think we were stealing her flipping dog, not saving its life!'

Paris turned around, distracted. 'Shall we get back now?'

'What's the matter? Did you scare yourself talking about that film?' Emily grinned, but Paris was already hurrying back up the path. 'Hang on a minute, wouldn't it be quicker to keep going down here and join the main road further along?'

'I want to go this way. Come on!'

'But—' Emily turned around and realised why Paris didn't want her to go down that path.

Strolling towards her, hand in hand like a pair of soppy teenagers, were her father and Miss Doyle.

She stopped dead. Every sound seemed to be magnified a

million times – the lonely birdsong, the patter of rain, the muted sound of their laughter.

As if they knew they were being watched, they suddenly looked up and saw her.

'Emily!' Her father made a move towards her. She turned, pushing past Paris and fled down the path, her trainers slipping in the wet leaves.

The next moment seemed to last a lifetime. Tess didn't realise she was still clinging to Jack's hand until he pulled away. 'I'd better go after her.'

She let him go. 'Do you want me to come with you?'

'I don't think that's a good idea, do you?' Jack let out a long ragged breath. 'Jesus, what a mess.' He turned to her. 'Will you be okay making your own way home?'

'Of course. Ring me later,' she called after him. But he'd already disappeared out of view.

He found her in the play park on the village green, slumped on a swing. She looked so heartbreakingly young, her long legs dragging on the ground.

'Emily?' She didn't reply. 'Emily, I want to explain.' He sat on the vacant swing beside her. She turned away from him. 'Look, I'm sorry you had to find out like that. We were going to tell you, honestly. You know I wouldn't do anything to deliberately hurt you – Emily, are you listening to me?'

'Go away,' she growled, so quietly he could barely hear her over the creak of the swing.

Jack opened his mouth to argue, then closed it again. What was the point? It would only antagonise her.

'Fine.' He stood up. 'We'll talk about it later. I'll see you at home, shall I?' There was no answer, just an imperceptible shrug of the shoulders. 'Don't stay out too long, will you? You'll get cold.'

He headed off across the play park, forcing himself to stay

nonchalant and not look back, even though his mind was racing with all kinds of terrors in which Emily didn't come home. What if she ran away? What if he never saw her again?

He fought the urge to rush back, haul her off the swing and drag her home, kicking and protesting but ultimately safe.

He reached the far end of the green and finally allowed himself to sneak a look over his shoulder at the forlorn, drooping figure on the swing.

Please come home, he prayed.

She sat on the swing all afternoon, too afraid to move. While she was here, everything around her was suspended, frozen. If she got up, it would all become real again and she didn't want that.

She felt utterly, devastatingly alone, more even than when her mum had died. The two people she'd trusted most had betrayed her. Now she had no one in the world to turn to.

Every time she closed her eyes she saw them again, holding hands, gazing into each other's eyes, as if no one else mattered. As if she didn't matter.

She felt such a fool, not knowing. It must have been going on for ages. They'd probably been laughing at her the whole time.

And to think she'd trusted Tess, confided in her about things she couldn't tell anyone else. She'd thought Tess was her friend. Now she realised she was only pretending to be nice to her so she could get close to her dad. How stupid could she be? She was probably the only one who didn't know what was going on.

It was late afternoon and getting dark when she finally went home. The cold and damp had seeped through her clothes right through to her bones, and her misery had crystallised into hard, implacable anger.

Her father was in the kitchen, loading the washing machine. She could hear Sophie playing upstairs.

He looked up as she walked in. His expression was carefully neutral but she could see the strain in his eyes. Good. She hoped she'd really worried him. He deserved to feel bad.

'You're back, then?' He sounded falsely jolly. 'Bet it was freezing out there?'

She ignored him and went to the fridge for some orange juice. She'd mentally rehearsed every bitter, cutting line she was going to say, but when she saw him again she was so angry she couldn't bring herself to speak.

He sighed and closed the washing-machine door. 'How long is this silent treatment going to go on? If you've got something to say, why don't you just come out and say it?'

She hitched herself on to the stool at the breakfast bar and filled her glass with juice, but still said nothing. She wanted to wind him up, to make him feel as angry as she felt.

She expected him to yell at her, but after a moment he went back to programming the machine. That showed how much he cared, didn't it? He couldn't even be bothered to lose his temper.

Emily stared at the glass in her hands. 'So how long's it been going on?'

'A week.'

'And when were you going to tell me? Or weren't you going to bother?'

'Of course we were going to tell you. We were just waiting for the right time.'

Emily snorted. 'And when was that going to be? A month? A year? Just before the wedding?'

'Don't be ridiculous.'

His dismissive remark made her hackles rise again. 'You're always lying to me,' she accused.

'That's not fair—'

'What about Charlie? You told me she was just someone from work and the next minute she'd practically moved in!' She stopped, a thought occuring to her. 'Is that why you split up with her?' She immediately saw from his guilty expression that it was. 'Did she find out you were shagging my teacher behind her back?'

'That's enough!' He so rarely shouted at her, it made her shrink back. 'I won't have you talking like that. You can show some respect.'

'Why? You never show me any!'

'I don't have to ask a fourteen-year-old's permission to live my life, do I? What I do is none of your business.'

'I'm not a kid.'

'Then stop acting like one!' He was losing his temper now, she could tell. A muscle pounded in his cheek.

'I suppose it was her idea to keep it a secret?' An image of Tess, all smiling and friendly, filled her mind. And all the time she was plotting to take her father away.

'And you wonder why, the way you're acting?'

'I think it's disgusting.'

'I don't really care what you think.'

She stared at him, furious. He used to care. It just showed how Tess had got to him, wheedled her way in between them.

'She's a bitch and I hate her.'

'You said that about Charlie. I'm not allowed to have anyone, am I?'

No, she wanted to shout. No, you're not allowed to have anyone. Not if it makes you turn against us.

Not if it makes you forget Mum.

'I'm not going to give her up, Em. Not like Charlie. It's different this time.'

'Are you in love with her or something?' Her mouth curled with contempt.

'Yes,' he said quietly. 'Yes, I think I am.'

She blundered to her feet, knocking the glass over. 'You can't!' she screamed. 'You can't say that, you can't!'

'Emily, listen. Just because I love Tess doesn't change the way I feel about you and Sophie. You still come first, you always will.' He reached for her but she pulled away. Panic clawed at her, clutching at her throat so she could hardly breathe.

'What about Mum?' The words were out before she could control them.

He flinched. 'What about her?'

What about her? Emily stared at him in disbelief. How could he even ask that question? It was like he'd already dismissed her.

'Emily, your mum's dead. Now, I wish that wasn't true as much as you do—'

'No, you don't! You're glad she's dead. I bet you never even loved her!'

His face lost its expression. 'Emily, don't say that. Don't ever say that.'

'It's true!' She backed away, out of his reach. 'How can you say you loved her when all you want to do is find someone else?' The words came tumbling out, angry and spiteful. She could see the raw pain in his eyes, but she wanted to hurt him, just like she was hurting.

'Emily, stop this. You don't know what you're saying.'

'Yes, I do. You never loved Mum. You never even—'

The stinging slap took them both by surprise. Emily recoiled and put her hand to her cheek. She could see the shock in her father's eyes, mirroring her own.

'Emily—'

'Leave me alone!' She stumbled backwards towards the doorway. 'I hate you! I wish you were dead instead of Mum!'

She thudded up the stairs. Just before she slammed her bedroom door, she heard his voice in the hall below.

'You know what? So do I.'

'Bloody hell, so what happened then?' Ros said. She'd dropped everything and come over as soon as Jack had phoned.

'Not much. She hasn't spoken to me since.' Jack collapsed back against the sofa cushions and nursed the drink Ros had given him. 'God, what have I done? A year ago I would never have raised my hand to her, and now—'

'Jack, you lost your temper. That doesn't make you a monster. Besides, from what you've told me, I'm not surprised you lost it.'

'That still doesn't make it right, does it?' Jack lifted his glass, his hand shaking. 'I feel I've let her down. And I've given her another reason to hate me. As if she needs one,' he said grimly.

'She'll get over it.'

'You think so? You didn't hear her. All those things she said were so cruel.'

'She was just lashing out because she was angry. And scared.'

'Scared?'

'I suppose she can see how serious you are about Tess. That's bound to be frightening.'

'But I thought she liked her?'

'Liking someone and wanting them to take your mum's place are two different things.'

'Tess could never take Miranda's place. She wouldn't want to.'

'I know that and so do you. But maybe Emily needs convincing?'

'If she ever listens to me again.' He looked up at the ceiling, then at Ros. 'Do you think she's right? Am I being disloyal to Miranda?'

Ros put her arm round his shoulders. 'Jack, no one could have loved Miranda more than you did. But she's gone now. And knowing her, she wouldn't have wanted you to be alone. I reckon if she could have picked someone, it would have been Tess. You two are made for each other.'

Jack managed a thin smile. 'I seem to remember you said that about Charlie.'

'Yes, well, I was wrong. And you don't have to look at me like that, I know I don't admit it very often. And if you breathe a word to Greg, I'll kill you.' She shook a warning finger under his nose.

'I think Emily might beat you to it.'

'She'll come round,' Ros promised.

The phone rang just as she was leaving. 'I expect that's Greg, fretting about me leaving him so long with the kids,' Ros smiled.

But it was Tess. 'I wondered if everything was all right?'

Jack suddenly remembered she'd asked him to call her and felt guilty. He mouthed goodbye to Ros as she let herself out. 'Quite peaceful at the moment. But only because Emily's barricaded herself in her room and won't speak to anyone.'

'Oh God. She hasn't calmed down, then?'

'It's all relative, isn't it? She's not actually shouting and throwing things now, but I think it's more simmering resentment than actual calm.' He felt very weary, exhausted by the day. He just wanted to go to bed and wake up and for it to be tomorrow.

Except he had the feeling tomorrow would be just as bad, if not worse.

'Would it help if I came round?'

About as much as throwing petrol on a chip-pan fire. 'Not unless you're a trained seige negotiator?'

'I'm afraid not.' There was a smile in her voice. 'Poor you. I feel so guilty.'

'Why should you feel guilty?'

'It's my fault you're going through this. I talked you out of telling the girls.'

'I don't think that would have helped somehow.' He didn't tell her about the things Emily had said. He didn't want to upset her.

He looked up at the sound of footsteps overhead. 'Hang on, I think something's stirring upstairs.' He lowered his voice. 'I'd better go.'

'Will you call me later?'

'I'll try.' He put the phone down and gazed nervously at the ceiling.

Chapter 33

That evening Tess went to visit her mother. She didn't bother calling first because she knew Margaret Doyle always had her flat spick and span, ready for visitors. She frowned on Tess' habit of only tidying up when she was expecting someone.

It took a while for her mother to answer the door. She looked rather flustered to see Tess.

'Teresa! What are you doing here?'

'That's a nice greeting!' Tess looked her up and down. There was something different about her. Her hair was set in soft, flattering waves around her face and under her usual beige cardigan she wore a blouse in a racy shade of eau-de-Nil. 'Are you going to invite me in, or do I have to stand out here freezing like a Jehovah's Witness?'

It was meant as a joke but Margaret looked as if she was seriously considering it. 'I suppose you'd better come in,' she said finally.

In the hall, Tess shook off her wet coat and sniffed the air. 'Something smells good?'

'I was just having a bit of dinner.'

'On your own? You don't usually go to all that trouble just for—' She stopped in the kitchen doorway. There were two plates on the kitchen table. Ronnie was filling the kettle at the sink.

'All right, lass?' he beamed at her. 'I was just making a brew, do you fancy one?'

Tess nodded, too dumbfounded by the flowery pinny around his waist to speak.

'Shame you weren't around just now, or you could've had something to eat with us. She cooks a grand piece of beef, your mum.' His blue eyes twinkled appreciatively at Margaret, who dimpled in response. Tess peered at her. If she didn't know better, she would swear her mother was blushing.

Margaret noticed Tess staring at her, pulled herself together and began clearing the plates.

Tess frowned at the bottle on the table. 'Is that wine?'

'It is, lass. Would you prefer a glass of that to tea? I think there's some left in the bottle, isn't there, Maggie?'

'No thanks.' Tess looked at her mother. 'I've never known you to drink wine?'

'I was very partial to a glass when your father was alive.' Margaret looked defensive. 'But there's no point opening a bottle just for yourself.'

'Why not? I do.'

'I know.' Margaret's severe look was back in place. 'And most of the time you end up drinking the lot.'

'I've been introducing your mother to the delights of New World wines,' Ronnie explained.

'Ronnie belongs to a wine club,' her mother added proudly, as if she'd announced he belonged to the Prime Minister's cabinet. 'I never knew there were such things.'

'Oh yes?' And what other delights had he been introducing her to? Tess wondered. She watched them moving around the kitchen together, fussing over the washing-up. She was sure Ronnie must be a regular visitor. He certainly seemed to know his way around her mother's kitchen; he put the dishes away exactly how Margaret liked them, something Tess hadn't managed in thirty-four years.

There was something very odd going on. It was as if her mother had been abducted by aliens and replaced by this strange, smiling creature with a taste for eau-de-Nil blouses and Chilean Chardonnay.

'Your hair looks nice,' she said.

'Do you think so?' Margaret patted her soft curls.

'Takes years off her, doesn't it?' Ronnie piped up. 'I've been telling her she suits it like that, but you know what your mother's like about compliments.'

He smiled at her. Fondly. Almost lovingly, in fact. Tess looked from one to the other and suddenly it all added up.

'I'm just going to the loo,' she said.

On the way back she sneaked into her mother's bedroom to take a look around. It looked just the way it always did – neat, clean, unadorned, with faded floral-print wallpaper and a pink silk eiderdown on the bed. There were photos of her grandchildren on her dressing table, alongside a neatly arranged tortoiseshell-backed hairbrush and comb set, and a bottle of Yardley's lavender water – and a make-up bag.

Tess rummaged quickly through it. As far as she knew her mother had made the same pot of face powder and pale-pink Rimmel lipstick last all her adult life, rationing it strictly for special occasions. But the make-up bag contained light-reflecting foundation, cream blusher, mascara and a new lipstick in a very flattering shade of warm coral. Max Factor, no less.

Tess tried it on the back of her hand. Either Ronnie was a cross-dresser, or her mother had been on an unheard-of spending spree in Boots.

'If you tell me what you're looking for, I can help you find it.' She jumped. Margaret stood in the doorway, her arms folded across her chest. No amount of light-reflecting make-up could hide her scowl. 'Got lost on your way to the bathroom, did you? You should know where it is by now.'

'I – I –' Tess looked around, searching for an excuse. There wasn't one. 'I was just trying to find out what's going on,' she said.

'Why didn't you just ask me?'

Tess opened and closed her mouth, then opened it again. 'Okay, then. What's going on?'

'None of your business,' Margaret said flatly.

'But I'm your daughter!'

'That doesn't give you the right to go prying into my affairs.' Margaret snatched the make-up bag away from her and put it back down on the dressing table.

Tess sat down on the bed. 'What's going on between you and Ronnie?'

'I don't know what you're talking about. He's just a friend from the Over Sixties club, that's all.' Her mother's sheepish expression gave her away.

'You've got lots of friends from the Over Sixties club, but I've never known you to invite any of them over for dinner. And how come he's allowed to call you Maggie? And what are his shirts doing hanging over there?' She suddenly noticed the row of crisply ironed shirts hanging up on the wardrobe doorknob, ready to be put away.

'All right, all right!' Margaret looked irritable. 'Since you're that bothered I'll tell you. Ronnie and I are engaged.'

'What! When? How?'

'He asked me to marry him at Christmas. When we were in London.'

So she wasn't lying when she said she'd gone with her fancy man! 'Does Frances know about this?'

Margaret shook her head. 'I met up with Ronnie after I'd left your sister's. We wanted to keep it quiet until we'd set a date for the wedding.'

'And have you?'

'Not yet. We're hoping for some time in the early summer. You can't afford to wait that long when you get to our age. That's why we've decided to live together now.'

'Live together!' Without thinking she glanced at the other side of the bed she was sitting on. Her father's side.

There were a packet of Rennies and a Len Deighton paperback on the bedside table. She shot to her feet.

'Don't look so shocked.' Her mother's eyes gleamed with amusement. 'It does happen these days.'

Maybe, but not to her mother. Margaret Doyle, sharing her bed with a man! And getting married! She never imagined in her wildest dreams she would ever see the day.

'I know it's probably come as a shock,' Margaret said.

'You could say that!'

'But I hope you and your sister can be happy for us?' Tess didn't answer. 'Ronnie's a nice man, once you get to know him.'

'I'm sure he is.' That wasn't the point. The point was her mother had made such a huge, life-changing decision and she hadn't been told. Just like Dan. Why was it that no one wanted to discuss anything with her these days?

'I'm lucky to find someone like him,' Margaret went on. 'Single men are difficult to come by once you get to my age. Ones who've still got all their faculties, anyway.'

Tess suppressed a shudder. She didn't want to think about Ronnie's faculties, or how well they worked.

'And we're company for each other. It's a long time since I had that.'

Tess was stung. 'You've got me.'

'I know, but you've got your own life.' That's a matter of opinion, Tess thought. It turned out what she had always thought of as her life had been built around other people's. And now they were all moving away from her.

'I didn't realise you were so lonely?' she said.

'You wouldn't, would you? I didn't know myself until I met Ronnie.' Margaret twisted the wedding ring on her finger. Her father's ring. 'I've been on my own for twenty-five years, Teresa. Longer than I was married. And in all that time I've never so much as looked at another man. Never thought I'd want to. Until now.' She smiled mistily. 'I know we're no Romeo and Juliet. We're both a bit old for that nonsense. But like I said, we're company for each other. You miss that when you get to my age.'

'Why didn't you tell me?'

'I don't know. I suppose I knew it was a bit foolish.' She smiled shakily. 'Anyway, look on the bright side. At least if I've got Ronnie, I won't be a burden to you in my old age!'

'Tea's up,' Ronnie called.

'Give him a chance. For my sake?' Margaret pleaded as they headed for the kitchen.

They drank their tea and chatted, and half an hour later Tess left, knowing she liked Ronnie. And she only had to look at the way he fussed around her mother to see he adored her. But that didn't stop her feeling hurt and upset.

Fairly or unfairly, her mother was always fixed in her mind as living alone, staying faithful to the man she'd lost more than twenty-five years before. A man who could never be replaced.

Until now. Now everything had changed, shifted around. Tess didn't know why it should unsettle her after so many years, but it did.

The light on her answer machine was blinking in the darkness when she got home. Tess dumped her bag on the floor and pressed the Play button.

'Hi, it's me.' Jack sounded weary. 'Just to let you know the war's still going on over here. Give me a call when you get in. Doesn't matter what time it is. I just need to hear a friendly voice.'

Tess went into the kitchen, found the half-empty wine bottle in the fridge and poured herself a glass. New World wines, indeed! What would Ronnie be introducing her mother to next: salsa dancing?

A stab of jealousy went through her and suddenly she thought of Emily. If she could feel like this after twenty-five years, how much worse must Emily be feeling after one? Her grief was still so raw. And she was so much younger than Tess, so vulnerable and unable to deal with her

367

emotions. No wonder she hated Tess and her father for what they'd done. She thought she was the centre of her father's life, just like Tess did her mother. To find out things had changed so dramatically, and no one had told her about it, must have hurt her more than anyone could imagine.

Heavy-hearted, she picked up the phone and dialled Jack's number.

'I don't believe I'm hearing this.' Jack paced the room. He'd come straight over after Tess' call. 'After everything that's happened, you're saying we shouldn't see each other any more?'

'I didn't say that.'

'Well, excuse me, but that's how it sounds. Would you mind explaining to me exactly what your mother's marriage has got to do with us?'

'I told you. Seeing her with Ronnie just made me realise how Emily must be feeling. This must be so hard for her. All this sneaking around behind her back, she must feel as if we've betrayed her.'

'Right now I don't care how she feels.'

She stared at him, shocked. 'You don't mean that.'

'Don't I? You didn't hear some of the things she said to me. Hurtful, spiteful things. About me and Miranda.'

'She was angry and hurt.'

'Sometimes I think she really believes she has the monopoly on pain.'

'That's teenagers for you. They're not exactly known for their generosity of spirit.'

Jack sat down on the sofa and reached for her hand. 'Ironic, isn't it? You're sticking up for her and she doesn't have a good word to say about you.'

'You get used to it.' Tess shrugged. 'Once you've read the obscene graffiti about yourself on a boys' toilet wall, insults don't seem to touch you.'

'How obscene?' Jack raised his brows questioningly. The old sparkle was there in his eyes. It would have been so easy to forget about Emily and all their problems and just enjoy being together, but Tess knew it wouldn't solve anything.

'Never you mind.' She tried to slip her hand from his, but Jack held on to it.

'I don't want to lose you,' he said. 'I'm a grown man. I'm not having my life dictated by a fourteen-year-old.'

'But if it's making her this unhappy—'

'She'll get over it. If I have to stop seeing you, I'm not sure I will.'

She saw the look in his eyes and her stomach did a backflip. She forced herself to stay calm. 'I'm not saying it's for ever. Just until the dust settles—'

'How long is that? Should we put our lives on hold until she's sixteen? Or eighteen? Or shall we just wait until she's married with kids of her own before we broach the subject? I love you, Tess. I never thought I could feel like this about anyone after Miranda died. I'm not prepared to give you up.'

How long had she dreamed of hearing him say those words? She wanted to ask him to say them again, just so she could bask in them.

'So you think we should just tough it out? Tell Emily she's got to like it or lump it?'

He looked defensive. 'Why not?'

'And what if she doesn't forgive you? What if this ruins your relationship for ever?'

'It will ruin our relationship anyway if she drives you away.'

'She won't.' She squeezed his hand reassuringly. 'I told you, if we just leave it for a few months, it might give her a chance to calm down. Anything could happen in that time. She might grow up a bit, see things differently—'

'Or you could decide you're better off without me?' Jack's voice turned cold. 'Are you sure that's not what all this is about? You've seen what Emily can be like and you've realised you don't need the hassle?'

'If I felt like that, would I be bothering to have this conversation?' she snapped back. 'I want this to last, Jack. That's why I want to do it properly. For everyone's sake.'

She could see him wavering. Part of her – the stupid, romantic part – wanted him to take her in his arms, tell her he couldn't go through with it, that he didn't think he could last a day, let alone a month, without her.

But her practical side knew it was never going to be like that. He could see the sense in what she was saying, even if he wasn't ready to admit it.

'How many months?' he said finally.

'I don't know – maybe six?'

'Six months!' He released her hand and began pacing again. 'That's a bloody lifetime! Why should I put my life on hold for that long? If there's one thing Miranda's death has taught me it's that life's short and you have to grab happiness while you can.'

Tess waited quietly for the storm to pass. Finally he calmed down and said, 'You're serious about this, aren't you?'

'It's the only way.'

He thought about it for a moment. 'Couldn't we meet in secret?'

Tess rolled her eyes. 'How do you think we got into this mess in the first place?'

'I suppose you're right,' he admitted grudgingly. 'It's still going to be bloody hard, though. I mean, Haxsall isn't exactly a seething metropolis. We're bound to bump into each other—'

'We're both adults. I'm sure we can manage to be civilised.'

'And what about when the six months are up?'

'Then we'll talk about it, and if we both still feel the same—'

'So you're saying you might not?'

'I'm saying *you* might not.'

He was silent for a moment. 'I must be stupid to agree to this,' he groaned.

Chapter 34

Jack sat in his office, looking down at the piece of bone in his hand. That harmless little fragment had changed everything. It had even made him rethink his future at Crawshaw and Finch.

It would be so simple to throw it away, pretend he'd never seen it. That would be the easy way out.

At least he had something to distract him. He didn't know how he would have got through the last five days if he hadn't had work to stop him going out of his mind. He'd thrown himself into it, spending fifteen-hour days making phone calls, preparing drawings and labouring on the computer. It helped him forget.

And it helped him avoid Emily. At least she was talking to him now, although things were still uneasy between them. But inside Jack still burned with anger. He was afraid if he had to look at her sulky face or listen to how badly life had treated her, he might say something he regretted.

Greg walked in while he was still deep in thought. 'Why aren't you in the boardroom? The Westpoint meeting's due to start in — what have you got there?' Jack put the bone down on the desk. Greg stared at it for a moment, then laughed. 'Sophie's missing treasure. Where did you find it?'

'In Bernard Sweeting's safe.'

Greg picked it up and turned it over in his hand. 'What was it doing in there, I wonder?'

'You tell me.'

He saw Greg's eyes flicker. 'Don't know what you're talking about.'

'Really? So it wasn't you who gave it to Bernard for analysis?'

'You know it wasn't.' Greg laughed uneasily. 'What is this? Is there some kind of conspiracy going on at Crawshaw and Finch?'

'If there is, you're right in the middle of it.'

There was a long silence. Then Greg sat down heavily in the chair opposite his, all the fight gone out of him. 'How did you find out?'

'I saw the trial pit up on the site. Bernard wasn't very good at hiding his tracks.'

'Stupid bugger. He always was too thorough for his own good.' Greg picked up the fragment of bone. 'I told him to get rid of this thing.' He looked at Jack. 'I suppose he's still got that bloody Environmental Impact Assessment report too?'

'No, he hasn't. I have.' Jack pulled the file out of his drawer and slapped it on the desk. 'Makes interesting reading, doesn't it? I'm amazed no one picked up on all this stuff earlier.'

'They wouldn't, would they? All the previous investigations were on a different part of the site. No one would ever have known it was there, if only—'

'If only Sophie hadn't dug that bone up. I'm amazed she didn't find anything else.' Jack flicked through the file in front of him. 'Quite a discovery, wasn't it? Traces of mosaic floor, fragments of pottery—'

'Don't rub it in,' Greg groaned.

'All pointing to this being the site of a Roman temple. Quite an important one, by all accounts.'

'I'm afraid so.'

Jack closed the file. 'So who else knows about this?'

'Bernard, of course. And Peter Jameson.'

Jack looked up sharply. 'Jameson knows?'

'Of course he knows. Who do you think told us to cover it up?'

'But why?'

'Work it out, Jack. If anyone finds out about this, all hell will break loose. The place will be swarming with archaeologists and the first thing they'll do is declare it a site of historical importance. Then it'll be goodbye, Westpoint.'

'So he told you to keep quiet about it?'

'He said in a couple of months it wouldn't make any difference. He promised he'd make it worth our while.'

Jack suddenly remembered Peter Jameson's new-found friendship with Greg. The cosy dinners, the games of golf, the invitations to his villa. It all made sense.

'You let him bribe you,' he said.

'Yes, I let him bribe me.' Greg's eyes were cold. 'You don't have to look so sanctimonious about it, Jack. We all know you'd never stoop so low.'

'I never thought you would, either.'

'Well, I did. And do you know why? Because it felt good to be noticed, instead of always being known as Jack Tyler's brother-in-law.'

Jack frowned. 'What are you talking about?'

'Oh, come on, Jacko! Do you have any idea what it's like, living in your shadow? No matter how hard I try, I know I'm never going to match up to you. Jack Tyler, the golden boy. Top of the class. The college babe magnet. The would-be senior partner.' His face was bitter. 'And what am I? Greg Randall, the also-ran.'

'Humphrey put you in charge of this project.'

'Only because you turned the job down! Everyone knows he asked you first, Jack. How do you think that makes me feel, being second best again?'

Jack stared at him. He'd always got on so well with his brother-in-law, he had no idea his resentment went so deep.

'Look, don't feel bad about it. You can't help being a hero.' Greg smiled at him. 'Anyway, I've proved my real worth, haven't I? I've screwed up again.' He stood up.

'Where are you going?'

'To see Humphrey and tell him about all this.'

'But you could lose your job.'

'Maybe. But we can't keep this hushed up, can we?' Jack didn't answer. 'To tell the truth, it'll be a relief to have it all in the open. I always hated lying. And I was crap at it. Just like everything else, really.'

'I'm sorry,' Jack said.

Greg shrugged. 'Like I said, don't feel bad. This was my mistake, not yours.'

He'd got to the door when Jack called him back. 'Wait. Don't go just yet. There might be another way . . .'

Humphrey had already opened the meeting by the time they arrived in the boardroom. Jack looked around at the men in suits ranged around the table. Peter Jameson was at the far end, looking smug. There was no sign of Bernard Sweeting.

Jack wasn't surprised. He'd been on stress leave for the past two weeks. The strain of keeping his findings a secret must have been too much for him. Bernard was a conscientious man, and good at his job. Just like Greg.

'Ah, Jack.' Jack felt a twinge of irritation as Humphrey greeted him and ignored Greg. 'I was just saying, it looks as if the public inquiry is in the bag. The opposition are in disarray now we've got the council on our side.'

'With any luck the whole thing should be wrapped up soon, then you can get the contractors on to the site,' Peter Jameson concluded. 'The quicker we get started, the better.'

I'll bet, Jack thought. He glanced at Greg, who cleared his throat and said, 'There may be a problem with that.'

Peter's smile didn't waver. 'What kind of problem, Greg?'

Greg reached over and topped up his glass from the water jug in the middle of the table. Only Jack could see

375

how much his hand was shaking. 'We've been doing some further investigations and we've come up with the possibility that the site may hold special archaeological interest.'

A ripple ran around the table. 'What kind of archaeological interest?' Humphrey asked.

'We're not quite sure yet.' Greg made a show of consulting his notes. 'But initial surveys lead us to believe it may be a Roman temple.'

He passed copies of the report around the table. There was much murmuring as everyone flicked through it. Peter Jameson didn't bother to open his, Jack noticed.

'Well,' Humphrey sat back in his seat. 'This puts rather a different spin on things, doesn't it?'

Jack glanced at Peter. He looked as if he was about to explode with frustration, but there was nothing he could do about it. If he tried to drop Greg in it, he would have to admit he already knew about the report himself.

'I wasn't aware we'd requested these extra environmental studies to be done?' He glared at Greg.

'You didn't,' Jack said. 'But it's just as well we did, isn't it? Or no one would ever have known it was there.'

'Quite.' Peter shot him a look of loathing. 'Couldn't we just build anyway? Surely if no one's found it by now they're not going to miss it for another couple of centuries,' he joked.

Greg regarded him steadily. 'I think the archaeological world might take a different view.'

'So do I,' Humphrey said. 'We're going to have to rethink this whole project in the light of these findings.'

The meeting broke up shortly after that. Jack left them still comparing notes outside the boardroom and went back to his office.

Vicky guiltily folded up her copy of the *Daily Mail* and began tapping on the keyboard as he approached. 'Meeting over already?' she asked.

'There didn't seem to be much more to say.' He looked around. 'Have you got any cardboard boxes, Vick?'

'There are probably some downstairs. Why, are you having a clear-out?'

'You could say that.'

Half an hour later, Humphrey walked in. 'Hello, Jack. Can I have a word?'

'Sure. Sit down – if you can find somewhere.' Jack cleared a pile of books from one of the chairs and Humphrey took it. He didn't look so fit and sprightly any more. He seemed to have aged twenty years in the last hour.

'That was quite a meeting, wasn't it?' he said.

'It was certainly interesting. Have you spoken to Jameson?'

'I didn't get the chance. He left in rather a hurry.' Humphrey frowned. 'D'you know, I had the strangest feeling he already knew what was in that report?'

'Really?' Jack deadpanned. 'How would he know?'

'I thought you could tell me?'

'I have no idea.'

'And even if you did, you wouldn't say anything?' Humphrey regarded him shrewdly. 'That's what I like about you, Jack. You're a loyal, honourable man. And there aren't many of them around these days.' He leaned back in his seat. 'That's why I wanted to offer you the senior partnership.'

Jack smiled. His whole career had been building up to this moment. But now it had happened, he felt nothing at all. 'I'm flattered. But I'm afraid you're going to have to find someone else. I'm leaving.'

'What? But you can't!' Humphrey stared at him in amazement. 'Don't you understand, I'm offering you the top job?'

'And I'm turning it down.'

Humphrey was silent for a while. 'May I ask why?'

'I just don't feel I fit in here any more.' He sat back on his heels and looked around his office. A year ago, the only way he would have been leaving it was to go on to a bigger and better one. But now . . . 'You told me once you expect one hundred and ten per cent from the people here and I don't think I can give that any more. I've got too much else going on in my life.'

He expected Humphrey to argue, but he didn't. 'I respect your decision, although I can't pretend I'm not disappointed,' he said heavily. 'So what are you planning to do with your life? Not giving up your career entirely, I hope?'

'God, no. I couldn't afford to do that. Actually, I'm thinking of starting up on my own.' It felt strange, saying it aloud. 'It's something I've been mulling over for a while now, and I quite like the idea of being my own boss.'

'It's not as easy as it looks, you know. What will you do for capital?'

'I've still got some money left over from the sale of the old house. And there was an insurance pay-out after Miranda's death.' It had sat in the bank for almost a year because he hadn't wanted to touch it. It didn't feel right. But he felt sure Miranda would approve of his plan.

Humphrey stood up. 'In that case, I hope it all works out for you. But I must say you've left me in a difficult position. Where am I going to find another senior partner?'

'How about Greg?'

'Who?'

Jack checked his impatience. 'Greg Randall. He's intelligent, ambitious, loyal. He deserves a chance.' And maybe with Jack out of the way he'd finally get it.

'Greg Randall, eh?' Humphrey considered it. 'I hadn't thought of him.'

No, Jack said to himself. That's the trouble, no one ever does.

★

The yard at Second Chance was deserted, although from one of the distant sheds came the muffled sound of hip-hop music punctuated by lots of swearing. Jack went round to what had been the office and peered in through the window. There was no sign of Melanie labouring over her keyboard. There wasn't even a keyboard. It was empty, apart from a pile of boxes filled with old files and other rubbish.

'Taking a last look round, are you?' He swung round. There was Reverend Dobbs. 'I suppose you couldn't resist having a gloat?'

'Not necessarily.' Jack rubbed at the dusty pane of glass with his sleeve. 'Looks like you've been having a clear-out?'

'No point in leaving it till the last minute, is there? You lot will be wanting to get started on the site as soon as you get your go-ahead.'

'What makes you think we'll get it?'

'Oh, come on! I may be a vicar but even the Almighty couldn't pull off a miracle like that. Of course you'll get it. Unless you've come to tell me you've changed your minds?'

Jack didn't answer. He looked up at the main building. 'See that crack in the wall up near the roofline? Looks like you've got some movement in the foundations. With any luck it's just a bit of settlement, but you'd have to check if it's still happening. If it is, you might need underpinning.' He looked around. 'And those sheds should go. You need some new workshops. Purpose-built, south-facing, with a bit more natural light so the lads can see what they're doing.'

'Nice idea. Maybe while we're at it we could put in a heated swimming pool too?' Sam gave him an odd look. 'Hello? This whole place will be reduced to rubble in a few weeks, or have you forgotten?'

'Like I said, not necessarily.' Jack looked around. 'Of course, you'd have to be careful about where you build, so

379

as not to upset the temple. But you should be all right over here.'

'Temple?' Sam followed him across the yard. 'Jack, have you been drinking? What are you talking about?'

'You mean you don't know about the Roman temple?' Jack regarded him with mock surprise. 'Perhaps you should ask the Westpoint consortium. They know all about it. They're having to hand this site over for archaeological investigations.'

A look of understanding passed across Sam's face. 'And you say this temple is somewhere around here?'

'So I believe. Right over there, in fact.' He pointed towards the other side of the field.

'Is that right?' Sam said slowly. 'And it's important, is it?'

'Very.'

'So it wouldn't be a good idea to build a shopping centre on top of it?'

'There's no way anyone would get permission. The archaeologists will have to open the whole site up. It could take years.'

'Really?' Sam scratched his chin thoughtfully. 'I don't suppose you'd like to stay for a cup of tea, would you? I'm sure we could track down the kettle.'

As they trudged towards the gate half an hour later, Jack said, 'Of course, now Westpoint can't build much more than a rabbit hutch here, they might be keen to get rid of the land. They might even be prepared to let you have this corner of it at a knockdown price.'

'It's worth asking, I suppose.'

'Can't do any harm.'

Sam glanced sidelong at him. 'And who found out about all this?'

'Let's just say I did some digging.'

'This wouldn't have anything to do with cracking safes, would it?'

'Reverend Dobbs! I'm surprised at you. You know that's illegal?'

Sam smiled. 'So why go to all this trouble? I expect it's cost your firm a few bob, losing that contract?'

'A wise man once said there's more to life than making money.'

'Sounds more like an idiot to me.' Sam grinned. 'Honestly, who'd come out with a thing like that?'

'The same idiot who'd spend his days hanging out with juvenile delinquents.'

'Ex juvenile delinquents, please.'

'And there's another reason,' Jack said. 'A purely selfish one.'

'What's that?'

'I want you to be my first client. I've decided to leave Crawshaw and Finch and set up on my own. I feel like doing something worthwhile for a change.'

'You won't get rich doing that. I should know.'

'Maybe not, but it's got to be better than building shopping centres no one wants. Anyway, maybe I'll get my reward in heaven. That's what you lot say, isn't it?'

'I'll put in a word for you at Head Office myself.'

They reached the gate. 'Fancy that,' Jack said, looking down the road. 'My car's still in one piece.'

Sam smiled. 'See?' he said. 'It's working already.'

Chapter 35

'Now are you sure you've remembered everything? What about all that stuff in the airing cupboard? Have you packed all that?'

'Yes, Mum!' Dan rolled his eyes heavenwards. 'I wish you'd stop fussing!'

'My only baby's leaving home. How can I not fuss?' She looked at the cases arranged around her. 'Have you packed enough jumpers? You don't know how cold it gets down there.'

'I'm going to Basingstoke, not Siberia!'

He might as well be going to Siberia, Tess thought. It felt far enough. She picked up a shirt and refolded it. It was early May and Dan was on study leave before his A Levels. And in spite of all her prayers that he'd change his mind, he'd decided to spend the time getting settled in down south with his father. He would be coming back in June to take his exams but basically, this was it. He was leaving home.

'Anyway, I'll be back in a few weeks if I've forgotten anything,' Dan reminded her.

Tess forced a smile. 'Don't expect to stay here, will you? I've already let your room to a bunch of asylum seekers!'

Dan laughed. She could tell in spite of his merry mood he wasn't looking forward to saying goodbye any more than she was. It was up to her to try and make it easy for him, no matter how hard it might be for her.

'I'm going to miss your rubbish jokes, Mum.'

'And I'm going to miss tidying up your mess.'

They were saved from getting maudlin when Phil stuck his head round the door. 'Hi. The front door was open so I let myself in.' He looked around the room. 'Blimey, I hope this is everything?'

'Almost.' Tess put the shirt back in the case and stood up. 'We've just got to unplumb the kitchen sink and that'll be it.'

'Why do I not feel you're joking?' Phil grinned. 'I'd better start packing the car.'

'Would you like a cup of tea?'

'No thanks, I'd rather get on our way so we miss the traffic.' He saw her desolate face. 'Oh well, maybe a quick cup wouldn't hurt.'

Tess hurried off to the kitchen to make it, relieved that she didn't have to watch Phil loading Dan's luggage into the car. She'd been hovering on the edge of tears ever since she dragged the suitcases out of the loft a week ago.

It's for the best, she told herself over and over again. Dan will have a great job, he'll be really happy, and Phil will look after him.

It was his turn now. She'd had Dan all to herself for nearly eighteen years. The time had come to share him.

She just hoped he was up to the job. Playing dad every other weekend was one thing, but he'd never been a full-time father.

She busied herself making tea. By the time she'd carried the tray through to the sitting room Phil had loaded the last of the luggage into the boot of his car. A people carrier, she noticed.

Tess frowned through the window. 'What happened to the Porsche?'

'I sold it. I thought that one might be more practical. I'm having it specially adapted so Dan can drive it.' He glanced at her anxiously. 'That's all right, isn't it?'

'It's very thoughtful of you.' Tess smiled back. Maybe Dan would be okay with Phil after all.

All too soon the time came to say goodbye. Tess stood on the doorstep to watch Phil as he loaded Dan's wheelchair into the boot. Dan was in his bedroom, taking a last look around to make sure he had everything.

'I flaming well hope so!' Phil said. 'There's no room for anything else in the car.' He looked at Tess. 'Are you okay?'

She nodded. 'I'm fine. You will look after him, won't you?'

'Of course I will.'

'You'll make sure he does his revision and his physiotherapy? Oh, and be careful if he gets a cold. It can so easily turn into something worse—'

'Tess, calm down. He's my son too, remember?'

Her smile wobbled and Phil pulled her into his arms for a reassuring hug. 'It'll be okay,' he whispered into her hair.

'I'm just worried I won't be able to say goodbye.'

'You could come with us for the weekend? Just to make sure Dan's settled in.'

Tess knew he was being kind and she appreciated it. 'He's not a child, Phil. He doesn't need me to hold his hand for him.' Not any more, she thought sadly.

'Here he comes.' He let her go and she turned around. Dan was coming down the path on his sticks, a bundle of rolled-up posters under his arm. Her little boy, so full of hope. She mustn't spoil this for him.

She fixed her smile back in place. 'I hope you've cleared all the coffee cups out from under your bed?'

'I think you'll find you're the one with all the cups under the bed, Mother.' He handed the posters to Phil. 'I'll be back in June. And you can always come and visit us before then, can't she, Dad?'

Dad. She'd never heard him call Phil that before. And from the emotional look on Phil's face, neither had he.

'Of course, son. Any time she likes.'

'I will. You wait, as soon as those summer holidays start,

384

I'll be down there all the time. Do they have beaches in Basingstoke?'

Phil smiled. 'We'll find one.'

He moved around to open the passenger door for Dan. Just as she'd been afraid she would, Tess hugged him fiercely, not wanting to let him go, trying to imprint the feel of him in her arms for ever.

As he pulled away, there were tears in his eyes. 'You will be all right on your own, won't you, Mum?'

'Who said I'll be on my own? I plan to find myself a toyboy the moment you're gone.'

'Why don't you ring Jack?'

A painful lump rose in her throat. She'd spent the last three months trying not to miss him. 'I can't. We had an agreement.'

'A stupid one, if you ask me. You miss him and I bet he misses you too.'

Does he? Tess was beginning to wonder. She hadn't heard from him at all in the past three months, and even though she knew that was what they'd agreed, part of her still worried that he hadn't even attempted to break it. She'd felt tempted, hundreds of times. She'd even gone as far as buying him a Valentine's card a couple of months back. It was still in her bedside drawer, unsigned and unsealed.

Also, Emily seemed far less moody and hostile at school these days. Maybe Jack had realised how easy his life was without Tess to complicate everything and decided they were better off without each other?

'We'll have to see, won't we?' she said.

She'd never known what it meant to put on a brave face until that moment. She stood at the front gate, waving madly until the car turned the corner and disappeared. Then she went back into the bungalow and closed the door.

The silence closed in on her immediately. She'd been on

her own millions of times, when Dan was at college or round at a friend's. But the house had never seemed as empty as it did now. It was as if he'd taken all the life and memories away with him.

She went into his room. It, too, looked strange and unfamiliar without all his clutter around. She thought about all the times she'd charged in to this very room, shouting at him to keep the noise down. Now she'd never hear it again. Next time Dan came he would be a visitor. There would be no more banging doors, no more loud music, no more troglodyte friends stomping through the house.

She sat down on the bed, looked at the big, empty spaces on the wall where his posters used to be, and cried.

Emily was on her way to the shop to buy a magazine when a car slowed down beside her and someone called her name.

It took her a moment to recognise the boy with the floppy fair hair leaning out of the passenger window. Then she realised it was Tess Doyle's son.

'Got a minute?' he asked.

She glanced past him at the fair-haired man behind the wheel. He shrugged.

'What for?'

'I want to talk to you.'

She turned away. 'I've got nothing to say.'

'No, but I have. And you're going to hear it.'

Emily started to walk away up the road. She didn't turn round, but she knew he was getting out of the car. It took him a long time to catch up with her, limping along on his sticks.

'I told you, I've got nothing to say to you.'

'Fine. I'll do all the talking then, shall I?' He sidestepped in front of her, blocking her way. 'Why do you hate my mum?'

'I don't.'

'You could have fooled me. So how come you stopped her seeing your dad?'

'That was nothing to do with me.'

'Like hell it wasn't! She really misses him, you know.'

He missed her too, Emily could tell. Even though things had settled down at home and he'd been busy setting up his new business over the past few months, she could tell he was miserable. Sometimes she'd wake up in the early hours to find all the lights still on and him sitting at his drawing board, staring into space. She knew he wasn't thinking about work.

She missed Tess too. They'd reached an uneasy truce at school, but it wasn't the same. Emily missed Tess' jokes, her laughter, the way she could talk to her about anything. Now she couldn't talk to her at all.

She'd screwed everything up and she knew it. But that didn't mean she was ready to admit it to Dan.

'So?' she said.

'So you could stop giving them both a hard time.' She was silent. 'Look, I know you're not keen on the idea of your dad having a girlfriend, but you can't keep him to yourself for ever. Apart from anything else, it's selfish.'

She glanced sideways at him. 'Oh yeah? How do you work that out?'

'Think about it. In a few years you'll probably have left home and be at college somewhere. Do you really want your dad to be lonely?'

'He'll have Sophie.'

'And what happens when she grows up and moves on? It's going to happen. I'm moving away myself and leaving my mum on her own, and I feel like shit for doing it. Do you want that?'

'Your mum's on her own?'

Dan nodded. 'But she wouldn't have to be if you'd given her the chance. And you could do a lot worse than my mum, you know. She's not that bad once you get to know her.'

Emily managed a half smile at that. She did like Tess. Very much. Or she had, until all this happened.

'They lied to me,' she said.

'Big deal. Adults do it all the time. Anyway, do you blame them? They knew you'd hit the roof when you found out.'

'They still shouldn't have lied.'

'I think they've worked that out for themselves,' Dan said wryly.

They reached the shop. Emily said, 'Anyway, it's finished now. It's been over for ages.'

'That's what you think.'

'What do you mean?'

'I mean my mum's still mad about your dad and I reckon he feels the same. The only reason they're not together is because they don't want to hurt you.'

'So?' Guilt made her snap.

'So maybe you should think about that.' Dan turned and limped away, leaving her open-mouthed.

That Saturday afternoon, her dad dropped them off at Auntie Ros' while he went to meet a potential client. He worked at the weekends a lot these days. He said he had to work long hours to get the business going, but Emily sometimes wondered if he was trying to avoid being at home.

Auntie Ros was attempting to tackle the housework and seemed relieved when Emily said she wanted to go shopping.

'I don't suppose you'd like to take these with you?' She looked down at the three small children jumping over the vacuum-cleaner hose at her feet.

'No thanks,' Emily smiled. Where she was going was no place for kids.

It was a warm day and the cemetery was busy. No funerals, but lots of people visiting graves. Emily thought about the last time she'd come here, with Tess. She'd been so kind to her, buying flowers and listening to her troubles. She'd even gone into battle with her dad on Emily's behalf.

She remembered them squaring up to each other on the front drive. That wasn't someone who was using her because she secretly fancied him. That was someone who cared about her enough to put her job on the line to stand up for her.

But that didn't quell the anxiety lurking in the pit of her stomach. She liked Tess and she was sure she hadn't used her to get to her dad. And yes, if she had to choose someone for him to get involved with, it would probably be Tess Doyle.

But that only made it worse. Emily could imagine them all living together, being happy. She could see Tess fitting seamlessly into their family. She could picture them all talking and laughing around the dining-room table.

That was what frightened her. Because the more comfortable Emily felt having Tess around, the more she might forget her mother. She'd already slipped from her father's mind. Emily owed it to her to keep her memory alive.

She turned the corner and saw him. A tall figure kneeling beside her mother's grave. Her heart lurched. She dodged behind a yew tree and watched him arranging flowers around the headstone.

So he hadn't forgotten her after all.

She wondered if she should sneak away but he looked up and saw her.

'Emily? What are you doing here?'

What do you think? All her old defences of sarcasm and bitterness sprang up, but she quelled them. 'Same as you. I thought you were working today?'

'I was. But then I decided to come here.' He straightened up and brushed the dirt off his knees. 'I've been tidying it up.'

'It looks all right.' Emily looked at the half-dead bunch of flowers he'd just taken from the grave. 'Who left those?'

'I did. Last week.'

'You came last week?'

'I come every week.'

'I didn't know that.'

'I don't tell you everything.'

She could have said something cutting, but she didn't. She gazed down at the roses. 'They were her favourites.'

'I know. I used to buy them for her every Friday before you were born.'

She kept her eyes fixed on the grave. 'Do you miss her?'

'Of course I miss her. Not a day goes by when I don't think about her.'

She glanced sideways at his profile and realised how badly she must have hurt him when she accused him of being glad her mother was dead. A lump rose in her throat. 'I'm sorry,' she mumbled. 'About those things I said.'

She felt his hand come down on her shoulder. 'It doesn't matter.'

'I can't help it. I just get – frightened.'

'Frightened of what, Em?'

'That you'll forget her.' She looked up at him, her eyes wet with tears. 'I'm scared that if you meet someone else, you might get to love them more than you loved her.'

His dark gaze softened. 'Do you really think that could happen?'

'It feels like you're trying to forget her,' she rubbed her eyes on her sleeve. 'That's why we moved house.'

'I wasn't trying to forget her. I was just trying not to miss her so badly.' His arm slid further around her shoulders. For once she didn't try to shrug him off. 'I don't want to forget her. We had some really special times, me and your mum. She'll always be there. Nothing could change that. And I wouldn't want it to.'

He hugged her close. It felt good to be back in his arms. Whatever happened, he would always be there for her and Sophie. Nothing could change that, either.

'Come on,' he said gruffly. 'Let's go home.'

She chose her moment carefully. They were on the M62, stuck in a traffic snarl-up as usual. Emily pretended to flick through the CDs.

'I spoke to Dan today.'

'Who?'

'You know – Miss Doyle's son?'

'Oh.' He didn't take his eyes off the road.

'He says he's left home.'

He missed a gear. 'Dan's gone? Already? I thought he wasn't leaving until the summer?'

'Well, he's gone, anyway.' She stared out of the window. 'His mum's very upset, he said.'

'I bet she is.' Jack's face was grim.

'Maybe you should call her?'

'Are you feeling all right?'

'I mean it.' Emily plucked at a loose thread on her sleeve. 'I wouldn't mind if you saw her again.'

He frowned. 'You don't sound too sure about that.'

Emily thought about it for a moment. It was going to be hard for her, seeing her father with another woman. But Dan was right. She had to stop being selfish.

And if there had to be someone else, she would rather it was Tess than anyone. 'She's all right really,' she said.

'She is, isn't she?' He was smiling. The first real smile she'd seen in weeks.

When they got back, the first thing he did was call Tess' number. Emily pretended not to listen as he stood there, hanging on to the phone.

Finally, he put it down. 'She's not there.' He looked disappointed.

'She must have gone out. She's not expecting you to call, is she?'

'No.'

'So she's not going to be sitting by the phone waiting, is

she? Don't panic, I'm sure she hasn't lined herself up with another bloke!'

'I suppose not.' He went on staring at the phone. Emily sighed.

'If you're that worried, why don't you go round there?' she said.

Tess looked at the phone and resisted the urge to call Dan. He'd phoned an hour ago to say they'd arrived safely and even though Tess had done her best to sound thrilled when he raved about his new home, she already missed him dreadfully. She'd tried going out for a walk to make herself think about something else, but it hadn't worked.

She decided to do what she always did in times of crisis and call her mother instead. She reached for the phone and was halfway through dialling the number when she remembered no one was home. She and Ronnie had gone on a honeymoon cruise of the Mediterranean. She'd got a postcard from them that morning, a colourful photo of the island of Madeira.

It made her smile to see it propped up on the mantelpiece. Margaret had never owned a passport or gone further than Scarborough for her holidays. Ronnie was opening up new horizons for her.

But it felt strange, not having her on the end of a phone whenever she needed her. She was lucky to catch her mother in these days. If she wasn't out at her conversational Italian classes, she was learning tennis or Tai Chi. Sometimes Tess felt like the old one, sitting at home feeling bitter and resentful that no one bothered to call her any more.

Not that she begrudged her mother her new life. She just wished she could be part of it. It felt as if everyone had moved on and left her behind.

But she couldn't sit moping about it. As Helen kept telling her, this was her chance to make a life of her own.

'Just think, you don't have any responsibilities any more,' she'd said. 'You can do what you like, when you like.'

Which all sounded wonderful, except that Tess couldn't think of a single thing she wanted to do. Maybe she should ask Ronnie and her mum if she could tag along to their Tai Chi class?

Her grumbling stomach told her it was time to eat, so she trailed into the kitchen in search of food. It wasn't until she was staring into an empty fridge that she realised she'd forgotten to go to the supermarket. All the fridge contained was some sliced ham that had curled up at the edges and a Tupperware container full of something that might once have been potato salad but was now curdled and dubious-smelling. And the usual half bottle of wine, of course. Tess resisted the urge to drink the lot.

This was ridiculous! Dan had only been gone a few hours and she'd already let herself go. If she carried on like this, by the end of the week she'd have stopped bothering to wash her hair or get dressed. She'd sleep all day and drink all night and probably live in her slobby old pyjamas. She might as well go out and buy those cats now, so they could eat her when she dropped down dead from starvation or alcohol poisoning.

Or she could just stop being over-dramatic and go out for a takeaway. She grabbed the car keys from the worktop before she could change her mind and decide it wasn't worth the bother.

She opened the front door and walked straight into Jack coming up the path, clutching a large flat pizza box.

'Jack!' She shot a quick look around, half expecting a vengeful Emily to appear from behind the hedge. 'What are you doing here?'

'I heard about Dan moving out,' he said. 'I came to see how you are.'

The tender concern in his face made her want to weep all over again. 'I'm fine.' Actually, I'm bloody terrible, she cried out inside. My mother's got herself a life, my son's left home and I'm all on my own. *And I miss you*. She hadn't realised how much until she saw him standing there, so tall and dark and damn good-looking it hurt.

He looked at her shrewdly. 'Are you sure about that?'

'I will be once I get a grip on myself and stop crying in his bedroom. I've had to hide the phone to stop myself calling him.' A thought occurred to her and she frowned. 'How did you know he'd gone?'

'Emily told me.'

'How did she find out?'

'She met Dan this morning. They had a good talk, apparently. He told her you missed me.' He gave her a look that made her toes curl inside her trainers. 'Is it true?'

'Jack—'

'Is it true?'

'Of course I miss you! But we agreed—'

'You shouldn't be on your own at a time like this,' he cut her off. 'Why don't you come round to our place? We're having a pizza.' He held up the box in front of her. The heavenly smell made her stomach groan.

'Jack—'

'Before you say anything else, it wasn't my idea.' He glanced back over his shoulder. For the first time Tess noticed Emily and Sophie were in the car, their faces pressed against the glass. Emboldened, Jack leaned across the pizza box and kissed her full on the mouth. 'We'd all like you to come,' he said quietly.

Tess looked from the girls back to him. 'In that case, I'd love to.'

It was only pizza. But it was a start.